Henning Mankell **FIREWALL**

Internationally acclaimed author Henning Mankell has written numerous Kurt Wallander mysteries. The books have been published in thirty-three countries and consistently top the bestseller lists in Europe, receiving major literary prizes (including the UK's Golden Dagger Award in 2000) and generating numerous international film and television adaptations. Born in a village in northern Sweden in 1948, Mankell divides his time between Sweden and Maputo, Mozambique, where he works as the director of Teatro Avenida.

KURT WALLANDER MYSTERIES by Henning Mankell

Faceless Killers

The Dogs of Riga

The White Lioness

Sidetracked

The Fifth Woman

One Step Behind

Firewall

FIREWALL

FIREWALL

HENNING MANKELL

Translated from the Swedish by

EBBA SEGERBERG

VINTAGE CRIME/BLACK LIZARD
Vintage Books
A Division of Random House, Inc.
New York

FIRST VINTAGE CRIME/BLACK LIZARD EDITION,
SEPTEMBER 2003

The Cataloging-in-Publication Data is on file at the Library of
Congress.

Vintage ISBN: 1-4000-3153-2

www.vintagebooks.com

Printed in the United States of America
10   9   8   7

"A man who strays from the path of understanding comes to rest in the company of the dead."

—Proverbs 21:16

FIREWALL

part one **THE CATALYST**

Chapter One

The wind died down toward evening, then stopped completely. He was standing on the balcony. Some days he could see a sliver of ocean between the buildings across the way. Right now it was too dark. Sometimes he set up his telescope and looked into the lighted windows of the other apartments. But he always started to feel as if someone was onto him and then he would stop.

The stars were very clear and bright.

It's already fall, he thought. *There may even be a touch of frost tonight, though it's early for Scania.*

A car drove by. He shivered and went back in. The door to the balcony was hard to close and needed some adjustment. He added it to the to-do list he kept on a pad of paper in the kitchen.

He walked into the living room, pausing in the doorway to look around. Since it was Sunday, the place was immaculately clean. It gave him a feeling of satisfaction.

He sat down at his desk and pulled out the thick journal he kept in one of the drawers. As usual, he began by reading his entry from the night before.

Saturday, the fourth of October, 1997. Gusty winds, 8–10 meters per second according to the National Weather Service. Broken cloud formations. Temperature at six o'clock: seven degrees Celsius. Temperature at two o'clock: eight degrees Celsius.

Below that he had added four sentences.

No activity in c-space today. No messages. C doesn't reply when prompted. All is calm.

He removed the lid of the ink pot and carefully dipped the nib in the ink. It had been his father's pen, one his father had saved from his early days as an assistant clerk at a bank in Tomelilla. He never used any other pen for writing in his journal.

The wind died away as he was writing. The thermometer outside the kitchen window read three degrees Celsius. The sky was clear. He made a note of the fact that cleaning the apartment had taken three hours and twenty-five minutes. That was ten minutes faster than last Sunday.

He had also taken a short walk down to the marina, after meditating in Saint Maria's church for thirty minutes.

He hesitated, then wrote, *Short walk in the evening.*

He pressed the blotting paper over the few lines he had just written, wiped off the pen, and replaced the lid of the ink pot.

Before shutting the journal, he glanced over at the old ship's clock that stood next to him on the desk. It was twenty minutes past eleven.

He walked out into the hall, put on his leather jacket, and pulled on an old pair of rubber boots. He stuck a hand in his pocket to make sure he had his wallet and his keys.

Once he was down on the street, he stood in the shadows for a while and looked around. There was no one there, just as he had expected. He started walking down to the left, as he usually did, crossing the highway to Malmö and heading down toward the department stores and the red brick building that housed the Tax Authorities. He increased his speed until he found his usual smooth evening rhythm. He walked quickly in the daytime to get his heart rate up, but the evening walks had a different purpose. This was when he tried to empty his mind, preparing for sleep and the day to come.

Outside one of the department stores, he passed a woman with a German shepherd. He almost always bumped into her on his evening walks. A car drove by at high speed, music blaring.

They have no inkling of what's in store for them, he thought. *All these hooligans who drive around permanently damaging their hearing with their obnoxious music. They don't know. They know as little as that woman out walking her dog.*

The thought cheered him up. He thought about the power he wielded, the sense of being one of the chosen. He had the power to do away with the hardened, corrupt ways of this society and create a new order, something completely unexpected.

He stopped and looked up at the night sky.

Nothing is truly comprehensible, he thought. *My own life is as incompre-*

hensible as the fact that the light I now see from the stars has been traveling for eons. The only source of meaning is my own course of action, like the deal that I was offered twenty years ago and that I accepted without hesitation.

He continued on his way, increasing his speed because his thoughts were making him excited. He felt a growing sense of impatience. They had waited so long for this. Now the moment was approaching when they would open the invisible dams and watch their tidal wave sweep over the world.

But not yet. The moment was not quite here, and impatience was a weakness he would not permit himself.

He turned and started back. As he walked past the Tax Authority, he decided to go to the cash machine in the plaza. He put his hand over the pocket where he kept his wallet. He wasn't going to make a withdrawal, just get an account balance and make sure all was as it should be.

He stopped in the light by the ATM and took out his card. The woman with the German shepherd was long gone. A heavily loaded truck drove past on the Malmö highway, probably on its way to one of the Poland ferries. By the sound of it, the muffler was damaged.

He fed his card into the slot, punched in his code, and selected the button for account balance. The machine returned his card and he slipped it back into his wallet. He listened to the whirring and clicking and smiled. *If they only knew,* he thought. *If people only knew what lay in store for them.*

The white slip of paper with his account balance slid out of the slot. He felt around for his glasses before he realized he had left them in his other coat. He felt a twinge of irritation at this oversight.

He walked over to the place under the street lamp where the light was strongest and studied the slip of paper.

There was Friday's withdrawal, as well as the cash he had taken out the day before. His balance was 9,765 kronor. Everything was in order.

What happened next came without warning.

It was as if he had been kicked by a horse. The pain was sudden and violent.

He fell forward with the white piece of paper clutched in his hand.

As his head hit the asphalt he had a final moment of clarity. His last thought was that he didn't understand what was happening.

Then a darkness enveloped him from all sides.

It was just past midnight on Monday, the 6th of October, 1997.

A second truck on its way to the night ferry drove by.

Then calm returned to the streets once more.

Chapter Two

When Kurt Wallander got into his car on Mariagatan in Ystad, on the morning of the 6th of October, 1997, it was with reluctance. It was a little after eight o'clock. He drove out of the city, wondering what had possessed him to say he would go. He had a deep and passionate dislike of funerals, and yet that was exactly what he was on his way to attend. Since he had plenty of time, he decided against taking the direct route to Malmö. Instead, he took the coastal highway toward Svarte and Trelleborg. He glimpsed the sea on his left-hand side. A ferry was approaching the harbor.

He thought about the fact that this was his fourth funeral in seven years. First there had been his colleague Rydberg, who died of cancer. It had been a protracted and painful end. Wallander had often visited him in the hospital where he lay slowly wasting away. Rydberg's death had been a huge blow. Rydberg was the one who had made a police officer out of him. He had taught Wallander to ask the right questions. Through watching him work, Wallander had slowly learned how to read the information hidden at the scene of a crime. Before he started working with Rydberg, Wallander had been a very average policeman. It was only after many years, after Rydberg's death, that Wallander realized he had become not only a stubborn and energetic detective, but a good one. He still held long, silent conversations with Rydberg in his head when he tackled a new investigation and didn't quite know how to proceed. He experienced a brief sense of loss and sadness at Rydberg's absence almost every day. Those feelings would never go away.

Then there was his father, who had died unexpectedly. He had collapsed from a stroke in his studio in Löderup. That was three years ago. Sometimes Wallander still had trouble grasping the fact that his father wasn't still in the studio, surrounded by the smell of turpentine and oil paint. The house in Löderup had been sold after his death. Wallander had driven past it a couple of times since then and seen that new people were living there. He had never stopped the car and taken a closer look. From time to time he went to his father's grave, always with an inexplicable feeling of guilt. These visits were getting less frequent. He had also noticed that it was getting harder for him to visualize his father's face.

A person who died eventually became a person who had never existed.

Then there was Svedberg, his colleague who had been so brutally murdered only one year ago. That had made Wallander realize how little he knew about the people he worked with. During the investigation he had uncovered a more complicated network of relationships in Svedberg's life than he would ever have been able to dream of.

And now he was on his way to funeral number four, the only one he didn't really have to go to.

She had called on Wednesday, just as Wallander was about to leave the office. It was late afternoon and he had a bad headache from concentrating on a depressing case involving smuggled cigarettes. The tracks seemed to lead to northern Greece, then went up in smoke. Wallander had exchanged information with both German and Greek police. But they had still not managed to arrest the smugglers. Now he realized that the driver of the truck that contained the smuggled goods probably had no idea what had been in his load. But he would end up going to jail, at least for a couple of months. Nothing else would come of it. Wallander was certain that smuggled cigarettes arrived daily in Ystad. He doubted they would ever be able to put a stop to it.

His day had also been poisoned by an argument with the district attorney, the man who was filling in for Per Åkeson, who had gone to Sudan a couple of years ago and seemed to be in no hurry to return. Wallander was filled with envy whenever he got a letter from Åkeson. He had done what Wallander had only dreamed of: starting over. Now Wallander was about to turn fifty and he knew, though he had trouble admitting such a thing to himself, that the decisive events of his life were already behind him. He would never be anything but a police officer. The best he could do in the years leading up to retirement was try to become better at solving crimes, and pass on his knowledge to the younger generation of his colleagues. But there were no life-altering decisions waiting for him, no Sudan.

He was just about to put his jacket on when she called.

At first he hadn't known who she was.

Then he realized she was Stefan Fredman's mother. Memories and isolated images from the events three years ago rushed back in the space of a few seconds. It was the case of the boy who had painted himself to look like a Native American warrior and set out to revenge himself on the men who had driven his sister insane and filled his younger brother with terror. One of the victims had been Stefan's own father. Wallander flinched at one of the last, most disturbing images, of the boy kneeling by his sister's dead body and crying. He didn't know what had happened afterward, except that the boy had been sent to a locked psychiatric ward rather than prison.

Now Anette Fredman had called to say the boy was dead. He had committed suicide by throwing himself out the window. Wallander had expressed his condolences and they had been genuine, though perhaps what he felt was a sense of hopelessness and despair rather than grief. But he still had not understood why she had called him. He had stood there with the receiver in his hand and tried to recall her face. He had only met her on two or three occasions in her home in a suburb of Malmö, when he had been struggling with the idea that a fourteen-year-old boy had committed these heinous crimes. She had been shy and tense. She had always seemed to be cringing, as if expecting everything to turn out for the worst. In her case, they often did. Wallander remembered that he had wondered if she were addicted to alcohol or prescription medication. But he didn't know. He could hardly remember her face. Her voice on the telephone sounded completely unfamiliar.

Then she told him why she was calling. She wanted Wallander to attend the funeral. There were so few people who were coming. She was the only one left now, except her youngest son, Jens. Wallander had, after all, been someone who wished them well.

He promised to be there. He changed his mind the moment he said the words, but by then it was too late.

Later he had tried to find out what happened to the boy after his admittance to the psychiatric ward. He spoke with one of Stefan's doctors. He was told that Stefan had been almost completely silent during the past few years, closed off from the outside world. But the boy who came smashing down onto that slab of concrete on the hospital grounds had worn full-blown warrior paints. That disturbing mask of paint and blood held little clue as to who the young person locked inside had really been, but it spoke volumes about the violent and largely indifferent society in which he had been formed.

Wallander drove slowly along the road. He had been surprised when he put on his suit that morning and found that the pants fit. He must have lost weight. Ever since being diagnosed with diabetes the previous year he had been forced to modify his eating habits, start exercising, and lose weight. At first he had been too extreme and had jumped on the bathroom scale several times a day, until he finally threw it out in a rage.

But his doctor had not let up, insisting that Wallander do something about his unhealthy eating habits and his almost total absence of exercise. His nagging had finally produced results. Wallander had bought a sweatsuit and sneakers and started taking regular walks. But when his colleague Martinsson had suggested they start running together, Wallander had refused. He drew the line at jogging. Now he had established a regular route for his walks that took about an hour. It went from Mariagatan through the Sandskogen park, and back. He forced himself out on a walk at least four times a week, and had also forced himself to stay away from his favorite hamburger places. Accordingly, his blood sugar levels had dropped and Wallander had lost weight. One morning as he was shaving in front of the mirror he noticed that his cheeks were hollow again. It was like getting his old face back after having worn an artificial padding of fat and bad skin. His daughter, Linda, had been delighted with the change when she saw him last. But no one down at the station had made any comments about his appearance.

It's as if we never really see each other, Wallander thought. *We work together, but we don't see each other.*

Wallander drove by Mossby beach, which lay deserted now that it was fall. He remembered the time six years ago when a rubber raft carrying two dead men had drifted ashore here.

On a whim, he slammed on the brakes and turned the car around. He had plenty of time. He parked and got out of the car. There was no wind and it was perhaps a couple of degrees above freezing. He buttoned his coat and followed the small trail that snaked out between the sand dunes to the sea. The beach was deserted, but there were traces of people and dogs—and horses—in the sand. He looked out over the water. A flock of birds was flying south in formation.

He still remembered exactly where they had found the bodies. It had been a difficult investigation that had led Wallander to Latvia. He had met Baiba in Riga. She was the widow of a Latvian police officer, a man Wallander had known and liked.

Then they had started seeing each other. For a long time he had thought it was going to work out, that she would move to Sweden. They had even started looking at houses. But then she had started to pull away. Wallander had thought jealously that she had met someone else.

He even flew to Riga once without telling her in advance so he could surprise her. But there had been no one else, just Baiba's doubts about marrying another police officer and leaving her homeland, where she had an underpaid but rewarding job as a translator.

So it had ended.

Wallander walked along the beach and realized that a year had gone by since he had last talked to her. She still sometimes appeared in his dreams, but he never managed to grab hold of her. When he approached her or put out his hand to touch her, she was gone. He asked himself if he really missed her. His jealousy was gone now; he no longer flinched at the thought of her with another man.

I miss the companionship, he thought. *With Baiba I managed to escape the loneliness I hadn't even been aware of.*

He returned to the car. *I should avoid deserted beaches in the fall*, he thought. *They make me depressed.*

Once he had taken refuge from his normal life in a remote part of northern Jylland. He had been on sick leave due to a deep depression and had thought he would never return to his work as a police officer in Ystad again. It was many years ago, but he could still recall in terrifying detail how he had felt. It was something he never wanted to experience again. That bleak and blustery landscape had seemed to awaken his worst fears.

He got in the car and continued on to Malmö. He wondered what the coming winter was going to be like, if there would be a lot of snow or if it would simply rain. He also wondered what he was going to do during the week of vacation he was due to take in November. He had talked to Linda about taking a charter flight to a warmer climate. It would be his treat. But she was still up in Stockholm, studying something—he didn't know what—and said she really couldn't get away. He had tried to think of other travel companions but had not managed to come up with anyone. He had almost no friends. There was Sten Widén, who raised horses on a ranch outside of Ystad, but Wallander wasn't sure he would be such a good travel companion. Widén drank constantly, while Wallander was struggling to keep his own once-considerable alcohol consumption to a minimum. He could ask Gertrud, his father's widow. But what would they talk about for a whole week?

There was no one else.

He would stay home and use the money to buy a new car. The Peugeot was getting old. It had started to make a funny sound.

*   *   *

He entered the suburb of Rosengård shortly after ten o'clock. The funeral was scheduled for eleven. The church was a modern building. Nearby some boys were kicking a soccer ball against a concrete wall. There were seven in all, three of them black. Three others also looked like they might have immigrant parents. The last one had freckles and unruly blond hair. The boys were kicking the ball around with enthusiasm and a great deal of laughter. For a split second Wallander felt an overwhelming urge to join them. But he stayed where he was. A man walked out of the church and lit a cigarette. Wallander got out of the car and approached him.

"Is this where Stefan Fredman's funeral is going to be held?" he asked.

The man nodded. "Are you a relative?"

"No."

"I didn't think there would be very many people here," the man said. "I take it you know what he did."

"Yes, I know," Wallander said.

The man looked down at his cigarette.

"Someone like him is better off dead."

Wallander felt himself getting angry.

"Stefan wasn't even eighteen years old. Someone that young is never better off dead."

Wallander realized he was yelling. The man with the cigarette looked at him with curiosity. Wallander shook his head angrily and turned around. At that moment the hearse drove up. The brown coffin was unloaded. There was only a single wreath of flowers on it. *I should have brought a bouquet,* Wallander thought.

He walked over to the boys, who were still playing soccer.

"Any of you know of a flower shop around here?" he asked.

One of the boys pointed into the distance.

Wallander took out his wallet and held up a hundred-crown note.

"Run over and buy me some flowers," he said. "Roses. And hurry back. I'll give you ten crowns for your troubles."

The boy looked at him with big eyes, but took the money.

"I'm a police officer," Wallander said. "A dangerous police officer. If you make off with the money, I'll find you."

The boy shook his head.

"Then why aren't you wearing a uniform?" he asked in broken Swedish. "You don't look like a policeman. Not a dangerous one, anyway."

Wallander got out his police badge and showed it to him. The boy studied it for a while, then nodded and set off. The rest of them resumed their game.

There's a good chance he won't be back, Wallander thought gloomily. *It's been a long time since civilians had any sense of respect for the police.*

But the boy returned with the roses, as promised. Wallander gave him twenty crowns, the ten he owed him and ten more for actually coming back, realizing that he was being overly generous. Shortly thereafter, a taxi pulled up and Stefan's mother got out. She had aged and was so thin she looked sick. A young boy of about seven stood by her side. He looked a lot like his brother. His eyes were wide and frightened. He still lived in fear from that time. Wallander walked over and greeted them.

"It's just going to be us and the minister," she said.

They walked into the church. The minister was a young man who was sitting on a chair next to the coffin, leafing through a newspaper. Wallander felt Anette Fredman suddenly grab hold of his arm.

He understood.

The minister got up and put his newspaper away. They sat down to the right of the coffin. She was still hanging onto Wallander's arm.

First she lost her husband, Wallander thought. Björn Fredman had been an unpleasant and brutal man who used to hit her and who frightened his children. But he had still been her husband and the father of her children. He was later murdered by his own son. Then her oldest child, Louise, had died. *And now here she is, about to bury her son. What's left for her? Half a life? As much as that?*

Someone entered the church behind them. Anette Fredman did not seem to hear anything, or else she was trying so hard to stay in control of herself that she couldn't focus on anything else. A woman was walking up the aisle. She was about Wallander's age. Anette Fredman finally looked up and nodded to her. The woman sat down a few rows behind them.

"She's a doctor," Anette Fredman said. "Her name is Agneta Malmström. She helped Jens a while back when he wasn't doing so well."

Wallander recognized the name, but it took him a moment to remember that it was Agneta Malmström and her husband who had provided him with the most important clues in the Stefan Fredman case. He had spoken to her late one night with the help of Stockholm Radio. She had been on a sailboat far out at sea, out past Landsort.

Wallander heard organ music, although he had not seen an organist. The minister had turned on a tape recorder.

Wallander wondered why he had not heard any church bells. Didn't funerals always start with the ringing of church bells? This thought was pushed aside when Anette Fredman's grip on his arm tightened. He cast a glance at the boy by her side. Should a child his age be attending a funeral? Wallander didn't think so. But the boy looked fairly collected.

The music died away and the minister started to speak. He started by reminding them of Christ's words, "let the little ones come unto me." Wallander concentrated on the wreath that lay on the coffin, counting the blossoms in order to keep the lump in his throat from growing.

The service was short. Afterward they approached the coffin. Anette Fredman was breathing hard, as if she were in the final few yards of a race. Agneta Malmström stood right behind them. Wallander turned to the minister, who seemed impatient.

"Why were there no church bells?" Wallander asked him. "There should be bells ringing as we walk out, and not a recording, either."

The minister nodded hesitantly. Wallander wondered what would have happened if he had pulled out his police ID. They started walking out. Anette and Jens Fredman went ahead of the others. Wallander said hello to Agneta Malmström.

"I recognized you," she said. "We've never met, but I've seen your face in the papers."

"She asked me to come. Did she call you, too?"

"No, I came of my own accord."

"What's going to happen to her now?"

Agneta Malmström shook her head slowly.

"I don't know. She's started drinking heavily. I have no idea how Jens is going to get on."

At this point they reached the vestibule, where Anette Fredman and Jens were waiting for them. The church bells rang. Wallander opened the church doors, taking one last look at the coffin. Some men were already in the process of removing it through a side door.

Suddenly a flash went off in his face. There was a press photographer waiting outside the church. Anette Fredman held up her hands to shield her face. The photographer turned from her and tried to get a picture of the boy. Wallander put out his arm to stop him, but the photographer was too quick. He got his picture.

"Why can't you leave us alone?" Anette Fredman cried.

The boy started to cry. Wallander grabbed the photographer and pulled him aside.

"What the hell do you think you're doing?" he yelled.

"None of your fucking business," said the photographer. He was about Wallander's age and had bad breath.

"I shoot whatever sells," he added. "Pictures of a serial killer's funeral sell. Too bad I didn't get here earlier."

Wallander reached for his police ID, then changed his mind and snatched the camera. The photographer tried to pull it out of his hands, but Wallander was stronger. In a split second he had opened the camera and pulled out the film.

"There have to be limits," Wallander said and handed the camera back to him.

The photographer stared at him, then hauled his cell phone out of his pocket.

"I'm calling the cops," he said. "That was assault."

"Go ahead," Wallander said. "Do it. I'm a detective with the homicide division in Ystad. Inspector Kurt Wallander. Please call my colleagues in Malmö and tell them whatever you want."

Wallander let the roll of film fall on the ground and broke it up with his foot. The church bells stopped ringing.

Wallander was sweaty and still enraged. Anette Fredman's shrill plea to be left alone echoed in his head. The photographer stared at the destroyed roll of film. The group of boys were still playing soccer.

When she had called, Anette Fredman had asked him to join them for coffee after the service. He had not been able to say no.

"There won't be any pictures in the paper," Wallander said.

"Why can't they leave us alone?"

Wallander had nothing to say. He looked over at Agneta Malmström, but she had nothing to say, either.

The apartment in the shabby rental building was exactly as Wallander remembered it. Agneta Malmström accompanied them. They sat quietly while they waited for the coffee to brew. Wallander thought he heard the clink of a glass bottle in the kitchen.

Jens was sitting on the floor playing quietly with a toy car. Wallander realized that Agneta Malmström found it all as depressing as he did, but there seemed to be nothing to say.

They sat there with their coffee cups. Anette Fredman sat across from them with shiny eyes. Agneta Malmström tried to ask her how she was managing financially now that she was unemployed. Anette Fredman answered in vague perfunctory phrases.

"We manage. Things will work out somehow. One day at a time."

The conversation died away. Wallander looked down at his watch. It was close to one o'clock. He got up and shook Anette Fredman's hand.

She burst into tears. Wallander was taken aback. He didn't know what to do.

"You go," Agneta Malmström said. "I'll stay with her a little while."

"I'll call to see how things are going," Wallander said. Then he awkwardly patted the boy's head, and left.

He sat in the car for a while before starting the engine. He thought about the photographer who was so sure the pictures of a serial killer's funeral would sell.

I can't deny that this is how it is now, he thought. *But I also can't deny that I don't understand a single bit of it.*

He drove through the fall landscape toward Ystad.

It had been a hell of a morning.

He parked the car and walked in through the doors of the police station shortly after two.

The wind had picked up from the east. A cloud belt was moving in over the coast.

Chapter Three

By the time Wallander reached the office, he had a headache. He looked through his desk drawers to see if he could find any tablets. He heard Hansson walk past his door whistling to himself. He finally found a crumpled packet of acetaminophen in the back of a drawer. He went to the lunchroom to get himself a glass of water and a cup of coffee. Some young police officers, who had been hired during the last couple of years, were sitting at one table talking loudly. Wallander nodded to them and said hello. He heard them talking about their time at the police academy. He walked back to his office and watched the two headache tablets slowly dissolve in the glass of water.

He thought about Anette Fredman, and tried to imagine what the future might hold for the little boy in the impoverished suburb of Rosengård who had played so quietly on the apartment floor. He had seemed as if he were hiding from the world, carrying within him his memories of a dead father and now two equally dead siblings.

Wallander drained the glass in front of him and immediately felt the headache lifting. He looked at a case folder that Martinsson had put on his desk, with "Urgent as all hell" written on a red Post-it note on the front. Wallander already knew the facts of the case. They had discussed it on the phone last week while Wallander was at a national police conference on new directions for policing the violence associated with the growing motorcycle-gang movement. Wallander had asked to be excused, but Chief Holgersson had insisted. She specifically wanted him on this. One of the gangs had just bought a farm outside of Ystad and they had to be prepared to deal with them in the future.

Wallander decided to return to being a police officer and opened the folder with a sigh. Martinsson had written a concise report of the events. When he'd gotten to the end of it, Wallander leaned back in his chair and thought about what he had just read.

Two girls, one nineteen, the other not more than fourteen, had ordered a taxi at a restaurant shortly after ten o'clock on a Tuesday evening. They had asked to be driven to Rydsgård. One of the girls was in the front seat. When they reached the outskirts of Ystad she asked the driver to stop the car saying she wanted to move to the back seat. When the taxi pulled over to the side of the road, the girl in the back-seat had pulled out a hammer and hit the driver in the head. The girl in the front seat had helped her companion by stabbing him in the chest with a knife. They had taken the driver's wallet and cell phone and left the car. The driver had been able to make an emergency call on the taxi radio despite his condition. His name was Johan Lundberg and he was sixty years old. He had been a taxi driver almost all his adult life. He had been able to give good descriptions of both girls. Martinsson had been able to get their names by describing them in turn to the restaurant patrons. Both girls had been arrested in their homes. Although they were so young, both were now being held in custody due to the severity and violence of the crime. Johan Lundberg had been conscious when he was admitted at the hospital, but later his condition had suddenly deteriorated. Now he was unconscious and the doctors were unsure of the prognosis. As a motive for the crime, according to Martinsson, the girls had only offered the brief explanation that they "needed money."

Wallander grimaced. He had never seen anything like it—two young girls involved in such meaningless brutality. According to Martinsson's notes, the younger girl had a high grade-point average. The older one was a hotel receptionist and had previously worked as a nanny in London. She had just enrolled at the local community college. Neither one of them had ever been involved with the authorities before.

I just don't get it, Wallander thought. *This total lack of respect for human life. They could have killed that taxi driver, it may even turn out that way if he dies in the hospital. Two girls. If they had been boys, maybe I could understand, if only because I'm used to it by now.*

He was interrupted by a knock on the door. His colleague Ann-Britt Höglund came in the door. As usual, she looked pale and tired. Wallander thought about the change she had undergone since first coming to Ystad. She had been one of the best of her graduating class at the Police Academy and had arrived with a great deal of energy and ambition. Today she still possessed a strong will, but she was changed. The paleness in her face came from within.

"Do you want me to come back later?" she asked.

"No, by all means."

She sat down gingerly in the rickety chair opposite him. Wallander pointed to the papers on his desk.

"Do you have anything to say about this?" he asked.

"Is it the taxi-driver case?"

"Yes."

"I've talked to the older girl, Sonja Hökberg. She gave me clear and strong answers, answered everything. And seemed completely without remorse. The other girl has been in custody with the social-welfare people because of her youth."

"Do you understand it?"

Höglund paused before answering.

"Yes and no. We already know that very young people are committing serious crimes these days."

"Forgive me, but I can't recall a previous case involving teenage girls attacking anyone with knives and hammers. Were they drunk?"

"No. But I don't know if that should surprise us. Maybe what should surprise us is that something like this didn't happen sooner."

Wallander leaned over the table.

"You'll have to run that last part by me again."

"I don't know if I can explain it."

"Give it a try."

"Women aren't needed in the workforce anymore. That era is over."

"But that doesn't explain why young girls have started assaulting taxi drivers."

"There has to be something more to it that we don't know. Neither one of us believes in the idea that people are born evil."

Wallander shook his head.

"I try to hang on to that belief," he said, "though at times it's a challenge."

"Just look at the magazines these young girls are reading. Now it's all about beauty again, nothing else. How to get a boyfriend and find meaning for life through his interests and dreams, that sort of thing."

"Weren't they always like that?"

"No. Think about your own daughter. Didn't she have her own ideas about what to do with her life?"

Wallander knew she was right. But he shook his head doubtfully anyway.

"I just don't know why they attacked Lundberg."

"But you should. Young girls are slowly starting to see through the messages society sends them. When they figure out they aren't needed, that in fact they're superfluous, they react just as violently as boys. And go on to commit crimes, among other things."

Wallander was quiet. He now understood the point Höglund had been trying to make.

"I don't think I can do a better job of explaining it," she said. "Don't you think you should talk to them yourself?"

"Martinsson already suggested it."

"Actually, I stopped by for another reason. I need your help on something."

Wallander waited for her to continue.

"I promised to give a talk to a local women's club here in Ystad. They're meeting Thursday evening. But I don't feel up to it anymore. There's too much going on in my life, and I can't seem to focus."

Wallander knew she was in the middle of agonizing divorce proceedings. Her ex-husband was constantly away due to his work as a machinery installer, which sent him all over the world. That meant the process was dragging on. It was over a year ago now that she had first told Wallander about the marriage ending.

"Why don't you see if Martinsson can do it?" Wallander said. "You know I'm hopeless at lectures."

"You would just have to tell them what it's like to be a police officer," she said. "And you'd only need to speak for half an hour to an audience of about thirty women. They'll love you."

Wallander shook his head firmly.

"Martinsson would be more than happy to do it," he said. "And he has experience in politics, so he's used to this kind of thing."

"I already asked him. He can't do it."

"Holgersson?"

"Same. There's just you."

"What about Hansson?"

"He would start talking about horse racing after a few minutes. He's hopeless."

Wallander realized he would have to say yes. He couldn't leave her in the lurch.

"What kind of women's club?"

"It started as a book club, I think, that grew into a society for intellectual and literary activity. They've been active for about ten years."

"And I would be there to talk to them about what it's like to be a police officer?"

"That's all. They'll probably ask you questions, too."

"Well, I don't want to do it, but I will since you're in a bind."

She was clearly relieved and pulled out a piece of paper.

"Here's the name and number of the contact person."

Wallander glanced at the note. The address was a building in the middle of town, not too far from where he lived. Höglund got to her feet.

"They won't pay you anything," she said. "But you'll get plenty of coffee and cake."

"I don't eat cake."

"If it's any consolation, this kind of public service is exactly what the National Chief of Police wants us to be doing. You know how we're always getting those memos about finding new ways of reaching out to the community."

Wallander thought briefly about asking her how she was doing in her personal life, but decided to let it pass. If she had any problems she wanted to discuss with him, she would have to be the one to bring them up.

"Weren't you going to attend Stefan Fredman's funeral?"

"I was just there. And it was exactly as depressing as you might imagine."

"How is the mother doing? I can't remember her name."

"Anette. She's certainly been dealt a bum hand in life. But I think she's taking good care of the one child she has left. Or trying to, at any rate."

"We'll have to wait and see."

"What do you mean by that?"

"What's the boy's name?"

"Jens."

"We'll have to wait and see if the name Jens Fredman starts popping up in our police reports in about ten years."

Wallander nodded. There was certainly that possibility.

Höglund left the room. Wallander got up to get a fresh cup of coffee. The young police officers were no longer in the lunchroom. Wallander walked over to Martinsson's office. The door was wide open, but the room was empty. Wallander returned to his office. His headache was gone. He looked out of the window. Some blackbirds were screeching over by the water tower. He tried to count them, but there were too many.

The phone rang and he answered without sitting down at his desk. It was someone calling from the bookstore to let him know that the book he had ordered had come in. Wallander couldn't recall ordering a book, but he said nothing. He promised to stop by and pick it up the following day.

It was as he was putting the phone down that he remembered what the book was. It was a present for Linda. A French book on restoring antique furniture. Wallander had read about it in some magazine he had picked up at the doctor's office. He was still convinced that Linda would return to her original idea of restoring furniture for a living, despite her subsequent experimentation with other careers. He had ordered the book and promptly forgotten about it. He pushed his coffee cup aside and decided he would call her later that evening. It had been several weeks since they had talked.

Martinsson walked into the room. He was always in a hurry and seldom knocked. Over the years Wallander had become more and more impressed by Martinsson's abilities as a police officer. His real weakness was that he would probably rather be doing something else. There had been several times in the past few years that he had seriously considered quitting. The most serious phase was spurred by an attack on his daughter at school. The offenders claimed it was for no reason other than that she was the daughter of a cop. That had been enough to push him over the edge. But Wallander had eventually been able to talk him out of leaving the job. Martinsson's greatest strengths were that he was both stubborn and sharp. But his stubborness was sometimes replaced by a certain impatience, and then his sharp wits were not enough. From time to time he turned out sloppy background reports.

Martinsson leaned against the door frame.

"I tried to call you," he said. "But your phone isn't turned on."

"I was in church," Wallander said. "I forgot to turn it on again."

"At Stefan's funeral?"

Wallander repeated the phrase he had told Höglund, that it was just as depressing as he could imagine.

Martinsson gestured to the folder on his table.

"I've read it," Wallander said. "And I still don't understand what drove these girls to pick up a hammer and a knife and attack someone like that."

"It says it right there," Martinsson said. "They needed the money."

"But why such violent methods? How is he, anyway?"

"Lundberg?"

"Who else?"

"He's still unconscious and in critical condition. They promised to call if there was any change. The prognosis doesn't look so good, though."

"Do you understand any of this?"

Martinsson sat down.

"No," he said, "I certainly don't. And I'm not so sure I want to."

"But we have to. If we're going to do our jobs, that is."

Martinsson looked at Wallander.

"You know how I feel on that subject. Last time you managed to talk me out of quitting. Next time I'm not so sure you will. It won't be as easy, that's for sure."

Martinsson might be right. It was a thought that worried Wallander. He didn't want to lose Martinsson as a colleague, just as he didn't want to see Höglund turn up in his office with her pink slip.

"Maybe we should go talk to this girl, Sonja Hökberg," Wallander said.

"One more thing."

Wallander sat back down in his chair. Martinsson had a few papers in his hand.

"I want you to look this over. The events occurred last night. I was on duty and saw no reason to get you out of bed."

"What happened?"

Martinsson scratched his forehead.

"A night patrolman called in around one o'clock saying that there was a dead man lying in front of one of the cash machines next to that big department store downtown."

"Which department store?"

"The one right next to the tax authority."

Wallander nodded in recognition.

"We drove out to take a look and confirm the report. According to the doctor the man hadn't been dead very long, a few hours at most. We'll get the autopsy report in a few days, of course."

"What happened?"

"That's the question. He had an ugly wound on his head, but whether somebody hit him or whether he injured himself by falling to the ground, I don't know. We couldn't tell."

"Was he robbed?"

"His wallet was still there, with money in it."

Wallander thought for a moment.

"Any witnesses?"

"No."

"Who was he?"

Martinsson looked in his papers.

"His name was Tynnes Falk. He was forty-seven years old and lived nearby. He was renting the top floor apartment in a building at number ten Apelbergsgatan."

Wallander raised his hand to stop Martinsson.

"Number ten Apelbergsgatan?"

"That's right."

Wallander nodded slowly. A couple of years ago, right after his divorce from Mona, he had met a woman during a night of dancing at the Hotel Saltsjöbaden. Wallander had been very drunk. He had gone home with her and woken up the next morning in a strange bed next to a woman he could hardly recognize. He had no idea what her name was. He had quickly thrown his clothes on and left and never met her again. But for some reason he was sure she had lived at 10 Apelbergsgatan.

"Do you recognize the address?" Martinsson asked.

"I just didn't hear you."

Martinsson looked at him with surprise.

"Was I mumbling?"

"Please continue."

"He was single—divorced, actually. His ex-wife still lives in town, but their children are scattered all over the place. One boy is nineteen and is studying in Stockholm. The girl is seventeen and is working as a nanny at an embassy in Paris. The wife has been notified of his death."

"Who did he work with?"

"He appears to have worked for himself. Some kind of computer consultant."

"And he wasn't robbed?"

"No, but he had just requested his account balance from the cash machine before he died. He was still holding the slip in his hand when we found him."

"So he hadn't made a withdrawal?"

"Not according to the printed receipt."

"Strange. The most reasonable thing to assume would be that someone was waiting for him to withdraw money and then strike when he had the cash."

"That occurred to me as well, of course, but the last time he made a withdrawal was on Saturday, and that wasn't a large sum."

Martinsson handed Wallander a small plastic bag containing the blood-spattered bank receipt. It had recorded the time as being two minutes past midnight. He handed it back to Martinsson.

"What does Nyberg say?"

"That nothing apart from the head wound points to a crime. He probably suffered a heart attack."

"Perhaps he had been expecting to see a higher amount than the one on the printout," Wallander said thoughtfully.

He stood up.

"Let's wait for the autopsy report. Until then we'll assume no crime was committed, so put it aside for now."

Martinsson gathered up his papers.

"I'll contact the lawyer who was assigned to Hökberg. I'll let you know when he can be expected down here so you can talk to her."

"Not that I want to," Wallander said. "But I guess I should."

Martinsson left the room and Wallander walked to the bathroom. He thought gratefully that at least his days of running to the bathroom due to elevated blood sugar were over.

For an hour he kept working on the smuggled cigarettes while the thought of the favor he had agreed to do for Höglund nagged at the back of his mind.

Two minutes past four Martinsson called to say that Sonja Hökberg and her lawyer were ready.

"Who is he?" Wallander asked.

"Herman Lötberg."

Wallander knew him. He was an older man who was easy to work with.

"I'll be there in five minutes," Wallander said and hung up.

He walked back over to the window. The blackbirds were gone and the wind had picked up. He thought about Anette Fredman and the little boy who had played so quietly on the floor. He thought about the boy's frightened eyes. Then he shook his head and tried to work out the questions he was going to ask Sonja Hökberg. From Martinsson's notes he learned she was the one who had sat in the back seat and hit Lundberg in the head with a hammer. There had been many blows, not just one. As if she had been in a blind rage.

Wallander grabbed a notebook and pen and left. When he was halfway there, he realized that he had left his glasses. He walked back.

There's really only one question, he thought as he returned to the conference room.

Why did they do it?

Their statement about needing money isn't enough.

There's another answer somewhere, a deeper answer that I have to find.

Chapter Four

Sonja Hökberg did not look anything like Wallander had expected. Afterward he couldn't quite recall what he had been expecting, but he knew it wasn't the person he had met in that room. Sonja Hökberg was seated when he came in. She was small and thin, almost to the point of transparency. She had shoulder-length blond hair and blue eyes. She could have been a poster child for innocence and purity. Nothing indicated that she was a crazed hammer-wielding murderer.

Wallander had been met by her lawyer outside the room.

"She's very much in control of herself," he said to Wallander. "But I'm not convinced she understands the gravity of the charges she's facing."

"It's not a matter of accusation; she's guilty," Martinsson said firmly.

"What about the hammer," Wallander asked. "Have we found it?"

"She put it under her bed. She hadn't even tried to wipe the blood off. The other girl got rid of her knife. We're still searching for it."

Martinsson left. Wallander stepped into the room with the lawyer. The girl looked at them expectantly. She didn't seem nervous at all. Wallander nodded to her and sat down. There was a tape recorder on the table. Wallander looked at her for a long time. She looked back.

"Do you have any gum?" she asked finally.

Wallander shook his head and looked over at Lötberg, who also shook his head.

"We'll see if we can get you some later," Wallander said and turned on the tape recorder. "But first we're going to have a little chat."

"I've already said what happened. Why can't I have some gum? I can pay for it," she said and held up a black purse with an oak-leaf clasp. Wallander was surprised that it hadn't been confiscated. "I won't talk until I get my gum."

Wallander reached over for the phone and called the reception desk. *Ebba will take care of this,* he thought. It wasn't until an unfamiliar woman's voice came on the line that he remembered that Ebba was retired now. Even though she had been gone for six months, Wallander had still not grown used to the new receptionist. She was a woman in her thirties named Irene. She had previously worked as an administrative assistant in a doctor's office, and she had already become well-liked at the police station. But Wallander missed Ebba.

"I need some gum," Wallander said. "Do you know anyone who would have any?"

"Yes," Irene said. "Me."

Wallander hung up and walked out to the reception desk.

"Is it for the girl?" Irene asked.

"Fast thinker," Wallander said.

He returned to the examination room, gave Sonja Hökberg the stick of gum, and realized he had forgotten to turn off the tape recorder through all of this.

"Let's begin," he said. "It's a quarter past four on October sixth, 1997. Kurt Wallander is questioning Sonja Hökberg."

"So do I have to tell you everything all over again?" she asked.

"Yes. Try to speak clearly and direct your words at the mike."

"What about the fact that I've already told you everything?"

"I may have some additional questions."

"I don't feel like going over it again."

For a moment Wallander felt thrown by her total lack of anxiety.

"Unfortunately you'll just have to cooperate," he said. "You have been accused of a very serious crime, and what's more, you have confessed. Right now you stand accused of assault in the third degree, but this already serious charge may be upgraded to something worse if the taxi driver's condition deteriorates further."

Lötberg gave Wallander a disapproving look but didn't say anything.

Wallander started at the beginning.

"Your name is Sonja Hökberg and you were born on February second, 1978."

"That makes me an Aquarius. What's your sign?"

"That doesn't concern us at present. You're here to answer my questions and that is all. Understand?"

"Do I look stupid?"

"You live with your parents at twelve Trastvägen, here in Ystad."

"Yes."

"You have a younger brother, Emil, born in 1982."

"He's the one who should be sitting in this chair, not me."

Wallander raised his eyebrows.

"Why do you say that?"

"He never leaves my things alone. He's always looking through my stuff. We fight a lot."

"I'm sure it can be trying to have a younger brother, but let's leave it for now."

She's still so composed, Wallander thought. Her nonchalance was starting to irritate him.

"Can you describe the events of last Tuesday evening?"

"It's such a drag to have to tell the same thing twice."

"That can't be helped. You and Eva Persson went out that evening?"

"There's nothing to do around here. I wish I lived in Moscow."

Wallander regarded her with surprise. Even Lötberg seemed startled.

"Why Moscow?"

"I just saw somewhere that exciting things often happen there. Have you ever been to Moscow?"

"No. Just answer my questions. So, you went out that night."

"You already know that."

"Were you and Eva good friends?"

"Why else would we have gone out together? Do I seem like the kind of person who would go out with people she didn't like?"

For the first time Wallander thought he could detect a note of emotion in her voice. Impatience.

"How long have you known each other?"

"Not very long."

"How long?"

"A few years."

"She's five years younger than you are."

"She looks up to me."

"What do you mean by that?"

"She's told me so herself. She looks up to me."

"Why is that?"

"You'll have to ask her yourself."

I will, Wallander thought. *I have a lot of things to ask her.*

"Can you tell me what happened that night?"

"Jesus Christ!"

"You have to, whether you want to or not. We can stay here all night if we have to."

"We had a beer."

"Even though Eva Persson is only fourteen?"

"She looks older."

"Then what happened?"

"We ordered another beer."

"And after that?"

"We called a cab. But you know all this. Why do you keep asking?"

"Had you already decided to attack this taxi driver?"

"We needed the money."

"For what?"

"Nothing in particular."

"Let me see if I have this straight: you needed money, but not for anything in particular."

"Right."

No, that's not right, Wallander thought. He had noticed a note of insecurity in her answer. He immediately grew more attentive.

"Normally, when you need money it's for something in particular."

"Not in our case."

Oh, yes it was, Wallander thought. But he decided to leave the matter for now.

"How did you come up with the idea of robbing a taxi driver?"

"We talked about it."

"At the restaurant?"

"Yes."

"So you hadn't talked about it earlier?"

"Why would we have done that?"

Lötberg was staring down into his hands.

"Would it be correct to say that you had no intention of assaulting the taxi driver before you went to the restaurant? Whose idea was it?"

"It was mine."

"Eva had no objections?"

"No."

This doesn't hang together, Wallander thought. *She's lying, but she's remarkably collected.*

"You ordered the taxi from the restaurant, then waited until it arrived. Is that correct?"

"Yes."

"But where did the hammer and knife come from? If you hadn't planned the attack in advance, I mean."

Sonja Hökberg looked steadily into Wallander's eyes.

"I always carry a hammer with me," she said. "And Eva always has a knife."

"Why?"

"You never know what's going to happen."

"What do you mean?"

"The streets are full of crazy people. You have to be able to defend yourself."

"So you mean to say you always go out with this hammer in your purse?"

"Yes."

"Have you ever used it before?"

Lötberg looked up.

"That question bears no relevance to this case," he said.

"What does that mean?" Sonja Hökberg asked.

"Relevance? That he has no business asking that question."

"I can answer anyway. I had never used the hammer before. But Eva cut someone once. Some creep who was trying to feel her up."

Wallander was struck by a sudden thought and veered away from his earlier line of questioning.

"Did you meet anyone at that restaurant? Had you made a date with anyone?"

"No."

"You don't have a boyfriend?"

"No."

That answer came a little too quickly, Wallander thought. He made a mental note of it.

"The taxi came and you left."

"Yes."

"What did you do then?"

"What do you think? We told him where we wanted to go."

"And you said you wanted to be driven out to Rydsgård. Why?"

"I don't know. We had to say something and that was the first thing that came to mind."

"Eva sat up front with the driver, and you sat in the backseat. Did you decide on that beforehand?"

"That was the plan."

"What plan?"

"That we would get the driver to stop because Eva wanted to get in the back seat with me. And that's when we were going to get him."

"So you had already decided to use your weapons?"

"Not if he had been younger."

"What would you have done then?"

"Then we would have got him to stop by pulling up our skirts and being suggestive."

Wallander noticed he had started to sweat. Her obvious detachment from the situation was starting to get to him.

"Suggesting what exactly?"

"What do you think?"

"You would entice him into thinking he could have sex with you?"

"You dirty old fuck."

Lötberg leaned forward.

"You should watch your language."

Sonja Hökberg looked over at him.

"I'll use whatever language I please."

Lötberg sat back again. Wallander decided to move on.

"But, as it happened, the taxi driver was an older man. You got him to stop. Then what?"

"I hit him in the head. Eva stabbed him with the knife."

"How many times did you strike him?"

"I don't know. A couple of times. I wasn't counting."

"You weren't afraid of killing him?"

"We needed the money."

"That wasn't what I was asking. What I want to know is, were you aware that the wounds you were inflicting could be fatal?"

Sonja Hökberg shrugged. Wallander waited but she didn't say anything. He didn't feel he had the energy to repeat the last question.

"You say you needed money. For what?"

"Nothing in particular. I told you."

"Then what happened?"

"We took his wallet and the cell phone and walked home."

"What happened to the wallet?"

"We divided up the cash. Then Eva threw it away somewhere."

Wallander looked briefly through Martinsson's notes. Johan Lundberg had been carrying around 600 kronor. They had found the wallet in a wastepaper basket after getting directions from Eva Persson. Sonja Hökberg had taken the cell phone. The police had found it in her bedroom.

Wallander turned off the tape recorder. Sonja Hökberg followed his movements with her eyes.

"Can I go home now?"

"No, as a matter of fact," Wallander said. "You are nineteen years old and that means you count as an adult in our courts. You have committed a felony, and you will be formally arraigned."

"And that means?"

"You'll have to stay here at the station."

"Why?"

Wallander looked at Lötberg, then stood up.

"I think your attorney can probably explain it to you."

Wallander left the room. He felt sick to his stomach. Sonja Hökberg had not been putting on an act in there. She had no sense of wrong-doing. Wallander walked into Martinsson's office and sat down in a chair. Martinsson was on the phone but gestured that he would be off soon. While Wallander waited he felt a strong urge to smoke. That almost never happened. But his meeting with Sonja Hökberg had been unusually disturbing.

Martinsson put the phone down.

"How did it go?"

"She confessed to everything. She's as cold as ice."

"Eva Persson is the same way and she's only fourteen."

Wallander looked at Martinsson with something like pleading in his eyes.

"What's happening to the world?"

"I don't know."

Wallander was visibly shaken.

"They're just young girls."

"I know, I know. And they have no remorse at all."

They were silent for a while and Wallander felt completely empty inside. Martinsson was the one who finally spoke.

"Do you understand now why I think of quitting so often?"

Wallander roused himself.

"And do you understand why it's so important that you don't?"

He got up and walked over to the window.

"How is Lundberg?"

"Still in critical condition."

"We have to get to the bottom of this, whether or not he dies. They didn't assault him like that just to get some cash. Either they needed the money for a specific purpose or the attack was about something else entirely."

"What could that have been?"

"I don't know. It's just a feeling that there's something deeper behind all this."

"Isn't the most probable scenario that they were a little drunk and concocted this mad plan to get some money? Without thinking of the consequences?"

"Why do you think that?"

"I'm just sure it wasn't a random act, like you said."

Wallander nodded.

"Well, we agree on that. But I want to know what their reasons were. Tomorrow I'll talk to Eva Persson, as well as her parents. Does either of them have a boyfriend?"

"Eva Persson said she had someone."

"Not Hökberg?"

"No."

"Then she's lying. She has someone and we'll find him."

Martinsson made some notes.

"Who will take that on—you or me?"

Wallander's response was immediate.

"I'll do it. I want to know what's going on in this country."

"Suits me fine."

"You're not completely off the hook, though. Not you, nor Hansson, nor Höglund. We have to find out the real reason for this attack. I'm convinced it was an attempted homicide, and if Lundberg dies, then it's murder."

Wallander returned to his office. It was half past five and already it was dark outside. He thought about Sonja Hökberg and why the two girls had needed money so badly. Had there been another reason entirely? Then he thought of Anette Fredman.

He still had work to do but felt he couldn't bear to stay in his office. He grabbed his coat and left. The sharp fall wind burned his face. He heard the strange engine noise again when he started the car. As he turned out of the parking lot, he decided to go shopping. His refrigerator was almost empty except for the bottle of champagne that he had won in a bet with Hansson. He could no longer remember what the bet had been. On an impulse he thought he would swing by the cash machine where the man had died the night before. He could do his shopping in one of the department stores nearby.

After parking the car, he walked up to the ATM and waited while a woman with a baby in a stroller withdrew some money. The concrete pavement was rough and uneven. Wallander looked around. There seemed to be no residential buildings nearby. In the middle of the night the plaza would be quite deserted. Even in the powerful streetlights, a man could scream and collapse onto the ground without anyone hearing or seeing him.

Wallander went into the nearest department store and found the food market. As usual, he found himself plagued by boredom and indecision as he inspected the shelves. He quickly filled up his basket with an assortment of items, paid, and left. When he started the car again, the mystery engine-noise seemed to increase. He took off his dark suit as soon as he was back in his apartment. He showered and noted that he was almost out of soap. He made some vegetable soup for dinner that tasted surprisingly good. He brewed some coffee, and took a cup out with him into the living room. He was tired. He flipped the channels without finding anything interesting, then reached for the phone and called Linda in Stockholm. She was sharing an apartment in Kungsholmen with two women he only knew by name. To make ends meet, she sometimes worked as a waitress in a nearby restaurant. Wallander had eaten dinner there the last time he was in town and had enjoyed the food. But he was surprised she could stand the music, which was oppressively loud.

Linda was twenty-six years old now. They had a good relationship, but he missed being able to see her regularly.

An answering machine came on. Neither Linda nor any of her roommates was home. The message was repeated in English. Wallander said who he was and that it wasn't anything important.

He put the phone down and stared down at his coffee. It was cold. *I can't keep living like this,* he thought irritatedly. *I'm only fifty years old, but I feel ancient and weak.*

He knew he should go for an evening walk and tried desperately to think of an excuse not to. Finally he put his sneakers on and headed out.

It was half past eight when he returned. The walk had cleared his mind and he no longer felt as dispirited as before.

The phone rang, and Wallander thought it must be Linda. But it was Martinsson.

"Lundberg has died. They just called from the hospital."

Wallander was silent.

"That means Hökberg and Persson have committed murder," Martinsson said.

"I know," Wallander said, "and we have a hell of a mess on our hands."

They decided to meet at eight o'clock the next morning.

There was nothing more to say.

Wallander stayed in front of the television and absentmindedly watched a news program. The dollar had gained more ground against the krona. The only story that managed to grab his attention was the piece on an insurance company, Trustor. It seemed bafflingly easy these days to drain the resources of an entire corporation without anyone catching on until it was too late.

Linda didn't call back. Wallander went to bed around eleven o'clock.

It took him a long time to fall asleep.

Chapter Five

Wallander woke up with a sore throat shortly after six o'clock on Tuesday, the seventh of October. He was sweating lightly and he knew it meant he was starting to come down with the flu. He stayed in bed for a while and debated whether or not he should stay home, but the thought of Johan Lundberg's death forced him up. He showered, drank some coffee, and swallowed some pills to reduce his fever. He tucked the bottle of pills into his pocket. Then, before heading out, he forced himself to eat a bowl of yogurt. The street lamp outside the kitchen window was swaying in the gusty wind. It was overcast and only a couple of degrees above freezing. Wallander rummaged around in his closet for a thick sweater. Then he put his hand on the phone and debated whether he should call Linda. It was too early. When he reached street level and was about to get in his car, he remembered that he had left a to-do list on the kitchen table. There was something on the list that he had been planning to buy today but he couldn't recall what it was. He decided he didn't have the energy to go get it.

Wallander took his usual route to the office, driving along the Österled. Each time he drove this way he felt guilty. He knew he should be out there walking to work, in order to keep his blood sugar at a healthy level. And even today he wasn't so weak from the flu that he couldn't have walked.

He parked outside the station and was in his office as the clock struck seven. Sitting at his desk, he suddenly remembered the item he had forgotten to buy. Soap. He immediately wrote it down on a piece of paper. Then he turned his thoughts to the case.

Some of the unpleasant feelings from the day before returned. He recalled Sonja Hökberg's complete lack of emotion. He tried to convince himself that she did in fact exhibit some signs of compassion that he simply had not been able to pick up, but to no avail. His experience in these matters told him he had not been mistaken. He got up and went to get a cup of coffee from the lunchroom. Since Martinsson was also an early riser, Wallander stopped by his office. As usual, the door was open. Wallander had often wondered how Martinsson got any work done. Wallander couldn't concentrate unless his door was bolted shut.

Martinsson nodded when Wallander stopped in the doorway.

"I thought you'd be here," he said.

"I don't feel so well today," Wallander said.

"A cold?"

"I always get a sore throat in October."

Martinsson, who always worried about getting sick, pulled his chair back a couple of inches.

"You could have stayed home today," he said. "This depressing Lundberg case is already solved."

"Only partially," Wallander objected. "We still don't have a motive. I don't believe that line that they needed extra money for nothing in particular. Have you found the knife yet?"

"Nyberg's in charge of that. I haven't talked to him yet."

"Call him."

Martinsson made a face.

"He's not easy to talk to in the morning."

"Then I'll call him myself."

Wallander reached for Martinsson's phone and tried Nyberg's home number. After a few moments he was automatically transferred to a cell phone. Nyberg answered, but it was a poor connection.

"It's Kurt. I just wanted to know if you've found the knife yet."

"How the hell are we supposed to find anything in the dark?" Nyberg answered angrily.

"I thought Eva Persson said where she had left it."

"We still have an area of several hundred cubic meters to comb. She just said she threw it somewhere in the Old Cemetery."

"Why don't you have someone bring her down?"

"If it's here, we'll find it," Nyberg said.

They ended the conversation.

"I didn't sleep well last night," Martinsson said. "My daughter Terese knows Eva Persson. They're almost the same age. And Eva Persson has parents too. What are they going through right now? From what I understand, Eva is their only child."

They both thought about what he had said. Then Wallander started a series of sneezes. Martinsson left quickly. The conversation was left hanging.

They gathered in one of the conference rooms at eight o'clock. Wallander sat in his usual spot at the end of the table. Hansson and Höglund were already there. Martinsson was standing by the window talking to someone on the phone, most likely his wife. Wallander had always wondered how they could have so much to say to each other after having had breakfast together only an hour before. The main feeling in the room was despondence. Lisa Holgersson walked in and Martinsson finished his conversation. Hansson got up and shut the door.

"Isn't Nyberg supposed to be here?" he asked.

"He's looking for the knife," Wallander said. "I think we can assume he'll find it."

Then he looked over at Holgersson, who nodded at him. He could start the meeting. He wondered briefly how many times he had found himself in exactly this situation. Up early in the morning, facing his colleagues across the conference table with a crime to solve.

They were waiting for him to begin.

"Johan Lundberg is now dead," he said. "In case anyone hasn't heard the latest."

He pointed to a copy of the local newspaper, the *Ystad Allehanda*, that was lying on the table. The taxi driver's death was announced in huge print on the first page.

Wallander continued. "This means the two girls, Hökberg and Persson, are charged with murder. We can't call it anything else, since Hökberg in particular was so precise in her explanations. They planned this and were carrying weapons. They were going to attack whichever taxi driver came their way. We've recovered the hammer, as well as Lundberg's empty wallet and his cell phone. The only thing missing is the knife. Neither one of the girls has denied the charges, nor shifted the blame to the other. I'm assuming we can hand the matter over to the district attorney tomorrow at the latest. Since Eva Persson is so young, her case will be handled by the juvenile courts. The autopsy results aren't in yet, but I think we can say that our role in this unfortunate case is as good as over."

Wallander finished and waited to see if anyone had anything to say.

"Why did they do it?" Lisa Holgersson finally asked. "It seems so unnecessary."

Wallander nodded. He had hoped someone would ask this question so he wouldn't have to find a way to pose it himself.

"Sonja Hökberg was very firm on this point," he said. "Both in her session with Martinsson and later with me. She said, 'We needed the money.' Nothing else."

"What for?"

Hansson asked the last question.

"We don't know why. They won't tell us. If Hökberg is to be believed, they didn't even know why themselves. They just wanted money."

Wallander looked around the table before he continued.

"I don't think they're telling the truth. At the very least, I know Hökberg is lying. I haven't yet spoken with Eva Persson, but I'm still convinced of it. They needed that money for something in particular. I also have the suspicion that Persson was doing what Hökberg told her to. That doesn't make her any less guilty, but I think it gives a clearer picture of their relationship."

"Does it even matter?" Höglund asked. "Whether they needed the money for clothes or something else?"

"I guess not, at this point. The district attorney certainly has enough evidence to convict Hökberg."

"They've never been in trouble with us before," Martinsson said. "I made a quick search of our database. And they were both doing well in school."

Wallander again had the feeling that they were taking the wrong approach to the case. Or at the very least, that they had been overly hasty in writing off other explanations for Lundberg's murder. But since he was unable to put this hunch into words, he said nothing. They still had a lot of work to do, and the reason for the murder could very well have to do with money. They simply had to keep their eyes open for other possibilities.

The phone rang and Hansson picked up. After listening for a moment he put the receiver down.

"That was Nyberg," he said. "They found the knife."

Wallander nodded and shut the folder lying in front of him.

"Naturally, we still need to speak to the parents and make sure we conduct a thorough background investigation, but I think we can safely forward the preliminary information to the district attorney's office."

Lisa Holgersson raised her hand to speak.

"We need to hold a press conference. We've been barraged by calls from the media. It is still unusual for two young girls to commit this kind of violent crime."

Wallander looked over at Höglund, but she shook her head. In the
past few years, she had often taken on the task of talking to the media,
a job he thoroughly despised. But not this time. Wallander understood.

"I'll do it," he said. "Do we have a time?"

"I'm going to suggest one o'clock."

Wallander made a note of it.

They divided up the tasks and brought the meeting to a close.
Everyone wanted the matter disposed of as quickly as possible. It was a
particularly wretched case, and no one wanted to spend more time on
it than was necessary. Wallander would pay a visit to the Hökberg
family. Martinsson and Höglund would talk to Eva Persson and her
parents.

Soon the room was empty. Wallander could feel the symptoms of his
flu getting worse. *At least maybe I'll infect a journalist,* he thought as he
dug around in his pockets for a tissue.

He bumped into Nyberg in the hallway. Nyberg was wearing boots
and a warm coat, his hair splayed in all directions. He was clearly in a
bad mood.

"I heard you found the knife," Wallander said.

"Looks like the county can no longer afford to pay for basic upkeep," Nyberg answered. "We were shin-deep in leaves. But we finally
found it."

"What kind of a knife?"

"Kitchen knife. Fairly big. The tip broke off, probably from hitting
a rib, so she must have used a surprising amount of force. But then
again, it was a cheap knife."

Wallander shook his head.

"It's hard to believe," Nyberg said. "I don't know what happened to
the basic respect for human life. How much money did they get?"

"We don't know yet, but probably around six hundred kronor. It
couldn't have been much more. Lundberg was at the beginning of his
shift, and he never carried a lot of change to start."

Nyberg muttered something under his breath and walked off. Wallander returned to his office. For a while he sat in his chair without
knowing what to do next. His throat hurt. Finally he opened the folder
with a sigh. Sonja Hökberg lived to the west of Ystad. He wrote down
the address, got up, and put on his coat. As he was leaving, the phone
rang. He picked up. It was Linda. The voices and clatter in the background made him think she was calling from the restaurant.

"I got your message this morning," she said.

"This morning?"

"I wasn't at home last night."

Wallander knew better than to ask her where she had spent the night. It would only make her get angry and slam down the phone.

"Well, I didn't call for any particular reason," he said. "I just wanted to know how you were doing."

"Good. How about you?'

"I've got a little cold. Otherwise things are the same. I was wondering if you had any plans to come down and visit soon."

"I don't have time."

"I'm happy to pay your fare."

"I told you, I don't have time. It's not about the money."

Wallander realized he would not be able to change her mind. She was as stubborn as he was.

"How are you doing, anyway?" she asked again. "Do you have any contact with Baiba these days?"

"That ended a long time ago. You know that."

"It's not good for you to go on like this."

"What do you mean by that?"

"You know what I mean. You're even starting to get a whiny tone in your voice. You never had that before."

"You think I sound whiny?"

"You're doing it right now. But I have a suggestion. I think you should contact a dating service."

"A dating service?"

"Where you can find someone. Otherwise you're going to turn into a whiny old man who worries about where I'm spending my nights."

She sees right through me, he thought. *I'm an open book.*

"You mean I should put an ad in the paper?"

"Yes, or use one of those agencies."

"I'll never do that."

"Why not?"

"I don't believe in them."

"And why not?"

"I don't know."

"Well, it was just a suggestion. Think it over. I have to get back to work."

"Where are you?"

"At the restaurant. We open soon."

They said goodbye and hung up. Wallander wondered where she had spent the night. A couple of years ago, Linda had been involved with a young man from Kenya who was in medical school in Lund. But that had ended. After that, he had not known very much at all about who she was dating, other than that every so often she started seeing someone new. He felt an unpleasant pinch of irritation and jealousy. Then he left the room. The thought of putting in a personal ad or getting in touch with a dating service had actually occurred to him before. But he had always rejected the idea. It was as if that would mean sinking to an unacceptable level of desperation.

The strong wind chilled him as soon as he walked outside. He got in his car and started the engine, listening to the strange noises that were only getting worse. Then he drove out to the townhouse where the Hökbergs lived. Martinsson's report had only given him the information that Sonja Hökberg's father was "self-employed." He still didn't know what that actually meant. Wallander got out of the car. The small patch of garden in the front was neat and tidy. He rang the doorbell. After a moment a man came to the door. Wallander knew at once that they had met before. He had a good memory for faces. But he didn't know when or where it had been. The man had also immediately recognized Wallander.

"It's you," he said. "I knew the police would be coming out, but I didn't expect it to be you."

He stepped aside to let Wallander enter. Wallander heard the sound of a TV coming from somewhere. He still had not managed to figure out where he had met this man before.

"I take it you remember me?" Hökberg asked.

"Yes," Wallander said. "But I have to say I'm having trouble placing you in the right context."

" 'Erik Hökberg' doesn't ring a bell?"

Wallander searched his memory. "I don't think so."

"What about 'Sten Widén'?"

Suddenly Wallander remembered. Sten Widén, with his horse farm in Stjärnsund. And Erik. The three of them had once shared a passion for the opera. Sten had been the most deeply involved, but Erik was a childhood friend of his and they had often sat around the record player as they listened to Verdi's operas.

"Yes, I remember now," Wallander said. "But your name wasn't Hökberg then, was it?"

"I took my wife's name. As a boy I was called Erik Eriksson."

Erik Hökberg was a large man. The coat hanger he held out to Wallander looked small in his hand. Wallander remembered him as thin, but now he was of substantial proportions. That must have been why it had been so hard to put two and two together.

Wallander hung up his coat and followed Hökberg into the living room. There was a TV in the middle of the room, but it was turned off.

The sound was coming from another room. They sat down. Wallander tried to think of how to start off.

"It's horrible what's happened," Hökberg said. "Naturally I have no idea what got into her."

"Had she ever been violent before?"

"Never."

"What about your wife? Is she home?"

Hökberg had collapsed into a heap in his chair. Behind the rolls of fat in his face Wallander thought he could sense the outline of another face from a time that now seemed endlessly distant.

"She took Emil and went to her sister in Höör. She couldn't stand to stay here. The reporters kept calling. They show no mercy. They called in the middle of the night, some of them."

"I'm afraid I have to speak to her."

"I know. I told her the police would come by."

Wallander wasn't sure how to proceed.

"You and your wife must have talked about what happened."

"She doesn't understand it any more than I do. It was a complete shock."

"You have a good relationship with Sonja?"

"There have never been any problems."

"And between her and her mother?"

"Same. They've had fights from time to time but only stuff you would expect. Nothing else, at least as long as I've known her."

Wallander furrowed his brow.

"What do you mean by that?"

"Didn't you know she was my stepdaughter?"

Wallander was sure that the information had not been in the report. He would have remembered it.

"Ruth and I had Emil together," Hökberg said. "Sonja was about two when I entered the scene. That was seventeen years ago. Ruth and I met at a Christmas party."

"Who was Sonja's biological father?"

"His name was Rolf. He never cared about her. He and Ruth were never married."

"Do you know where he is?"

"He died a few years ago. He drank himself to death."

Wallander looked for a pen in his coat pocket. He had already realized that he had forgotten both his glasses and notebook. There was a pile of old newspapers on the glass table.

"Do you mind if I tear off a piece?"

"Can't the police afford to stock office supplies anymore?"

"That's a good question. As it happens I've forgotten to bring my notebook."

Wallander used a magazine as a writing pad. He saw that it was an English-language financial magazine.

"Do you mind if I ask you what you do for a living?"

The answer came as a surprise.

"I play the stock market."

"I see. What exactly does that entail?"

"I trade stocks, options, foreign currency. I also place some bets, mainly on English cricket games. Sometimes American baseball."

"So you mean you gamble?"

"Not the usual kind. I never place bets on horses. But I guess you can call trading stocks another form of gambling."

"And you do all this from home?"

Hökberg got up and gestured for Wallander to follow him. When they reached the adjoining room, Wallander paused in the doorway. There was not simply one TV in this room; there were three. Various numbers flashed past in a dark ribbon on the bottom of each screen. On one wall was a row of clocks showing the time in other parts of the world. It was like stepping into an air traffic control tower.

"People always say technology has made the world smaller," Hökberg said. "I think that's debatable. But the fact that it's made my world bigger is beyond dispute. From this flimsy townhouse at the edge of Ystad, I can reach all the markets in the whole world. I can connect to betting centers in London or Rome. I can buy options on the Hong Kong market and sell American dollars in Jakarta."

"Is it really so simple?"

"Not completely. You need permits, good contacts, and knowledge. But when I step into this room I'm in the middle of the world. Whenever I choose. Strength and vulnerability go hand in hand."

They returned to the living room.

"I would like to see Sonja's room," Wallander said.

Hökberg led him up the stairs. They walked past a room that Wallander assumed belonged to their boy, Emil. Hökberg pointed to a door.

"I'll wait downstairs," he said. "If you don't need me, that is."

"No, I'll be fine."

Wallander heard Hökberg's heavy steps recede down the stairs. He pushed open the door. There was a sloping ceiling in the room and one of the windows was slightly open. A thin curtain wafted in the wind. Wallander knew from experience that the first impression was often the most valuable. A closer examination could reveal dramatic details that were not immediately visible, but the first impression was something he always came back to.

A person lived here in this room. She was the one he was looking for. The bed was made, heaped with pink flowery cushions. On one of the walls was a shelf covered with teddy bears. There was a mirror on the closet door and a thick rug on the floor. There was a desk by the window, but there was nothing on its surface. Wallander stood in the doorway for a long time and looked into the room. This was where Sonja Hökberg lived. He entered the room, knelt by the bed, and looked underneath. There was a thin covering of dust everywhere except in one spot where an object had left an outline of itself. Wallander shivered. He suspected it was the spot where the hammer had been found. He got up and opened the drawers of the desk. None of them was locked. There weren't even any locks. He didn't know exactly what he was looking for. Maybe a diary or some photographs. But nothing in the drawers caught his attention. He sat down on the bed and thought about his meeting with Sonja Hökberg.

There was something that had struck him as soon as he saw her room from the doorway.

Something didn't add up. Sonja Hökberg and her room didn't go together. He couldn't imagine her here among all the pink cushions and teddy bears. But it was her room. He tried to figure out what it could mean. Which was closer to the truth—the indifferent girl he had met at the police station, or the room where she had lived and hidden a hammer under her bed?

Many years ago Rydberg had taught him how to listen. *Each room has its own life and breath. You have to listen for it. A room can tell you many secrets about the person who lives there.*

At first Wallander had been skeptical about Rydberg's advice, but in time he had come to realize that Rydberg had imparted a crucial knowledge.

Wallander's head was starting to ache, particularly in his temples. He got up and opened the closet door. There were clothes on the hangers and shoes on the floor. On the inside of the closet door was a poster from a movie called *The Devil's Advocate*. The starring role was played by Al Pacino. Wallander remembered him from *The Godfather*. He shut the closet door and sat down on the chair by the desk. That gave him a new angle from which to view the room.

There's something missing, he thought. He remembered what Linda's room had looked like as a teenager. Of course there had been some stuffed animals. But above all there were the pictures of her idols, who changed from time to time but were always there in some form or another.

There was nothing like that in Sonja Hökberg's room. She was nineteen, and all she had was a movie poster in her closet.

Wallander remained for a few minutes, then left the room and walked back down the stairs. Hökberg looked at him carefully.

"Did you find anything?"

"I just wanted to have a look around."

"What's going to happen to her?"

Wallander shook his head.

"She'll be tried as an adult, and she's confessed to the crime. They're not going to be easy on her."

Hökberg didn't say anything. Wallander could see he was pained.

Wallander took down the number for Hökberg's sister-in-law in Höör.

Then he left the townhouse and drove back to the station, feeling worse and worse. He was going to go home after the press conference and crawl into bed.

When he walked into the reception area, Irene waved him over. Wallander saw that she was pale.

"What's happened?" he asked.

"I don't know," she said. "They were looking for you, and as usual you didn't have your phone with you."

"Who was looking for me?"

"Everyone."

Wallander lost his patience.

"What do you mean, 'everyone'? Give me some names, dammit!"

"Martinsson. And Lisa."

Wallander went straight to Martinsson's office. Hansson was in there.

"What's happened?"

Martinsson answered.

"Sonja Hökberg has escaped."

Wallander stared at him in disbelief.

"Escaped?"

"It happened about an hour ago. We've put all available personnel on the search, but she's gone."

Wallander looked at his colleagues.

Then he took off his coat and sat down.

Chapter Six

It didn't take Wallander long to understand what must have happened.

Someone had been sloppy, someone had disregarded the most basic security measures. But above all, someone had forgotten the fact that Sonja Hökberg was not the innocent young girl she appeared to be; that she had committed a brutal murder only a couple of days before.

It was easy to recontstruct the chain of events. Sonja Hökberg was supposed to be moved from one room to another. She had met with her lawyer and was to be brought back to the holding cell. While she was waiting to be moved, she had asked to go to the bathroom. When she came back out she saw that the officer on guard had turned his back to her and was engaged in conversation with someone in one of the neighboring offices. She had then simply walked the other way. No one had tried to stop her. She had walked straight out through the front hall. No one had seen her. Not Irene, not anyone else. After about five minutes, the officer in charge of her had gone into the bathroom and discovered that she was gone. He had then looked into the room where she had talked to her lawyer, and then he'd alerted security. At that point Sonja Hökberg had had ten minutes to do her disappearing act, and that had been more than enough time.

Wallander groaned and felt his headache worsen.

"I've alerted all available personnel," Martinsson said. "And I called her father. You had just left the house. Did you discover anything that might tell us where she's headed?"

"Her mother is staying with her sister in Höör."

He gave Martinsson the number.

"She can hardly be planning to go there on foot," Hansson said.

"She has a driver's licence," Martinsson said, with the telephone receiver pressed against his ear. "She could hitch a ride, steal a car."

"The first person we have to talk to is Eva Persson," Wallander said. "And that's going to happen pronto. Juvenile or not, she's going to tell us everything she knows."

Hansson got up to leave and almost collided with Lisa Holgersson, who had only just heard of the disappearance. While Martinsson was talking on the phone with Sonja Hökberg's mother, Wallander told Holgersson how the escape had taken place.

"This is simply unacceptable," she said when Wallander had finished.

Holgersson was furious. Wallander liked that about her. He thought about how their previous chief, Björk, would always start worrying about his own reputation at times like these.

"These things are not supposed to happen," Wallander said. "But they do. The most important thing right now is to track her down. Then we'll have to scrutinize our security practices and figure out who's responsible for the mistakes in this case."

"Do you think there's a danger of more violence?"

Wallander thought for a moment. He saw an image of her room and all the stuffed animals sitting in a row.

"We don't know enough about her at this point," he said. "But additional violence cannot be ruled out."

Martinsson put the phone down.

"I've just talked to her mother," he said. "And our colleagues in Höör. They know what to do."

"I'm not sure any of us knows that," Wallander objected. "But I want that girl picked up as soon as possible."

"Was the escape planned?" Holgersson asked.

"Not according to the officer in charge," Martinsson answered. "I think she took advantage of the situation."

"Oh, it was planned," Wallander said. "She was waiting for the right moment, that's all. Has anyone spoken to her attorney? Could he be of any help?"

"I don't think anyone's thought of that yet," Martinsson said. "He left the station when he was done talking to her."

Wallander got up.

"I'll talk to him."

"What about the press conference?" Holgersson asked. "What should we do about that?"

Wallander looked down at his watch. It was twenty minutes past eleven.

"We'll do it as planned, but I'm afraid we'll have to give them the latest developments."

"I guess I should be there," Holgersson said.

Wallander didn't answer. He returned to his office, his head throbbing. Every time he had to swallow it hurt.

I should be lying in bed, he thought. *Not out running around after teenage girls who murder taxi drivers.*

He found some tissues in a desk drawer and wiped himself down as well as he could. He was running a temperature and sweating profusely. Then he called Sonja Hökberg's lawyer, Lötberg, and told him what had happened.

"This is unexpected," Lötberg said when Wallander had finished.

"What this is is a problem," Wallander said. "Do you have any information that might help us?"

"I don't think so. It was hard to connect with her. She seemed very calm on the surface but as to what was going on underneath I have no idea."

"Did she mention a boyfriend? Anyone she wanted to see?"

"No."

"No one?"

"She asked about Eva Persson."

Wallander paused.

"She didn't ask about her parents?"

"Actually, no."

This fact struck Wallander as strange, and reminded him of the feeling her room had given him. His sense that something didn't quite add up about Sonja Hökberg was growing stronger.

"Of course I'll be in touch if she contacts me," Lötberg said.

They finished the conversation and Wallander was left with the image of her room in his head. *It was a child's room,* he thought. *Not the room of a nineteen-year-old.* It was still the room of a ten-year-old, as if the room had suddenly stopped aging even though Sonja was still growing.

He couldn't develop this insight any further, but he knew it was important.

It took Martinsson less than half an hour to arrange Wallander's meeting with Eva Persson and her mother. Wallander was shocked when he saw the girl. She was short and hardly looked older than twelve. He looked at her hands and tried unsuccessfully to imagine her holding a knife and forcefully plunging it into the chest of her victim. But he soon discovered that there was something about her that reminded him of Sonja Hökberg. At first he couldn't put his finger on it, but then he realized what it was.

The look in her eyes, the same indifference.

Martinsson left them alone. Wallander would have liked Höglund to be present, but she was out in the field somewhere, trying to organize the search for Sonja Hökberg as efficiently as possible.

Eva Persson's mother looked like she had been crying. Wallander felt sorry for her. He shuddered to think what she was going through. He got right to the point.

"Sonja has escaped. I want you to tell me where you think she's gone. Think carefully before you say anything, and make sure you tell the whole truth. Understand?"

Eva Persson nodded.

"Where do you think she's gone?"

"Home, probably. Where else would she have gone?"

Wallander couldn't tell if she was telling the truth or being arrogant. He realized his headache was making him impatient.

"If she had gone home, we would already have found her," he said and raised his voice a little. Eva Persson's mother seemed to retreat into herself.

"I don't know where she is."

Wallander opened his notebook.

"Who are her friends? Who does she normally associate with? Does she know anyone who has a car?"

"Normally it's just her and me."

"What about her other friends?"

"There's Kalle, I guess."

"What's his last name?"

"Ryss."

"His name is Kalle Ryss?"

"Yes."

"I don't want to hear a single lie, do you understand?"

"What the fuck are you screaming at me for, you old bastard?!"

Wallander almost exploded, perhaps reacting most strongly to being called an "old bastard."

"Just tell me who he is."

"He's a surfer. He goes to Australia a lot, but he's home right now working for his dad."

"What does the dad do?"

"He owns a hardware store."

"And he's friends with Sonja?"

"They used to go out."

Wallander continued questioning her but Eva Persson was unable to think of anyone else that Sonja Hökberg might have been likely to contact. She didn't know where Sonja would be likely to go. In a last attempt to get some more information, Wallander turned to Eva's mother but she only said she knew very little about Sonja.

"You must have known something about her—she was your daughter's best friend."

"I never liked her."

Eva Persson turned to her mother and hit her in the face. It happened so fast that Wallander had no time to stop her. Eva's mother started screaming and Eva continued hitting her and yelling obscenities. She bit Wallander's hand but he still managed to tear them apart.

"Get rid of that old hag!" she yelled. "I don't want to see her anymore!"

At that moment Wallander lost control of himself. He slapped Eva Persson hard in the face. The girl was knocked to the ground. Wallander quickly left the room with his palm stinging. Lisa Holgersson came hurrying down the hallway and stared questioningly at him.

"What happened in there?"

Wallander didn't answer. He looked down at his hand. It had turned red and was still hurting.

Neither one of them noticed the journalist who had arrived early for the press conference. During the chaotic events of the last few minutes he had managed to come right up to the doorway unnoticed. He snapped a few pictures and made a note of what he observed. A headline was starting to take shape in his head.

When the press conference finally started, it was half an hour late. Lisa Holgersson had been holding onto the hope that a patrol car would spot Sonja Hökberg. Wallander, who had not been harboring any illusions about the likelihood of this, had wanted to start the press conference on time. His reasons were only partly due to his doubts about finding Sonja. It was also because his flu was now starting to break out in full force.

At last he managed to convince her to go ahead. The reporters were only going to get irritated and make things more difficult for them.

"What do you want me to tell them?" she asked him as they walked into the large conference room where the meeting was to be held.

"Nothing," Wallander said. "I'll handle it. I just want you to be present, that's all."

Wallander excused himself and went to the bathroom. He rinsed his face off with cold water, then returned to the conference room. He flinched when he saw how many reporters were assembled. He walked up to the small podium, followed by Holgersson. They sat down and Wallander looked out over the sea of faces. He recognized some of them. He even knew some of the reporters' names, but most of them were complete strangers.

What should I tell them? he wondered. *Even when you think you know what you're going to say, it never comes out exactly the way you had imagined.*

Lisa Holgersson welcomed the reporters and introduced Wallander.

I hate this, he thought bitterly. *I don't just dislike it, I hate all these meetings with the media even though I know it's a fact of life.*

He counted silently to three before he began.

"Several days ago a taxi driver in Ystad was robbed and brutally assaulted. As you know, he recently died due to the severity of the wounds that were inflicted. Two people have since been charged with the crime and they have both confessed. Since one of the assailants is a juvenile, we will not be releasing any names at this press conference."

One of the reporters raised his hand.

"Isn't it true that the assailants were both women?"

"I'll get there, don't worry," Wallander said.

The reporter was young and pushy.

"This press conference was supposed to start at one o'clock and it's already past one-thirty. Don't you realize that we have deadlines to meet?"

Wallander ignored this question.

"The charges in this case have been upgraded to murder," he said. "There's no reason for us not to disclose the fact that this was an unusually brutal killing. It is therefore particularly comforting that we were able to resolve the investigation as quickly as we did."

Then he took a deep breath. It felt like diving into a pool without knowing how deep the water was.

"Unfortunately, there has recently been a complication due to the fact that one of the assailants has escaped. We have, however, every expectation of catching her shortly."

At first there was complete silence in the room. Then it exploded in questions.

"What's her name?"

Wallander looked over at Holgersson, who nodded.

"Sonja Hökberg."

"Where was she being detained?"

"Here at the police station."

"How could that happen?"

"We're conducting an internal inquiry into the matter."

"What do you mean by that?"

"Exactly what you think it means. That we're investigating how Sonja Hökberg was able to escape from our custody."

"Would it be correct to characterize her as dangerous?"

Wallander hesitated.

"We don't know yet if she poses a threat to the public."

"Surely she either poses a threat or she doesn't? Which is it?"

Wallander was starting to lose his temper, something that had happened innumerable times this day. He wanted to bring the proceedings to a close so he could go home and go to bed.

"Next question."

The reporter was not going to give up.

"I want a definite answer. Is she dangerous or not?"

"I've already given you an answer. Next question."

"Is she armed?"

"We don't know."

"How was the taxi driver killed?"

"With a knife and a hammer."

"Have you recovered the murder weapons?"

"Yes."

"Can we see them?"

"No."

"Why not?"

"For technical reasons linked to the progress of the investigation. Next question."

"Have the police been alerted nationwide?"

"At this point there is only regional involvment. And that's all we have to tell you for the moment."

Wallander's closing words were met with a storm of protest. Wallander knew there were an endless number of more or less important questions left, but he got up and pulled Chief Holgersson up with him.

"That will have to do for now," he hissed.

"Shouldn't we stay longer?"

"Then you'll have to take over. They got the information they need. They'll fill in the rest better than we could have done."

Reporters from TV and radio stations wanted interviews. Wallander had to wade through a throng of microphones and camera lenses.

"You'll have to deal with this yourself," he said to Holgersson. "Or Martinsson. I have to go home."

They had reached the hallway. She looked at him with surprise.

"You're going home?"

"I give you permission to lay your hand on my brow, if you like. I'm sick. I have a temperature. There are other officers here who are more than capable of finding Hökberg, and of answering all these damned questions from the media."

He left without waiting for a response. *What I'm doing is wrong,* he thought. *I should stay and try to sort out this chaotic situation. But I just don't have the energy.*

He reached his office and put on his coat. A note left on the desk caught his attention. It was in Martinsson's handwriting.

"According to pathologist's report, Tynnes Falk died from natural causes. No crime. Shelve it for now."

It took Wallander a couple of seconds to remember that this was in reference to the man who was found dead by the cash machine.

One less thing to worry about, he thought.

He left the station by slipping out through the garage in order to avoid reporters. The wind was very strong now. He had to hunch over and run straight into it to get to his car. When he turned the key, nothing happened. He tried several times, but the engine was completely dead.

He took off the seat belt and left the car without bothering to lock the door. On his way back to Mariagatan he remembered the book he was supposed to pick up. But that would have to wait. Everything would have to wait. Right now all he wanted to do was sleep.

When he woke up, it was as if he had come running out of a dream at full speed.

He had been in the middle of a press conference, but this one had been held at Sonja Hökberg's house. Wallander had not been able to answer a single question. Then he had suddenly spotted his father sitting in the very back of the room. His father seemed completely undisturbed by the TV cameras in the room and was calmly painting his favorite fall landscape.

That was the point when Wallander woke up. He lay awake for a moment, listening for sounds. The wind blew against the window. He turned his head. The clock on his bedside table read half past six. He had been sleeping for almost four hours. He tried to swallow. His throat was still swollen and sore, but his temperature seemed to have gone down. He knew that Sonja Hökberg was still on the loose. Someone would have called him otherwise. He got up and went out into the kitchen. There was the reminder to buy soap. He added the book he had to pick up to the list. Then he made some tea. He looked for a lemon but didn't find one. There were just some old tomatoes and a half-rotten cucumber in the vegetable bin. He threw out the cucumber. When the tea was ready he brought the cup with him out into the living room.

He reached for the phone and called the station. The only person he managed to get hold of was Hansson.

"How's it going?"

Hansson sounded tired when he answered.

"She's disappeared without a trace."

"No one's seen her?"

"No one, nothing. The National Chief of Police has called and expressed his displeasure."

"I don't doubt it. But I suggest we ignore him for the moment."

"I heard you're sick."

"I'll be fine by tomorrow."

Hansson told him how the investigation was proceeding. Wallander had no objections to the way things were being handled. They had declared a regional search for Hökberg and had alerted the rest of the force in case they had to operate nationally. Hansson promised to call if anything new developed.

Wallander put the phone down and put on a compact disc with Verdi's *La Traviata*. He lay down on the couch and closed his eyes. He thought about Eva Persson and her mother, the girl's violent outburst and her puzzlingly indifferent gaze. Then the phone rang. Wallander sat up and turned the music down.

"Kurt?"

He recognized the voice immediately. It was Sten Widén, one of Wallander's few close friends and probably the oldest.

"It's been a while."

"It's always been a while when we talk to each other. How are you doing? When I tried to reach you at the station someone said you were sick."

"I have a sore throat. It's nothing."

"I thought it would be nice to see you."

"Now is not the best time. Have you seen the news?"

"I never watch the news or read the paper. Apart from the results of the latest horse race, of course."

"Someone managed to escape from custody. I have to find her. Then we can meet."

"I wanted to say goodbye."

Wallander felt something constrict in his stomach. Was Sten sick? Had his alcohol abuse finally managed to ruin his liver?

"Why? Why do you need to say goodbye?"

"I'm selling my place and taking off."

The last few years Sten Widén had talked about leaving. The horse ranch he had inherited from his father had stopped being profitable many years ago. Wallander had listened to his dreams of starting a new life on countless occasions, but he had never taken Widén seriously, just as he never took his own dreams seriously. That had apparently been a mistake. When Sten was drunk, as he often was, he tended to exaggerate. But right now he seemed sober and full of energy. The normal slowness of his speech was gone.

"Is this for real?"

"Yes. I'm going."

"Where?"

"I don't know yet, but I'll make up my mind soon."

Wallander was no longer tensing up his stomach, but now he felt envy instead. Sten Widén's dreams had turned out to have more life in them than his own.

"I'll come by as soon as I can. Maybe in a few days."

"I'll be home."

When the conversation was over, Wallander sat deep in thought for a long time. He couldn't hide from his own envy. His own dreams of leaving his work as a police officer behind felt extremely remote. What Sten was doing right now, Wallander could never do.

He drank the rest of his tea and then carried the cup into the kitchen. The thermometer outside the window read one degree above freezing. It was cold for the beginning of October.

He walked back to the sofa. The music was still playing softly. He reached for the remote control and directed it at the stereo.

At the same time the power went out.

At first he thought it was a blown fuse, but after feeling his way over to the window he saw that even the street lamps had gone out.

He returned to the sofa in the dark and waited.

What he didn't know was that a large part of Scania lay in darkness.

Chapter Seven

Olle Andersson was sleeping when the phone rang.

He tried to turn on the bedside lamp but it wouldn't go on. That told him what the phone call was about. He turned on the strong flashlight he always kept beside his bed and lifted the receiver. As he had guessed, the call was from the Sydkraft main office, staffed around the clock. It was Rune Ågren. Olle Andersson had already known that Ågren was the one on duty that night, the eighth of October. He was from Malmö and had worked for various utility companies for over thirty years. He was due to retire next year. He got straight to the point.

"Twenty-five percent of Scania is without power."

Olle Andersson was surprised. Even though there had been gusty winds the past few days, there had been nothing close to a storm.

"The devil only knows what happened," Ågren continued. "But it's the Ystad power substation that's been affected. You'd better get dressed and go down there to take a look."

Olle Andersson knew it was urgent. In the complicated network that conveyed electricity to cities and houses across the countryside, the Ystad power substation was one of the central points of connection. If anything happened to it, most of Scania would be affected one way or the other. Someone was always in charge of making sure that didn't happen. This week Olle Andersson was on call for the Ystad area.

It took him nineteen minutes to reach the substation. The area was completely dark. Every time the power went out and he was out looking for the problem he was struck by the same thought: that as little as a hundred years ago this impenetrable darkness had been the norm. The advent of electricity had changed everything. No person still living could remember what life had been like before. But Andersson would also think about how vulnerable society had become. In the worst-case scenario, one single snag in the power grid could plunge a third of the country into darkness.

"I'm here," he told Ågren on his radio transmitter.

"Hurry up, then."

The power substation stood in the middle of a field. It was surrounded by a barbed-wire fence. At regular intervals there were NO TRESPASSING and DANGER! HIGH VOLTAGE signs. He hunched over against the wind, carrying a set of keys in his hand and wearing some glasses he had constructed himself. He had attached two small and powerful flashlights to the frames. He found the right keys and stopped in front of the gates. They were open. He looked around. There was no other car, no sign of a person. He took up his radio again and called Ågren.

"The gates have been busted open," he said.

Ågren had trouble hearing him because of the wind. Andersson had to repeat himself.

"It doesn't look like anyone's here. I'm going in."

It wasn't the first time something like this had happened. The gates had been broken open before, and it was always reported to the police. Sometimes the police managed to apprehend the guilty party, usually drunk teenagers on a vandalism kick. But they had also discussed the possibility of someone bent on sabotaging the power-distribution grid. In fact, Andersson had been in a meeting only this last September in which one of the Sydkraft safety engineers had talked about instituting a whole new set of security measures.

He turned his head. Since he had his handheld flashlight as well, three spots of light traveled across the metal frame of the substation. A little gray building set deep among the steel towers was the heart of the structure. It housed the transformers. It had a thick steel door that could only be opened with two different keys, or by the use of powerful explosives. Andersson had marked the various keys on his keychain with colored bits of tape. The red key went to the gates, the yellow and blue were for the steel door of the transformer building. He looked around. The place was deserted. The only thing he heard was the wind. He started walking but stopped after only a few steps. Something had caught his attention. He looked around. Was there anyone behind him? He could hear Ågren's raspy voice coming from the radio that dangled from his jacket. He didn't bother to answer. What was it that had made him stop? There was nothing out there in the darkness, at least nothing he could see. There was, however, a bad smell, but that probably came from the fields, he thought. The farmer must have fertilized them recently. He continued toward the transformer building. The bad smell still lingered. Suddenly he stopped short. The steel door was ajar. He took a few steps back and clutched the radio.

"The door's open," he said. "Can you hear me?"

"I hear you. What do you mean the door is open?"

"Just what I said."

"Is anyone there?"

"I don't know. It doesn't look like it's been forced."

"Then how could it be open?"

"I don't know."

The radio was quiet. Andersson felt very alone. Ågren spoke up.

"Do you mean the door is unlocked?"

"That's what it looks like to me. And there's a strange smell."

"You'll have to go see what it is. There's a lot of pressure right now from above to get this thing cleared up. The bosses keep calling and asking what the hell happened."

Andersson took a deep breath and walked all the way up to the door, opened it further and directed his flashlight inside. At first he didn't know what he was looking at. The stench was overwhelming. Slowly it dawned on him what had happened. The power had gone out in Scania this October evening because a burned corpse lay among the power lines.

He stumbled backward out of the building and called for Ågren to come in.

"There's a corpse in the transformer building."

A few seconds went by before Ågren replied.

"Can you repeat that?"

"There's a burned body in there. A person has short-circuited the entire region."

"Are you serious?"

"You heard me. Something must have gone wrong with the relay safety."

"We'll call the police. You stay where you are. We'll try to reconnect the power grid to bypass you."

The radio went dead. Andersson realized he was shaking. He couldn't believe what had happened. What could drive a person to go down to a power substation and commit suicide with high voltage electrical current? It was like choosing execution by the electric chair.

He felt sick to his stomach and tried to keep himself from throwing up by walking back to the car.

The wind was still gusty, and now it had started to rain.

*   *   *

The police in Ystad were alerted shortly after midnight. The officer who took the call from Sydkraft wrote down the information and made a quick decision. Since a death was involved, he called Hansson, who was the senior officer on duty. He promised to drive out right away. He had a candle by the phone. He knew Martinsson's phone number by heart. It took Martinsson a while to pick up since he was sleeping and had no idea the power was off. He listened to what Hansson had to say and knew it was a serious matter. When the conversation was over, he called Wallander.

Wallander had fallen asleep on the sofa while he had been waiting for the power to come back on. When the phone rang and woke him up it was still dark. He inadvertently knocked the phone down onto the floor as he was reaching for the receiver.

"It's Martinsson. Hansson just called me."

Wallander sensed that something serious had happened. He held his breath.

"A body has been found on one of Sydkraft's stations outside Ystad."

"Is that why there's no power?"

"I don't know. But I thought you should be notified, even if you are sick."

Wallander swallowed. His throat was still sore but he felt no fever.

"My car has broken down," he said. "You'll have to pick me up."

"I'll be there in ten minutes."

"Make that five," said Wallander. "If it's true the whole region is without power."

He got dressed in the dark and went down to wait on the street. It was raining. Martinsson arrived in seven minutes. They drove through the dark city. Hansson was waiting by one of the roundabouts at the outskirts of town.

"It's one of the substations just north of the waste management plant," Martinsson said.

Wallander knew where it was. He had been on a walk in a forest close by a few years ago, when Baiba had been visiting.

"What exactly happened?"

"I don't know any details. Sydkraft made an emergency call claiming to have found a dead body out there when they were investigating the power outage."

"Is it affecting a large area?"

"According to Hansson, one quarter of Scania is without power."

Wallander looked at him in disbelief. Blackouts were rarely so large.

It happened occasionally after a big winter storm. It had happened after the hurricane in the fall of 1996. But not when the weather was like this.

They turned off the main road. It was raining more heavily now. Martinsson's windshield wipers were on full speed. Wallander regretted not having his raincoat or his boots, which he kept in the back of his car, now stuck down at the station.

Hansson stopped the car. Flashlights were on in the dark. Wallander saw a man in overalls who was gesturing for them to follow him.

"This is a high-voltage station," Martinsson said. "It won't be a pretty sight."

They stepped out into the rain. The wind was stronger out here in the open fields. The man who came toward them was clearly shaken. Wallander no longer had any doubts that something serious had occurred.

"In there," the man said and pointed behind him.

Wallander went ahead. The rain whipped him in the face and made it hard to see. Martinsson and Hansson were somewhere behind him. Their shaken guide was walking to one side.

"In there," he repeated, when they stopped in front of the transformer building.

"Is anything still live in there?" Wallander asked. "I mean the power lines."

"Nothing. Not anymore."

Wallander took Martinsson's flashlight and went in. He could smell it now, the stench of scorched human flesh. It was a smell he had never been able to get used to, although he had been exposed to it on frequent occasions when houses burned down and people were trapped inside. *Hansson will probably be sick to his stomach*, Wallander thought absently. *He can't take the smell of burned bodies.*

The corpse was completely blackened and sooty. The face was gone. The body was trapped in a mess of lines, switches, and circuit breakers.

Wallander moved aside so Martinsson could take a look.

"Oh, Christ," Martinsson groaned.

Wallander called out to Hansson to get Nyberg on the line and organize the backup they needed.

"And tell them to bring a generator," he said. "We'll need it to get some light in here."

He turned back to Martinsson.

"What's the guy's name, the one who discovered the body?"

"Olle Andersson."

"What was he doing here?"

"Sydkraft had sent him down here to take a look. They always have repairmen on call in case of emergencies."

"Have a chat with him. See if you can get some specifics on the sequence of events from him. And don't walk around too much in here or Nyberg will be on your case."

Martinsson took Andersson with him to one of the cars. Wallander was left alone. He crouched down and shone his flashlight on the body. Nothing remained of the clothes. It was like looking at a mummy, or a body that had been fished out of a bog after a thousand years. But this person had only been dead for a few hours. He tried to think back to when the power had been cut off. That had been some time around eleven. Now it was almost one o'clock in the morning. If this body had caused the outage then this had happened about two hours ago.

Wallander got up and let his flashlight rest on the floor. What had happened here? A person goes to a remote power substation and causes a major blackout by killing him- or herself. Wallander made a face. That made no sense. The questions were starting to pile up. He bent down to pick up the flashlight. The only thing to do was to wait for Nyberg.

At the same time something was bothering him. He let the beam of light from the flashlight travel over the blackened remains. He didn't know what was causing this feeling, but it was as if he was sensing something that was no longer there. But that *had* been there.

He walked out of the building and studied the reinforced steel door. He could see no signs of a forced entry. There were two impressive locks. Wallander started walking back the way he had come. He tried to retrace his steps exactly so he wouldn't interfere with any tracks that might be there. When he reached the gates he examined the lock. It had been broken and forced open. What did that mean? The gates had been clumsily cut open, but a reinforced steel door had posed no problem?

Martinsson was sitting in Andersson's car. Hansson was making phone calls from his own car. Wallander tried to shake the rain off his coat and got into Martinsson's car. The engine was running and the windshield wipers were still on high. He turned up the heat. His throat ached. He turned the radio on to get the latest news. He listened and began to realize the enormity of what was happening.

A quarter of Scania was without power. It was dark from Trelleborg to Kristianstad. The hospitals were using their emergency generators, but otherwise the power outage was total. A Sydkraft executive had been reached and had said that the problem had been located. He was expecting the power in most areas to be restored in half an hour.

There won't be any power coming from here in half an hour, that's for sure, Wallander thought. He wondered if the executive really knew what had happened. *I have to let Lisa Holgersson know about this.* He reached for Martinsson's cell phone and dialed her number. It took a while for her to answer.

"Wallander here. Have you noticed the power's off?"

"A blackout? I was sleeping."

Wallander outlined the situation for her. She became fully alert.

"Do you want me to come down there right away?"

"I think you should get in touch with Sydkraft and explain that their power problem now also involves a police investigation."

"What do you think has happened? Is it a suicide?"

"I don't know."

"What about sabotage? A terrorist act?"

"I don't think we can answer that question yet. We can't rule any of these things out yet."

"I'll call Sydkraft. Keep me posted."

Wallander hung up. Hansson came running through the rain over to his car. Wallander opened the door.

"Nyberg is on his way. How did things look in there?"

"Pretty bad. There was nothing left, not even a face."

Hansson didn't answer. He ran back through the rain to his own car.

Twenty minutes later, Wallander saw the lights from Nyberg's car appear in the rearview mirror. Wallander stepped out of the car and greeted him. Nyberg looked tired.

"What is it that's happened, exactly? I couldn't get a coherent sentence out of Hansson."

"We have a dead body in there. Burned to a crisp. There's nothing left."

Nyberg looked around.

"That's what usually happens when high-voltage transformers are involved. Is that why the power's out?"

"Seems so."

"Does that mean half of Scania will be waiting for me to finish?"

"We can't take that into consideration. I think they're working on restoring the power anyway, just not by means of this substation."

"We live in a vulnerable society," Nyberg said and immediately started commandeering his crew of technicians.

Erik Hökberg said the same thing, Wallander thought. *We live in a*

*vulnerable society. His computers will have been shut off by this, if he sits up
with them at night trying to make more money.*

Nyberg worked quickly and efficiently. Soon all the spotlights were
up and running, connected to a noisy generator. Martinsson and Wallander went back to the car. Martinsson flipped through his notes.

"Andersson was called by some central command employee called
Ågren. They had pinpointed the blackout to this substation. Andersson lives in Svarte. It took him twenty minutes to get here. He found
that the gates to the area had been tampered with, but that the steel
door was simply unlocked. When he looked in, he saw what had happened."

"Did he see anything else?"

"There was no one here when he arrived and he didn't meet anyone
walking around."

Wallander thought for a moment.

"We have to get to the bottom of this question of the keys," he said.

Andersson was talking with Ågren on the radio when Wallander got
into his car. He immediately finished the conversation.

"I know that you're shaken by this," Wallander said.

"I've never seen anything so terrible. What happened, exactly?"

"We don't know that yet. Now, when you arrived on the scene, the
gates had been forced open but the steel door had been opened
without any visible use of force. How do you explain that?"

"I can't."

"Who else has copies of these keys?"

"Only another repairman called Moberg. He lives in Ystad. And the
main office, of course. But the security is always very tight."

"But someone did unlock the steel door?"

"That's what it looks like."

"I take it these keys can't be copied."

"The locks are made in the United States. They're supposed to be
impossible to jimmy."

"What's Moberg's first name?"

"Lars."

"Is it possible someone forgot to lock the door?"

Andersson shook his head.

"That would be grounds for instant dismissal. The security checks
are very thorough. If anything, security has increased in the past few
years."

Wallander had nothing else to ask for the moment.

"I'd like you to remain here for now," he said. "In case any other questions come up. I'd also like you to call Lars Moberg and ask him if he still has the keys for this place. The ones that open the steel door."

Wallander left the car. It was no longer raining as hard. The conversation with Andersson had increased his sense of anxiety. It was still possible that someone wanting to commit suicide had decided to come out here to this substation, but the facts were starting to speak against this hypothesis; among other things, the fact that the steel door had been opened with keys. Wallander realized where this thought was leading: murder. The victim had then been disposed of in the power lines to cover up the crime.

Wallander walked into the strong spotlights. The photographer had just finished taking his pictures and video clips. Nyberg was kneeling by the body. He started muttering irritably when Wallander happened to block his light.

"What's your take on this?"

"That it's taking the pathologist an awfully long time to get out here. I want to move the body to see if there's anything behind it."

"I mean your take on what could have happened."

Nyberg thought for a while before answering.

"It's a macabre way for someone to choose to commit suicide. If it's murder, it's unusually brutal. It would be the equivalent of executing someone in the electric chair."

That's right, Wallander thought. *That leads us to the possibility that it's an act of revenge. Taking revenge through executing someone in a very special kind of electric chair.*

Nyberg continued to work. One of his technicians had started to search the area between the building and the gates. The pathologist arrived, a woman Wallander had met several times before. Her name was Susann Bexell and she was a woman of few words. She immediately got down to business. Nyberg got his thermos from his bag and had a cup of coffee. He offered Wallander some. Wallander decided to accept. They would get no more sleep that night anyway. Martinsson turned up at their side, wet and frozen. Wallander passed him his cup of coffee.

"They're starting to restore power," Martinsson said. "Parts of Ystad already have some light. I have no idea how they managed to do that."

"Has Andersson spoken to his colleague Moberg about the keys?"

Martinsson walked off to find out. Wallander saw that Hansson was sitting frozen behind his steering wheel. He walked over and told Hansson to return to the station. Most of Ystad was still dark, after all, and he would be able to do more good there than here. Hansson nodded gratefully and drove off. Wallander walked over to the pathologist.

"Have you learnt anything about him?"

Susann Bexell looked over at him.

"Just enough to tell you you're wrong. This isn't a man, it's a woman."

"Are you sure?"

"Yes, but I'm not going to answer any other questions for now."

"I just have one more question. Was she dead when she wound up here, or was it the power that killed her?"

"I don't know that yet."

Wallander turned around thoughtfully. He had been assuming the victim was a man.

At that moment the crime technician who had been searching the area came over to Nyberg with something in his hand. Wallander joined them.

The object was a woman's handbag.

Wallander stared at it.

At first he thought he was making a mistake.

Then he knew he had seen it on a previous occasion. More specifically, yesterday.

"I found it to the north by the fence," said the technician, whose name was Ek.

"Is the body in there a woman?" Nyberg asked with surprise.

"Not only that," Wallander said. "Now we know who she is."

The handbag had recently rested on a desk inside the interrogation room. It had a clasp that looked like an oak leaf.

He wasn't making a mistake.

"This purse belongs to Sonja Hökberg," he said. "She's the one who's lying in there."

It was ten minutes past two. The rain had picked up again.

Chapter Eight

The power in Ystad was restored shortly after three o'clock. At that time Wallander was still working with the crime technicians at the substation. Hansson called from the police station and told him the news. In the distance, Wallander could see lights come on on the outside of a barn.

The pathologist had finished her work, the body had been removed, and Nyberg had been able to continue his forensic investigation. He had asked Olle Andersson to explain the complicated network of lines and switches inside the transformer building. Outside, his technicians worked to find any traces that might have been left behind. It was still raining, which made for difficult working conditions. Martinsson slipped in the mud and cut his elbow. Wallander was shaking with cold and longed for his rubber boots.

Soon after the power in Ystad was restored, Wallander took Martinsson with him to one of the police cars. There they mapped out the information they had gathered so far. Sonja Hökberg had escaped from the police station about thirteen hours earlier. She could have made it to the substation on foot, but neither Wallander nor Martinsson thought it plausible. After all, it was eight kilometers to Ystad.

"Someone should have seen her," Martinsson said. "Our cars were out looking for her."

"Double-check to see if a squad car came down this way and saw someone."

"What's the alternative?"

"That someone gave her a ride. Someone who left her and drove off."

They both knew what that implied. The question of how Sonja

Hökberg had died was still the most pressing. Did she commit suicide or was she murdered?

"The keys," Wallander said. "The gates were forced, but not the door. Why?"

They both searched in their thoughts for a rational explanation.

"We need a list of anyone who could possibly have had access to the keys," Wallander continued. "I want every key accounted for. Who had them, and what they were doing last night."

"I have trouble getting all this to hang together," Martinsson said. "Sonja Hökberg commits murder. Then she gets murdered in turn? Suicide makes more sense."

Wallander didn't answer. There were a number of thoughts in his head, but they weren't linking up with each other. He went over and over the one and only conversation he had had with Sonja Hökberg.

"You talked to her first," Wallander said. "What was your impression of her?"

"Same as you. That she felt no remorse, and could just as well have killed an old taxi driver as a bug."

"That doesn't suggest suicide to me. Why would she kill herself if she felt no remorse?"

Martinsson turned off the windshield wipers. Through the windshield they could see Olle Andersson waiting in his car, and beyond him Nyberg was helping to move a spotlight. His movements were abrupt. Wallander understood that he was both angry and impatient.

"Well, is there anything that suggests it was murder?"

"No," Wallander answered. "There's nothing to suggest either possibility, therefore we have to keep them both open. But I think we can rule out accidental death."

The conversation died away. After a while, Wallander asked Martinsson to make sure the investigative team was ready to meet at eight o'clock in the morning. Then he got out of the car. The rain had stopped. He felt how tired he was, and how cold. His throat ached. He walked over to Nyberg, who was wrapping up work in the transformer building.

"Have you found anything?"

"No."

"Does Andersson have anything to say?"

"About what? Forensic investigations?"

Wallander counted silently to ten before continuing. Nyberg was in a very bad mood. Saying the wrong thing would make him impossible to talk to.

"He can't determine what happened," Nyberg said after a while.

"The body caused the power break, but whether it was a dead body or a living person who was thrown down there only the pathologist can say. And even she may not be able to tell."

Wallander nodded. He looked down at his watch. It was half past three. There was no point in staying any longer.

"I'm going to take off now. But we have a meeting at eight o'clock."

Nyberg muttered something unintelligible in reply. Wallander took that to mean he would be there. Then he returned to the car, where Martinsson was making notes.

"We're going," he said. "You'll have to take me home."

They returned to Ystad in silence. When Wallander got back to his apartment he started a bath. While the bathtub was filling up, he swallowed the last of his painkillers and added "pills" to the list on the kitchen table. He wondered helplessly when he would next be able to go by the drugstore.

His body thawed out in the warm water. He dozed off for a couple of minutes, his mind a blank. But then the images returned. Sonja Hökberg and Eva Persson. In his thoughts, he slowly went through the events. He proceeded cautiously so as not to forget anything. Nothing made any sense. Why had Johan Lundberg been killed? What had motivated Sonja Hökberg and made Eva Persson go along with it? He was sure it wasn't a random impulse. They needed the money for something very particular, or else it was about something entirely different.

There had only been about thirty kronor in the handbag that they had found at the substation. The money from the robbery had been confiscated by the police.

She was desperate, he thought. *Suddenly she sees a chance to get away. It's ten o'clock in the morning. Nothing could have been planned in advance. She leaves the police station and disappears for thirteen hours. Her body is later found eight kilometers from Ystad.*

How did she get there? She could have hitched a ride. But she could also have called someone to come pick her up. And then what? Does she ask to be driven to a spot where she commits suicide? Or is she murdered? And who has access to the keys that open the door, but not the ones for the gates?

Wallander got up out of the bath. *There are two central questions,* he thought. *If she had decided to commit suicide, why pick the substation, and how did she get the keys? And if she was murdered, then why?*

Wallander crawled into bed and pulled up the blankets. It was half past four. His head was spinning and he realized he was too tired to think. He had to sleep. Before turning out the light, he set his alarm clock. He then pushed the clock as far away from his bed as possible, so he would be forced to get out of bed to turn it off.

When he woke up he felt as if he had only been sleeping for a couple of minutes. He tried to swallow. His throat was still sore but seemed better than it had the day before. He felt his forehead. The fever was gone, but he was congested. He walked out to the bathroom and blew his nose, avoiding his reflection in the mirror. His whole body ached with fatigue. While he was waiting for the water to boil so he could make coffee, he looked out the window. It was still windy, but the rain clouds were gone. It was five degrees Celsius. He wondered absently when he would have time to do anything about his car.

They met in one of the conference rooms at the police station shortly after eight. Wallander looked at Martinsson's and Hansson's tired faces and wondered what his own face must be like. Lisa Holgersson, however, who also could not have slept many hours, seemed undismayed. She called the meeting to order.

"We need to be perfectly clear about the fact that last night's power outage was one of the most serious ever to have hit Scania. That displays the extent of our vulnerability. What happened should have been impossible, but it happened anyway. Now the authorities, power companies, and law enforcement will have to discuss how security can be stepped up. This is just by way of introduction."

She nodded to Wallander to continue. He gave a brief summation of the events.

"In other words, we don't know what happened," he said finally. "We don't know for sure if it was an accident, suicide, or murder, even if we can reasonably rule out an accident. She was either alone or had someone with her who had broken in through the outside gates. After that they apparently had access to keys. The whole thing is strange, to say the least."

He looked around at the others gathered around the table. Martinsson said he had confirmed that several police cars had on several different occasions driven along the road that led out to the power substation while they were looking for Sonja Hökberg.

"Then we know this much," Wallander said. "Someone drove her out there. Were there any car tracks found?"

He directed that question to Nyberg, who sat at the other end of the table with bloodshot eyes and wild hair. Wallander knew how much he was looking forward to his retirement.

"Apart from our own cars and that of Andersson, we found tracks belonging to two other vehicles. But there was a hell of a rainstorm last night and the impressions weren't too clear."

"But two other cars had been there?"

"Andersson seemed to think one of them could have belonged to his colleague, Moberg. We're still checking on it."

"That leaves one set of car tracks unaccounted for?"

"Yes."

Ann-Britt Höglund, who hadn't said anything up to this point, now raised her hand.

"Could it really be anything other than murder?" she asked. "Like all of you, I have a hard time imagining that Sonja Hökberg would have committed suicide. And even if she had decided to end her life, I can't imagine she would have chosen to *burn* herself to death."

Wallander was reminded of an incident that had occurred a few years earlier. A young woman from a Central American country had burned herself to death by pouring gasoline over herself out in the middle of a linseed field. It was one of his worst memories. He had been present. He had seen the girl set fire to herself. And he had not been able to do anything.

"Women take pills," Höglund was saying. "They rarely shoot themselves. And I don't think they throw themselves on power lines very often, either."

"I think you're right," Wallander answered. "But we have to wait for the pathologist's report. Those of us who were out there last night weren't able to determine what happened."

There were no other questions.

"The keys," Wallander said. "We need to make sure none of the keys were stolen. That's the first thing we need to establish."

Martinsson volunteered to check on the keys. Then they ended the meeting and Wallander went to his office. On his way there, he got a cup of coffee. The telephone rang. It was Irene from reception.

"There's someone here to see you," she said.

"Who is it?"

"His name is Enander and he's a doctor."

Wallander searched his mind without being able to come up with a face.

"Send him to someone else."

"I've tried that, but he insists on speaking to you. And he says it's urgent."

Wallander sighed.

"I'll be right out," he said and put the phone down.

The man waiting for him in the reception area was middle-aged. He had cropped hair and was dressed in a sweatsuit. Wallander noted his firm handshake. The doctor said his name was David Enander.

"I'm very busy right now," Wallander said. "The power outage last night has created a lot of chaos. I can spare about ten minutes. What is it you wanted to see me about?"

"I'd like to clear up a misunderstanding."

Wallander waited for him to continue, but he didn't. They walked to his office. The armrest came off the chair that Enander sat down in.

"Let it be," Wallander said. "The chair's broken."

David Enander got right to the point.

"I'm here about Tynnes Falk, who died a few days ago."

"That case is closed, as far as we're concerned. He died of natural causes."

"That's the misunderstanding I wanted to clear up," Enander said and stroked his cropped hair with one hand.

Wallander saw he was anxious about something.

"I'm listening."

David Enander took his time. He chose his words carefully.

"I've been Tynnes Falk's physician for many years. He became my patient in 1981—that is, more than fifteen years ago. He first came to me because of a rash on his hands. At that time I was working in the epidermal clinic at the hospital, but I opened a private practice in 1986 and Falk followed me there. He was rarely sick. His skin rash disappeared, but I continued with his regular checkups. Falk was a man who wanted to know the state of his health. He took great care of himself. He ate well, exercised, and had very regular habits."

Wallander wondered what Enander was driving at and felt a growing impatience.

"I was away when he died," Enander continued. "I only found out last night when I returned."

"How did you hear it?"

"His ex-wife called me."

Wallander nodded for him to continue.

"She said the cause of death was a massive coronary."

"That's what we were told."

"The only thing is, that can't possibly be true."

Wallander raised his eyebrows.

"And why not?"

"It's very simple. As little as ten days ago I did a complete physical workup on Falk. His heart was in wonderful condition. He had the physical stamina of a twenty-year-old."

Wallander thought this through.

"So what is it you're saying? That the pathologist made a mistake?"

"I'm aware of the fact that a heart attack can in rare cases strike a perfectly healthy person. But I can't accept that this happened in Falk's case."

"What else could he have died of?"

"That, I don't know. But I wanted to straighten out this misunderstanding. It wasn't his heart."

"I'll pass on what you've told me," Wallander said. "Was there anything else?"

"Something must have happened," Enander said. "I don't know if I'm right about this, but I gather he had a head wound. I think he was probably attacked. Killed."

"Nothing points to that conclusion. He wasn't robbed."

"All I know is, it wasn't his heart," Enander repeated firmly. "I'm neither a pathologist nor a forensic specialist, so I can't tell you what killed him. But it wasn't his heart. I'm sure of it."

Wallander made a note of Enander's phone number and address. Then he got up. The conversation was over. He didn't have any more time.

Wallander saw Enander back out to the reception area, then returned to his office. He put the notes about Tynnes Falk in a drawer and used the following hour to write up the events of the night before.

As he typed, he thought about the fact that he had once thought of his computer with distaste. But then one day he suddenly realized it actually made his work easier. His desk was no longer drowning in random notes jotted on odd bits of paper. He still typed with two fingers and often made mistakes, but now when he worked on his reports he no longer had to use white-out to erase all of his mistakes. That in itself was a huge relief.

At eleven o'clock, Martinsson came in with a list of all the people who had keys to the power substation. There were five names. Wallander glanced at them.

"Everyone can account for their keys," Martinsson said. "None of them have let them out of their possession. Apart from Moberg, no one has been out to the substation in the past few days. Should I look into what they were doing during the time that Sonja Hökberg was missing?"

"Let's wait on that," Wallander said. "Before the forensic reports come back, we can't do much except wait."

"What should we do with Eva Persson?"

"She should be questioned more thoroughly."

"Are you going to do that?"

"No, thanks. I thought we would leave that to Höglund. I'll talk to her."

By noon, Wallander had brought Höglund up to date on the Lundberg case. His throat was feeling better, but he was still tired. After trying to start his car up a couple of times, he called a service station and asked them to pick up the car. He left the keys with Irene and walked down into town to have lunch. At the next table, people were talking about the power outage. Afterward he went by the drugstore and bought soap and painkillers. When he returned to the station his car was gone. He called the mechanic, but they still hadn't identified the problem. When he asked how much the repair was going to cost, the answer was vague. He hung up and decided that enough was enough. He was going to get a new car.

Then he let himself sink down into his thoughts. He was suddenly convinced that Sonja Hökberg had not ended up at that substation by accident. And it was no coincidence that it was one of the most vulnerable points in Scania's power-distribution system.

He reached for the list that Martinsson had given him. Five people, five sets of keys.

Olle Andersson, line repairman
Lars Moberg, line repairman
Hilding Olofsson, power manager
Artur Wahlund, safety manager
Stefan Molin, technical director

The names still told him as little as they had when he'd first looked them over. He called Martinsson, who picked up immediately.

"These key guys," he said. "You haven't by any chance looked them up in the police register, have you?"

"Should I have?"

"Not at all, but I know you're very thorough."

"I can do it now, if you like."

"Hold off on it. There's nothing from the pathologist?"

"I don't think they'll be able to say anything until tomorrow at the earliest."

"Then plug in the names. If you have time."

In contrast to Wallander, Martinsson loved his computer. If anyone at the station was having a computer problem they always turned to him for help.

Wallander turned back to the Lundberg murder case. At three o'clock, he went to get some coffee. He was no longer so congested; his throat was basically back to normal. Hansson told him that Höglund was talking to Eva Persson. *Everything is flowing nicely,* he thought. *For once we have time for everything we need to do.*

He had just sat down with his paperwork when Chief Holgersson turned up at his door. She had one of the evening papers in her hand. Wallander could see from her face that something had happened.

"Have you seen this?" she asked, and handed him the newspaper.

Wallander stared at the photograph. It was a picture of Eva Persson sprawled on the floor of the interrogation room. It looked as if she had fallen.

He felt a knot form in his stomach when he read the accompanying text.

Well-known policeman assaults teenage girl. We have the pictures.

"Who took this picture?" Wallander asked in disbelief. "There were no journalists around, were there?"

"There must have been."

Wallander had a vague recollection of the fact that the door to the hallway had been slightly open, and there might have been a shadow of a person there.

"It was before the press conference," Holgersson said. "Maybe one of the reporters came early and was hanging around the hallway."

Wallander was paralyzed. He had often been involved in scuffles and fistfights in his thirty-year career, but that had always been during a difficult arrest. He had never jumped anyone in the middle of an interrogation, however irritated he had become.

It had only happened once, and just that once there had been a photographer present.

"There's going to be trouble here," Holgersson said. "Why didn't you say anything?"

"She was attacking her mother. I slapped her to keep her from hurting her mother."

"That's not the story the picture tells."

"That's how it was."

"Why didn't you tell me?"

Wallander had no answer.

"I hope you understand I'm forced to order an investigation into this."

Wallander heard the disappointment in her voice. It angered him. *She doesn't believe me,* he thought.

"Am I suspended from my job?"

"No, but I want to hear exactly what happened."

"I've already told you."

"Eva Persson gave a different account of the incident to Ann-Britt. She said your assault came out of the blue."

"In that case she's lying. Ask her mother."

Holgersson hesitated before answering.

"We did," she said finally. "She says her daughter never hit her."

Wallander was quiet. *I'm going to quit,* he thought. *I'm going to quit the force and leave this place. And I'm never coming back.*

Chief Holgersson waited for an answer, but Wallander didn't say anything.

Finally she left the room.

Chapter Nine

Wallander immediately left the station.

He wasn't sure if he was running away or just going out for air. He knew he was right about what had happened, but Chief Holgersson didn't believe him and that upset him.

It was only after he got outside that he remembered he didn't have a car. He swore. When he was upset he liked to drive around until he had calmed down again.

He went down to the liquor store and bought a bottle of whiskey. Then he went straight home, unplugged the phone, and sat down at the kitchen table. He opened the bottle and took a couple of deep draughts. It tasted bad. But he felt he needed it. If there was one thing that made him feel helpless, it was being accused of something he didn't do. Holgersson hadn't spelled it out for him, but he wasn't wrong about her doubts. *Maybe Hansson had been right all along,* he thought angrily. *You should never have a woman for a boss.* He took another swig. He was starting to feel better, and was even starting to regret the fact that he had come straight home. That could be interpreted as a sign that he was guilty. He plugged the phone back in. He felt a sense of childish impatience over the fact that no one had called him. He dialed the number to the police station and Irene picked up the phone.

"I just wanted to let you know I've gone home for the day," he said. "I have a cold."

"Hansson has been asking for you, and Nyberg. Also people from several newspapers."

"What did they want?"

"The papers?"

"No, Hansson and Nyberg."

"They didn't say."

She probably has the paper in front of her right now, Wallander thought. *She and all the rest of them. It wouldn't surprise me if no one's talking about anything else. And I'll bet some of them are downright happy about the fact that that bastard Wallander has finally gotten what's been coming to him.*

He asked Irene to put him through to Hansson's office. It took a while before he picked up. Wallander suspected that Hansson had been poring over some complicated gambling sheets that were supposed to get him that big jackpot, but that never helped him do much more than break even.

"How are the horses doing?" Wallander asked when Hansson picked up, to let him know that the story in the evening papers hadn't affected him.

"What horses?"

"You're not betting on horses these days?"

"No, not right now. Why do you ask?"

"It was just a joke. What was it you wanted to ask me?"

"Are you in your office?"

"I'm at home with a cold."

"I wanted to tell you that I've worked out the times that our cars went up and down that road. I've talked to the drivers, and no one saw Sonja Hökberg. All in all that stretch of road was covered four times."

"Then we know she didn't walk. She must have caught a ride. The first thing she did when she left the station was call someone. Or else she walked to someone's house first. I hope Ann-Britt knew to ask Eva Persson about that, about who could have given Sonja Hökberg a ride. Have you talked to Ann-Britt yet?"

"I haven't had time."

There was a pause. Wallander decided to be the first to bring it up.

"That picture in the paper wasn't too flattering, I suppose."

"No."

"The question is what a photographer was doing floating around the hallways like that. They're always brought in as a group for the press conferences."

"It's strange that you didn't notice someone taking pictures."

"With today's cameras it's not so easy."

"What happened, exactly?"

Wallander told him what had happened. He used exactly the same words that he had used when he talked to Holgersson. He didn't add or omit anything.

"There were no witnesses?" Hansson asked.

"No one apart from the photographer, and he's going to lie. Otherwise his picture wouldn't be worth anything."

"You'll have to make a public rebuttal and tell your side."

"And how well would that work? An aging police officer's word against a mother and her daughter? It'll never work."

"You forget that this particular girl committed murder."

Wallander wondered if that was really going to help. A policeman using excessive force was always a serious matter. That was his own opinion. It didn't help that the details of the situation had been quite unusual.

"I'll think about it," he said, and asked Hansson to connect him with Nyberg.

Several minutes later, Nyberg came on the line. Wallander had taken a few more swigs from the whiskey bottle and was starting to feel tipsy, but the pressure was lifting from his chest.

"Have you seen the papers?" Wallander asked.

"Which paper?"

"The picture? The picture of Eva Persson?"

"I don't read the evening papers, but I heard about it. I understand she had been in the process of attacking her mother."

"That's not what the picture indicates."

"What does that matter?"

"It means I'm in big trouble. Lisa is going to set up a formal investigation."

"So then the truth comes out. Isn't that what you want?"

"I just wonder if the media will buy it. Who cares about an old policeman when there's a young fresh-faced murderess involved?"

Nyberg sounded surprised. "Since when do you care what they write in the paper?"

"Maybe I still don't. But it's different when they publish a picture saying I've punched out a young girl."

"But she's committed murder."

"It still makes me uncomfortable."

"It'll blow over. Look, I just wanted to confirm that one of the car prints was from Moberg's car. That means all sets of car tracks have been accounted for except for one, but I can say that the unknown car is a common model."

"So we know someone drove her out there. And left her."

"There's one other thing," Nyberg said. "Her handbag."

"What about it?"

"I've been trying to figure out why it was so far away, over by the fence."

"Don't you think he just threw it there?"

"But why? He couldn't have expected us not to find it."

Nyberg was right. This was important.

"You mean, why didn't he just take it with him? Especially if he was hoping the body wouldn't be identified."

"Something like that."

"What would the answer be?"

"That's your job. I'm just telling you the facts. The handbag lay fifteen meters from the door of the transformer building."

"Anything else?"

"No. We didn't manage to get any other prints or tracks."

The conversation was over. Wallander lifted up the bottle of whiskey but then quickly put it down. He had had enough. If he kept drinking he would cross a line he didn't want to cross. He walked out into the living room. It felt strange to be home in the middle of the day. Was this what retirement would be like? The thought made him shiver. He walked over to the window and looked out at the street. It was already getting dark. He thought about the doctor who had paid him a visit, and about the man who had been found dead next to the cash machine. Wallander decided to call the pathologist the following day and tell him what Enander had said about not accepting a heart attack as the reason for Falk's death. It wouldn't change anything, but at least then he would have passed on the information.

He switched to thinking about what Nyberg had said about Sonja Hökberg's handbag. There was really only one conclusion, and it was one that brought out his keenest investigative instincts. *The bag lay there because someone had wanted it to be found.*

Wallander sat back down in his sofa and thought it through. *A body can be burned beyond recognition,* he thought. Especially if it is burned with a high-voltage charge that can't be controlled. A person who is executed in the electric chair is boiled from the inside out. Sonja Hökberg's murderer knew it would be hard to identify her body. That's why the handbag was left behind.

It still didn't explain its position over by the fence, however. Wallander thought it all through again, but still could not come up with an explanation that accounted for this fact. He abandoned the question of the bag. In any case, he was proceeding too quickly. First they had to confirm that Sonja Hökberg had actually been murdered.

He returned to the kitchen and made some coffee. The phone was silent. It was four o'clock. He sat down at the kitchen table with his cup of coffee and called in again. Irene told him that the papers and TV had been calling all afternoon. She had not given out his phone number: it had been unlisted for a couple of years now. Wallander thought again that his absence was going to be interpreted as an admission of guilt, or at least as a sign of deep embarrassment about the matter. *I should have stood my ground and stayed put,* he thought. *I should have talked to every damned reporter who called and told them the truth, that both Eva Persson and her mother were lying.*

The moment of weakness was over. He was starting to get angry. He asked Irene to put him through to Höglund. He should have started with Holgersson and told her once and for all that her suspicious attitude was unacceptable. But he put the phone down before there was an answer.

Right now he didn't want to talk to either one of them.

Instead, he dialed Sten Widén's number. By the time he picked up, Wallander had almost had time to regret it. But he was fairly sure Widén would not yet have seen the picture in the papers.

"I was thinking of stopping by," Wallander said. "The only problem is, my car is broken."

"I'll pick you up if you like."

They decided on seven o'clock. Wallander glanced in the direction of the whiskey bottle, but didn't touch it.

The doorbell rang. Wallander jumped. No one ever came by his house unannounced. It was probably a reporter who had found his address somehow. He put the bottle of whiskey in a cabinet and opened the door. But it wasn't a reporter. It was Höglund.

"Is this a bad time?"

He stood by to let her in and turned his face away so she wouldn't smell the alcohol on his breath. They sat down in the living room.

"I have a cold," Wallander said. "I didn't have the energy to keep working."

She nodded, but he didn't think for a second that she believed him. She had no reason to. Everyone knew Wallander always kept working in spite of whatever fevers or ailments he was suffering from.

"How are you holding up?" she asked.

The moment of weakness is over, Wallander thought. *Even if it just retreated for now and I know it's still in there. But I'm not going to show it.*

"If you're referring to the picture in the paper, I know it looks bad. How can a photographer make his way unseen all the way into our interrogation rooms?"

"Lisa is very concerned."

"She should listen to what I have to say," Wallander said, "She should support me, not immediately believe everything they say in the paper."

"She can't just ignore what's in the picture."

"I'm not saying she should. I hit the girl, but only because she was laying into her mother."

"You know of course that they have a different story."

"They're lying. But maybe you believe them?"

She shook her head.

"The question is only how to prove that they're lying."

"Who's behind it?"

Her answer came quickly and firmly.

"The mother. I think she's smart. She sees an opportunity to turn the attention away from her daughter's deeds. And now that Sonja Hökberg is dead, they can try to pin everything on her."

"Not the bloody knife."

"Oh, but they can. Even though it was recovered with Eva's help, she can claim that Sonja was the one who used it against Lundberg."

Höglund was right. The dead can't speak. And there was a large color photograph of a policeman who had knocked a girl to the ground. The picture was somewhat fuzzy, but no one could have any doubts as to what it depicted.

"The district attorney's office has demanded as quick an investigation as possible."

"Who in particular?"

"Viktorsson."

Wallander didn't like him. Viktorsson had only been in Ystad since August, but Wallander had already had a couple of run-ins with him.

"It's going to be one person's word against another."

"Except that there's two them, of course."

"The strange thing is that Eva Persson doesn't even like her mother," Wallander said. "It was clear when I spoke to her."

"She's probably realized she's in deep trouble, even though she's a juvenile and won't go to jail. Therefore she's declared a temporary truce with her mother."

Wallander suddenly felt he couldn't keep talking about the subject any longer. Not right now.

"Why did you stop by?"

"I heard you were sick."

"But not at death's door. I'll be back tomorrow. Tell me instead what you learned from your conversation with Eva Persson."

"She's changed her story."

"But she can't possibly know Sonja Hökberg is dead?"

"That's what's so strange."

It took a while for Wallander to understand what Höglund had just said. Then it dawned on him. He looked at her.

"You're thinking something?"

"Why does one change one's story? Eva Persson couldn't have known that Hökberg was dead when I started questioning her. But that's when she changed her whole story. Now Hökberg is the one who did everything. Eva Persson is innocent. They were never going to rob a taxi driver. They weren't going out to Rydsgård. Hökberg had suggested they visit her uncle who lived in Bjäresjö."

"Does he exist?"

"I've called him. He claims he hasn't seen Sonja in five or six years."

Wallander thought this over.

"In that case, there's only one explanation," he said. "Eva Persson would never have been able to rescind her confession and fabricate another story if she wasn't sure that Sonja would never be able to contradict it."

"I can't find another explanation either. Naturally I asked her why she hadn't said all this earlier."

"What was her answer?"

"That she hadn't wanted all the blame to fall on Sonja."

"Since they were friends?"

"Yes."

They both knew what it meant. There was only one possible explanation: that Eva Persson knew that Sonja Hökberg was dead.

"What are you thinking?" Wallander asked.

"That there are two possibilities. One is that Sonja could have called Eva after she left the station. She could have told her she was planning to commit suicide."

Wallander shook his head.

"That doesn't sound likely."

"I don't think so either. I don't think she called Eva Persson. I think she called someone else."

"Someone who later called Eva Persson and told her Sonja was dead?"

"It's possible."

"Was anyone monitoring her calls?" Wallander asked.

"I asked Hansson to check the log. But she may still have her cell phone. It wouldn't surprise me if no one thought to take it away from her."

"This could mean that Eva Persson knows who killed Sonja. Assuming it was a murder."

"Could it have been anything else?"

"It's doubtful. But we have to wait for the autopsy report."

"I tried to get a preliminary report, but I guess it takes time to work with badly burned bodies."

"I hope they realize it's urgent."

"Isn't it always?"

She looked down at her watch and got up.

"I have to get home to the kids."

Wallander thought he should say something to her. He knew from his own life what a hellish experience it was to end a marriage.

"How are things going with the divorce proceedings?"

"You've been through it yourself. You know what it's like."

Wallander walked her to the door.

"You should have a whiskey," she said. "You need it."

"I already have," Wallander replied.

At seven o'clock, Wallander heard a car honk down below. Through his kitchen window he could see Sten Widén's rusty old van. Wallander stuffed the whiskey bottle in a plastic bag and went down.

They drove out to the farm. As usual, Wallander asked to see the stables first. Many of the stalls were empty. A girl of about seventeen was hanging up a saddle when they came in. She finished and they were left alone. Wallander sat down on a bale of hay. Sten Widén leaned against a wall.

"I'm leaving," he said. "The ranch has been put up for sale."

"Who do you think will buy it?"

"Someone crazy enough to think he'll make money on it."

"Do you think you can get a good price?"

"No, but it will probably be enough. If I live cheaply I can probably survive on the interest."

Wallander was curious to know how much money was involved, but couldn't think of the right way to ask.

"Have you decided where to go?" he asked instead.

"First I have to sell. Then I'll decide where to go."

Wallander got out the bottle of whiskey.

"You'll never be able to live without your horses," he said. "What will you do?"

"I don't know."

"You're going to drink yourself to death."

"Or else it'll be just the opposite. Maybe that's when I'll be able to kick the bottle for good."

They left the stables and walked across the yard to the house. It was a chilly evening. Wallander felt his usual pang of envy. Sten was on his way toward an unknown but surely different future. He, on the other hand, was splashed across the front pages of the paper for assaulting a fourteen-year-old girl.

Sweden has become a place that people try to escape from, he thought. *The ones who can afford to. And those who can't afford it join the hordes who scavenge for enough money to leave.*

How had that happened? What had changed?

They sat down in the untidy living room that also served as an office. Widén poured himself a glass of cognac.

"I've been thinking about becoming a stage technician."

"What do you mean?"

"Exactly what I say. I could go to La Scala in Milan and work the curtain."

"You don't really think they operate the curtain by hand anymore, do you?"

"Well, I'm sure the occasional prop is still moved by hand. Think about being able to be backstage every night and hear that singing without paying a penny for it. I would even work for free."

"Is that what you're going to do?"

"No. I have a lot of ideas. Sometimes I even think about heading up to northern Sweden and burying myself in some cold and unpleasant heap of snow. I just don't know. The only thing I know is that the ranch is going to be sold and I'll have to go somewhere. What about you?"

Wallander shrugged without answering. He had had too much to drink. His head was starting to feel heavy.

"Are you still chasing moonshiners?"

Widén had a teasing tone in his voice. Wallander felt himself get angry.

"Murderers," Wallander said, "People who kill others by crushing their heads with a hammer. I take it you heard about that taxi driver?"

"No."

"Two little girls beat and stabbed a taxi driver to death the other day. They're the kind of people I chase. Not moonshiners."

"I don't understand how you can keep at it."

"I don't either. But someone has to do it, and I probably do it as well as anybody else."

Widén looked smilingly at him.

"You don't have to get so defensive. Of course I think you're an excellent policeman. I've always thought so. I just wonder if you're going to make time for anything else in your life."

"I'm not a quitter."

"Like me?"

Wallander didn't answer. He was suddenly aware of the distance between them and wondered how long it had really been there without their knowing it. Once upon a time they had been very close. Then they had grown up and gone their separate ways. When they'd met up years later, they thought they could build on the friendship they'd once had. They had never seen that the continuation of that friendship was totally different. Only now could Wallander see it clearly. Widén had probably also come to the same conclusion.

"One of the girls who killed this taxi driver had a stepfather," Wallander said. "Erik Hökberg."

Widén looked at him with surprise.

"Seriously?"

"Seriously. It looks like the girl has now been murdered herself. I don't have the time to take off, even if I wanted to."

He tucked the whiskey bottle back into the plastic bag.

"Could you call a cab for me?"

"Are you going already?"

"I think so."

A wave of disappointment washed over Widén's face. Wallander felt the same. Their friendship had come to an end. Or rather: they had finally discovered that it had ended a long time ago.

"I'll take you home."

"No," Wallander said. "You've had some drinks."

Widén didn't argue. He went over to the phone and called the cab company.

"It'll be here in ten minutes."

They went out. It was a clear fall evening with no wind.

"What did we expect?" Widén said suddenly. "When we were young, I mean."

"I've forgotten. But I'm not the kind to look back very often. I have enough on my hands with the present, and my worries for the future."

The taxi arrived.

"Make sure you write and tell me what happens," Wallander said.

"Will do."

Wallander climbed into the back seat.

The car drove through the darkness toward Ystad.

Wallander had just stepped into his apartment when the phone rang. It was Höglund.

"Are you home now? I've tried to call you a million times. Why isn't your cell phone turned on?"

"What's happened?"

"I tried the coroner's office in Lund again. I spoke to the pathologist. He didn't want to be held to this, but he's found something. Sonja Hökberg had a skull fracture in the back of the head."

"Was she dead when she hit the power lines?"

"Maybe not, but probably unconscious."

"Could she have hurt herself somehow?"

"He was pretty sure it could not have been self-inflicted."

"That settles it," Wallander said. "She was murdered."

"Haven't we known that all along?"

"No," Wallander said. "We suspected it, but we haven't known it until now."

Somewhere in the background a child started crying. Höglund was in a hurry to get off the phone. They arranged to meet at eight the next morning.

Wallander sat down at the kitchen table. He thought about Widén and Sonja Hökberg, but above all about Eva Persson.

She must know, he thought. *She knows who killed Sonja Hökberg.*

Chapter Ten

Wallander was catapulted from sleep at around five o'clock on Thursday morning. As soon as he opened his eyes in the dark he knew what had awakened him. It was something that had slipped his mind: his promise to Höglund. Today was the day he was supposed to give a speech at the Ystad women's literary society about life as a police officer.

He lay paralyzed in the darkness. How could he have forgotten about it so completely? He had nothing prepared, not even any scribbled notes.

He felt the anxiety grip in his stomach. The women he was going to address would almost certainly have seen the pictures of Eva Persson. And Höglund must have called them by now to tell them he was speaking in her place.

I can't do it, he thought. *All they are going to see is a brutal man who assaulted a young girl. Not the person I actually am. Whoever that is.*

As he lay in bed he tried to plot a way out of his dilemma, but he soon realized there was no way to get out of this. He got up at five-thirty and sat down at the kitchen table with a pad of paper in front of him. He wrote the word *Lecture* at the top of the page. He asked himself what Rydberg would have told a group of women about his work, but in the back of his mind he suspected that Rydberg would never have gotten himself roped into something like this in the first place.

By six o'clock he had still only written that one word. He was about to give up when he had a sudden thought. He could tell them about what they were involved in right now: the investigation of the taxi driver's death. He could even start by telling them about Stefan Fredman's funeral. A few days in a policeman's life—the way it really was, without any editing. He made a few notes. He wouldn't be able to avoid the whole incident with the photographer, and so his speech could seem like a defense. But in a way of course it was. It was a chance for him to tell it the way it had happened.

He put down his pen at a quarter past six. He was still anxious about the evening, but he no longer felt quite so helpless. He called the repair place and asked about his car. The conversation was depressing. Apparently they were considering taking the whole engine apart. The clerk promised to call him with a price quote later that day.

The thermometer outside read seven degrees Celsius. There were a soft wind and some clouds, but no rain. Wallander watched an old man slowly walking down the street. He stopped by a garbage can and leafed through its contents with one hand without finding anything. Wallander thought back to his visit with Widén. All traces of envy were gone. It had been replaced by a vague sense of melancholy. Widén was going to disappear from his life. Who was left who connected him to his earlier life? Soon there would be no one.

Wallander forced himself to halt this train of thought and left the apartment. On his way to the station he kept thinking about what he should say in his speech. A patrol car pulled up alongside him and the officer asked him if he wanted a ride. Wallander thanked him but declined the offer. He wanted to walk.

A man was waiting for him in the reception area. When Wallander walked past, the man turned to face him. Wallander recognized his face but was unable to place it in a context.

"Kurt Wallander," he said. "Do you have a minute?"

"That depends. Who are you?"

"Harald Törngren."

Wallander shook his head.

"I was the one who took the picture."

Wallander realized he remembered the man's face from the press conference.

"You mean, you were the one skulking around the hallway."

Harald Törngren smiled. He was in his thirties and had a long face and short hair.

"I was looking for a bathroom and no one stopped me."

"What do you want?"

"I thought you might like to comment on the picture. I'd like to interview you."

"You'd never write what I say anyway."

"How do you know that?"

Wallander thought about asking Törngren to leave. But he saw an opportunity and decided to take it.

"I want a third party present," he said.

Törngren kept smiling.

"A witness to the interview?"

"I've had bad experiences with reporters before."

"As far as I'm concerned, you're welcome to have ten witnesses."

Wallander looked down at his watch. It was twenty-five minutes past seven.

"I'll give you half an hour. No more."

"When?"

"Right now."

They walked in together. Irene said that Martinsson had already come in. Wallander told Törngren to wait while he went to Martinsson's office. He was doing something on his computer. Wallander quickly explained the situation.

Martinsson seemed to hesitate.

"As long as you don't flare up."

"Do I usually say things I don't mean?" Wallander objected.

"It happens."

Martinsson was right.

"I'll keep it in mind. Come on."

They sat down in one of the smaller conference rooms. Törngren put his little tape recorder on the table. Martinsson kept himself in the background.

"I spoke to Eva Persson's mother last night," Törngren said. "They have decided to press charges against you."

"For what?"

"For assault. What's your reaction?"

"There was never any question of assault."

"That's not what they say. And I have a picture of what happened."

"Do you want to know what happened?"

"I'd be delighted to hear your version."

"It's not a version. It's the truth."

"It's their word against yours, you know."

Wallander was starting to realize the impossibility of what he was trying to do and regretted allowing the interview. But it was too late now. He simply told Törngren him what happened. Eva Persson had attacked her mother and Wallander had tried to separate them. The girl had been wild. He had slapped her.

"Both the mother and the girl deny this."

"Nonetheless, it's what actually happened."

"Do you really expect me to believe that she started hitting her mother?"

"Eva Persson had just confessed to murder. It was a tense moment. At such times unexpected things can happen."

"Eva Persson told me last night that she had been forced to confess."

Wallander and Martinsson looked at each other.

"Forced?"

"That's what I said."

"And who forced her to do this?"

"The officers who interrogated her."

Martinsson was upset.

"That's the damndest thing I ever heard," he said. "We most certainly do not coerce anyone during our interrogations."

"I'm just repeating what she said. She now denies everything. She says she's innocent."

Wallander looked hard at Martinsson, who didn't say anything else. Wallander felt completely calm.

"The pre-investigation is far from complete," he said. "Eva Persson is tied to the crime, and even if she has decided to retract her confession it doesn't change anything at this point."

"You're saying she's lying."

"I can't answer that."

"Why not?"

"Because in order to do so I would have to reveal information about an ongoing investigation. Information that is still classified."

"But you are claiming she's lying?"

"Those are your words. I can only tell you what actually happened."

Wallander was starting to see the headlines. But he knew what he was doing was right. Eva Persson and her mother were cunning, but it wasn't likely to help them in the long run. Nor would exaggerated and emotional newspaper coverage.

"The girl is very young," Törngren said. "She claims she was pulled into these tragic events by her much older friend. Doesn't that sound plausible? Couldn't Eva Persson be telling the truth?"

Wallander considered telling the truth about Sonja Hökberg. The most recent events had not yet been made public, but he decided against saying anything. It would still give him an advantage.

"You and your newspaper are not the ones in charge of this investigation. We are. If you wish to draw your own conclusions and arrive at your own judgment, we can't stop you. But the reality is probably going to turn out to be something quite different. Not that it will be given much space in your paper."

Wallander let his hands fall palms down on the table to signal the end of the interview.

"Thank you for your time," Törngren said and started putting his tape recorder away.

"Martinsson will show you out," Wallander said.

He left the room without shaking hands. While he was getting his mail he tried to judge how the interview with Törngren had gone. Was there something he should have added? Was there something he should have expressed differently? He carried a cup of coffee back to his office with the mail tucked under his arm. He decided that the conversation with Törngren had gone well, even if he couldn't control what eventually showed up in the newspaper report. He sat down and started going through the mail. There was nothing that couldn't wait. He reminded himself of Enander's visit, shuffled through his notes in the top desk drawer, and called the coroner's office in Lund. He was lucky and was immediately put through to the pathologist in question. Wallander briefly described Enander's visit. The pathologist listened carefully and took down the relevant information. He ended the conversation after he had promised to notify Wallander if any of the new information was likely to lead to the revision of the conclusions of the autopsy.

At eight o'clock, Wallander got up and went to the large conference room. Lisa Holgersson was already there, as well as the attorney Lennart Viktorsson. Wallander felt a surge of adrenaline when he caught sight of him. Most people would probably keep a low profile after ending up on the front page of the newspaper. Wallander had gone through his moment of weakness the day before when he left the station early. But now he was ready for battle. He sat down in his chair and started speaking.

"As you all know, the evening papers ran a photograph of Eva Persson last night in which she had fallen down because I had slapped her. Although both the girl and her mother claim otherwise, what happened was that the girl was hitting her mother in the face and I was trying to intervene. She was in a fury. To snap her out of it, I slapped her. It was just hard enough to knock her off balance and she fell. This is also what I told the reporter who snuck into the station. I met with him this morning, as Martinsson can report."

He paused before continuing and looked around at the people gathered at the table. Chief Holgersson seemed put out. He sensed that she had wanted to be the one to bring it up.

"I've been told that there will be an internal investigation of the matter, which is fine with me. But now I think we should turn our attention to the matter at hand: Lundberg's murder and sorting out what actually happened to Sonja Hökberg."

Holgersson started speaking as soon as he was finished. Wallander didn't like the expression on her face. He still felt like she was letting him down.

"I think it goes without saying that you will no longer be allowed to question Eva Persson," she said.

Wallander nodded.

"Even I understand that much."

I should really have said more, he thought. *That a police officer's first duty is to stand by his colleagues—not uncritically, not at any price. But as long as it is a question of one person's word against another. This lie is easier for her than standing up for the uncomfortable truth.*

Viktorsson lifted his hand and interrupted Wallander's train of thought.

"I will of course be following this internal investigation very closely, and I suggest that we consider Eva Persson's new version of the events seriously. It's quite possible that things happened as she says, that Sonja Hökberg was solely responsible for the planning and execution of the assault."

Wallander couldn't believe his ears. He looked around the room, trying to elicit support from his closest colleagues. Hansson, in his checkered flannel shirt, looked lost in thought. Martinsson was rubbing his chin, and Höglund was slumped in her chair. No one met his gaze, but he decided to interpret from what he saw that they were still with him.

"Eva Persson is lying," he said. "Her first story is the true one. That's the version we will also be able to prove, if we get down to business and do our jobs."

Viktorsson wanted to go on, but Wallander didn't let him. He doubted that most people had been informed of what Höglund had called him about last night.

"Sonja Hökberg was murdered," he said. "The pathologist has informed us that fractures consistent with a strong blow to the back of the head have been found. It may have been the cause of death; at the very least it knocked her unconscious. Thereafter she was thrown in among the power lines. At any rate, we no longer need to have any doubts about whether or not she was murdered."

He had been correct. Everyone in the room was surprised.

"I should emphasize that this is the pathologist's preliminary report," he continued. "There may be more information forthcoming."

No one said anything, and he felt he had control of the proceedings now. The photograph in the papers nagged at him and gave him renewed energy. But he still couldn't get over Holgersson's open distrust of him.

He continued to give a thorough overview of the investigation to date.

"Johan Lundberg was murdered in what appears to be a hastily planned and executed robbery. The girls have said they needed money, but not for anything in particular. They make no attempts to conceal themselves from the police after the deed. When we bring them in, both of them confess almost immediately. Their stories are consistent with each other and neither one of them appears repentant. We also find the murder weapons. Then Sonja Hökberg escapes from the police station in what seems like a spur-of-the-moment decision. Twelve hours later she turns up murdered in one of the Sydkraft power substations. Establishing how she got there will be of crucial importance for us. We also don't know why she was murdered. But parallel to these events, something else happens that must also be considered crucial: Eva Persson recants her earlier confession. She now lays the entire blame for what happened on Sonja. She gives new information that cannot be checked because Sonja is now dead. The question is how Eva Persson knew this—and she must have known it. Information about the murder has still not been publicly released. The people who know about it are very few in number; yesterday that number was even smaller. Yet that was when Eva Persson suddenly changed her story."

Wallander finished and sat back in his chair. The level of attentiveness in the room had risen sharply. Wallander had managed to isolate the decisive issues.

"What did Sonja Hökberg do when she left the station?" Hansson asked. "That's what we need to find out."

"We know she didn't walk to the substation," Wallander said. "Even if it will be hard for us to prove with one-hundred-percent certainty. But we have to assume she was driven."

"Aren't we proceeding a little too quickly?" Viktorsson asked. "She could have been dead when she got there."

"I haven't finished yet," Wallander said. "Of course that is a possibility."

"Is there anything that speaks against this assumption?"

"No."

"Isn't it in fact the most logical conclusion? What reasons do we have to assume she went there willingly?"

"Only that she knew the person who drove her there."

Viktorsson shook his head.

"Why would anyone seek out a power substation located in the middle of a field? Wasn't it raining the whole time? Doesn't this tell us that she was in fact killed somewhere entirely different?"

"You're proceeding too quickly," Wallander said. "We're trying to lay all the alternatives on the table. We shouldn't be zeroing in on any of them just yet."

"Who gave her the ride?" Martinsson said. "If we know that, we'll know who killed her, even if we still don't know why."

"That will have to come later," Wallander said. "My thought is that Eva Persson couldn't have found out about Sonja's death through anyone other than the person who killed her. Or, at the very least, from a witness."

He looked over at Holgersson.

"That means Eva Persson is our key to figuring out what happened. She's a juvenile and she's lying, but now we have to turn up the heat. I want to know how she learned of Sonja's death."

He stood up.

"Since I won't be involved in Eva Persson's questioning, I'll be attending to other matters in the meantime."

He quickly left the room, pleased with his exit. He knew it was a childish display, but he also thought it would hit its mark. He assumed Höglund would be the one who would be given the responsibility of talking to Eva Persson. She knew what to ask; he didn't have to prepare her.

Wallander picked up his coat and left. He would be using his time to check something else. Before leaving the station he tucked two photographs from the case file into his pocket. He walked down toward the center of town. One aspect of the whole case had continued to bother him: Why had Sonja Hökberg been killed, and why had it taken place in such a way as to cut power to large parts of Scania? Had that really been a coincidence?

He crossed the main square and ended up on Hamngatan. The restaurant where Sonja and Eva had had their beers wasn't open yet. He peeked in through a window. There was someone in there, and it was a man he recognized. He knocked on the pane of glass. The man continued his work behind the counter. Wallander knocked harder and the man looked up. When he recognized Wallander he smiled and opened the door.

"It's not even nine o'clock yet," he said. "Do you want pizza already?"

"Sort of," Wallander said. "A cup of coffee would be nice. I need to talk to you."

István Kecskeméti had come to Sweden from Hungary in 1956. He had operated a number of restaurants in Ystad, and Wallander had made it a habit to eat at one of them when he didn't have the energy to cook for himself. He talked a lot at times, but Wallander liked him. He was also one of the few people who knew about Wallander's diabetes.

"You don't stop by very often," István said. "When you come, we're closed. That means you want something other than food."

He raised his arms and sighed.

"Everyone comes to István for help. Sports clubs and charities, someone who wants to start a cemetery for animals—they all want money. They all promise some advertising in return. But how is advertising in a pet cemetery going to help a pizzeria?"

He sighed again before continuing.

"Perhaps you also want something? Do you want me to give a donation to the Swedish police force?"

"Answers to a couple of questions will do fine," Wallander said. "Last Wednesday—were you here?"

"I'm always here. But last Wednesday is a while ago."

Wallander put the two photographs on the table. The lighting was poor.

"See if you recognize either one of these faces."

István took the photographs with him to the bar area. He looked at them for a long time before he returned.

"I think so."

"Did you hear about the taxi murder?"

"A terrible thing—how can it happen? And such young people." István suddenly understood the connection.

"These two?"

"Yes. And they were here that evening. It's very important that you tell me everything you remember. Where they sat, who they were with, that kind of thing." István clearly wanted to be of help. He strained to remember that evening, while Wallander waited. István picked up the photographs and started walking around the restaurant. He walked slowly and searchingly. *He's looking for his guests,* Wallander thought. *He's doing exactly what I would have done. The question is whether he'll find them.*

István stopped by a table close to the window. Wallander got up and walked over to it.

"I think they sat here," he said.

"Are you sure?"

"Pretty sure."

"Who sat in which seat?"

István looked troubled. Wallander waited again while István walked around the table a couple of times. Then, as if he were handing out menus, he put down the photographs of Sonja Hökberg and Eva Persson in front of their seats.

"Are you sure?"

"Yes."

But Wallander saw him wrinkle his brow. He was still trying to remember something.

"There was something that happened that evening," he said. "I remember them because I had doubts about one of them being eighteen years old."

"She wasn't," Wallander said. "But forget it."

Wallander waited. He saw how István was struggling to remember. "Something happened that evening," he repeated.

Then he suddenly remembered what it was. "They switched," he said. "At one point that evening, they switched seats."

Wallander sat down in the chair where Sonja Hökberg had spent the first part of the evening. From that seat, he could see a wall and the window facing out onto the street. But most of the restaurant was behind him. When he switched seats he saw the front door. Since a pillar and a booth hid most of the rest of the room, he only had a clear view of one table. It was a table for two.

"Did anyone sit there?" he asked and pointed to the table. "Did anyone sit down at the same time as the girls switched seats?"

István thought back.

"Actually, yes," he said. "Someone did come in and sit there, but I'm not sure if it was when they changed seats or not."

Wallander realized he was holding his breath.

"Can you describe him? Did you know who he was?"

"I had never seen him before, but he's easy to describe."

"What do you mean?"

"Well, he was Chinese. Or at least he looked Asian."

Wallander was quiet. This could be important.

"Did he stay here after the girls left in the taxi?"

"Yes, at least an hour."

"Did they have any kind of contact?"

István shook his head.

"I don't know. I didn't notice anything, but it's possible."

"Do you remember how the man paid his bill?"

"I think it was by credit card, but I'm not sure."

"Good," Wallander said. "I want you to find that charge slip."

"I've already sent it in. I think it was American Express."

"Then we'll find your copy," Wallander said.

He felt a sense of urgency. *Sonja Hökberg saw someone walking down the street,* he thought. *She changed places in order to see him. He was Asian.*

"What is it you're looking for?" István asked.

"I'm just trying to understand what must have happened," Wallander said. "I haven't gotten any further than that."

He said goodbye to István and left the restaurant.

A man of Asian descent, he thought.

He sensed that he was close to something important. He sped up. He was in a hurry.

Chapter Eleven

W hen Wallander arrived at the station he was out of breath. He had walked quickly because he knew Höglund was in the process of interrogating Eva Persson. He had to tell her what he had learned at István's restaurant so he could get her to ask the questions that now needed to be asked. Irene handed him a large heap of phone messages that he shoved unread into his pocket. He called the room where Höglund was questioning Eva Persson.

"I'm almost done here," she said.

"Not so fast," Wallander said. "I have a few more questions for you. Take a break. I'll drop by."

She seemed to sense that it was important and promised to do as he asked. Wallander was waiting impatiently for her in the hallway when she emerged from the room. He got right to the point, telling her about the seat changes and the man who had been sitting at the only table that Sonja Hökberg had a clear view of. When he finished, he saw that she was not convinced.

"An Asian man?"

"Yes."

"Do you really think this is important?"

"Sonja Hökberg changed seats because she wanted to have eye contact with someone. That has to mean something."

She shrugged.

"I'll talk to her about it. But what is it exactly that you want an answer to?"

"Why they changed places, and when. Try to see if she's lying. And did she notice the man who sat behind her?"

"It's hard to see anything going on inside her."

"Is she sticking to her new story?"

"Sonja Hökberg both hit and stabbed Lundberg. Eva Persson knew nothing in advance."

"How did she react when you told her Sonja is dead?"

"She tried to act sad, but didn't do a very good job. I think actually she was quite shocked."

"So you don't think she knew anything?"

"No."

Höglund got up to continue her work. She turned around in the doorway.

"The mother has hired a lawyer. He's already filed charges against you. His name is Klas Harrysson."

Wallander didn't recognize the name.

"He's a young ambitious lawyer from Malmö. He seems very sure of himself."

Wallander was overcome by a wave of tiredness. Then the anger came back, as well as the feeling of being treated unfairly.

"Did you get anything new out of her?"

"I honestly think Eva Persson is a little stupid, but she's sticking to her story—the later version—and she's not changing anything. She sounds like a recording."

Wallander shook his head.

"There's something deeper going on with Lundberg's murder," he said. "I'm convinced of it."

Höglund returned to continue questioning Eva Persson and Wallander went back to his room. He tried to find Martinsson without success. Hansson wasn't in, either. Then he leafed through the telephone messages that Irene had handed to him. Most of the callers were reporters, but there was also a message from Tynnes Falk's ex-wife. Wallander put the message aside, then called Irene and told her to hold all incoming calls for a while. He called information and was given the phone number for the American Express office. He started to explain what he wanted and was transferred to someone called Anita. She asked to return his call as a security check. Wallander put down the phone and waited. After a few minutes he remembered that he had asked Irene to hold all incoming calls. He swore and dialed the American Express number. This time they managed to arrange the security callback and Wallander was finally able to ask for the information he needed.

"I hope you realize it will take us some time to do this," Anita said.

"As long as you understand how important it is."

"I'll do what I can."

When the conversation was over, Wallander immediately called the car shop. After a few minutes, the clerk he had spoken with came on the line and quoted him a price that made him speechless. He was told the car would be ready the following day. It was the replacement parts that were expensive, not the labor. Wallander agreed to come and pick up the car at twelve.

He remained idle for a while after putting the receiver down. In his thoughts he was in the interrogation room with Höglund. It bothered him that he couldn't be there. Höglund could be a bit soft when it came to applying real pressure. Moreover, he had been unfairly treated by Holgersson. She had not given him the benefit of the doubt, something he couldn't forgive her for.

To get the time to pass, he dialed the number for Tynnes Falk's ex-wife. She picked up almost immediately.

"This is Wallander. Am I speaking with Marianne Falk?"

"I'm so glad you called. I've been waiting for you."

She had a high-pitched, pleasant-sounding voice. It occurred to Wallander that she sounded like Mona. He felt a distant, brief pull of emotion. Was it sadness?

"Has Dr. Enander been in touch with you?" she asked.

"I've talked to him."

"Then you know Tynnes didn't die of a heart attack."

"I'm not sure we can rule out that possibility."

"Why not? He was attacked."

She sounded very firm. Wallander's curiosity was piqued.

"You don't sound surprised."

"I'm not. Tynnes had many enemies."

Wallander pulled a pen and some paper toward him.

"What kind of enemies?"

"I don't know. But he was constantly on guard."

Wallander searched his memory for the information that had been in Martinsson's report.

"He was some kind of computer consultant, isn't that right?"

"Yes."

"That doesn't sound so dangerous."

"I think it depends on what you do."

"And what did he do, exactly?"

"I don't know."

"And yet you're convinced he was attacked?"

"I knew him well, although we didn't live together. This past year he was especially anxious."

"But he never told you why?"

She hesitated before answering.

"I know it sounds very strange that I can't be more specific," she said, "even though we lived together for a long time and had two children."

" 'Enemy' is a strong word to throw around in casual conversation."

"Tynnes traveled extensively. He had always done so. I have no idea what people he must have met, but sometimes he came home very excited. At other times when I met him at Sturup airport he was clearly worried."

"But he must have said something, like why he had enemies, or who they were?"

"He was a quiet man. But I could read the deep-seated anxiety in his face."

Wallander started wondering if the woman he was speaking to wasn't a bit high-strung.

"Was there anything else?"

"It wasn't a heart attack. I want the police to find out what really happened."

Wallander thought for a moment before answering.

"I've made a note of what you've said. We'll be in touch if we need to ask you anything else."

"I'm expecting you to find out what happened. We were divorced, Tynnes and I, but I still loved him."

The conversation was over. Wallander wondered briefly if Mona would also say she still loved him, though they were divorced and she was now married to another man. He doubted it. Then he wondered if she had ever really loved him. He brushed these thoughts aside angrily and went through in his head what Marianne Falk had told him. Her sense of anxiety seemed genuine. But she had not really been able to say anything concrete. He still didn't have a clear sense of who Tynnes Falk had been. Wallander looked for Martinsson's report, then called the coroner's office in Lund. The whole time, he was listening for Höglund's footsteps outside his door. It was the conversation with Eva Persson that was his primary interest right now. Tynnes Falk had died of a heart attack, and that fact wasn't altered by an ex-wife who was convinced he had been surrounded by enemies. Wallander spoke once more with the pathologist who had conducted the autopsy on Tynnes Falk. He told him about his conversation with Marianne Falk.

"It's not unheard of that heart attacks come seemingly from out of nowhere," the pathologist said. "The autopsy clearly revealed this as the cause of death. Neither Falk's wife's words nor what his doctor said changes my view in any way."

"And the head wound?"

"That was caused by hitting the asphalt."

Wallander thanked him and hung up. As he closed Martinsson's report, he had the nagging feeling that he had overlooked something, but he decided to ignore it. He couldn't spend time worrying about the products of other people's imagination.

He poured himself another cup of coffee in the lunchroom. It was almost half past eleven. Martinsson and Hansson were still out. No one knew where they were. Wallander returned to his office, impatient and irritated. Widén's decision to get out was needling him. It was as if he had ended up in a race he never thought he could win, but one in which he also didn't want to end up last. It was an unclear thought, but he knew what was bothering him. He felt that time was rushing away from him.

"I can't live like this," he said out loud to himself. "Something has to change."

"Who are you talking to?"

Wallander turned around. Martinsson stood in the doorway. Wallander hadn't heard him come in. No one at the station moved as quietly as Martinsson.

"I was speaking to myself," Wallander said firmly. "Don't you ever do that?"

"I talk in my sleep, according to my wife. Maybe that's the same thing."

"What do you want?"

"I've checked everyone who had access to the substation keys. No one has a previous record with us."

"Not that we expected them to," Wallander said.

"I've been trying to figure out why the gates were forced," Martinsson said. "I can only think of two possibilities: one, that the key to the gates was missing. Two, someone's trying to confuse us and throw us off the track."

"For what reason?"

"Vandalism, destruction for its own sake, I don't know."

Wallander shook his head.

"The steel door was unlocked. As I far as I can tell, there's also the possibility that the person who forced the gates was not the same person who unlocked the door."

Martinsson wrinkled his brow.

"And how would you explain that?"

"I can't explain it. I'm only presenting you with another alternative."

The conversation died away and Martinsson left. It was twelve o'clock. Wallander continued to wait. Höglund turned up at twenty-five minutes past twelve.

"One thing you can't accuse that girl of is talking too fast," she said. "I've never heard a young person who talked so slowly."

"Maybe she was afraid of saying the wrong thing," Wallander said.

Höglund sat down in his visitor's chair.

"I asked her about what you told me," she began. "But she never saw a Chinese person."

"I didn't say Chinese, I said Asian."

"Well, she never saw anyone like that. They changed seats because Sonja complained about a cold draft from the window."

"How did she react when you asked her that question?"

Höglund looked worried.

"Just as you would expect. The question took her by surprise and her answer was a pure lie."

Wallander hit the table.

"Then we know," he said. "There's a connection here to the man who came into the restaurant."

"What kind of connection?"

"We don't know. But it certainly wasn't an impulse murder."

"I just don't know how we're going to get any further."

Wallander told her about his call to the American Express office.

"That will give us a name," he said. "And if we have a name, we will have made good progress. While we're waiting on that, I'd like you to visit Persson's home. I want you to take a look at her bedroom. And where's her father?"

Höglund checked her notes.

"His name is Hugo Lövström. According to his daughter, he's a homeless drunk. She's filled with hate, that girl. I don't know who she hates more, her mother or her father."

"They have no regular contact?"

"It doesn't look like it."

Wallander thought about it.

"We don't see clearly yet," he said. "We have to find the real reasons behind all this. It may be that I'm simply too naive, that young people today—even girls—don't see anything wrong with murdering people. In that case, I give up. But not just yet. Something else must have driven them to do this."

"Maybe we should be looking at it from all angles," Höglund said.

"What do you mean?"

"Maybe we should be looking a little more closely at Lundberg."

"Why? They couldn't have known who their taxi driver was going to be."

"You're right."

But Wallander saw that she was thinking about something. He waited.

"There's just this possibility," she said thoughtfully, "that maybe it was an impulsive act after all. They ordered a taxi. Perhaps one or both of them suddenly recognized Lundberg."

Wallander saw what she was getting at.

"You're right," he said. "There is that possibility."

"We know the girls were armed," she said, "with both a hammer and a knife. It seems as if all young people these days carry some kind of weapon. The girls realize that Lundberg is their driver. Then they kill him. It could have happened like this, even if it seems unlikely."

"Not more unlikely than anything else," Wallander said. "Let's try to establish if they had any earlier contact with Lundberg."

Höglund got up and left. Wallander reached for his pad of paper and tried to jot down the basic outline of what Höglund had said. At one o'clock, he still felt as if he had not gotten any further. He was hungry and walked out to the lunchroom to see if there were any sandwiches left. They were gone. He picked up his coat from his office and left the station. This time he had remembered to bring his cell phone and to instruct Irene to let calls from American Express through. He went to the diner closest to the station. He noticed that customers there recognized him. He was sure that the picture in the paper had been a topic of discussion in most Ystad homes. He felt self-conscious and ate in a hurry. When he was back on the street his phone rang. It was Anita.

"We've found the information you were looking for," she said. "The card number belongs to someone called Fu Cheng."

Wallander stopped and wrote it down on a scrap of paper in his pocket.

"It's a Hong Kong-based account," she continued. "There's only one problem. It's a false account."

Wallander frowned.

"He stole it?"

"Worse. The account is completely fabricated. American Express has never opened an account with Fu Cheng."

"What does that mean?"

"Well, it's good that we discovered it so quickly. The restaurant owner will unfortunately not get his money. Hopefully he has fraud insurance."

"Does that mean Fu Cheng doesn't exist?"

"Oh, I'm sure he exists, but he has a fake credit card, as well as a fake address."

"Why didn't you tell me this from the start?"

"That's what I was trying to do."

Wallander thanked her and hung up. A man who maybe came from Hong Kong had turned up at István's restaurant in Ystad and paid with a fake credit card. At some point he had made eye contact with Sonja Hökberg.

He hurried back to the office. He could no longer put off the next task: preparing the lecture he had promised to give. Even though he had decided to speak plainly about the murder investigation he was involved in, he still needed to write down the points he wanted to touch on. Otherwise his nervousness would get the better of him.

He started writing but had trouble concentrating. The image of Sonja Hökberg's charred body kept returning. He reached for the phone and called Martinsson.

"See if you find anything on Eva Persson's father," he said. "Hugo Lövström. He's supposed to live in Växjö. A homeless alcoholic, apparently."

"In that case it'll be easier to locate him through our colleagues in Växjö," Martinsson replied. "I'm also in the process of checking out Lundberg."

"Did you think of that on your own?" Wallander was surprised.

"Höglund asked me to. She's just left to go check out Eva Persson's home. I don't know exactly what she expects to find."

"I have another name for your computers," Wallander said. "Fu Cheng."

"What was that?"

Wallander spelled it.

"Who's that?"

"I'll explain later. We should have a meeting this afternoon. I suggest half past four. It'll be short."

"His name is Fu Cheng? That's it?" Martinsson asked.

Wallander didn't bother to reply.

Wallander used the rest of the afternoon to plan his lecture. After working on it for only a short while, he had already started to hate what he had written. The year before, he had given a lecture at the National Police Academy about his experiences as a crime fighter. It had been a complete disaster in his own opinion. But many students had come up to him afterward to thank him. He had never been able to figure out what they were thanking him for.

At half past four he gave up. Now it was up to fate. He picked up his notes and headed for the conference room. No one was there yet. He tried to gather his thoughts and come up with a clear summary of the events of the case so far, but he was distracted.

It doesn't hang together, he thought. *Lundberg's murder doesn't fit with these two girls. Nor does Sonja's murder. This whole investigation lacks a common foundation, even though we know what happened. What we don't have is the crucial "why."*

Hansson arrived with Martinsson in tow, and Höglund came in behind them. Wallander was glad that Holgersson didn't turn up. It was a short meeting. Höglund told them about her visit to Eva Persson's house.

"Everything seemed very normal," she said. "It's an apartment on Stödgatan. Her mother works as a cook at the hospital. The girl's room was what you'd expect."

"Did she have any posters on the wall?" Wallander asked.

"Just some pop stars I didn't recognize," Höglund said. "But nothing unusual. Why do you ask?"

Wallander didn't answer.

The transcript of Höglund's conversation with Eva Persson was already prepared and Höglund distributed copies to everyone. Wallander told them of his visit to István's restaurant and the subsequent discovery of the stolen credit card.

"We need to find this man," he said. "If for no other reason than to be able to effectively rule out any involvement on his part with this case."

They continued to sift through the day's work. Martinsson told them what he had done, then Hansson. Hansson had talked to Kalle Ryss, whom Eva Persson had called Sonja's boyfriend. But he hadn't said anything of interest, other than that he knew very little about Sonja.

"He said she was very secretive," Hansson said. "Whatever that means."

After twenty minutes, Wallander tried to sum up the state of the investigation. He stressed the fact that he thought they had more work ahead of them than they expected.

The meeting was over shortly before five. Höglund wished him good luck.

"They're going to accuse me of being a violent misogynist," Wallander complained.

"I don't think so. You have a good reputation."

"I thought that was destroyed a long time ago."

Wallander went home. There was a letter from Per Åkeson in Sudan. He put it on the kitchen table to be opened later. Then he showered and changed. He left the apartment at six-thirty and walked to the place where he was supposed to meet all these unknown women. He stood for a moment staring up at the lighted house before he had the courage to enter.

When he reemerged from the house it was past nine o'clock. He was drenched in sweat. He had talked longer than he had planned to, and there had been more questions than he had expected. But the women there had inspired him. Most of them were his age, and their attentions had flattered him. When he left, part of him had actually wanted to stay longer.

He walked home slowly. He hardly knew anymore what he had actually told them. But they had listened to him. That had been the most important thing.

There was one woman in particular who stood out in his mind. He had exchanged a few words with her right before he left. She had said her name was Solveig Gabrielsson. Wallander had trouble getting her out of his head.

When he got home, he wrote down her name. He didn't know exactly why.

The phone rang before he'd even taken his coat off. He answered it.

It was Martinsson.

"How did the lecture go?" he asked.

"Good, I think. But that can't be why you're calling."

"I'm just here working," Martinsson said slowly. "There's this phone call from the coroner's office in Lund that I don't quite know what to do with."

Wallander caught his breath.

"Do you remember Tynnes Falk?" Martinsson asked.

"The man by the automatic teller. Yes, of course I do."

"Well, it seems as if his body has disappeared."

Wallander frowned.

"I thought dead bodies only disappeared into coffins."

"One would think so, but it appears in this case that someone has actually stolen the corpse."

Wallander didn't know what to ask next. He tried to think.

"There's one other thing," Martinsson said. "It's not just that the body has gone missing. Something was left in its place on the stretcher in the morgue."

"What was that?"

"A broken relay."

Wallander wasn't exactly sure what that was, other than that it had something to do with electricity.

"It's not just an ordinary relay," Martinsson continued. "It's large."

Wallander's heart was beating faster. He sensed what was coming.

"And where does one normally find large relays?" he asked.

"In power substations, just like the one where Sonja's body was found."

Wallander was silent.

They had finally found a connection.

But not the kind he had been expecting.

Chapter Twelve

Martinsson was waiting in the lunchroom.

It was ten o'clock on Thursday evening. The faint sound of a radio came from the control room that handled all the incoming emergency calls. Otherwise, it was completely quiet. Martinsson was drinking a cup of tea and eating some rusks. Wallander sat down across from him without taking off his coat.

"How did your lecture go?"

"You've already asked me that."

"I used to enjoy public speaking, but I don't know if I'd be any good at it anymore."

"I'm sure you'd still be better at it than me. But since you're asking, I can tell you that I had nineteen middle-aged women listening with bated breath to bloodthirsty stories about our socially responsible profession. They were very nice and asked me polite and friendly questions that I answered in a manner that even the National Chief of Police would not have been able to fault. Does that give you the picture?"

Martinsson nodded and brushed the crumbs from his mouth before pulling out his notes.

"I'll take it from the top. At nine minutes to nine the phone rings in the control room. The officer in charge puts the call through to me, since he knows it doesn't involve sending out any patrol cars. If I hadn't been here, the caller would probably have been told to call back tomorrow morning. The caller's name was Pålsson. Sture Pålsson. I don't know what his position was, but he's in charge of the coroner's office in Lund. Anyway, at around eight o'clock he checked the morgue and noticed that one of the lockers—do they call them lockers?—wasn't fully closed, and when he pulled out the stretcher, the body was gone and an electrical relay was in its place. He called home to the janitor who had been working there that day. His name was Lyth. He was able to confirm that the body had been there at six o'clock when he left for the day. The body seems to have disappeared sometime between six and eight. On one side of the morgue there's a back entrance that opens onto the yard. When Pålsson checked the door, he saw that the lock had been broken. He immediately called the Malmö police. The whole thing went very fast. A patrol car was there within fifteen minutes. When they heard that the body in question was from Ystad and had been the subject of a criminal investigation, they told Pålsson to contact us, which he did."

Martinsson put his notes down.

"The task of finding the body falls primarily to our colleagues in Malmö," he continued. "But I guess it's also something that we have to deal with."

Wallander turned the matter over in his mind. It was a strange and unpleasant incident. He felt his sense of anxiety grow stronger.

"We'll have to assume that our colleagues will think of searching for fingerprints," he said. "I don't know exactly what category this kind of crime falls into. Desecration of the dead? But there is a good chance they won't take it as seriously as we would like. Did Nyberg manage to secure any fingerprints from the substation?"

Martinsson thought about it.

"I think so. Would you like me to call him?"

"Not right now. But I'd like our Malmö colleagues to look for fingerprints on the relay and around the morgue. "

"Right now?"

"I think that would be best."

Martinsson left to go make the phone call. Wallander poured himself a cup of coffee and tried to understand exactly what this meant. A connection had emerged, but it was not one he would have expected and it could still turn out to be an unlikely coincidence. He had experienced such things before. But something told him it wouldn't be the case here. Someone had broken into a morgue and stolen a dead body, leaving an electrical relay in its place. It made Wallander think of something Rydberg had said many years ago, when they first started working together: "Criminals often leave a greeting at the scene of the crime. Sometimes it's deliberate, sometimes by accident."

This is no mistake, Wallander thought. *No one just happens to be carrying a big electrical relay around. It's even less likely that someone would accidentally leave it on a gurney in a morgue. It was supposed to be found, and it was hardly a message meant for the pathologists. It was left for us.*

This led to the other question: Why had the body been stolen? He had heard of cases where the bodies of people who had been members of strange sects were removed. That hardly applied in the case of Tynnes Falk, although it couldn't be entirely ruled out. But there was really only one wholly plausible explanation: the body had been removed in order to conceal something.

Martinsson returned.

"We're in luck," he said. "They've put the relay in a plastic bag."

"Any prints?"

"They're working on it right now."

"No signs of the body?"

"No."

"No witnesses?"

"Not as far as I know."

Wallander told him what he had been thinking. Martinsson agreed with his conclusions. The relay was a deliberate message, and the body had been removed in order to conceal something from them. Wallander also told him about Enander's visit and the phone call from Falk's ex-wife.

"I didn't put too much stock in what they told me," he conceded. "You have to be able to trust the coroner's report."

"Just because the body's been stolen doesn't mean Tynnes Falk was murdered."

Martinsson was right.

"I still have trouble seeing any other reason to remove the body except to conceal the manner of death," he said.

"What do we do now?"

"We need to determine who Tynnes Falk was," Wallander said. "Since we closed the case so quickly, we had no need to examine his life closely. But when I talked to the ex-wife she said that Falk was nervous and that he claimed to have many enemies. In fact, she said a number of things that led me to believe he was a complicated person."

Martinsson made a face.

"A computer consultant with enemies?"

"That was what she said. And none of us has spoken to her in any detail."

Martinsson was carrying the file folder that contained all the information they had on the Falk case.

"We never talked to his kids," he said, checking the report. "We never talked to anyone, since we concluded he had died of natural causes."

"That's what we're still assuming," Wallander said. "It's as plausible at this stage as anything else. What we have to acknowledge, however, is that there is some kind of connection between him and Sonja Hökberg. Perhaps even to Eva Persson."

"Why not also with Lundberg?"

"You're right. Maybe also with the taxi driver."

"At least we know that Tynnes Falk was already dead when Sonja Hökberg was killed," Martinsson said. "He's not our man."

"And if we assume Falk was murdered, the killer may be the same person who killed Hökberg."

Wallander's sense of anxiety increased. They were delving into something they didn't understand. *We have to find the part where it comes together,* he thought. *We have to go deeper.*

Martinsson yawned. Wallander knew he was often asleep by this time.

"The question is whether we can really get much further," he said. "We're not in a position to send people out to look for a lost body."

"We should take a look at his apartment," Martinsson said, stifling a new yawn. "He lived alone. We can start there and then talk to the wife."

"Ex-wife. He was divorced."

Martinsson got up.

"I have to get some sleep. How's the car?"

"It'll be ready tomorrow."

"Do you want a ride?"

"No, I'm going to stay for a while."

Martinsson hesitated.

"I know it must have upset you," he said. "The whole business with the picture in the paper."

Wallander looked at him closely.

"What's your take?"

"On what?"

"Whether or not I'm guilty?"

"Clearly you slapped her. But I believe you. She was attacking her mother and you were trying to restrain her."

"Well, my mind's made up," Wallander said. "If they try to pin it on me, I'm quitting."

He was surprised by his own words. It had never occurred to him before to quit if the internal investigation came back with a guilty verdict.

"In that case, we'll be swapping roles," Martinsson said.

"How do you mean?"

"Then I'll be the one trying to convince you to stay."

"You'll never do it."

Martinsson didn't reply. He took the folder and left. Wallander stayed at the table. After a little while, two patrol officers on the night shift walked through the room. They nodded at him. Wallander listened absently to their conversation. One of them was thinking of buying a motorcycle in the spring.

Once they had poured themselves coffee and left, Wallander was alone again. Without being completely aware of it, he had already arrived at a decision.

He looked down at his watch. It was almost half past eleven. He knew he should wait until the morning, but the sense of urgency was too great.

He left the station shortly before midnight, a set of pass keys in his pocket.

It took him ten minutes to walk to Apelbergsgatan. There was a soft breeze, and it was a few degrees above freezing. It was overcast. The town felt deserted. Some heavily laden trucks barrelled past him on their way to the Polish ferries. It occurred to Wallander that it was about this time of night that Falk had died.

Wallander stood in the shadows and looked at the apartment building at 10 Apelbergsgatan. The top floor was dark. That was where Falk had lived. The apartment below was also dark, but in the first-floor apartment the lights were on. Wallander shivered. That was where he had once fallen asleep in the arms of a total stranger. He had been so drunk he hadn't even known where he was.

He fingered the pass keys in his pocket and hesitated. What he was about to do was unnecessary as well as unlawful. There was no reason not to wait until the morning, when he could arrange to get the keys to the apartment. But his sense of urgency wouldn't let up. And it was something he had learned to trust over the years.

The front door to the building was unlocked. The stairway was dark. He turned on the flashlight he had remembered to bring with him and listened for any sounds before starting up the stairs. There were two doors on the top floor. The one to the right was Falk's. He listened again, putting his ear up against both doors. Nothing. Then he gripped the little flashlight between his teeth and got out the passkeys. If Falk had outfitted his door with specialty locks, he would have been forced to give up at the outset. But Falk had only ordinary locks. *That doesn't fit with what she said,* he thought. *That Falk was worried and had many enemies. She must have exaggerated.*

It took him longer than he'd expected to get the door open. The pass keys felt unfamiliar in his hands and he had started to sweat. When the door finally opened, he thought he heard breathing coming at him from out of the darkness. But then it was gone. He stepped into the hall and shut the door softly behind him.

The first thing he always noticed about an apartment was the smell. But here there wasn't one, as if the apartment was new and no one had moved in yet. He made a mental note of it and started to walk through the apartment with the flashlight in his hand, expecting to find someone in there at any moment. Only when he had assured himself that he was alone did he take off his shoes, shut all the curtains, and turn on a lamp.

Wallander was in the bedroom when the phone rang. He flinched and held his breath. The answering machine in the living room picked up and he hurried over to it. But the caller didn't leave a message. Who had called? Who called a dead person in the middle of the night?

Wallander walked over to one of the windows that looked out onto the street. He peeked out through a tiny slit in the curtains. The street was empty. He tried to penetrate the shadows with his gaze, but he didn't see anyone.

He started his search in the living room after turning on the desk lamp. Then he stood in the middle of the room and looked around. *This is where Tynnes Falk lived,* he thought. *His story starts with a clean and well-ordered living room that is the very opposite of everyday chaos. There is leather furniture, a collection of maritime art on the walls. There's a big bookcase along one wall.*

He walked over to the desk. He saw an old brass compass laid out next to a green writing pad. Some pens lay neatly lined up next to an antique oil lamp made of clay.

Wallander continued out into the kitchen. There was a coffee cup on the counter and a small notepad on the kitchen table. Wallander turned on the light and looked at the pad. DOOR TO BALCONY, he read. *Maybe Tynnes Falk and I have a lot in common,* he thought. *We both keep notepads in our kitchens.* He walked back out into the living room and tried to open the balcony door. It was stiff. Falk hadn't gotten around to fixing it. He continued into the bedroom. The double bed was made. Wallander knelt and looked underneath it. He saw a pair of slippers.

He opened the closet and pulled out all the dresser drawers. Everything he saw had been neatly arranged. He walked back out into the living room. Slipped in underneath the answering machine were its instructions. When he was sure he could listen to the messages without erasing anything, he put on a pair of rubber gloves and pressed the button.

First there was a message from someone called Jan who asked Tynnes Falk how he was doing. He sounded young—maybe a teenager. He didn't say when he was calling. Then there were two calls from someone who only breathed on the other end. Wallander had the feeling it was the same person both times. The fourth call came from a tailor's shop in Malmö to let Falk know his pants were ready. Wallander made a note of the name. Then came the most recent call from the person who only breathed. Wallander listened to the whole thing one more time and wondered if Nyberg could somehow determine if the mystery calls were from the same person.

He put the instruction manual back in its place. There were three photographs on the desk, two of them probably of Falk's children. There were a boy and a girl. The boy was sitting on a rock in a tropical setting, smiling at the camera. He was probably around eighteen years old. Wallander turned it over. *Jan 1996, the Amazon.* That must have been the boy who'd left the message on the answering machine. The girl was a little younger. She sat on a bench surrounded by pigeons. Wallander turned that picture over and read *Ina, Venice, 1995.* The third photograph was of a group of men in front of a white stone wall. It was slightly out of focus. Wallander turned it over but found nothing written on it. He studied the men's faces. They were of varying ages. To the far left there was a man who looked Asian. Could he be the man from the restaurant? Wallander put the photograph down and tried to think. He tucked the photo into his pocket.

Then he lifted the green writing pad and found a newspaper clipping. *How to make fish fondue.* He went through the drawers, which were characterized by the same meticulous order. He found a thick diary in the third drawer. Wallander opened it to the last entry. On Sunday, the fifth of October, Tynnes Falk had noted that the wind had died down and that it was three degrees Celsius. The sky was clear and he had cleaned the apartment. It had taken him three hours and twenty-five minutes, which was ten minutes faster than the last time.

Wallander frowned. The notes about the housecleaning perplexed him.

Then he read the last line: *A short walk in the evening.*

Did that mean he had already been on a walk, or was he about to head out?

Wallander glanced at the entry for the previous day:

"Saturday, the fourth of October, 1997. Gusty winds all day. According to the meteorological institute wind speed is 8 to 10 meters per second. Broken cloud formations. The temperature at six A.M. was 7 degrees Celsius. By two o'clock up to 8, but in the evening back down to 5. C-space has been quiet. No messages. C doesn't answer. Everything calm."

Wallander read the last lines without understanding what they meant. He flipped through the diary and saw that all the entries were similar, giving information about the weather as well as "c-space." Sometimes all was quiet, sometimes there were messages, but what kind of messages they were Wallander never figured out. Finally he shut the book and put it back.

He thought it was strange that Falk had not written a single name anywhere, not even those of his children.

He wondered if Tynnes Falk had been crazy. The diary entries seemed consistent with those of a manic or confused person.

Wallander got up and walked over to the window again. The street was still empty. It was already past one o'clock.

He made one last search of the desk and found some business material. It seemed that Tynnes Falk was a consultant who helped corporate clients choose and install the right computer systems for their businesses. Wallander couldn't tell exactly what that involved, but he noted that a number of prominent companies, including several banks and Sydkraft Power, had been among his clients.

There was nothing really surprising anywhere.

Wallander closed the last drawer.

Tynnes Falk is a person who doesn't leave any traces, he thought. *Everything is impersonal, well-ordered, and impenetrable. I can't find him.*

Somehow Sonja Hökberg's murder was connected to Tynnes Falk's death, and to the fact that his body had now disappeared.

There was also possibly a connection to Johan Lundberg.

Wallander took out the photograph that he had slipped in his pocket. Then he put it back. He wanted to make sure no one found out about his late-night visit. In case he later had Falk's ex-wife let them in, he didn't want anything to be missing.

Wallander walked around the apartment and turned out all the lights, then opened all the curtains. He listened carefully for sounds before opening the door. He checked the outside of the door, but the pass keys hadn't left any marks.

*   *   *

Once he was back out on the street, he paused and looked around. No one was in sight, the town was quiet. He started walking home. It was twenty-five minutes past one o'clock.

He never saw the shadow quietly following him at a distance.

Chapter Thirteen

Wallander woke up when the phone rang.

He sprang out of bed as if he had been lying in wait for the call rather than deeply asleep. As he put the receiver to his ear, he glanced at the time. A quarter past five.

"Kurt Wallander?"

The voice on the other end was unfamiliar to him.

"Speaking."

"I'm sorry for calling so early. I would like to ask you some questions regarding that alleged assault."

Wallander was suddenly completely alert. He sat up. The man told him his name and the name of the paper he worked for. Wallander realized he should have foreseen the possibility that a reporter would try to get hold of him early in the morning. If one of his colleagues had wanted to reach him, they would have tried the cell phone. At least that number was still private.

But it was too late now. He had to say something.

"I've already explained that it wasn't assault."

"So do you mean that the photograph is a lie?"

"It doesn't tell the whole truth."

"Would you care to tell it now?"

"Not as long as I'm involved in the investigation."

"But you must be able to say something?"

"I already have. It wasn't assault."

Wallander hung up and unplugged the phone. He could already see the headlines: *Defensive silence from police. Officer hangs up on reporter.* He sank back onto the pillows. The streetlamp outside his window was swaying in the wind. The light flickered across the wall.

He had been dreaming something when the phone rang. The images slowly returned from his subconscious.

They were images from last fall, when he had taken a trip to the Östergötland archipelago. He had been invited to stay with the postman who delivered mail out in the islands. They had met during one of the worst cases Wallander had ever been involved in. He had accepted the invitation somewhat hesitantly. One early morning, the postman took him to explore one of the remote little islands on the edge of the archipelago, where craggy rocks poked out of the sea like fossilized creatures from the ice age. As he had wandered around the small island on his own, he had experienced a remarkable feeling of clarity. He had often returned to this moment in his thoughts since that time. He had often longed to experience the feeling again.

The dream is trying to tell me something, he thought. *I just don't know what.*

He stayed in bed until a quarter to six, when he got up and plugged the phone back in. While he drank a cup of coffee he tried to go through everything that had happened in his head, trying to make sense of the new connection drawn between Sonja Hökberg's death and the man whose apartment he had searched the night before.

At seven o'clock he gave up trying to make sense of it and went in to the station. It was colder than he had been expecting. He hadn't yet become accustomed to the fact that it was fall. He wished he had put on a warmer sweater. As he walked, he felt his left foot getting wet. When he stopped and looked at the shoe, he discovered a tear in the sole. It made him furious. He had to restrain himself from tearing off both of his shoes and continuing in bare feet.

When he came into the reception area, he asked Irene who else was already in. She said that both Martinsson and Hansson had arrived. Wallander asked her to send them in to see him. Then he changed his mind and decided to meet them in one of the conference rooms. He asked her to make sure Höglund joined them when she came in.

Martinsson and Hansson entered the room at the same time.

"How did the lecture go?" Hansson asked.

"Let's not waste our time on that," Wallander said irritably, then felt guilty that he had taken his bad mood out on Hansson.

"I'm tired," he said.

"Who isn't?" Hansson said.

Höglund opened the door and stepped in.

"That's some wind," she said as she took off her jacket.

"It's fall," Wallander said. "All right, let's start. Something happened last night that dramatically alters the investigation."

He nodded to Martinsson, who told the others about the disappearance of Tynnes Falk's body.

"At least this is something new," Hansson said when Martinsson had finished. "I don't think we've ever had a stolen body before. I know there was that rubber raft. But not a dead body."

Wallander made a face. He remembered the rubber raft that had floated ashore on Mossby beach after it had mysteriously and by still-unclear means disappeared from the police station.

Höglund looked at him.

"So are we to accept a connection between the man who died near the cash machine and Lundberg's murder? That seems ludicrous."

"Yes," Wallander said. "But I don't think we can avoid working with this assumption for now. I think we should also be prepared for the fact that this will be a difficult case. We thought we were dealing with an unusually brutal but clear-cut case of murder. We then saw this first scenario dissolve when Sonja Hökberg escaped and was later found dead at the power substation. We were aware of the fact that a man had been found dead by a cash machine, but we had already declared that case closed from lack of evidence that any crime had been committed. This conclusion still cannot be ruled out. Then the body disappears, and someone puts an electrical relay in its place."

Wallander interrupted himself and thought back to the questions he had regarding Sonja's and Eva's visit to the restaurant and the identity of the Asian man. Now he saw that they should actually start from a totally different angle.

"Someone breaks into a morgue and steals a dead body. We can't be sure of the reasons, but it seems probable that someone wants to conceal something. At the same time the relay is left as a kind of message. It wasn't left by accident. The person who removed the body wanted us to find it."

"Which can only mean one thing," Höglund said.

Wallander nodded.

"That someone wants us to see a connection between Sonja Hökberg and Tynnes Falk."

"Couldn't it be a red herring?" Hansson objected. "Someone who's read about how the girl was burned to death?"

"Our colleagues in Malmö have assured me the relay is large and heavy," Martinsson said. "It's hardly the kind of thing you carry around with you in a briefcase."

"We have to proceed step by step," Wallander said. "Nyberg will examine the relay and determine whether or not it originates from our substation. If it does, then we're home free."

"Not necessarily," Höglund said. "It could still be a symbolic act."

Wallander shook his head.

"I just don't get that feeling in this case."

Martinsson called Nyberg while the others went to get coffee. Wallander told them about the reporter who had woken him up that morning.

"It'll blow over soon," Höglund said.

"I hope you're right, but I'm not so sure."

They returned to the conference room.

"Listen up," Wallander said. "We have to get serious with Eva Persson. It doesn't matter anymore that she's a juvenile. We've got to throw away the kid gloves and start getting some real answers. That will be up to you, Ann-Britt. You know what questions to ask, and you're not going to give up until she starts telling the truth."

They continued planning the next stages of the investigation. Wallander suddenly realized he had completely recovered from his cold. His strength was returning. They finished around half past nine. Hansson and Höglund disappeared down the hall to their various tasks. Wallander and Martinsson were going to examine Tynnes Falk's apartment together. Wallander was tempted to tell him about his visit the night before, but he decided against it. He knew that one of his faults was his tendency not to tell his colleagues about all the steps he took in his detective work. But he had also given up hope a long time ago that he would ever be able to change this aspect of his personality.

While Martinsson was arranging getting keys to the apartment, Wallander went to his office with the newspaper that Hansson had earlier thrown on the table. He flipped through it to see if there was anything about himself. The only thing he found was a small item about a police officer suspected of use of excessive force against a juvenile offender. His name did not appear anywhere, but his sense of outrage returned.

He was about to put the paper aside when his gaze fell on the personal ads. He started reading. There was an ad from a divorced fifty-year-old woman who said she felt lonely now that the kids were grown up. She listed her main interests as travel and classical music. Wallander tried to imagine what she looked like, but he kept seeing the face of a woman named Erika whom he had met a year ago at a roadside café in Västervik. He had thought about her from time to time since then, without being able to say why. Irritably he tossed the paper into the trash. But just before Martinsson came into the room he fished it up, tore out the page with the ad and slipped it into one of his drawers.

"His ex-wife's meeting us there with the keys," Martinsson said. "So you want to walk or take the car?"

"The car," Wallander said. "I have a hole in my shoe."

Martinsson gave him an amused look.

"What would the National Chief of Police say about that?"

"We've already instituted his ideas about community policing," Wallander answered. "Why not expand the idea to include barefoot policing?"

They left the station in Martinsson's car.

"How are things with you?" Martinsson asked.

"I'm pissed off," Wallander said. "You'd think you get used to all this but you don't. During my years in the force I've been accused of almost everything, with the possible exception of being lazy. You'd think you develop a defensive shield, but you don't. At least not in the way you'd hope."

"Did you mean what you said yesterday?"

"What did I say?"

"That you'd leave if they found you guilty."

"I don't know. I don't think I have the energy to think about it right now."

Wallander didn't want to talk more about it and Martinsson knew to leave him alone. They pulled up outside 10 Apelbergsgatan, where a woman was waiting for them.

"That must be Marianne Falk," Martinsson said. "I guess she kept her name after the divorce."

Martinsson was about to open the car door when Wallander stopped him.

"Does she know what's happened? About the body being missing?"

"Someone notified her."

They stepped out of the car. The woman standing there in the wind was very well dressed. She was tall and slender and reminded Wallander vaguely of Mona. They said hello. Wallander had the feeling she was worried. He immediately became more alert.

"Have they found the body yet? How can things like this happen?"

Wallander let Martinsson answer.

"It's very unfortunate, of course."

"'Unfortunate'? It's unacceptable. What do we have a police force for, anyway?"

"There's a question," Wallander said. "But I think we should deal with that another time."

They went into the building and walked up the stairs. Wallander felt uncomfortable. Had he left anything behind the night before?

Marianne Falk walked ahead of them. When she came to the top landing, she stopped and pointed to the door. Martinsson was right behind her. Wallander pushed him aside. Then he saw. The door to the apartment was wide open. The locks he had taken so much trouble with the night before, trying not to leave any traces of his visit, had been broken with something like a crowbar. Wallander listened for sounds. Martinsson was right beside him. Neither one of them was carrying a weapon. Wallander hesitated. He signaled them to go down to the apartment below.

"There could be someone in there," he whispered. "We had better get some backup."

Martinsson picked up his phone.

"I want you to wait in your car," Wallander said to Marianne Falk.

"What's happened?"

"Just do as I say. Wait in your car."

She disappeared down the stairs. Martinsson was talking to someone at the station.

"They're on their way."

They waited motionless on the stairs. There were no sounds coming from the apartment.

"I told them not to turn on the sirens," Martinsson whispered.

Wallander nodded.

After eight minutes Hansson came up the stairs with three other officers. Hansson had a gun. Wallander took a gun from one of the other policemen.

"Let's go in," he said.

The hand that was holding the gun shook slightly. Wallander was afraid. He was always afraid when he was about to enter a situation where anything was possible. He established eye contact with Hansson, then pushed the door open and called out into the apartment. There was no answer. He shouted again. When the door behind them opened, he jumped. An older woman looked out. Martinsson forced her back inside. Wallander called out a third time without getting an answer.

Then they went in.

The apartment was empty. But it was not the apartment he had left the night before with an impression of meticulous order. Now all the drawers were pulled out and emptied on the floor. Paintings on the wall hung askew and the record collection lay jumbled on the floor.

"There's no one here," he said. "Let's get Nyberg and his people here as soon as possible. I don't want us disturbing the area more than we have to."

Hansson and the others left. Martinsson went to talk to the neighbors. Wallander stood in the doorway to the living room and looked around. How many times had he stood like this in an apartment where a crime had been committed? He couldn't say. Without being able to put his finger on it, he knew something was missing. He let his gaze slowly travel through the room. When he was looking at the desk for the second time he realized what it was. He took off his shoes and approached the table.

The photograph was gone, the one of the group of men against the white stone wall. He bent over and looked under the desk. He slowly lifted the pieces of paper that had fallen to the ground. But it was gone.

At the same moment he realized something else was gone too. The diary.

He took a step back and held his breath. *Someone knew I was here*, he thought. *Someone saw me come and go.*

Was it an instinctive sense of this that had made him walk up to the windows twice and look out at the street? There had been someone out there he hadn't been able to see. Someone hidden deep within the shadows.

He was interrupted in his thoughts by Martinsson.

"The woman next door is a widow by the name of Håkansson. She hasn't seen or heard anything unusual."

Wallander thought about the time he was drunk and had ended up spending the night in the apartment below.

"Talk to everyone who lives here. Find out if anyone has seen anything."

"Can't we get someone else to do it? I have a lot to do as it is."

"It's important that it's done right," Wallander said. "Not that many people live here, anyway."

Martinsson disappeared again and Wallander waited. A crime technician turned up after twenty minutes.

"Nyberg is on his way," he said. "But he was in the process of doing something out at the substation that seemed to be important."

Wallander nodded.

"Take a look at the answering machine," he said. "I want you to get everything that you can out of it."

The officer wrote it down.

"The whole apartment should be videotaped," Wallander continued. "I want this apartment examined down to every last detail."

"Are the people who live here away?" the officer asked.

"The person who lived here was the man who was found dead by the cash machine," Wallander said. "It's very important that the forensic investigation is thorough."

He left the apartment and walked out onto the street. There were no clouds in the sky. Marianne Falk was smoking in her car. When she saw Wallander she got out.

"What's happened?"

"There's been a break-in."

"I wouldn't have believed someone could have such utter disrespect for the dead."

"I know you were divorced, but were you familiar with his apartment?"

"We had a good relationship. I visited him here many times."

"I'm going to ask you to return later today," Wallander said. "When the forensic team is done I want to you to walk through the apartment with me. You might be able to spot something that's gone missing."

"Oh, I doubt that." Her answer came quickly and unwavering.

"Why do you say that?"

"I was married to him for many years. I knew him fairly well then, but not later on."

"What happened?"

"Nothing. He just changed."

"In what way?"

"I didn't know what he was thinking anymore."

Wallander looked at her thoughtfully.

"But you may still be able to notice if something's gone. You said yourself that you visited him here many times."

"I could probably tell you if a lamp or a painting was missing, but nothing else. Tynnes had many secrets."

"What do you mean by that?"

"Just what you think it means. I didn't know what he was thinking or what he did. I tried to explain this to you during our first telephone conversation."

Wallander was reminded of what he had read in Tynnes's diary the night before.

"Do you know if your ex-husband kept a diary?"

"I'm sure he didn't."

"Did he ever keep one?"

"Never."

So she's right about one thing, he thought. *She didn't know what he was up to, at least not that he had a diary.*

"Was your ex-husband interested in outer space?"

Her surprise seemed completely genuine.

"Why do you ask that?"

"I was just wondering."

"When we were young we used to sometimes look up at the stars together, but I can't remember any other signs of interest after that."

Wallander switched to a new topic.

"You said before that he had many enemies, and that he seemed worried about something."

"Yes, he actually said that to me."

"What else did he say?" Wallander asked.

"That people like him always had enemies."

"Was that all he said?"

"Yes."

" 'People like me always have enemies'?" he repeated.

"Yes."

"What did he mean by that?"

"I've already told you that I no longer understood him."

A car pulled over to where they were standing and Nyberg got out. Wallander decided to end the conversation for now and wrote down her phone number. He said he would be in touch later in the day.

"One last question: Can you think of any reason why someone would steal his body?"

"Of course not."

Wallander nodded. He had no more questions.

When she had climbed into her car and backed out of her parking space, Nyberg came over to him.

"What's happened?" he asked.

"A break-in."

"Do we really have time for this right now?"

"It's connected to the other events. I don't know exactly how yet, but I'd like to see if you find anything in there."

Nyberg blew his nose before answering.

"You were right, by the way. Once our colleagues in Malmö brought in that relay it was obvious. The substation workers were able to show us exactly where it used to fit."

Wallander suppressed his excitement.

"Room for doubt?"

"None at all."

Nyberg went into the building. Wallander looked down the street in the direction of the department stores and the cash machine.

The connection between Sonja Hökberg and Tynnes Falk was confirmed. But what it meant he didn't yet know.

He started walking back to the police station. After only a few yards he picked up the pace.

Anxiety drove him on.

Chapter Fourteen

After he returned to the station, Wallander tried to construct a reliable outline of the now-chaotic mix of details. But the various events remained sharply separated in his mind. They collided only to quickly continue on their separate ways.

Shortly before eleven, he went to the bathroom and washed his face in cold water. That was also something he had picked up from Rydberg.

Nothing is better for you when your impatience is threatening to take over your mind. Nothing is ever better than cold water.

Then he continued on into the lunchroom to get more coffee. But the coffee machine was broken, as it often was. Martinsson had at some point suggested that they all pitch in to buy a new one. His argument was that no one could reasonably expect good police work from officers without reliable access to coffee. Wallander looked unhappily at the machine and remembered that he had a tin of instant coffee somewhere in his desk. He returned to his room and started looking for it. He finally found it in the bottom drawer together with some shoe cleaner and a couple of frayed gloves.

Then he compiled a list of all the events of the case. He made a timeline in the margin. He was trying to break through the surface of the case to the layer that he knew had to be there that connected all the events.

When he was finished, he felt as if he were looking at an evil and incomprehensible fairy tale. Two girls went out and had some beers. One of the girls was so young that she had no business being served in the first place. Some time during that evening, they traded places. This happened at the same time that an Asian man came into the restaurant and sat down at a nearby table. This man paid with a false credit card in the name of Fu Cheng, with a Hong Kong address.

After a couple of hours, the girls ordered a taxi, asked to be driven to Rydsgård, and attacked the driver. They took his money and left, each going separately to her home. When they were picked up by the police they immediately confessed, sharing the blame and saying their motive was money. The older of the two girls then took advantage of a momentary lapse in security and escaped from the police station. Later her burned corpse was found at the power substation outside Ystad. In all likelihood she was murdered. The substation in turn was an important link in the power distribution grid for southern Sweden. When Sonja Hökberg died, she plunged much of the region of Scania into darkness. After this event, Eva Persson retracted her earlier confession and changed her story.

At the same time as these events, a parallel story was unfolding. There was a possibility that this parenthesis, this minor story, was in fact connected to the very heart of the other occurrence somehow. A divorced computer consultant by the name of Tynnes Falk cleaned his apartment one Sunday and then went for an evening walk. He was later found dead in front of an automatic teller machine nearby. After a preliminary investigation that included a conclusive autopsy report, the police eliminated any suspicions of possible crime and considered the case closed. Later the body was removed from the morgue and an electrical relay from the Ystad substation was left in its place. Falk's apartment was also robbed in conjunction with these latest events, and at least a diary and a photograph were missing.

At the periphery of all these events, figuring as a face in a group photograph and as a customer in a restaurant, was an Asian man.

Wallander read through everything he had just written. He knew it was too early to draw any conclusions, but while he had been sketching out his summary of the events he had also seen a new connection. If Sonja Hökberg had been murdered, it had to be because someone wanted to make sure she didn't talk. Tynnes Falk's body had also been removed in order to conceal something. This was the common denominator.

The question is, What needs to be covered up, Wallander thought, *and by whom?*

Wallander was about to push his notes aside when something popped into his head. It was something Erik Hökberg had said, something about the vulnerability of modern society. Wallander took a new look at his notes, starting at the beginning.

What happened if he placed the events surrounding the power

substation at the center? With the grisly aid of a human body, someone had managed to disrupt the power in large areas of southern Sweden. It could therefore be viewed as sabotage. And why had the electrical relay been placed on the gurney when Falk's body was stolen? The only reasonable explanation was that someone had wanted the connection between Sonja Hökberg's fate and Tynnes Falk to be made perfectly clear. But what did this connection mean?

Wallander pushed his notes aside in a gesture of irritation. It was too early to even think of reaching a conclusion. They had to keep searching for more clues, without preconceived ideas.

He drank his coffee, absently rocking back and forth in his chair. Then he reached for the page he had ripped out of the newspaper and kept looking through the personal ads. *What would I say in an ad?* he wondered. *Who would be interested in a fifty-year-old policeman with diabetes and increasing doubts about his career choice? Someone who isn't particularly interested in walks in the forest, evenings in front of the fire, or sailing?*

He put down the page and started writing.

His first attempt was somewhat disingenuous: *Fifty-year-old police officer, divorced, grown daughter, tired of being lonely. Appearance and age don't matter, but you should enjoy opera and the comforts of home. Send your answer to "Police '97."*

Lies, he thought. *Appearance does matter. I'm not looking to end my loneliness. I want companionship. That's something completely different. I want someone to sleep with, someone who will be there when I want her. And who will leave me alone when I feel like it.* He tore up the paper and started writing again. This time the ad was more truthful: *Fifty-year-old police officer, diabetic, divorced, grown daughter, wishes to meet someone to spend time with. The woman I'm looking for is attractive, has a good figure, and is interested in sex. Send your answer to "Old Dog."*

Who would respond to something like that? he wondered. *Hardly anyone stable.*

He turned over the page so he could start afresh, but was almost immediately interrupted by a knock on the door. It was already noon, and Höglund was at the door. He realized too late that the personal section of the newspaper was still lying on the table. He snatched it up and threw it in the trash, but he sensed she had seen what he was doing. It irritated him.

I'm never going to write a personal ad, he thought angrily. *The chances are too great that someone like Höglund would answer.*

She looked tired.

"I've just finished questioning Eva Persson," she said and sat down heavily.

Wallander pushed all thoughts of personal ads aside.

"How was she?"

"She didn't change her story. She insists that Sonja both stabbed and hit Lundberg."

"I asked how she was."

Höglund thought about it before answering.

"She was different. She seemed more prepared for the questions."

"How did you get that impression?"

"She spoke faster. Many of her answers seemed as if she had prepared them in advance. It was only when we got to the questions she wasn't expecting that she started speaking in that slow, apathetic way. That's how she protects herself, giving herself time to think. I don't know how intelligent she is, but she's clear-headed. She keeps track of her lies. I didn't catch a single instance of self-contradiction in the two hours that we were at it. That's pretty impressive."

Wallander pulled over his notepad.

"We'll take the most important stuff now, your impressions. The rest I'll read about in your report."

"It's totally apparent to me that she's lying. Quite honestly I don't understand how a fourteen-year-old girl can be so hard-boiled."

"Because she's a girl?"

"I think it would be unusual even for a boy her age."

"You didn't managed to budge her?"

"No, not really. She sticks to her new story that she was innocent and claims she only said what she said because she was afraid of Sonja. I tried to get her to tell me why she was afraid, but she wouldn't. All she said was that Sonja could be very tough on you."

"She's probably right about that."

Höglund checked her notes.

"She denied taking any calls from Sonja, or anyone else, after Sonja's escape from the station."

"When did she find out Sonja was dead?"

"Erik Hökberg called her mother."

"Did Sonja's death come as a shock?"

"She claims it did, but I certainly couldn't tell. Maybe she was surprised. She had no explanation as to why Sonja would have gone out to the substation, nor as to who could have taken her there."

Wallander got up and walked over to the window.

"Did she really have no reaction? No sorrow, no evidence of pain?"

"In my opinion she was controlled and totally cold. Many of her answers were prepared in advance, some pure lies. But I did get the impression that she wasn't surprised about what had happened, even though she claims she was."

Wallander was struck by a thought that seemed important.

"Did she seem afraid of anything happening to her?"

"No, I thought about that. I don't think what happened to Sonja made her worried for her own life."

Wallander returned to the desk.

"Let's assume that's the case. What does that mean?"

"It means Eva Persson is at least partially telling the truth. Not about Lundberg's murder, since I'm convinced she was an active participant. But I don't think she had much of an idea what else Sonja was involved in."

"And what would that be?"

"I don't know."

"Why did they switch seats in the restaurant?"

"Because Sonja complained of a cold draft. She won't change her line on that."

"And the man who was sitting behind them?"

"She claims not to have seen him or anyone else. She also says she didn't notice Sonja having contact with anyone other than her."

"She didn't see anyone as they were leaving the restaurant?"

"No. That may even be true. I don't think she could ever qualify for the title of The World's Most Observant Person."

"Did you ask her if she had ever heard of Tynnes Falk?"

"She claimed never to have heard the name."

"Was she telling the truth?"

Höglund paused.

"There might have been a slight hesitation on her part, but I can't say for sure."

I should have talked to her myself, Wallander thought helplessly. *If Eva Persson had been holding something back, I would have seen it.*

Höglund seemed to be reading his thoughts.

"I don't have your certainty about these things. I wish I could give you a better answer."

"We'll get to the bottom of all this sooner or later. If the main entrance is closed, you try the back door."

"I've been trying to make sense of it," Höglund said. "But nothing hangs together."

"It will take time," Wallander said. "I just wonder if we need reinforcements. We just don't have the manpower we need, even if we shelve our other duties and concentrate on this case."

Höglund looked at him with surprise.

"I never thought I'd hear you say that. Normally you always insist on us carrying out the investigation alone."

"Maybe I've changed my mind. I just want to make sure we're able to carry out the footwork necessary in this investigation. I'll talk to Lisa about it. If she hasn't already suspended me, that is."

"You know that Eva Persson is still sticking to that story as well. That you hit her without any provocation."

"Of course she is. If she's lying about everything else she might as well lie about that, too."

Wallander got up. He told her briefly about the break-in at Tynnes Falk's apartment.

"Has the body been found yet?"

"Not as far as I know."

Höglund was still sitting.

"Do you understand any of this?"

"No," Wallander said, "It worries me. Don't forget that a large area of Scania was left without power."

They walked out into the hallway together. Hansson looked out of his room to say that the police in Växjö had located Eva Persson's father.

"According to their report, he lives in a run-down shack somewhere between Växjö and Vislanda. Now they're wondering what it is we want to know."

"Nothing for now," Wallander said. "We have other more important questions to cover."

They decided to meet at half past one, when Martinsson would have returned. Wallander went back to his room and called the mechanic. His car was ready. He left the police station and walked down Frihemsgatan toward Surbrunn square. A gusty wind came and went.

The mechanic's name was Holmlund, and he had worked on many of Wallander's cars over the years. He loved motorcycles, had a number of missing teeth, and spoke with such a strong Scanian accent that Wallander had trouble understanding him. His appearance hadn't changed a bit since Wallander had first met him. Wallander still couldn't tell if he was fifty or sixty.

"It's going to cost you," Holmlund said and smiled his toothless smile. "But you'll recoup some of the cost if you sell the car as soon as possible."

Wallander drove away. The noise from the engine was gone. The thought of getting a new car excited him. The only question was if he was going to stay with a Peugeot or try a new brand. He decided to ask Hansson, who knew as much about cars as he did about horseracing.

Wallander drove down to a fast-food kiosk down by Österleden and ate. He tried to read a newspaper but couldn't concentrate on it. His thoughts kept returning to the case. He had been trying to find a new focal point and had considered the blackout as a potential candidate. Then they weren't only looking at a murder but a highly calculated form of sabotage. But what if he tried to form a center around something else, like the man who had appeared at the restaurant? He had made Sonja Hökberg trade places. He had a forged identity. And now he might have turned up in a photograph in Tynnes Falk's apartment—a photograph that had since been stolen. Wallander cursed himself for not taking the photograph himself as he had been intending to. Then he could have asked István to identify the man.

Wallander put down his fork and called Nyberg's cell phone. He was about to hang up when Nyberg answered.

"Have you by any chance come across a group photo?" he asked. "Something with a large group of men?"

"I'll ask."

Wallander waited and picked at the essentially tasteless piece of fried fish in front of him.

Nyberg returned to the phone.

"We have a photo of three men holding up a number of salmon for the camera. A fishing trip in Norway from 1983."

"Is that all?"

"Yes. How would you know that he would have a photograph like that, anyway?"

He's not stupid, Wallander thought. Luckily he had prepared an answer ahead of time.

"I didn't know. I'm trying to find as many pictures as I can of Falk's aquaintances."

"We're almost done here," Nyberg said.

"Found anything interesting?"

"It seems to be a standard case of breaking-and-entering. Possibly a drug addict."

"No clues?"

"We have some fingerprints but they could all belong to Falk. I'm not sure how we're going to verify that, now that the body is gone."

"We'll find him sooner or later."

"I doubt it. When someone steals a body it's normally in order to bury it."

Nyberg was right. Wallander had an idea but Nyberg got there first.

"I asked Martinsson to look up Falk in the police files. We couldn't rule out the possibility that we already had something on him."

"And what did he find?"

"He was there, actually. But not his fingerprints."

"What had he done?"

"According to Martinsson, Falk had been sued and fined for property damage."

"In connection with what?"

"You'll have to get the details from Martinsson," Nyberg said irritably.

They finished the conversation. It was ten minutes past one. Wallander filled up the car and returned to the station. Martinsson walked in at the same time.

"None of the neighbors seemed to have heard or seen anything unusual," Martinsson said as they walked across the parking lot together. "I managed to talk to all of them. Many are retired and home most of the day. One of them was a physical therapist about your age."

Wallander had no comments to make. Instead, he brought up what Nyberg had said.

"What was all that business about Falk inflicting property damage?"

"I have the paperwork in my office. It was something about a mink farm."

Wallander looked at him with curiosity but didn't say anything. He read the report in Martinsson's office. Tynnes Falk had been arrested by the police in 1991, slightly north of Sölvesborg. One night, a mink farmer had discovered that someone was opening the cages. He had called the police and two patrol cars had been dispatched. Tynnes Falk had not been working alone, but he was the only one who was caught. He had immediately confessed and given as his motivation the fact that he was vehemently opposed to animals being slaughtered for fur. He had, however, denied acting on behalf of any organization and had never given the names of his accomplices.

Wallander put down the report.

"I thought only young people did things like this," he said. "Falk was over forty in 1991."

"I suppose we could be more sympathetic to their cause," Martinsson said. "My daughter is a Greenpeace supporter."

"There's a difference between wanting to protect the environment and taking away a mink farmer's livelihood."

"These organizations teach you to have an enormous respect for animal life."

Wallander didn't want to be dragged into a debate he felt he would eventually lose. But he was perplexed by Tynnes Falk's involvement in animal-rights activism.

* * *

Wallander returned to his office and called Marianne Falk. An answering machine picked up, but as he started to leave his message her voice came on the line. They agreed to meet in the apartment on Apelbergsgatan around three o'clock. Wallander arrived in plenty of time. Nyberg and his forensic team had already left. A patrol car was parked outside. As Wallander was walking up the stairs to the apartment, the door to the apartment below, the one he would rather have forgotten about, suddenly opened. The door was opened by a woman who looked familiar, but he wasn't sure.

"I saw you when I looked out the window," she said, smiling. "I just wanted to say hello. If you even remember me, that is."

"Of course I do," Wallander said.

"You know, you never got in touch with me like you promised."

Wallander couldn't remember making any promises but he knew it was possible. When he was drunk and strongly attracted to a woman, he was capable of promising almost anything.

"Things came up," he said. "You know how it is."

"I do?"

Wallander mumbled something.

"Do you want to come in for a cup of coffee?"

"As you may have heard, there's been a break-in upstairs. I don't have time right now."

She pointed to her door.

"I had a security door put in several years ago. Almost all of us did. Everyone except Falk."

"Did you know him?"

"He kept to himself. We said hello if we met on the stairs. But that was it."

Wallander suspected she wasn't telling the truth but decided not to ask anything else. The only thing he wanted was to get away.

"I'll have to take a rain check on that coffee," he said.

"We'll see," she said.

The door closed. Wallander was sweating. He rushed up the last flight of stairs. At least she had pointed out a significant fact. Most people in the building had put in security doors, but not Tynnes Falk, the man whom his wife said was anxious and sure he was surrounded by enemies.

The door had not been repaired yet. Wallander walked into the apartment and saw that Nyberg and his team had left the chaos intact.

He walked into the kitchen and sat down by the table. It was very quiet in the apartment. He looked down at his watch. It was ten to three. He thought he could hear footsteps on the stairs. *Tynnes Falk was probably too cheap to have it put in,* he thought. *Security doors cost somewhere between ten and fifteen thousand crowns. Or maybe Marianne Falk is wrong. There were no enemies.* But Wallander was doubtful. He thought about the mysterious notations in the diary. There was also the facts that Tynnes Falk's body had been stolen from the morgue and that someone had broken into his apartment and stolen at least the diary and a photograph.

That could only mean one thing. Someone didn't want the picture or the diary to be studied too closely.

Wallander cursed himself once again for not removing the picture when he had had the chance.

He heard footsteps on the stairs outside the apartment. That had to be Marianne Falk. The door to the apartment softly opened and Wallander got up to greet her. He left the kitchen and stepped into the hall.

He sensed the danger instinctively and pulled back.

But it was too late.

A violent explosion ricocheted through the apartment.

Chapter Fifteen

Wallander threw himself to one side.

It was only later that he realized his quick reflexes had saved his life, after Nyberg and the forensic team had extracted the bullet in the wall next to the front door. In the subsequent reconstruction of events, and above all from examining the entry hole in Wallander's jacket, they were able to determine what had happened. Wallander had walked into the hall to greet Marianne Falk. He had turned toward the front door only to sense that something behind it constituted a threat—that the person behind the door was not Marianne Falk. Wallander had jerked backward and tripped on the rug in the hallway. That had been enough to let the bullet aimed at his chest pass between his body and his left arm. It had torn through his jacket, leaving a small but distinct hole.

That evening he got out the measuring tape and measured the distance from his shirt sleeve to where he thought his heart was. Seven centimeters. The conclusion he came to, as he was pouring himself a glass of whiskey, was that the rug had saved his life. It reminded him of the time long ago when he had been stabbed. He had been a young officer in Malmö. The blade had penetrated his chest within eight centimeters of his heart. At the time he had created a kind of mantra for himself. *There is a time for living, a time for dying.* Now he was struck by the worrying fact that his margin of survival during the past thirty years had decreased by exactly one centimeter.

He still didn't know exactly what had happened or who had fired the shot. Wallander had not been able to catch a glimpse of more than a shadow behind that door—a rapidly moving figure that seemed to dissipate the moment the shot ricocheted through the apartment and he found himself on the floor of the closet among Tynnes Falk's coats.

He thought he had been hit. He thought the cry that he heard as the deafening roar of the shot was still echoing in his ears must be his own. But it had come from Marianne Falk, who had been knocked down on the stairs by the fleeing shadow. She had not managed to get a good look at him either. She had heard the shot but thought that it came from below. Therefore she stopped and turned around. Then when she heard someone approach from behind, she turned back, but as she was turning she was hit in the face and tumbled over backwards.

Perhaps most remarkable was the fact that neither of the two officers in the patrol car stationed outside the building saw anything. The assailant must have left the building by the front entrance, since the door to the cellar was locked. But the officers claimed not to have seen anyone leave the building. They had seen Marianne Falk go in, then they had heard the shot without immediately knowing what it was. But they had not seen anyone leave.

Martinsson grudgingly accepted this fact, after having the whole building searched. He forced all the nervous senior citizens and the somewhat more controlled physical therapist to have their apartments scrutinized by policemen, who peeked into every closet and under every bed. There was no trace of the assailant anywhere. If it hadn't been for the bullet buried in the wall, Wallander would have started to think it had all been his imagination.

But he knew it was real, and he knew something else he didn't yet want to admit to himself. He knew that the rug had been even more of a blessing than he'd first thought. Not only because it let him escape the bullet, but because his fall had convinced the assailant that he had hit his mark. The bullet that Nyberg extracted from the wall had been the kind that formed a crater-like wound in its victim. When Nyberg showed it to Wallander, the latter instantly understood why the marksman had fired only one shot. He had been convinced that one bullet would have been fatal.

A regional alert had gone out at once, but everyone knew it wouldn't lead to anything, because no one knew who they were looking for. After all, neither Marianne Falk nor Wallander had been able to give a description of the assailant. Wallander and Martinsson sat down in the kitchen while Nyberg's team worked on the bullet. Wallander had handed over his jacket to them as well. His ears still hurt from the loud explosion. Lisa Holgersson arrived with Höglund, and Wallander had to explain all over again what had happened.

"The question is why he fired," Martinsson said. "There's already been a break-in here. Now an armed assailant returns."

"We can perhaps speculate that it was the same person," Wallander said. "But why did he return? I can't see any other explanation than that he's looking for something—something he didn't manage to get the first time he was here."

"Aren't we forgetting something else?" Höglund asked. "Who was he trying to kill?"

Wallander had asked himself the same question from the very beginning. Did this have anything to do with the night he'd come here to search the apartment? Had it been a mistake to look out of the window? Had someone been out there watching him? He knew he should tell them about it, but something kept him from doing so.

"Why would anyone want to shoot me?" Wallander asked. "I think it was just plain bad luck that I was here when he returned. What we should ask ourselves is what he came back for, which in turn means that Marianne Falk should be brought back here as soon as possible."

Marianne Falk had gone home to change her clothes.

Martinsson left the apartment with Holgersson. The forensic team was finishing up. Höglund stayed in the kitchen with Wallander. Marianne Falk called to say she was on her way.

"How does it feel?" Höglund asked.

"Not too good. You know what it's like."

A couple of years ago Höglund had been shot down on a field outside of Ystad. That had partly been Wallander's fault, since he had commanded her to advance without realizing that the suspect had picked up a gun Hansson had dropped a little earlier. Höglund had been seriously injured and it had taken her a long time to recover. When she returned to her post, she was a changed person. She had told Wallander about the fear that now surfaced in her dreams.

"At least I wasn't hit," Wallander said. "I was stabbed once. But so far I've never stopped a bullet."

"You should talk to someone. There are support groups."

Wallander shook his head impatiently.

"No need," he said. "And I don't want to keep talking about it now."

"I don't understand why you always have to be so bullheaded about these things. You're a good police officer, but you're only human like the rest of us. You can think what you like. But you're wrong."

Wallander was surprised by her eruption. She was right. When he stepped into his role as a policeman, he tended to forget about the person inside.

"I think at the very least you should go home."

"What good would that do?"

At the same moment, Marianne Falk returned to the apartment.

Wallander saw an opportunity to get rid of Höglund and her annoying questions.

"I'd prefer to talk to her alone," he said. "Thanks for your help."

"What help?"

Höglund left. Wallander felt dizzy when he stood up.

"What happened back there?" Marianne Falk asked.

Wallander saw a big bruise starting on the left side of her jaw.

"I arrived shortly before three o'clock. I heard someone at the door. I thought it was you, but that wasn't the case."

"Who was it?"

"I don't know. Apparently you don't, either."

"I never had a chance to get a look at him."

"But you're sure it was a man?"

She was surprised by the question and took a moment to answer.

"Yes," she said finally. "It was a man."

Wallander knew she was right, without being able to prove it.

"Let's start in the living room," he said. "I want you to walk around and make a note of everything. Tell me if you think something's gone. Then go on to the next room. Take your time and feel free to open drawers and look behind curtains."

"Tynnes would never have allowed that. He was so secretive."

"We'll talk later," Wallander interrupted her. "Start with the living room."

He could see she was trying her utmost to do as he said. He stood in the doorway and looked at her as she walked around the room. The longer he looked at her, the more beautiful she seemed to him. He wondered what kind of a personal ad he would have to write in order to get her to answer. She continued into the bedroom. He watched for signs of hesitation. When they returned to the kitchen, thirty minutes had gone by.

"Did anything seem to be gone?"

"No, nothing that I could see."

"How well did you know the apartment?"

"We never lived here together. He moved here after the divorce. He called sometimes and we had dinner together. But the kids saw him a lot more than I did."

Wallander tried to remember the facts that Martinsson had laid out for him when they first discussed Falk's case.

"Does your daughter live in Paris?"

"Ina is only seventeen years old. She's working as a nanny at the Danish Embassy. She wants to learn French."

"What about your son?"

"Jan? He's a student in Stockholm. He's nineteen."

Wallander turned the conversation back to the apartment.

"Do you think you would have noticed something being missing?"

"Only if it had been something I had seen before."

Wallander nodded, then excused himself. He went into the living room and removed one of the three china roosters sitting on a window ledge. When he came back into the kitchen he asked her to go through the living room one more time.

She discovered that the rooster was missing almost at once. Wallander realized they weren't going to get any further. She had a good memory, even if she didn't know what Falk kept in his closets.

They sat down in the kitchen. It was almost five o'clock and the fall darkness was blanketing the city.

"Tell me more about his work," Wallander said. "I know he was self-employed and worked with computer systems."

"He was a consultant."

"So what does that mean?"

She looked at him with surprise.

"Our whole country is run by consultants these days. Soon, even party leaders will be replaced by consultants. Consultants are highly paid executives who fly around to various companies and come up with solutions for their problems. If things go badly, they take the blame. But they're highly paid for their suffering."

"And your husband was a consultant who specialized in computer systems?"

"I would appreciate it if you didn't refer to Tynnes as my husband."

Her comment made Wallander impatient.

"Can you give me some more details of what he did?"

"He was very good at designing internal computer systems for companies."

"What does that mean?"

She smiled for the first time.

"I don't think I can explain it to you if you don't even have the most basic understanding of how computers work."

She was right.

"Who were his clients?"

"As far as I know, he did a lot of work for banks."

"Any particular bank?"

"I don't know."

"Who would know?"

"He had an accountant."

Wallander felt around in his pockets for a piece of paper to write the name on. All he found was the receipt for the work on the car.

"His name is Rolf Stenius and he has an office in Malmö. I don't know his address or phone number."

Wallander put his pen down. He had a feeling that he had over-looked something and he tried to catch a hold of the thought. Marianne Falk pulled out a packet of cigarettes.

"Do you mind if I smoke?"

"Not at all."

She got a saucer from a cupboard and lit up.

"Tynnes would be turning in his grave right now if he knew about this. He hated cigarettes. The whole time we were married he always chased me out onto the street to smoke. I guess this is my chance for revenge."

Wallander took the opportunity to change the topic of conversation.

"When we talked the first time, you said he had enemies, and that he was anxious."

"Yes, he gave that impression."

"It's possible to see if a person is anxious or not. But you can't just observe that a person has enemies. He must have said something to you."

She paused before giving her answer. She smoked and looked out the window. It was dark outside.

"It started a couple of years ago," she said. "I noticed that he was anxious, but also excited. As if he were in a kind of manic state. He started making strange comments. For example, if I were here having coffee with him he could say something like, 'If people knew what I was doing they would kill me.' Or, 'You can never know how close your pursuers are.'"

"He actually said those things?"

"Yes."

"But he never gave you an explanation?"

"No."

"Did you ask him what he meant?"

"He would get upset and tell me to be quiet."

Wallander thought carefully before continuing.

"Let's talk a little about your two children. Do you think either one of them has experienced these things that you describe? The anxiety or the talk about enemies?"

"I doubt it. They didn't have that much contact with him. They lived with me, and Tynnes wasn't always that eager to have them over. I don't say these things in order to be mean. I think both Jan and Ina would agree with me."

"He must have had some friends."

"They were very few. I realized after our wedding that I had married a hermit."

"Who knew him besides you?"

"I know he used to have regular contact with a woman who was also a computer consultant. Her name is Siv Eriksson. I don't have her number, but she has an office in Skansgränd, next to Sjömansgatan. They worked on some assignments together."

Wallander made a note of the name. Marianne Falk put out her cigarette.

"One last question," Wallander said. "At least for now. A couple of years ago Tynnes was caught by the police as he was letting minks out of their cages on a mink farm. He was later charged and fined for this."

She looked at him with genuine surprise.

"I've never heard a word about that."

"Does it make sense to you?"

"That he was letting minks out of their cages? Why on earth would he do that?"

"So you don't know if he was in contact with organizations who specialize in this kind of thing?"

"What kind of organizations would that be?"

"Militant environmental groups. Animal-rights activists."

"I'm having trouble taking this all in."

Wallander nodded. He knew she was telling the truth. She got up.

"I'll need to speak to you again," Wallander said.

He walked her out. She stopped by the hole in the wall.

"Do you carry a weapon in self-defense?"

"No."

She shook her head, stretched out her hand and said good-bye.

"One more thing," Wallander said. "Did Tynnes show any interest in outer space?"

"What do you mean by that?"

"Spaceships, astronomy, that kind of thing."

"You've already asked me that, and I'll give you the same answer. We did look at the night sky together a couple of times when we were young, but Tynnes was not the kind of person who usually lifted his head up just to look at the stars. If he ever did, it was probably just to make sure they were still there. He was pragmatic rather than romantic by nature."

She turned and went down the stairs. Wallander returned to the apartment and sat down on a chair in the kitchen. That was the same place where he had first had the feeling he was overlooking something. It was Rydberg who had taught him to listen to his inner alarm system. Even in the highly technical and rational world of police work, intuition was of crucial importance.

He sat without moving for a few minutes. Then he finally caught hold of it. Marianne Falk had not been able to find anything that was missing. Could that mean that the man who first broke into the apartment and later fired the shot at Wallander was in fact coming to return something? Wallander shook his head at the idea. He was about to get up when he jumped. Someone was knocking on the door. Wallander's heart was racing. It was only when the knocking stopped that he realized it could hardly be someone announcing his intention to kill him. He went out into the hall and opened the door. There was an elderly man holding a cane on the landing.

"I'm looking for Mr. Falk," he said in a stern voice. "I have a complaint."

"May I ask who you are?" Wallander asked.

"My name is Carl-Anders Setterkvist and I own this building. There have been a number of complaints from the other residents lately about excessive noise and loud visits by military men. I would prefer to speak to Mr. Falk about it personally, if possible."

"Mr. Falk is dead," Wallander said brutally.

Setterkvist looked at him with surprise.

"Dead? Whatever do you mean?"

"I'm a police officer," Wallander said, "Homicide division. There's been a burglary here. But Tynnes Falk is dead. He died last Monday. There are no military personnel running up and down these stairs, they're police."

Setterkvist seemed to be trying to judge if Wallander was telling the truth or not.

"I would like to see your identification badge, please," he said finally.

"Our badges disappeared a long time ago," Wallander answered, "but you can see my identification card."

He took it out of his pocket, and Setterkvist studied it carefully.

Wallander told him briefly what had happened.

"How unfortunate," Setterkvist said. "What will happen to the apartments?"

Wallander frowned.

"The apartments?"

"I simply mean that it's difficult when new people move in. One wants to know what kind of people they are before renting out the place, especially in this kind of building with a number of elderly tenants."

"Do you live here yourself?"

Setterkvist was clearly insulted.

"I live in a house outside of town."

"You said 'apartments.'"

"What else would I have said?"

"Do you mean that Falk rented more than one apartment?"

Setterkvist made a gesture indicating that he wanted to be let in to the apartment. Wallander stepped aside.

"I'd just like to remind you that it's so messy in here because there's been a burglary."

"I've been the victim of a burglary myself," Setterkvist answered calmly. "I know how it is."

Wallander ushered him into the kitchen.

"Mr. Falk was an excellent tenant," Setterkvist said. "He was never late with the rent. At my age one is never surprised by anything, but I must admit I was a little shaken by the complaints that have come pouring in these past few days. That is why I had to come in person."

"He rents more than one apartment from you?" Wallander asked again.

"I have a wonderful old building by Runnerström Square," Setterkvist said. "Falk had a small apartment in the attic there. He said he needed it for his work."

That would explain the absence of computers, Wallander thought. *There certainly isn't anything in this apartment to suggest he worked here.*

"I need to see that office," Wallander said.

Setterkvist thought for a moment and then pulled out the largest set of keys Wallander had ever seen. But Setterkvist knew exactly which keys he needed. He removed them from the key chain.

"I'll write out a receipt," Wallander said.

Setterkvist shook his head.

"One has to be able to trust people," he said. "Or rather, one has to be able to rely on one's own judgment."

Setterkvist marched off, while Wallander called the station and arranged for someone to come out and help him seal the apartment. Then he walked straight down to Runnerström Square. It was close to seven o'clock. The wind was still gusty. Wallander was cold. Martinsson had lent him a spare coat, but it was thin. He thought about the bullet. It still seemed unreal. He wondered what his reaction would be in a couple of days, when the realization of how close to death he had been finally sunk in.

The building at Runnerström Square was a three-story, turn-of-the-century building. Wallander walked to the other side of the street and stared up at the attic windows. No lights were on. Before he walked to the front door, he looked around. A man cycled past, and then Wallander was alone. He walked across the street and let himself in. He heard music coming from one apartment. He turned on the light in the stairwell. When he had climbed the stairs all the way to the attic floor he found only one apartment door on the landing. It was a security door without a name or mail slot. Wallander listened, but he heard nothing. Then he unlocked the door. He paused in the doorway and listened again. For a split second he thought he heard someone breathing in the darkness and he almost jumped out before he realized it was his imagination. He turned on the light and let the door close behind him.

It was a large room, almost completely empty. The only furniture was a desk and a chair. There was a large computer on the desk. Wallander approached it and saw that there was something resembling a blueprint on the desk next to the computer. He turned on the desk lamp.

It took him a moment to understand what it was.

Then he realized he was looking at a blueprint of the power sub-station where Sonja Hökberg had been killed.

Chapter Sixteen

Wallander held his breath.

At first he thought he was mistaken. It had to be a blueprint of something else. Then all doubt disappeared. He knew he was right. He carefully lay the paper back on the desk, next to the computer. He could see his own face reflected in its large dark screen. There was a phone on the desk. He thought he should call someone, either Martinsson or Höglund. And Nyberg. But he didn't lift the receiver. Instead he started walking around the room slowly. *This is where Tynnes Falk worked,* he thought. *Behind a reinforced steel door that would have been very hard for someone to open without a key. This is where he worked as a computer consultant. One evening his body is found next to a cash machine. His body disappears from the morgue, and now I find a blueprint for the power substation next to his computer.*

For one breathtaking moment he thought he sensed the connection. But the myriad of facts was too confusing. Wallander kept walking around. *What is here?* he thought, *and what is missing? There is a computer, a chair, a desk, and a lamp. There are a telephone and a blueprint, but no shelves, no binders, no books. There isn't even a pen.*

After making a round he returned to the desk and turned the lampshade so that the beam of light was directed at the wall. He turned it so the light illuminated each wall in turn. The light was strong, but he didn't see any hiding places. He sat down in the chair. The silence around him was overwhelming. If Martinsson had been here, Wallander would have asked him to turn on the computer. Martinsson would have loved that job. But Wallander didn't dare touch it himself. Again he thought that he should call him, and again he hesitated. *I have to understand how this hangs together,* he thought. *That's the most important thing right now. New connections have been revealed in a much shorter span of time than I would have thought. The problem is that I can't see the pattern yet.*

It was now almost eight. He finally decided to call Nyberg.

It couldn't help that it was already evening and Nyberg had been working for the past few days with no sleep. Someone else would probably have decided that the investigation of the apartment could wait until the following day, but Wallander was plagued by a sense of urgency that was only growing stronger. He called Nyberg on his cell phone. Nyberg listened without saying anything. He made a note of the address, and once they ended the conversation, Wallander made his way to street level to wait for him.

Nyberg arrived alone. Wallander helped him carry his bags up.

"What am I looking for here?" Nyberg asked once they were in the apartment.

"Prints. Secret compartments."

"Then I won't need anyone else for now. Can we wait on the photography and videotape?"

"Do it in the morning."

Nyberg nodded and took off his shoes. He took out a pair of custom-made plastic shoes from one of his bags. Nyberg had always been frustrated with the protective shoe covers that were commercially available. A couple of years ago he had finally designed his own and found someone to make them. Wallander assumed he had paid for them out of his own pocket.

"Are you good at computers?" he asked.

"I know as little as the next man about how they actually work," Nyberg said. "But I can probably get it started for you."

Wallander shook his head.

"Martinsson would never forgive me if I let anyone else deal with it."

Then he showed Nyberg the paper lying on the table. Nyberg saw at once what it was. He looked questioningly at Wallander.

"What does this mean? Did Falk kill the girl?"

"He was already dead when she was murdered," Wallander answered.

Nyberg nodded.

He got a magnifying glass out of his bags and sat down at the table. He studied the blueprint while Wallander waited silently.

"This is not a copy," Nyberg said finally. "It's an original."

"Are you sure?"

"Not completely, but almost."

"That would mean someone should be missing it."

"I don't know if this is right or not," Nyberg said, "but I talked to that guy Andersson about the security procedures at the power company. It should have been nearly impossible for anyone to make a copy of this blueprint, much less steal it."

Nyberg had brought up an important point. If the blueprint had been stolen from files at the power company, that could yield more clues.

Nyberg set up his spotlights. Wallander decided to leave him alone. "I'm going into the station. Call me if you need me."

Nyberg didn't answer. He was already lost in his work.

Once Wallander was down on the street, he realized his mind was making a slightly different decision. He wasn't going to go straight down to the station. Marianne Falk had talked about a woman named Siv Eriksson. She should be able to tell him more about Falk's work as a consultant. She lived nearby, or at least her office was there. Wallander left his car where it was. He took Långgatan toward the center of town, then turned right on Skansgränd. The streets were deserted. He turned around twice, but there was no one behind him. The wind was still strong and he was cold. While he was walking he started thinking about the bullet. He wondered when what had happened was going to hit him for real, and he wondered how he would react.

When he arrived at the building that Marianne Falk had described to him, he saw the sign by the door at once. SERKON. SIV ERIKSSON, CONSULTANT.

The office should be on the second floor. He pushed the buzzer and crossed his fingers. If it were only her office, he would have to find her home address somehow.

But someone picked up almost at once. Wallander announced who he was and what he wanted. The woman who had answered didn't say anything, but the door unlocked. Wallander went in.

She was waiting for him in the doorway when he came up the stairs. Although the light in the hallway was strong for his eyes, he recognized her at once.

He had met her the evening before when he had given his lecture. He had been introduced to her, but had of course forgotten her name. It flashed through his mind that it was odd that she hadn't explained who she was. She must have known that Falk was dead.

It threw him for a moment. Was it possible that she still did not know? Was he going to be announcing a death?

"I'm sorry to bother you," he said.

She let him into the apartment. There was the smell of an open fire coming from somewhere. Now he saw her clearly. She was in her forties, with medium-length dark hair and sharp features. He had been much too nervous when he met her to notice her appearance, but the woman he now saw made him self-conscious, the way he always felt when he saw someone he found attractive.

"I should explain why I've come," he said.

"I already know that Tynnes is dead. Marianne phoned me."

Wallander noticed that she seemed sad. He felt relieved. He had never been able to get used to the task of notifying someone of a death.

"As colleagues you must have been close," he said.

"Yes and no," she said. "We were close, very close. But only when it came to work."

Wallander wondered briefly if their collegiality had actually extended to more than that, and it made him feel an inexplicable pang of jealousy.

"I assume you must have an important matter to discuss with me, since you're here after hours," she said, handing Wallander a hanger.

He followed her into a tastefully arranged living room. There was a fire burning in the open fireplace. Wallander got the feeling that both the furniture and paintings were expensive.

"Can I get you anything?"

Whiskey, Wallander thought. *I really need it.*

"That won't be necessary," he said.

He sat down in a dark-blue sofa while she sat in a chair across from him. She had shapely legs. He became aware of the fact that she had noticed his gaze.

"I came straight from Falk's office," Wallander said. "He didn't seem to have anything except a computer."

"Tynnes was an ascetic. He wanted everything around him as pared back and minimalist as possible. It helped him work."

"That's my real reason for coming down here: to ask you what his work consisted of. What your work consisted of, I should say."

"We worked together on some things, but not all the time."

"Then let's start by talking about what he did when he worked alone."

Wallander regretted not having called Martinsson. There was a good chance he was going to get answers that he wouldn't be able to understand.

It still wasn't too late to call him, but for the third time this evening Wallander decided to let it go.

"I should warn you, I don't know much about computers," Wallander said. "You'll have to be very clear, or I won't be able to follow you."

She looked at him and smiled.

"That surprises me," she said. "From your lecture last night I gathered that computers are a police officer's best friend."

"That doesn't apply to me personally. Some of us still have to engage in the old-fashioned business of talking to people, not just running names through various databases. Or sending e-mail messages back and forth."

She got up and walked over to the hearth, then bent down to adjust the logs. Wallander watched her, but quickly lowered his gaze when she turned around.

"What exactly do you want me to tell you? And why?"

Wallander decided to start with the second question.

"We're no longer convinced that Falk died of natural causes, even though the autopsy report pointed fairly conclusively to a heart attack."

"A heart attack?"

Her surprise seemed genuine. Wallander immediately thought of the doctor who had come to see him.

"There was nothing wrong with his heart. Tynnes was in excellent shape."

"That's what I've heard. That's one of the reasons we wanted to reevaluate the case. The question then becomes what else this could be. An attack, perhaps, or simply an accident."

She shook her head doubtfully.

"Not an attack. Tynnes would never have let anyone get close enough for that."

"What do you mean?"

"He was always on his guard. He often talked about how he felt vulnerable in public. So he was prepared, and I know he was quick on his feet. He was quite advanced in some martial art that I forget the name of."

"He could split bricks with his bare hands?"

"Sort of."

"So you believe it was an accident?"

"Yes, it had to be."

Wallander nodded silently before continuing.

"There were additional reasons for my visit, but I think we'll put those aside for now."

She poured herself a glass of wine and carefully put it down on the armrest.

"I suppose you realize that makes me curious."

"Unfortunately I can't share any more information with you."

That's a lie, Wallander thought. *I could tell her a lot more if I wanted. For some reason I'm enjoying having some power over her, however small.*

She interrupted his thoughts.

"What else was it you asked me?"

"About his work."

"Right. He was a highly accomplished developer of computer systems."

Wallander waited for more.

"He designed computer programs for various businesses. Sometimes he just customized and improved existing systems. When I say he was highly accomplished, I mean it. He had several offers from important companies both in Asia and North America. But he always declined, even though it would have meant a great deal of money."

"Why did he do that?"

A look of anxiety flitted across her face.

"I actually don't know."

"Did you ever talk about it?"

"He always told me about the offers he received, and the amounts of money they were offering. If it had been me, I would have accepted them on the spot. But not him."

"And he never told you why?"

"He just didn't want to. He didn't think he needed to."

"He must have had plenty of money."

"I don't think that was it. Sometimes he needed to borrow from me."

Wallander frowned. He sensed they were nearing an important point.

"He didn't say anything else?"

"No, nothing. He just didn't need the extra work, he said. If I tried to keep asking, he inevitably cut me off. He could be quite aggressive at times. He set the limits, not me."

What was the real motivation for saying no? Wallander wondered. *It doesn't make sense.*

"What determined the kind of project you would work on together rather than individually?"

Her answer surprised him.

"The degree of tedium involved."

"I don't understand."

"Some parts of our kind of work will always be somewhat tedious. Tynnes could be impatient, and he often parceled out the more mundane tasks to me so that he could turn his full attention to the most challenging and interesting parts of the project. Especially if it involved something on the cutting edge, something that hadn't been addressed before."

"And you accepted this arrangement?"

"You have to live with your own limitations. It was never as boring for me as for him. I didn't have his extraordinary talents."

"How did you first meet?"

"Until the age of thirty I was a housewife. Then I divorced and got an education. Tynnes gave a lecture in one of my classes. I was fascinated by him, and I asked if he had any work for me. At first he said no, but a year later he called me. Our first project was designing a security system for a bank."

"And what did that involve?"

"Today money is transferred between accounts at an astonishing speed, between private persons and companies, between the banks of various countries, and so on. There are always people out there who want to disrupt these transfers for their own ends. The only way to thwart them is to stay a step ahead. It's a constant battle."

"That sounds very difficult."

"It is."

"It also sounds like a task that would be too big for a lone computer consultant in Ystad, however gifted."

"One of the advantages of the new technology is that you can be in the middle of things no matter where you're located. Tynnes was in constant contact with companies, computer manufacturers, and other programmers all around the world."

"From his office here in Ystad?"

"Yes."

Wallander was unsure of how to proceed. He still didn't feel that he had a good grasp of Falk's work, but he also saw the futility in continuing this conversation without Martinsson present. They should also get in touch with the IT-division at the national police headquarters.

Wallander decided to change the subject.

"Did he have any enemies?"

He watched her face carefully while he asked the question. But he couldn't see anything other than surprise.

"Not as far as I know."

"Did you notice a change in him recently?"

She thought for a while before answering.

"He was the same as always."

"And how was that?"

"Moody. He always worked a great deal."

"Where did you two meet to discuss your work?"

"Here. Never in his office."

"Why not?"

"I think Tynnes was somewhat of a germophobe, to be honest. I think he didn't want anyone leaving dirt on his floor. He was manic about maintaining cleanliness."

"Falk seems to have been a very complicated man."

"Not when you got to know him. He wasn't so different from other men."

Wallander looked at her with interest.

"And what are men like, exactly?"

She smiled.

"Is that your personal question, or are we still discussing Tynnes?"

"I'm not here to ask personal questions."

She sees right through me, Wallander thought.

"Men are often childish and vain, although they deny it."

"That's a rather broad characterization."

"I mean what I say."

"So Falk was like that?"

"Yes. But not always. He could be very generous, for example. He always paid me more than he had to. But you could never predict his moods."

"He had once been married and had children."

"We never talked about his family. It was only after about a year that I even heard he had one."

"Did he have any outside interests, apart from his work?"

"None that I knew about."

"Any friends?"

"He had some friends that he corresponded with via e-mail. I never saw him get so much as a postcard through the regular mail."

"How can you know that if you were never at his office?"

She made a little gesture of applause.

"Good question. His mail came to my address, as it happens. But nothing was ever sent to him."

"Nothing?"

"Yes, literally nothing. The whole time I've known him nothing ever came for him. No letter, no bill. Nothing."

Wallander frowned.

"This is a bit confusing. He used your address, but no mail ever actually came for him?"

"From time to time he got junk mail, but that was all."

"He must have had another postal address as well, then."

"Probably, but I don't know what it was in that case."

Wallander thought about Falk's two apartments. There had been nothing in the office at Runnerström Square, but he couldn't remember seeing any mail at Apelbergsgatan either.

"We'll have to look into this," he said. "Falk makes a secretive impression."

"I guess some people don't like getting mail, while others love the sound of another letter coming through the mail slot."

Wallander had no more questions. Falk was a mystery. *I'm proceeding too quickly,* he thought. *First we have to see what's in his computer. If he had a life that's where we'll find it.*

She poured herself more wine and asked him if he had changed his mind. Wallander shook his head.

"You said you were close. Did you ever visit him at home?"

"No."

That answer came a little too quickly, Wallander thought. Perhaps there had been something between Falk and his female assistant after all.

Wallander saw that it was already nine o'clock. The fire had burned down to glowing coals.

"I take it there's been no mail for him in the past few days?"

"No, nothing."

"And how would you sum up everything that's happened?"

"I don't know. I thought Tynnes would live to a ripe old age. It must have been an accident."

"You don't think he could have had some illness you didn't know about?"

"Yes, of course that's possible. But I don't think so."

Wallander wondered if he should tell her about the disappearance of Falk's body. But he decided to wait. He switched tracks.

"There was a blueprint of a power substation on his desk. Do you know anything about that?"

"I hardly even know what one is."

"It's a structure just outside Ystad belonging to Sydkraft Power."

She thought hard.

"He did some work for Sydkraft several years ago," she said. "But I wasn't involved."

Wallander had a thought.

"I'd like you to make a list of all the jobs he had recently," he said. "Both those he worked on alone and those you worked on together."

"How far back should I go?"

"Start with this year."

"Tynnes may have had projects I didn't know about."

"I'll talk to his accountant," Wallander said. "He must have given him the information. But I'd still like to see your list."

"Right away?"

"Tomorrow is fine."

She got up and stirred the embers in the fire. Wallander tried to compose a personal ad in his head that would tempt Siv Eriksson to reply. She returned to her chair.

"Are you hungry?"

"No. I'm on my way out."

"It doesn't seem as if my answers have helped you."

"I know more about Tynnes Falk than I did before I came. Police work requires patience."

He knew he should get up and leave. He had no more questions. He finally got to his feet.

"I'll get in touch tomorrow," he said. "Do you think you could fax the list of clients to the police station?"

"How about an e-mail attachment?"

"That would be fine as well, though I have no idea how to read those or even what address I have."

"I can find that out."

She followed him out. Wallander put on his coat.

"Did Falk ever talk to you about mink farming?" he asked.

"Why on earth would he ever have done that?" she asked.

"I was just wondering."

She opened the front door. Wallander felt a strong urge not to leave.

"You gave a great lecture," she said. "But you were very nervous."

"I think that's par for the course when you're standing on your own in front of so many women."

They said good-bye. Wallander walked down the stairs. Just before he opened the door to the street, his cell phone rang. It was Nyberg.

"How fast can you get here?"

"Pretty fast," Wallander said. "Why do you ask?"

"I think you'd better come over."

Nyberg hung up. Wallander's heart beat faster. Nyberg would only have called if it was important.

Something had happened.

Chapter Seventeen

I t took Wallander less than five minutes to return to the building at Runnerström Square. When he had walked up all the stairs he saw Nyberg smoking on the landing outside the apartment. That was when Wallander realized how extremely tired Nyberg was. He never smoked unless he was about to collapse from exhaustion. The last time that had happened was a couple of years ago during the difficult homicide investigation that led to the capture of Stefan Fredman.

Nyberg put out the cigarette with his foot and nodded to Wallander to follow him in.

"I started looking at the walls," Nyberg said. "There was a discrepancy. It happens sometimes in old buildings; renovations end up changing the original floor plan. But I started measuring the room anyway, and found this."

Nyberg led Wallander to the far end of the room. A part of the wall jutted into the room at a sharp angle.

"I started knocking on the walls," Nyberg continued. "It sounded hollow. Then I saw this."

Nyberg pointed to the floor. Wallander crouched down. If you looked closely you could see that the baseboard had been sawed loose from the floor. There was also a thin crack in the wall that had been carefully taped over and painted.

"Have you looked to see what's behind this wall?"

"I wanted to wait for you."

Wallander nodded. Nyberg carefully pulled away the tape, revealing a door about one and a half meters high. Then he stepped aside. Wallander pushed open the door, which gave way without a sound. Nyberg shone his flashlight into the opening.

The concealed room was bigger than Wallander had imagined. He wondered if Setterkvist knew about this. He took Nyberg's flashlight and looked around. He soon found the light switch.

The room was maybe eight square meters, with no windows but a small air vent. It was completely empty except for a table that looked like an altar. There were two candles on it and a photograph on the wall depicting Tynnes Falk. Wallander got the feeling that the picture had been taken in this very room. He asked Nyberg to hold the flashlight while he went closer to study the photograph. Falk was staring straight into the camera. His expression was serious.

"What's that in his hand?" Nyberg asked.

Wallander took out his glasses and then peered up at the photo again.

"I don't know what you think," he said finally straightening out his back. "But it looks to me as if he has a remote control in his hand."

They switched places. Nyberg came to the same conclusion. It was a remote control.

"Tell me what I'm looking at," said Wallander. "I'm at a loss."

"Did he worship himself?" Nyberg asked in a confounded tone of voice. "Was the man a lunatic?"

"I don't know," Wallander said.

They turned their attention to the rest of the room, but there was nothing else to look at. Wallander put on a pair of rubber gloves and carefully removed the picture. He looked on the back, but there was no writing. He handed the picture over to Nyberg.

"You'll have to look it over."

"Maybe this room is part of a series of rooms," Nyberg suggested doubtfully. "Like a series of Chinese boxes. Maybe there's another secret room somewhere."

They searched the room together but found nothing. The walls were solid.

They returned to the first room.

"You haven't found anything else?" Wallander asked.

"No. It seems as if the room was cleaned recently."

"Falk was a clean freak," Wallander said. He recalled both the diary entries and what Siv Eriksson had told him.

"I don't think I can do much more tonight," Nyberg said. "But I'll come back tomorrow to finish up."

"We'll also bring in Martinsson," Wallander said. "I want to know what's in that computer."

Wallander helped Nyberg collect his things.

"How the hell can someone worship himself?" Nyberg asked when they had finished and were ready to leave.

"I can give you countless examples of it," Wallander said.

"At least I won't have to deal with this any more in a couple of years," Nyberg said. "Lunatics who pray to their own image."

They loaded all the bags into Nyberg's car. Wallander nodded to him and watched him drive off. The wind had picked up. It was close to ten thirty. He was hungry, but the thought of going home and cooking something was not appealing. He got in the car and drove to a fast-food kiosk that was still open. When his food came, some boys had started playing a noisy video game. He decided to take his hot dogs and mashed potatoes out to the car. With the very first bite he managed to spill something on Martinsson's coat. His reaction was a desire to open the car door and throw everything on the ground. But he managed to calm himself down.

Once he had finished eating, he wasn't sure if he should go home or down to the station. He needed to sleep, but his anxiety wasn't letting up. He drove to the station. There was no one in the lunchroom, but the coffee machine had been fixed. Someone had written an angry note about not pulling too hard on the levers.

What levers? Wallander thought helplessly. *I put my cup down and push a button. I've never even seen a lever.* He took his coffee and went back to his office. The hallway was deserted. He had no idea how many late nights he had spent there alone.

Once, when he was still married to Mona and Linda was a young child, Mona had turned up at his office fuming and told him he had to make a choice between his family and his work. That time, he had immediately gone home with her. But there had been many times when he had chosen to stay on and work.

He took Martinsson's coat with him to the bathroom and tried to clean it, but without success. Then he returned to his office and spent a half-hour making notes about his conversation with Siv Eriksson. When he was done, he yawned and stretched. It was half past eleven and he knew he had to go home and try to sleep, but he forced himself to read through what he had written. He kept thinking about Falk's strange personality and his secret room with an altar for worshipping his own image. And the fact that no one knew where he had his mail sent. Then he thought about something Siv Eriksson had said that had stuck in his mind.

Tynnes Falk had declined a number of lucrative job offers because he felt he had enough as it was.

Wallander checked the time. Twenty minutes to midnight. He wanted to talk to Marianne Falk to ask about Falk's will but decided it was too late to call, even though something told him she wasn't asleep yet.

Wallander yawned. He put on his coat and turned off the light. As he was walking out through the reception area, one of the officers on the night shift stuck his head out of the control room.

"I think I have something for you," he said.

Wallander shut his eyes tightly and hoped it wasn't anything that would keep him up all night. Then he walked over and took the receiver that the man held out to him.

"Someone has discovered a body," the officer said.

Not another one, Wallander thought. *We can't handle it. Not right now.* He held the receiver to his ear.

"Kurt Wallander. What seems to be the matter?"

The man speaking on the other end was clearly agitated. He was screaming into the phone. Wallander held the receiver farther from his ear.

"Please speak more slowly," Wallander said. "Clearly and slowly. Otherwise we're not going to be able to get anywhere. What is your name, please?"

"My name is Nils Jönsson. There's a dead man on the street."

"Where are you?"

"In Ystad! I tripped over him. He's naked and he's dead. It's horrible! I shouldn't have to see things like this. I have a weak heart!"

"Calm down," Wallander said. "Nice and easy, now. You say there's a naked dead man on the street?

"Isn't that what I said?"

"Yes, you did. Now tell me what street you're on."

"I don't know. It's a fucking parking lot!"

Wallander shook his head.

"Is it a street or a parking lot?"

"I guess it's something in between."

"And where is it?"

"I'm on my way from Trelleborg to Kristianstad. I was going to fill up the car and then he was just lying there."

"So you're calling from a gas station?"

"I'm in my car."

Wallander had begun to hope the man was simply intoxicated and imagining things. But his agitation seemed real.

"What can you see from your car?"

"I think it's a department store."

"Is there a name?"

"I can't see any. I took the exit."

"What exit?"

"The one for Ystad, of course!"

"From Trelleborg?"

"From Malmö. I was on the main highway."

A thought had come crawling out of Wallander's subconscious, though he had trouble believing it could be true.

"Can you see a cash machine from your car?" he asked.

"That's where he is. On the sidewalk."

Wallander held his breath. The man kept talking and Wallander handed the phone to the officer who had been listening in the background.

"It's the same place Falk was found," Wallander said. "The question is simply if we've found him again."

"Who do you want me to send down there?"

"Call Martinsson and Nyberg. How many patrol cars are out right now?"

"Two. One is in Hedeskoga checking a domestic dispute. Some birthday party that got out of hand."

"The other?"

"Downtown."

"Tell them to head to the parking lot on Missunnavägen as soon as possible. I'll get there on my own."

Wallander left the station. He was freezing in the thin coat. During the short car ride he wondered what he was about to see. But deep down he was sure it was Tynnes Falk who had been returned to the place of his death.

Wallander and a patrol car arrived almost simultaneously. A man jumped out of a red Volvo when they arrived. He was waving his arms. Wallander got out and the man approached him shouting and pointing. He had bad breath.

"Wait here," he ordered.

Then he walked over to the cash machine. It was Tynnes Falk. He was lying on his stomach with his hands tucked underneath his chest. His head was turned to the left. Wallander told the other officers to seal off the area. He also asked them to take down Nils Jönsson's information, something he didn't have the energy to do himself. He didn't expect Jönsson to have anything important to tell them. The person or persons who had returned Falk's body would most likely have chosen a time when no one could see them.

Wallander had never seen anything like this before. The reconstruction of a death, a body returned to the scene of the killing.

He didn't understand it. He walked slowly around the body as if he were expecting Falk to rise to his feet.

One could say I'm looking at a divine figure, he thought. *You worshipped yourself, Tynnes Falk. According to Siv Eriksson, you were planning to become a very old man. But you didn't even live as long as I have.*

Nyberg arrived in his car. He stared at the body for a full minute, then looked over at Wallander.

"Wasn't he already dead? Then how did he end up back here? Was this where he wanted to be buried?"

Wallander didn't know what he should say in response to these questions. He saw Martinsson park behind one of the patrol cars, and he walked over to meet him.

Martinsson got out of his car. He was dressed in a sweatsuit. He eyed the stain on the coat Wallander was wearing with disapproval, but he didn't say anything.

"What's happened?"

"Tynnes Falk has come back."

"Is that your idea of a joke?"

"I'm just telling you what's happened. Tynnes Falk is lying in the same spot where he died."

They walked over to the cash machine. Nyberg was talking on the phone to a member of his forensic team. Wallander wondered gloomily if he was going to have to see Nyberg faint again.

"There's one important thing I want you to check out," Wallander told him. "See if you think he's lying in the same position as when he was first found."

Martinsson nodded and slowly circled the body. Wallander knew he had an excellent memory. Martinsson shook his head.

"He was lying farther away from the machine before. And one leg was bent."

"Are you sure?"

"Yes."

Wallander thought for a moment.

"We really don't need to wait for a doctor this time," he said after a while. "Falk was pronounced dead over a week ago. I think we can turn him over without being accused of any wrongdoing."

Martinsson hesitated, but Wallander insisted. He saw no reason to wait. Once Nyberg had taken a few photographs of the body, they turned it over. Martinsson flinched and drew back. A few seconds went by before Wallander realized why. Two fingers were missing. The index finger on the right hand and the ring finger on the left. He got up.

"What kind of animals are we dealing with?" Martinsson groaned. "Body snatchers? Corpse mutilators? Necrophiliacs?"

"I don't know, but clearly this means something. Someone went to a lot of trouble to steal the body and now to return it here."

Martinsson was pale and Wallander pulled him aside.

"We need to get hold of the night guard who discovered the body the first time," he said. "We also need a copy of the security guards' schedule so we can establish the times when they pass by this area. Then we'll be in a better position to zero in on the time that he was brought back here."

"Who found him this time?"

"A man called Nils Jönsson form Trelleborg."

"Was he getting cash?"

"He says he stopped to fill up the car."

Wallander walked over and talked to the officer who had taken down Jönsson's information. As Wallander had expected, he had said nothing of interest.

Martinsson came over with information from the security company.

"Someone came by here around eleven," he said.

It was now half past twelve. Wallander recalled that the first time Falk was found the call had come in to the station around midnight. Nils Jönsson said he had discovered the body around a quarter to twelve.

"The body can only have been here for about an hour," Wallander said. "And I have a decided feeling that the people who brought him back knew exactly when the guards came by."

" 'The people'?"

"It has to be more than one person," Wallander said. "I'm convinced of it."

"What do you think the chances are of finding a witness?"

"Negligible. There aren't many residential buildings in this area where someone might have looked out a window. And who comes down here late at night?"

"People out walking their dogs."

"Maybe."

"They may at least have noticed a car or some unusual activity. People with dogs tend to have habitual natures, and they'd notice something out of the ordinary."

Wallander agreed. It was worth a try.

"We'll put an officer down here tomorrow night," he said. "He can talk to all those dogwalkers and joggers that pass by."

"Hansson loves dogs," Martinsson said.

So do I, Wallander thought. *But I'll be thankful if I don't have to stand out here tomorrow night.*

A car slowed down and stopped by the police tape. A young man in a sweatsuit that looked like the one Martinsson was wearing stepped out. Wallander felt like he was slowly being surrounded by the members of a soccer team.

"That's our security guard," Martinsson said. "The one from last Sunday. He was off tonight."

He walked over to talk to him. Wallander went back to the body.

"Someone has cut off two of his fingers," Nyberg said. "It gets worse and worse."

Wallander nodded.

"I know you aren't a doctor," he said. "But you used the word 'cut'?"

"Both of them look like clean cuts. There is a small possibility it could have been another kind of instrument if it was powerful enough. The pathologist should be able to tell us. She's on her way."

"Susann Bexell?"

"I don't know for sure."

The doctor arrived after a half-hour. It was Bexell. Wallander explained the situation to her. The canine unit that Nyberg had requested arrived shortly thereafter. They were supposed to search for the missing fingers.

"I really don't know what I'm supposed to be doing out here," Bexell said when Wallander had finished telling her everything. "If he's dead, there's not much I can do."

"I need you to look at his hands. Two fingers are missing."

Nyberg had started smoking again. Wallander was surprised he wasn't feeling more exhausted himself. The dog and his officer had started their work. Wallander had a vague recollection of a time when a dog had found a blackened finger. How long ago was that? He couldn't say. Five, maybe ten years ago.

Bexell worked quickly.

"I think someone cut these fingers off with pruning shears," she said. "But whether that happened here, or in some other location, I can't say."

"It definitely wasn't here," Nyberg said.

No one disputed his opinion, nor did anyone bother to ask how he was able to arrive at this conclusion.

Bexell finished up and directed the work of loading the body into the morgue van.

"Hopefully the body won't disappear this time," Wallander said. "It would be nice if they could actually bury it this time."

Bexell and the morgue van left the scene. The dog had given up on the search.

"He would have found a couple of fingers," his trainer said. "That's an easy job for him."

"I still want the area searched again tomorrow," Wallander said, thinking of Sonja Hökberg's handbag. "The person who removed them may have discarded them a little farther away. Just to make our job harder."

It was a quarter to two and the security guard had gone home.

"He agreed with me, " Martinsson said. "The body was in a different position before."

"That could mean one of two things," Wallander said. "Either they simply couldn't be bothered to arrange it in the original position, or they didn't know what that was."

"But how could that be? And why did they bring it back here?"

"I don't know. But I don't think there's any use in staying here. We need to sleep."

Nyberg was packing up his bags for the second time this evening. The area would remain cordoned off until the next day.

"I'll see you tomorrow at eight," Wallander said.

Then they went their separate ways.

Wallander went home and made himself a cup of tea. He drank about half a cup and then went to bed. His back and legs ached. The streetlamp swayed outside his window.

Just as he was about to fall asleep, he was jerked back into consciousness. At first he didn't know what it was. He listened for noise, but then he realized the disturbance had come from within.

It was something to do with the fingers that had been cut off.

He sat up in bed. It was twenty minutes past two.

I have to know now, he thought. *It can't wait until tomorrow.*

He got out of bed and walked out into the kitchen. The phone book lay on the table.

It took him less than a minute to find the phone number he was looking for.

Chapter Eighteen

Siv Eriksson was sleeping.

Wallander hoped he wasn't tearing her from a dream she didn't want to leave. She answered the phone after the eleventh ring.

"This is Kurt Wallander."

"Who?"

"I came by last night."

She seemed to be waking up slowly.

"Oh, the policeman. What time is it?"

"Half past three. I wouldn't have called if it wasn't urgent."

"What's happened?"

"We found the body."

There was a scratchy sound on the other end. He thought she was probably sitting up in bed.

"Come again?"

"We have found Falk's body."

Wallander realized as he was saying this that he had never told her about it being missing in the first place. He was so tired it had slipped his mind.

So he told her. She listened without interrupting him.

"Do you really expect me to believe all this?" she said when he was finished.

"I know it sounds strange, but every word is true."

"Who would do something like that? And why?"

"That's what we're trying to find out."

"And the body lay where it was found the first time?"

"Yes."

"Oh my God!"

He heard her breathing hard.

"But how could it have gotten there?"

"We don't know that yet, but I'm calling because I'm hoping you'll help me with something else."

"Are you planning to come over?"

"Talking on the phone is fine."

"What is it you want to know? Don't you ever sleep, by the way?"

"Things have a tendency to get a little hectic at times. Now, the question I'm going to ask you will seem a little odd."

"Well, that's no surprise. I think everything about you is a little odd, if you don't mind my being completely honest while we're talking like this in the middle of the night."

Her comment threw him.

"I don't understand."

She laughed.

"Don't take it to heart. I didn't mean it so seriously. It's just that I find it funny when people who are obviously thirsty decline a drink, and people who are dying of hunger won't accept any food. That's all."

"I wasn't thirsty or hungry. If you're referring to me, that is."

"Who do you think?"

Wallander wondered why he couldn't tell her the truth. What was he afraid of? He didn't think she believed him.

"Have I offended you?" she asked.

"Not at all," he said. "Can I ask you my question?"

"Of course."

"Could you tell me how Tynnes Falk used a computer keyboard?"

"Was that your quesiton?"

"Yes. I would appreciate an answer."

"He used a keyboard the way anyone would."

"But people often type in different ways. The stereotype of a policeman, for example, is someone slowly pecking away at an old typewriter with one finger."

"I see what you're getting at."

"Did he use all his fingers when he was typing?"

"I don't think many people do."

"So he probably only used a couple of fingers?"

"Yes."

Wallander held his breath. He was about to find out if his hunch had been correct.

"Which fingers did he use?"

"I have to think about it. To make sure I'm right."

Wallander waited with excitement.

She was fully awake by now and he knew she was trying to do her best to help him.

"I think I'd like to call you back," she said. "There's something I'm not sure about. I think it'll be easier if I sit down at the computer. That will jog my memory."

Wallander gave her his home phone number.

Then he waited at the kitchen table. His whole head ached. *Tomorrow I have to try to get an early night,* he thought. *Whatever happens.* He wondered how Nyberg was doing. If he was sleeping, or tossing restlessly.

Ten minutes later the phone rang. He wondered nervously if it could be a journalist but decided it was too early for that. They didn't normally call before half past four in the morning. He picked up the receiver. She launched directly into what she had to say.

"It was the index finger on the right hand and the ring finger on the left hand."

Wallander felt a stir of excitement.

"Are you absolutely certain?"

"Yes. It's a pretty unusual way of typing, but that's what he did."

"Good," Wallander said. "That confirms something for us."

"You have to understand that you've made me very curious."

Wallander considered telling her about the missing fingers, but decided to hold off.

"Unfortunately I can't tell you anything more at this point. Perhaps later."

"What do you think is going on?"

"We're still working on that one," Wallander said. "Don't forget to fax me that list of clients tomorrow. Good night."

"Good night."

Wallander got up and walked over to the window. The temperature had risen to about seven degrees Celsius. The wind was still strong, and there was a light rain. It was four minutes to three. Wallander went back to bed, but the missing fingers danced in front of his eyes for a long time before he managed to sleep.

The man waiting in the shadows by Runnerström Square was counting his breaths. He had learnt to do so as a child. Breathing and patience were connected. A person had to know when it was best to wait.

Listening to his own breaths was also a way to keep his anxiety in check. There had been too many unanticipated turns of events. He knew it wasn't possible to have total control over a situation, but

Tynnes Falk's death had been a huge blow. Now they were busy reorganizing. Control would soon be achieved, which was just as well since time was running out. But if there was no more interference, they would be able to stay on track with their original schedule.

He thought about the man who lived far away in tropical darkness. A man he had never met, yet one he both feared and respected. He held everything in his hand.

There could be no mistakes.

Mistakes would not be tolerated.

But there were no grounds for his anxiety. Who would be able to break into the computer that functioned as the heart of the operation? It was simply a failure of confidence.

If there had been any mistake so far, it was that he had not managed to kill the policeman in Falk's apartment. But even so, they were safe. The policeman probably didn't know anything.

Of course, Falk himself had often said that nothing and no one is ever completely safe. And he had been right. Now he was dead. No one could ever be totally safe.

They had to take care. The man who now stood alone at the helm had told him to hold off and see what happened next. If the policeman was attacked a second time it would only attract unnecessary attention.

He had kept watch outside the building on Apelbergsgatan, and when the policeman made his way to Runnerström Square he had followed him. He had been expecting this, that they would discover the secret office. A little later, another policeman had arrived. He had been carrying bags. The first policeman had then left the apartment, only to return about an hour later. Then they had both left Falk's office before midnight.

He had continued to wait, all the while counting his breaths. Now it was three o'clock in the morning and the Square was completely deserted. He was cold. He decided that it was very unlikely that anyone would come by at this time. Finally he slid out of the shadows and walked across the street. He unlocked the front door and ran soundlessly up the stairs. He had his gloves on when he unlocked the door to the apartment. He walked in, turned on his flashlight, and looked around. They had found the door to the inner room, but he had expected as much. Without really knowing why, he had developed a kind of respect for the policeman he had tried to kill. The man's reaction had been very quick despite the fact that he was no longer young. He must have learnt this early in life.

It was always a mistake to underestimate an opponent.

He trained the flashlight on the computer and started it up. The monitor came on, and after a while he was able to search out the file that showed him when the computer was last booted up. Six days ago. The policemen had not touched it.

It was too soon to feel safe, however. It could simply be a question of time. They might be planning to use a specialist. That caused him a pang of anxiety, but the bottom line was that no matter who they used they would not be able to break the codes. Not in a thousand years. Someone with an extreme sense of intuition might have some luck, but how likely was it when they didn't even know what they were looking for? They couldn't imagine what this computer was set up to do, not in their wildest dreams.

He left the apartment as silently as he had come and melted back into the shadows.

When Wallander woke up the next morning, he felt as if he had overslept. But when he looked at the clock it was only five minutes past six o'clock. He had slept for three hours. He fell back against the pillows. His head was pounding from lack of sleep. *I need ten more minutes,* he thought. *Make that seven. I just can't get up right now.*

But he forced himself up and walked unsteadily out to the bathroom. His eyes were bloodshot. He stepped into the warm spray of water in the shower and leaned against the wall like a horse. He slowly came back to life.

At five minutes to seven he was in the parking lot at the station. It was still raining softly. Hansson was unusually early. He was in the reception area flipping through a newspaper. He was also wearing a suit and tie, although his normal outfits consisted of wrinkled corduroy pants and shirts that hadn't been ironed.

"Is it your birthday?" Wallander asked.

Hansson shook his head.

"I happened to see myself in the mirror the other day. Not a pretty picture. I thought I should try to make more of an effort. Anyway, it's Saturday today. We'll see how long it lasts."

They walked over to the lunchroom together and had the obligatory cup of coffee. Wallander told him what had happened during the night.

"That's crazy," Hansson said when he finished. "What kind of a sicko dumps a corpse on the street?"

"That's what we're paid to find out," Wallander said. "By the way, you're in charge of looking out for dogs tonight."

"What do you mean?"

"It's Martinsson's idea. He says someone out walking a dog might have noticed something unusual along Missunnavägen last night. We thought you could be posted there just to stop them as they walk by."

"Why me?"

"You like dogs, don't you?"

"I have dinner plans tonight. It's Saturday night, remember?"

"You'll be able to do both. It's fine if you get there shortly before eleven."

Hansson nodded. Even though Wallander had never liked him very much, he had to commend him for his willingess to put in the time when needed.

"I'll see you at eight in the conference room," Wallander said. "We need to review and discuss the latest events."

"It doesn't seem like we do anything else. And where does it get us?"

Wallander sat down at his desk, looked over his notes, and let himself sink deeply into thought. *Nothing in all of this makes any sense,* he thought. *I can't find a beginning or end. I have no idea why all these people have died. But there has to be a motive in here somewhere.*

He got up and walked over to the window, coffee cup in hand.

What would Rydberg do? he thought. *Would he have had any advice in this situation? Or would he feel as lost as I do?*

He received no answer. Rydberg remained silent.

It was half past seven. Wallander sat down again. He had to prepare for their meeting. After all, he was the one who had to lead the work. In order to try to gain a new perspective on the events, he backtracked. Which events lay at the bottom of all this? What were the possible connections? It was like charting a solar system where the planets circled not a sun, but a black hole.

There's a main figure in all this, he thought. *There's always a lead character. Not everyone is of equal importance. Some of the people who have died are minor players. But who is who, and how am I supposed to tell them apart? What story is being enacted?*

He was back where he started. The only thing he felt sure of was that the taxi driver's murder was not a potential center, nor a catalyst for the events that followed.

That left Tynnes Falk. There was a connection between him and Sonja Hökberg, indicated by the electrical relay and the blueprint of the power substation. That's what they had to concentrate on. The connection was tenuous and inexplicable, but it was there.

He pushed away his notes. *I can't see anything in what I've written,* he thought despondently.

He sat there for a few more minutes. He heard Höglund laugh in the hallway. That didn't happen every day. Finally he gathered up his papers and headed to the conference room.

They did a thorough review of the material, a task which took almost three hours. The tired and somewhat despondent feeling in the room slowly dissipated.

Nyberg walked in at half past eight. He sat down at the opposite end of the table without saying a word. Wallander looked at him, but Nyberg shook his head. He had nothing urgent to announce.

"Could someone be laying out false tracks deliberately?" Höglund wondered while they were taking a short break to stretch their legs. "Maybe this is all very simple when it comes down to it. Maybe we just need a motive."

"And what would that be?" Martinsson asked. "A person who robs a taxi driver has very different motives from one who burns a young woman to death, thereby causing blackouts in large parts of Scania. We should also keep in mind that we don't even know for sure whether Falk was murdered. My inclination is still to chalk it up to a natural death, or at the most an accident."

"It would be easier if he was murdered," Wallander said. "Then we could be sure that we're dealing with a series of criminal events."

They closed the windows and sat back down at the table.

"It seems to me that the most serious event so far is that someone tried to shoot you," Höglund said. "It's not very often that a burglar is willing to kill someone who crosses his path."

"I don't know if I would call it more serious than anything else here," Wallander objected. "But it does say something about the degree of ruthlessness in the people who are behind all this. Whatever it is they're really trying to do."

They continued discussing the various crimes, turning each in as many directions as possible. Wallander didn't say much but listened attentively to the others. During other difficult investigations, it had sometimes been a casually thrown-out phrase, or even a rephrasing of something, that had caused the whole case to break open. They were looking for openings now, and, not least, a center.

During the final hour, each person went through the tasks he or she had completed and what was still waiting to be done. Shortly before eleven Wallander realized they could go no further.

"This is going to take time," he said. "It's possible that we're going to need more personnel. I'll talk to Holgersson about it. I don't think there's any use staying here any longer, though that doesn't mean we get to take the weekend off. We need to keep going."

Hansson left to speak to a prosecutor who had demanded to be kept up to date. Martinsson went to his office to call home. Wallander had asked him earlier to accompany him to the office on Runnerström Square when the meeting was over. Nyberg sat at the table for a while longer, pulling at his thin wisps of hair. Then he got up and walked out without saying a word. Höglund was the only one left. Wallander realized she wanted to talk to him about something, so he closed the door.

"I've been thinking about something," she said. "That man who shot at you."

"Yes?"

"He saw you. And he didn't hesitate for a second."

"I'd rather not think too much about that."

"But maybe you should."

Wallander looked at her closely.

"What do you mean?"

"I just think maybe you should be extra careful. He may have been taken by surprise, but I don't think we can rule out that he thinks you know something. And he may try again."

Wallander was surprised that he hadn't considered this himself. It frightened him.

"I don't want to scare you," she said. "But I had to say it."

He nodded.

"I'll think about it. The question is what he thinks I know."

"Maybe he's right. Maybe you're just not aware of what you know."

Another thought came to Wallander.

"Maybe we should post some officers at Apelbergsgatan and Runnerström Square. No patrol cars, nothing too noticeable. Just in case."

She agreed with him and left to arrange it. Wallander was left with his fear. He thought about Linda. Then he shook out his arms and shoulders and walked out to the reception area to wait for Martinsson.

They stepped into the apartment at Runnerström Square shortly before noon. Although Martinsson was mainly interested in the computer, Wallander wanted to show him the secret room with the altar first.

"Too much time in cyberspace makes people a little strange," Martinsson said, shaking his head. "This whole apartment gives me the creeps."

Wallander didn't answer. He was thinking about Martinsson's choice of words. *Cyberspace.* Could that be '*c-space*'? The strange word Tynnes Falk had used in his diary.

C-space is quiet. No messages from his friends.

What message was he waiting for? Wallander thought. *I'd give a lot to know that right now.*

Martinsson took off his coat and sat down at the computer. Wallander stood behind him peering over his shoulder.

"This programming looks pretty complicated," Martinsson said once the computer had been turned on. "I don't recognize the code. Some of this may be more than I can handle."

"I'd still like you to do what you can. If you get stuck, we'll call in the technology division of the National Police and get some of their computer whizzes on it."

Martinsson didn't answer. He was absorbed by his task, staring straight ahead at the screen. Then he got up and walked around to look at the computer from the back. As Wallander watched him, he returned to the chair. The screen had come alive with a number of symbols flitting by. Then it settled into an image of the night sky.

Cyberspace. At least Falk is consistent, Wallander thought.

"The computer seems to automatically connect with a server when you turn it on," Martinsson said. "Do you want me to talk you through what I'm doing?" he added.

"I don't think I'd be able to follow you."

Wallander put on his glasses and leaned closer to the screen as Martinsson tried to open one of the files on the hard drive. After clicking on the file, Martinsson frowned.

"What happened?" Wallander asked.

Martinsson pointed to a corner of the screen where a cursor was blinking.

"I'm not one-hundred-percent sure about this," he said slowly. "But I think someone was just notified that we tried to open this file."

"How could that happen?"

"Well, this computer is connected to others."

"And someone at the other end of one of those could now have seen what we're trying to do?"

"Yes, something like that."

"Where is this person?"

"He could be anywhere," Martinsson said. "A remote ranch in California. An island off the coast of Australia. Or in an apartment in this building."

Wallander shook his head in bafflement.

"When you're hooked up to the Internet, you're in the middle of the world wherever you are," he quoted.

Martinsson had started working on the file again. After about ten minutes he pushed back his chair.

"Everything's locked," he said. "There are complicated codes and barriers to everything. There's no way in."

"So you give up?"

Martinsson smiled.

"Not just yet," he said.

Martinsson resumed his tapping on the keyboard but stopped almost at once.

"What is it?"

Martinsson looked at the screen with surprise.

"I'm not sure, but I think someone else used this computer only a few hours ago."

"Can you find out for sure?"

"I think so."

Wallander waited while Martinsson kept working. After about ten minutes, he got up.

"I was right," he said. "Someone was using this computer yesterday. Or rather, last night."

They looked at each other.

"That means someone other than Falk has access to the material on this computer."

"And that someone didn't have to break in to the apartment to get to it," Martinsson said.

Wallander nodded.

"How does that change the picture?" Martinsson asked.

"We don't know yet," Wallander said. "It's too early."

Martinsson sat back down at the computer and kept working.

They took a break at half past four. Martinsson invited Wallander to come home with him and have dinner. They were back at the apartment at half past six. Wallander realized that his presence was superfluous, but he didn't want to leave Martinsson totally alone.

Martinsson kept working until ten o'clock. Then he finally gave up.

"I'm not getting through," he said. "I've never seen any security systems that looked like this. There's the electronic equivalent of miles and miles of barbed wire in here. That and impenetrable firewalls."

"Well, that's that then. We'll give the National Police a call."

"I guess," Martinsson said hesitantly.

"Do we have a choice?"

"We do, actually," Martinsson said. "There's a young man called Robert Modin who lives in Löderup. Not so far from where your father used to live."

"Who is he?"

"He's a nineteen-year-old kid like any other, except he just got out of jail a couple of weeks ago."

"And why is he an interesting alternative?"

"Because he managed to break into the Pentagon supercomputer about a year ago. He's considered one of the best hackers in Europe."

Wallander thought it over. There was something appealing about Martinsson's suggestion. He didn't take long to make up his mind.

"Get him," he said. "Meanwhile I'll check up on Hansson and the dog-walkers."

Martinsson got in his car and drove toward Löderup.

Wallander looked around on the dark street. A car was parked a few blocks away. Wallander lifted his hand in greeting.

Then he thought about what Höglund had said about being careful. He looked around again, then headed up toward Missunnavägen. The light rain had finally stopped.

Chapter Nineteen

Hansson had parked his car outside the tax authority building. Wallander saw him from a distance. He was leaning against a streetlight reading the newspaper. *You can tell from here he's a cop*, Wallander thought. *No one can fail to see he's on the job, though it's not clear what he's up to. But he's not dressed warmly enough. Apart from the golden rule of making it through the day alive, there's nothing more important in the policeman's codebook than dressing warmly when working outside.*

Hansson was completely absorbed in his newspaper. He didn't notice Wallander until he was right next to him. Wallander saw he was reading the racing section.

"I didn't hear you," Hansson said. "I wonder if my hearing is going."

"How are the horses today?"

"I suppose I'm living in a fantasy land, like most people. I think one day I'll sit there with all the right numbers. But see, the horses don't run the way they're supposed to. They never do."

"And how are the dogs?"

"I only just got here. I haven't seen anyone yet."

Wallander looked around.

"When I first got here, this part of town was still an empty field," he said. "None of this was here."

They started walking along the street. Wallander told him about Martinsson's valiant efforts to break the code of Falk's computer. They got to the cash machine and stopped.

"It's funny how quickly you get used to things," Hansson said. "I can hardly remember life before these machines. Not that I have any idea how they actually work. Sometimes I imagine a little man sitting inside, someone who counts out all the cash and sends it through to you."

Wallander thought again about what Erik Hökberg had said, about how vulnerable society had become. The blackout a few days ago had proved him right.

They walked back to Hansson's car. They still didn't see any people out walking their dogs.

"I'm going now. How was the dinner?"

"I never went. What's the point of eating if you can't have a glass or two?"

Wallander was about to leave when Hansson brought up a conversation he had had earlier in the day with the district attorney.

"Did Viktorsson have anything to say?" Wallander asked.

"Not really."

"But he must have said something."

"He just said he couldn't see any reason to narrow the investigation at this point. The case should still be attacked on all fronts. Without preconceived ideas."

"Policemen never work without preconceived ideas," Wallander answered. "He should know that by now."

"Well, that was what he said."

"Nothing else?"

"No."

Wallander had the feeling that Hansson was holding something back. He waited, but Hansson didn't add anything.

"I think half past twelve should do it," Wallander told him. "I'm leaving now. I'll see you tomorrow morning."

"I should have worn warmer clothes. It's a chilly night."

"It's fall," Wallander said. "And soon enough it'll be winter."

He walked back into town. The more he thought about it, the more he was convinced of the fact that Hansson hadn't told him everything. By the time he got back to Runnerström Square he realized it could only mean that Viktorsson had made a comment about him, about the alleged assault and the ongoing internal investigation.

It irritated Wallander that Hansson hadn't told him what he had said, but it didn't surprise him. Hansson spent his life trying to be everyone's friend. Wallander suddenly felt how tired he was. Or perhaps he was simply despondent.

He looked around. The undercover police car was still parked in its spot. Apart from that, the street was deserted. He unlocked his car and got in. Just as he was about to start the engine his cell phone rang. He fished it out of his pocket. It was Martinsson.

"Where are you?"

"I went home."

"Why? Couldn't you get a hold of Molin?"

"Modin. Robert Modin. No, I started feeling like it wasn't such a good idea after all."

"Why not?"

"You know how it is. There are regulations stipulating that we can't simply bring in whoever we want on a case from outside the force. And Modin has been convincted of a crime—even if his jail time was only a month or so."

Martinsson was getting cold feet. That had happened before. At times it had even led to conflicts between them. Sometimes Wallander thought Martinsson was too careful. He never used the word "cowardly," but that was what he meant deep down.

"Strictly speaking, we should get Viktorsson's approval first," Martinsson continued. "At the very least we should talk to Lisa."

"You know I'll take full responsibility on this," Wallander said.

"Even so."

Martinsson had clearly made up his mind on the matter.

"Give me Modin's address," Wallander said. "That way you'll be absolved of all responsibility."

"You don't think we should wait?"

"No. Time is running out and I want to know what's in that computer."

"What you really need to do is sleep, you know. Have you looked in the mirror recently?"

"Yes, I know," Wallander said. "Now give me the address."

He found a pen in the glove compartment, which was stuffed full of papers and folded-up paper plates from fast-food kiosks. Wallander wrote down what Martinsson said on the back of a gas receipt.

"It's almost midnight," Martinsson said.

"I know," Wallander said. "See you tomorrow."

He hung up and put his phone down on the passenger seat. But before he started the engine, he thought about what Martinsson had said. He was right about one thing. They needed to sleep. What was the point of going out to Löderup in the middle of the night? Robert Modin was probably sleeping. *I'll let it go until tomorrow,* he thought.

He started the car and headed east in the direction of Löderup.

He drove fast to try to wake himself up. He wasn't even acting on his own decisions anymore.

He didn't need to consult the scrap of paper with the address. He'd known exactly where it was even as he had been writing it down. It was an area only a few kilometers from where his father's house had been. Wallander also had the feeling that he had met Robert Modin's father before somewhere. He rolled down the window and let the cold air wash over his face. He was irritated with both Hansson and Martinsson right now. *They're bending to pressure,* he thought. *Kowtowing to their boss.*

He turned off the main highway at a quarter past twelve. There was a good chance that he was about to arrive at a dark house whose inhabitants were sleeping. But his anger and irritation had chased the tiredness away from his own body. He wanted to see Robert Modin. And he wanted to take him to Runnerström Square.

He arrived at the house, which was in a rural area. There was a large garden, and a paddock to one side with a lone horse. The house was whitewashed. There were a jeep and a smaller car parked in front. There were still lights on in several of the downstairs windows.

Wallander turned off his engine and got out of the car. At the same time, the porch light came on and a man walked out of the house. Wallander had been right. They had met before somewhere.

He walked over and greeted the man, who was around sixty, thin and slightly bowed. His hands didn't feel like a farmer's.

"I recognize you," Modin said. "Your father lived not too far from here."

"I know we've met before," Wallander said. "But I can't remember the context."

"Your father was out walking in one of the fields around here," Modin said. "He was carrying a suitcase."

Wallander remembered that time. His father had had one of his episodes of confusion and had decided to go to Italy. He had packed his suitcase and started walking. Modin had seen him tromping through the mud and had called the police station.

"I haven't seen you since he passed away," Modin said. "The house is sold, of course."

"Gertrud moved to be close to her sister in Svarte. I don't even know who ended up buying the place."

"It's some man from up north who claims to be a businessman," Modin said. "I suspect he's actually a moonshiner."

Wallander had an image of his father's studio converted into a brew house.

"I guess you've come on account of Robert," Modin said suddenly. "I thought he had paid for his sins?"

"I'm sure he has," Wallander said. "Though you're right that I'm here to see him."

"What's he done now?"

Wallander heard the dread in the father's voice.

"Nothing, nothing. In fact, it seems he may be able to help us with something."

Modin looked surprised at this, but also relieved. He nodded at the door and Wallander followed him inside.

"The wife's sleeping," Modin said. "She wears earplugs."

Wallander remembered that Modin was a surveyor. He didn't know how he knew this.

"Is Robert here?"

"He's at a party with some friends. But he has his phone with him." Modin showed him into the living room.

Wallander jumped. One of his father's paintings was hanging over the sofa. It was the landscape motif without the wood grouse in the foreground.

"He gave it to me," Modin said. "Whenever it snowed a lot, I would go over and shovel his driveway for him. Sometimes I stopped by and we talked. He was an unusual man, in his own way."

"That's an understatement," Wallander said.

"I liked him. There aren't too many of his kind anymore."

"He wasn't always easy to deal with," Wallander said. "But I miss him. And it's true that old men like him are getting more rare. One day there won't be any left."

"Who *is* easy to deal with, anyway?" Modin said. "Are you? I don't think I could say that about myself. Just ask my wife."

Wallander sat down on the couch. Modin was cleaning out his pipe.

"Robert is a good boy," he said. "I thought he was given a harsh sentence, even if it was only a month. The whole thing was just a game to him."

"I don't know the whole story," Wallander said, "other than that he broke into the Pentagon's computer network."

"He's very good with computers," Modin said. "He bought his first one when he was nine years old, with money he had saved up from picking strawberries. Then he was swallowed up by it. But as long as he continued to do all right in school, it was fine with me. Of course my wife was against it from the start, and now she feels justified by what happened."

Wallander had the feeling that Modin was a somewhat lonely person, but however much he would have liked to sit and chat with him, Wallander had to move on. There was no time to waste.

"I need to get a hold of Robert as soon as possible," he said. "His computer expertise may help us with a case."

Modin puffed on his pipe.

"Can I ask in what way?"

"I can only tell you that it involves some complicated computer programming we'd like his opinion on."

Modin nodded and got up.

"I won't ask any more questions."

He walked out into the hall. Soon Wallander heard him speaking on the phone. He twisted around on the couch to look at his father's painting.

Modin came back.

"He's on his way," he said. "They're in Skillinge, so it'll be a little while."

"What did you tell him?"

"Not to worry, but that the police needed his help with something."

Modin sat down again. His pipe had gone out.

"It must be important, since you're here in the middle of the night."

"Some things can't wait."

Modin understood that Wallander didn't want to say anything more about it.

"Can I get you anything?"

"Some coffee would be nice."

"In the middle of the night?"

"I'm planning to put in a couple more hours of work. But I'm fine without it."

"Of course you should have some coffee," Modin said.

They were sitting in the kitchen when a car pulled up outside the house. The front door opened and Robert Modin came in.

Wallander thought he looked like he was thirteen years old. He had short hair, round glasses, and a slight build. He was probably going to look more and more like his father as he got older. He was wearing jeans, a dress shirt, and a leather jacket. Wallander got up and shook his hand.

"I'm sorry I bothered you in the middle of a party."

"We were about to leave anyway."

Modin was standing in the doorway to the living room.

"I'll leave you two to talk," he said and left.

"Are you tired?" Wallander asked.

"Not particularly."

"Good. There's something I want you to take a look at. I'll explain while we drive."

The boy was on his guard. Wallander tried to smile.

"Don't worry."

"I just have to change my glasses," Robert Modin said.

He walked upstairs to his room. Wallander walked out into the living room and thanked Modin for the coffee.

"I'll make sure he gets home safely. But I have to take him with me to Ystad right now."

Modin looked worried again.

"Are you sure he's not involved with anything?"

"I promise. It's like I told you—there's just something I want him to look at."

Robert Modin came back and they left the house. It was twenty minutes past one. The boy got in on the passenger side and moved Wallander's phone.

"Someone called you," Robert said.

Wallander checked his voice mail. It was Hansson. *I should have brought the phone in with me,* Wallander thought.

He dialed Hansson's number. It took a while before anyone answered.

"Were you sleeping?"

"Of course I was sleeping. What do you think? It's half past one in the morning. I was there until half past twelve. At that point I was so tired I thought I was going to pass out."

"You tried to call."

"I think we actually got something."

Wallander sat up.

"Someone saw something?"

"There was a woman with a German shepherd. She said she saw Tynnes Falk the night he died."

"Good. Did she see anything else?"

"Very observant woman. Her name is Alma Högström. She's a retired dentist. She said she often used to see Tynnes Falk in the evenings. He also used to take walks, apparently."

"What about the night the body was put back?"

"She said she thought she saw a van that night. Around half past eleven. It was parked in front of the cash machine. She noticed it because it wasn't parked in the parking lot."

"Did she see the driver?"

"She said she thought she saw a man."

"Thought?"

"She wasn't sure."

"Can she identify the van?"

"I've asked her to come into the station tomorrow."

"Good," Wallander said. "This may actually give us something."

"Where are you? At home?"

"Not exactly," Wallander answered. "I'll see you tomorrow."

*   *   *

It was two o'clock by the time Wallander pulled up outside the building in Runnerström Square. Wallander looked around. If anything dangerous were to happen, Robert Modin would also be at risk. But there was no one around. The rain had stopped.

Wallander had tried to explain the situation on the way from Löderup. He simply wanted Robert to access the information on Falk's computer.

"I know you're very good at this sort of thing," Wallander said. "I don't care about your business with the Pentagon. What I care about is what you know about computers."

"I should never have been caught," Robert suddenly said in the dark. "It was my own fault."

"What do you mean?"

"I was sloppy about cleaning up after myself."

"Cleaning up?"

"If you break into a secured area, you always leave a trace. It's like cutting a fence. When you leave you have to try to fix it so no one can see you were there. But I didn't do that well enough, and that's why I was caught."

"So there were people in the Pentagon who could see that a young man in Löderup had paid them a visit?"

"They couldn't see who I was or what my name was. But they knew it was my computer."

They went into the building and walked up the stairs. Wallander realized he was tensed up in anticipation of something. Before unlocking the door to the apartment, he listened for noise. Robert Modin watched him closely, but said nothing.

Once inside, Wallander turned on the light and pointed to the computer. He gestured for Robert to sit in the chair. Robert sat down and turned on the machine without hesitation. The usual succession of numbers and symbols started flickering across the screen. Wallander hung back. Robert's fingers were hovering above the keyboard as if he were about to launch into a piano concert. He kept his face very close to the screen, as if he were searching for something Wallander couldn't see.

Then he started tapping on the keyboard.

He kept at it for about a minute, then turned off the computer without warning and turned to face Wallander.

"I've never seen anything like this," he said simply. "I'm not going to be able to get through this."

Wallander sensed the disappointment, both in himself and in the boy.

"Are you sure?"

The boy shook his head.

"At the very least I need to sleep first," he said. "And I'll need a lot of time. Without being rushed."

Wallander realized the futility of bringing him out here in the middle of the night. Martinsson had been right. He grudgingly admitted to himself that it was Martinsson's hesitation that had spurred on his actions.

"Do you have anything else planned for tomorrow?"

"I can be here all day."

Wallander turned off the light and locked the door. Then he followed the boy out to the patrol car and asked the officer on duty to drive him home. Someone would be by to pick him up around noon the following day, when he had had a chance to sleep.

Wallander drove back to Mariagatan. It was almost three by the time he crawled into bed. He fell asleep quickly, after deciding he would not go in to the office before eleven the next morning.

The woman had been by the police station on Friday, shortly before one o'clock.

She had asked for a map of Ystad, and the receptionist had told her to try either the local Tourist Information office or the bookstore. The woman had thanked her politely, then asked to use the bathroom. The receptionist pointed it out to her. The woman had locked the door and opened the window. Then she closed it again, but only after covering the fasteners with tape. The cleaner who had been there Friday evening didn't notice anything.

Early Monday morning, around four o'clock, the shadow of a man ascended the wall of the station and disappeared through the bathroom window. The corridors were deserted. Only the faint sound of a radio came from the control room. The man had a map in his hand that had been obtained by breaking into a computer at an architectural firm. He knew exactly where to go.

He pushed open the door to Wallander's office. A coat with a large yellow spot on the front hung on the back of the door.

The man walked over to the desk. He looked at the computer for a moment before flicking it on. What he was about to do would take about twenty minutes, but he wasn't worried that anyone would come in during that time. It was very easy to go into Wallander's files and examine the material there.

When the man was done, he turned off the light and carefully opened the door. The hallway was empty.

He left the same way he had come.

Chapter Twenty

On Sunday morning, the twelfth of October, Wallander woke up at nine o'clock. Even though he had slept only six hours he felt fully rested. Before going in to the station, he decided to take a walk. The rain from the night before was gone. It was a fine and clear autumn day. It was almost nine degrees Celsius.

He walked through the front doors of the police station at a quarter past ten. Before going to his office, he walked past the control room and asked who of his colleagues had come in.

"Martinsson is here. Hansson had to go pick someone up. Höglund hasn't been in yet."

"I'm here," Wallander heard her voice behind his back. "Did I miss anything?"

"No," Wallander said. "But why don't you come with me?"

"I'll just take my coat off."

Wallander told the officer on duty that he needed a patrol car to be sent out around noon to pick up Robert Modin. He gave the directions.

"Make sure it's an undercover car," he added. "That's very important."

A few minutes later, Höglund stepped into his office. She looked a little less tired today. He thought about asking her how things were going at home, but then as usual he wondered if it was the right moment. Instead, he told her about the potential eyewitness that Hansson had found and was bringing in as they spoke. He also told her about Robert Modin, who would perhaps be able to help them access the information in Falk's computer.

"I remember him," she said when Wallander had finished talking. "Do you think he'll find something important in that computer?"

"I don't think anything. But we have to know what Falk was up to. Who was he? It seems as if more and more people today are really electronic personalities."

He went on to talk about the woman Hansson was bringing down to the station.

"She'll be the first person we have who has actually seen anything," Höglund said.

"We'll keep our fingers crossed."

She was leaning against the door frame. It was a newly acquired habit. Usually she came right in and sat in his visitor's chair.

"I did some thinking last night," she said. "I was watching TV, but I couldn't concentrate. The kids had gone to bed."

"Your husband?"

"My ex-husband. He's in Yemen right now, I think. Anyway, I turned off the TV and sat at the kitchen table with a glass of water. I tried to picture everything that had happened, as simply as possible, stripped of unnecessary details."

"That's an impossible task," Wallander said. "I mean the part about the details. You can't know what's unnecessary at this point."

"You're the one who's taught me to weigh facts against each other and discard what's less important."

"What was your conclusion?"

"Certain things seem firmly established—for example that there is a connection between Falk and Sonja Hökberg. The electrical relay gives us no choice in that department. But there's something about the timing of events that points to a possibility we haven't yet discussed."

"And what would that be?"

"That Tynnes Falk and Sonja Hökberg may not have had anything to do with each other directly."

Wallander saw where she was going. It could be important.

"You mean they are only indirectly connected? Via someone else?"

"The motive may lie somewhere entirely removed from them both, since Falk was dead himself when Hökberg was burned to death. But the same person who killed her later moved his body."

"That still doesn't tell us what we're looking for," Wallander said. "There's no common denominator."

"I've been thinking that maybe we have to start at the beginning," Höglund said thoughtfully. "With Lundberg, the taxi driver."

"Do we have anything on him?"

"His name doesn't appear in any register we have. I've spoken to a few of his colleagues and his widow, and no one had anything bad to say about him. He drove his taxi all day and spent his time off with his family. A normal, peaceful Swedish existence that came to an unexpectedly brutal end. What hit me last night while I was sitting in the kitchen was that it seemed a bit too pretty. There isn't a single smear anywhere. If you don't have anything against it I'd like to keep digging in his life for a while."

"That sounds good. We have to get to the bottom of this case in some way. Did he have kids?"

"Two boys. One of them lives in Malmö, the other still lives here in town. I was going to try to get hold of them today."

"Go ahead. If for no other reason than that it would be useful to determine once and for all if Lundberg's murder was a simple robbery or not."

"Are we meeting today?"

"I'll let you know if we do."

She disappeared out the door. Wallander thought about what she had said, then went out to the lunchroom and helped himself to coffee. He picked up a copy of the day's paper that was lying on a table. Once he got back to his office he started leafing through it absently, but he stopped when something caught his eye. An ad for a dating service, with the unoriginal name of "Computerdate." Wallander read the ad thoroughly. Without hesitating he turned on his computer and quickly threw an ad together. He knew if he didn't do it now he would never get around to it. No one would ever have to know. He could be completely anonymous. He tried to write something as simple and direct as possible: *Policeman, divorced, one child, seeking companionship. Not marriage, but love.* He chose the name *Labrador* rather than *Old Dog.* He printed it out and saved a copy on his hard drive. He put it in an envelope, wrote the address, and affixed a stamp. Then he put it in his pocket. Once he was done, he realized he actually felt excited about it. He would probably not get any replies, or if he did they would be ones he would immediately discard. But the sense of excitement was there. He could not deny it.

Then Hansson appeared in the doorway.

"She's here," he said. "Alma Högström, our witness."

Wallander got up and followed him to one of the small conference rooms. Alma Högström was a fit-looking woman in her mid seventies. A German shepherd was lying on the floor next to her. The dog regarded them suspiciously. Wallander greeted her, sensing that she had dressed up for her visit to the police station.

"Your willingness to speak to the police on this matter is greatly appreciated," he said. "Especially given that it is a Sunday."

He marvelled at the stilted phrases that had just left his mouth. How could he still sound so dry and impersonal after all these years?

"If the police need any information one may have, surely it is one's duty to try to be of assistance."

She's even worse than I am, he thought with a sigh. *It's like watching a bad film from the thirties.*

Slowly they went through what she thought she had seen. Wallander let Hansson do the questioning while he wrote down her answers.

She had observed a dark van at half past eleven. She was sure of the time because she had just looked down at her watch.

"It's an old habit," she said apologetically. "It's ingrained in me by now. I always had one client in the chair and a whole waiting room full of others. Time always went too fast."

Hansson tried to get her to identify the kind of van it had been. He had brought along a folder he had assembled himself a few years ago. It had pictures of different models of cars, as well as a color chart. Naturally there were all kinds of computer programs for this now, but Hansson, like Wallander, had trouble adjusting his work habits.

After a while they concluded it had possibly been a Mercedes. Either navy blue or black.

She hadn't seen the license plates or if there was a driver or not. But she had seen a shadowy figure behind the van.

"Well, I wasn't the one who saw him," she explained. "It was my dog, Steadfast. He pricked up his ears and strained in that direction."

"I know it may be hard to describe what you saw," Hansson said. "But I'd like you to try. Was it a man or a woman?"

She thought for a long time before answering.

"The figure was not wearing a skirt," she said finally. "So I guess I think it was a man."

Hansson continued.

"What happened after that?"

"I took my usual walk."

Hansson spread a map on the table. She described her route.

"That means you passed by the cash machine on your way back. Was the van gone then?"

"Yes."

"When was that?"

"About ten past twelve."

"And how do you know that?"

"I got home at twenty-five minutes past twelve. It takes me fifteen minutes to walk home from that spot."

She showed him where she lived on the map. Wallander and Hansson agreed with her. It would take about that long.

"But you didn't see anything in that area when you walked home?" Hansson continued. "And your dog didn't react in any way?"

"No."

"Isn't that surprising?" Hansson said to Wallander.

"The body must have been stored at a low temperature," Wallander said. "Then it wouldn't have a smell. We can ask Nyberg, or one of the canine units."

"I'm very glad I didn't see anything," Alma Högström said firmly. "It's terrible even to imagine it. People delivering dead bodies in the middle of the night."

"Did you know that this man you normally saw during your evening walks was called Falk?" Wallander asked.

Her answer came as a surprise.

"He was my patient once upon a time. He had good teeth. I only saw him a couple of times, but I have a good memory for faces and names."

"He often took walks at night?" Hansson asked.

"I used to meet him several times a week. He was always alone. I said hello sometimes, but he didn't seem to want to be disturbed."

Hansson had no more questions. He looked over at Wallander, who nodded.

"We may be in touch if we need anything else," he said. "If you think of anything in the meantime, we would of course like to hear from you."

Hansson followed her out, while Wallander remained seated.

He thought about what she had told them. Nothing had really emerged that helped them make more sense out of the case.

Hansson came back and picked up his folders.

"A black or navy blue Mercedes van," he said. "I guess we should look into cars that have been stolen recently."

Wallander nodded.

"And talk to one of the canine units about the question of smell. At least we have a fixed time for the event. That counts for a lot at this stage."

Wallander returned to his office. It was a quarter to twelve. He called Martinsson and told him what had happened during the night. Martinsson listened without saying a word. It irritated Wallander but he managed to control himself. Instead he said he would meet Martinsson in the reception area and give him the keys to the apartment.

"Maybe I'll learn something," Martinsson said when they met. "Watching a real master climb the firewalls."

"I assure you the responsibility is still all mine," Wallander said. "But I don't want him to be left alone."

Martinsson noticed Wallander's gentle irony and immediately became defensive.

"We can't all be like you," he said. "Some of us actually take police regulations seriously."

"I know," Wallander said patiently. "And of course you're right. But I'm still not going to Viktorsson or Lisa for permission on this."

Martinsson disappeared out the front doors.

Wallander felt hungry. He walked down into town and had lunch at István's Pizzeria. István was very busy. They never had a chance to talk about Fu Cheng and his fake credit card. On the way back to the station, Wallander posted his letter to the dating service. He continued on in the firm conviction that he would not be receiving a single reply.

He had just reached his office when the phone rang. It was Nyberg. Wallander went back out into the hallway. Nyberg's office was on the floor below. When Wallander got there, he saw the hammer and knife that had been used in Lundberg's murder lying on Nyberg's desk.

"As of today I've been a policeman for forty years," Nyberg intoned grumpily when he came in. "I started on a Monday, but of course my meaningless anniversary has to fall on a Sunday."

"If you're so sick of your job, you should just quit," Wallander shot back.

He was surprised that he'd lost his temper. He had never done so with Nyberg before. In fact, he always tried to be as tactful as possible around his irascible colleague.

But Nyberg didn't seem to take offense. He looked at Wallander with curiosity.

"Well, well," he said. "I thought I was the only one around here with a temper."

"Forget it. I didn't mean it," Wallander mumbled.

That made Nyberg angry.

"Of course you meant it. That's the whole point. I don't know why people have to be so afraid of showing a little temperament. And anyway, you're right. I'm just bitching."

"Maybe that's what we're all reduced to in the end," Wallander said.

Nyberg pulled the plastic bag with the knife over toward him with impatience.

"The results of the fingerprinting have come back," he said. "There are two different sets on this knife."

Wallander leaned in attentively.

"Eva Persson and Sonja Hökberg?"

"Exactly."

"So Persson may not be lying in this particular case?"

"It seems it's at least a possibility."

"That Hökberg is responsible for the murder, you mean?"

"I'm not implying anything. That's not my job. I'm just telling you the facts. It's a legitimate possibility, that's all."

"What about the hammer?"

"Only Hökberg's prints. No one else's."

Wallander nodded.

"That's good to know."

"We know more than that," Nyberg said, leafing through the papers that were strewn across his desk. "Sometimes the pathologists exceed even their own expectations. They have determined that the blows were inflicted in stages. First he was hit with the hammer, then with the knife."

"And not the other way around?"

"No. And not at the same time."

"How can they determine that?"

"I only know the approximate answer to that, but it's hard to explain."

"Does this mean Hökberg switched weapons in the middle of her attack?"

"I think so. Eva Persson had the knife in her purse, but she gave it to Sonja when asked."

"Like an operation," Wallander said with a shudder. "The surgeon asking for tools."

They thought about this for a moment. Nyberg broke the silence.

"There was one more thing. I've been thinking about that bag out at the power substation. It was lying in the wrong place."

Wallander waited for him to continue. Nyberg was an excellent and thorough forensic technician, but he could also sometimes show unexpected investigative skills.

"I went out there," he said, "and I brought the bag with me. I tried to throw it to the spot by the fence where it had been found, but I could never throw it that far."

"Why not?"

"You remember what the place looks like. There are towers, poles, high voltage lines and barbed wire everywhere. The bag always got stuck on something."

"That means someone must have walked all the way over there?"

"Maybe. But the question then is, Why?"

"You have an idea?"

"The most natural explanation would be that the bag was placed there deliberately and that someone wanted it to be found—but maybe they didn't want it to be found immediately."

"Someone wanted the body to be identified, but not immediately?"

"Yes, that's what I was thinking. But then I discovered something. The place where the bag was found is in the direct beam of one of the spotlights."

Wallander sensed where Nyberg was going, but said nothing.

"I'm simply wondering now if the bag was there because someone had been searching through it, looking for something."

"And maybe found something?"

"That's what I think, but it's your job to figure these things out."

Wallander got up.

"Good work," he said. "You may just have hit on something."

Wallander went back up the stairs and stopped by Höglund's office. She was bent over a stack of papers.

"I want you to contact Sonja Hökberg's mother," he said. "Find out what Sonja normally had in her purse."

Wallander told her about Nyberg's idea and she nodded.

Wallander didn't bother to wait while she made the call. He felt restless, and he started back toward his office. He wondered how many miles he had covered by walking to and fro in these corridors all these years. He heard the phone in his office and hurried over. It was Martinsson.

"I think it's time for you to come down here," he said.

"Why?"

"Robert Modin is a proficient young man."

"What's happened?"

"Exactly what we were hoping for. We're in. The computer has opened its doors."

Wallander hung up.

It's finally happened, he thought. *It's taken some time, but we finally did it.*

He took his coat and left the station.

It was a quarter to two on Sunday, the twelfth of October.

part two **THE FIREWALL**

Chapter Twenty-one

Carter woke up at dawn because the air conditioning unit suddenly stopped. He lay tensed between the sheets listening to the darkness. There was the constant drone of cicadas, and a dog barked in the distance. The power had gone out again. That happened every other night here in Luanda. Savimbi's bandits were always looking for ways to cut the power to the city. In a few minutes the room would be filled with stifling heat. But he didn't know if he had the energy to go down to the room past the kitchen and start up the generator. He didn't know what was worse: the unbearable heat or the throbbing noise from the generator.

He turned his head and looked at the time. It was a quarter past five. He heard one of the guards snoring outside. That was most likely José. As long as Roberto kept himself awake, it didn't matter. Carter shifted his head and felt the muzzle of his gun under the pillow. When it came down to it, beyond the guards and fences, this was his real protection against the countless burglars hiding in the dark. He understood them, of course. He was a white man, he was wealthy. In a poor and downtrodden country like Angola, crime was a given. If he had been one of the poor, he would have robbed people himself.

Suddenly the air conditioning started up again. That meant it wasn't the bandits who had caused the problem, it was simply a technical glitch. The power lines were old, left over from colonial times under the Portuguese. How many years ago that was he could no longer remember.

Carter had trouble falling asleep again. He thought about the fact that he was about to turn sixty. It was in many ways a miracle that he had reached this age given his unpredictable and dangerous lifestyle.

He pulled away the sheet and let the cool air touch his skin. He didn't like to wake up at dawn. He was most vulnerable during these hours before sunrise, left to the dark and his own memories. He could get worked up over old wrongs that had been done to him. It was only when he focused his thoughts on the revenge he was planning that he could calm himself again. But by then several hours had often passed. The sun would be up, the guards would have started talking, and Celine would be unlocking the door to the kitchen in order to come in and make his breakfast.

He pulled the sheet back up over his body. His nose started to itch and he knew he was about to sneeze. He hated to sneeze. He hated his allergies. They were a weakness he despised. The sneezing could come at any time. Sometimes it interrupted him in the middle of a lecture and made it impossible for him to continue.

Other times he broke out in hives. Or else his eyes kept tearing up.

He pulled the sheet all the way up over his mouth. This time he won out. The need to sneeze died away. He started thinking about all the years that had gone by and all that had taken place that had led to his lying in a bed in Luanda, capital of Angola.

Thirty years earlier, he had been a young man working at the World Bank in Washington, D.C. He had been convinced that the bank had the potential to do good in the world, or at the very least shift the balance of justice in the Third World's favor. The World Bank had been founded to provide the huge loans that were needed in the poverty-stricken parts of the world and that exceeded the capacity of individual nations and banks. Although many of his friends at the University of California had told him he was wrong, that no reasonable solutions to the economic inequality of the world were addressed at the World Bank, he had maintained his beliefs. At heart he was no less radical than they. He too marched in the antiwar demonstrations. But he had never believed in the potential of civil disobedience to change the world. Nor did he believe in the small and squabbling socialist organizations. He had come to the conclusion that the world had to be changed from within the existing social structures. If you were going to try to shift the balance of power, you had to stay close to its source.

But he had a secret. It was what had made him leave Columbia University and go to California. He had been in Vietnam for one year, and he had liked it.

He had been stationed close to An Khe most of the time, along the important route westward from Qui Nhon. He knew he had killed many soldiers during that year and that he had never felt remorse over this. While his buddies had turned to drugs for solace, he had maintained a disciplined approach to his work. He had known that he was going to survive the war; that he would not be among the bodies sent home in plastic sacks. And it was then, during the stifling nights patrolling the jungle, that he had arrived at his belief that you had to stay close to the source of power in order to affect it. Now, as he lay in the wet heat of the Angolan night, he sometimes experienced the feeling that he was back in the jungle. He knew he had been right.

He had understood fairly quickly that there was going to be an opening at the executive level in Angola, and he had immediately learnt Portuguese. His career climb had been meteoric. His bosses had seen his potential, although there were others with more experience who had applied for the same post. He had been appointed to a desirable position with little or no discussion.

That was his first contact with Africa, with a poor and shattered country. He didn't count his days in Vietnam. He had been an unwelcome intruder there. Here he was welcome. At first he spent his time listening, seeing, and learning. He had marveled at the joy and dignity that flourished among the hardships.

It had taken him almost two years to see that what the Bank was doing was completely wrong. Instead of helping the country to gain true independence and enable the rebuilding of the war-torn land, the Bank merely served to protect the very rich. He noted that the people around him treated him with deference because of his high rank. Behind the radical rhetoric there were only corruption, weakness, and greed. There were others—independent intellectuals and the odd politician—who saw what he saw. But they were not in positions of power. No one listened to them.

At last he could stand it no longer. He tried to explain to his superiors that the strategies of the Bank were misinformed. But he received no response, despite making transatlantic flights time and time again to persuade those at the top in the head office. He wrote countless memos but never received anything other than well-meaning indifference. At one of these meetings, he finally sensed he had become labeled as difficult. Someone who was beginning to fall outside the pale. One evening he spoke with his oldest mentor, a financial analyst named Whitfield who had followed his career since his undergraduate days and who had helped recruit him. They met for dinner at a small restaurant in Georgetown, and Carter had asked him straight out: Was he alienating everyone? Was there really no one who could see that he was right and that the Bank was wrong? Whitfield had answered just as candidly, and told him he was asking the wrong question. It didn't matter if Carter was right or not. What mattered was Bank policy.

The following evening, Carter had flown back to Luanda. A dramatic decision was taking shape in his head, as he leaned back into his comfortable first-class seat.

It took several sleepless nights for him to see what it was that he actually wanted.

It was also at this time that he met the man who would play a decisive role in convincing him that he was doing the right thing. In hindsight, Carter had often marveled at the mixture of conscious decisions and random coincidences that made up a person's life.

It had been an evening in March in the middle of the 1970s. He had been suffering a long period of sleeplessness as he searched for a way out of his dilemma. One evening he felt restless and decided to go to Metropol, one of the restaurants down in Luanda's harbor. He liked going there because there was little chance he would run into anyone from the Bank. Or any of Angola's elite, for that matter. At Metropol he was usually left in peace. At the next table, that night, had been a man who spoke very poor Portuguese, and since the waiter couldn't speak English, Carter had stepped in to translate.

Then the two of them had started talking. It turned out that the man was Swedish and was in Luanda on a consulting project commissioned by the state-owned telecom sector, which was grossly neglected and underdeveloped. Carter could never say afterward exactly what it was that sparked his interest in this man. He usually maintained an element of reserve in his interactions with others, assuming that most of the people he met were his enemies. But there had been something about this man that lowered his guard, even though Carter was a suspicious person by nature.

It had not taken long for Carter to understand that the man, who soon joined him at his own table, was highly intelligent. He was not merely an able engineer and technician, but someone who seemed to have read up on and understood much of Angola's colonial history and present political situation.

The man's name was Tynnes Falk. Carter had only learned this when it was late and they had said good-bye. They had been the last to leave the establishment. A lone waiter was slumped half-asleep at the bar. Their chauffeurs were waiting outside. Falk was staying at the Hotel Luanda. They decided to meet the following evening.

Falk had only intended to stay in Luanda for the three months that the project was expected to take, but after it was over, Carter offered him a new consulting project. It was mainly an excuse to retain him, so that they could continue their conversations.

Falk therefore returned to Luanda two months later. That was when he told Carter he was unmarried. Carter had likewise remained unmarried, though he had lived with a succession of women and fathered three girls and one boy, whom he almost never saw. In Luanda he now had two black lovers. One was a professor at the local university, the other the ex-wife of a cabinet minister. He kept these liaisons secret, except from his staff. He had avoided forming relationships within the Bank. Since Falk seemed very lonely, Carter helped him into a suitable relationship with a woman named Rosa, who was the daughter of a Portuguese businessman and his Angolan housekeeper.

Falk had started to feel at home in Africa. Carter got him a nice house with a garden and a view of Luanda's beautiful harbor. He also wrote a contract that rewarded Falk excessively for the minimal work he was expected to perform.

They continued their conversations. Whatever subject they discussed in those long tropical nights, they always found that their political and moral opinions coincided almost exactly. It was the first time Carter had met anyone whom he could confide in fully. Falk felt the same way.

It was during these long African nights that the plan began to take shape. Carter listened with fascination to the surprising things Falk told him about the electronic world where he lived and worked. Through Falk, he had come to understand that he who controlled electronic communication controlled everything. It was especially what Falk told him about how wars would be fought in the future that excited him. Bombs would be nothing more than computer viruses smuggled into the enemy's storehouse of weapons. Electronic signals could eliminate the enemy's stock markets and telecom networks. The time of nuclear submarines was over. Future threats would come barrelling down the miles of fiberoptic cables that were slowly entangling the world like a spiderweb.

They were in agreement about the need for patience, from the beginning. Never to rush. One day their time would come. And then they would strike.

They complemented each other. Carter had contacts. He knew how the Bank functioned. He understood the details of the financial world and how delicate the economic balance of the world really was. Falk was the technician who could translate ideas into practical reality.

They spent the evenings together for many months, refining their plans.

They had been in regular contact during the past twenty years. From the very beginning they had known the time was not quite at hand. One day it would be.

Carter was jerked out of his thoughts by a sudden noise and instinctively reached for the gun under his pillow. But it was only Celine, who was fumbling with the locks on the kitchen door. Irritated, he thought that he ought to fire her. She made too much noise getting his breakfast ready. The eggs were never cooked the way he liked them, and she was ugly, fat, and stupid besides. Celine could neither read nor write and had nine children. Her husband spent most of his time chatting in the shade of a tree. If he wasn't drunk.

Once, Carter had been convinced that these were the people who would create the new order. But he didn't believe it any longer. And then it was just as well to destroy the world, smashing it into bits.

The sun had already pulled itself up over the horizon. Carter thought again about what had happened. Tynnes Falk was dead. That which should never have happened, had happened. They had always been aware of the fact that something beyond their control might occur and interfere with their plans. They had included this in their calculations and had taken every precaution they could think of. But they had never been able to imagine that one of them might die. A meaningless and unplanned death. But this was what had happened. When Carter first got that call from Sweden, he had refused to believe it was true. But he had been forced to accept it at last. His friend Tynnes Falk no longer existed. It hurt him and changed all their plans. And it had happened at the worst possible time—right when they were about to strike. Now he was the only one left on the threshold of the great moment. But life always consisted of more than carefully laid plans and conscious decisions. There were always coincidences.

Their great operation already had a name in his head: *Jacob's Marsh*.

On one rare occasion, Falk had drunk a lot of wine and started talking about his childhood. He had grown up on an estate where his father was some kind of caretaker. There had been a marsh next to a particular strip of forest. It had been bordered by beautiful, chaotic wildflowers, according to Falk. He had played there many times as a child, watching the dragonflies and having the best times in his life. He had explained why it was called Jacob's Marsh. A long time ago a man named Jacob had drowned himself there due to unrequited love.

The marsh had acquired extra significance for Falk later in life, not least after his meeting with Carter and the realization that they shared some of their most fundamental understandings of life. The marsh became a symbol for the chaos of life, where the only way open in the end was to go and drown yourself. Or at the very least make sure everyone else did.

Jacob's Marsh. That was a good name. Not that the operation needed a name, but it was a way to honor Falk's memory. A gesture only Carter would be able to appreciate.

He stayed in bed a few more moments and thought about Falk. But when he realized he was starting to get sentimental he got up, took a shower, and went down to the dining room to eat his breakfast.

He spent the rest of the morning in his living room, listening to some Beethoven string quartets until he couldn't stand Celine's clatter in the kitchen any longer. Then he went to the beach and took a walk. His chauffeur and bodyguard, Alfredo, walked a short distance behind him. Whenever Carter went into Luanda and saw the social disintegration, garbage heaps, poverty, and misery he felt the action he was taking was justified.

He walked along the ocean and looked back at the decomposing city from time to time. Whatever rose from the ashes after the fire he was going to start would be better than this.

He was back at the house shortly before eleven. Celine had gone home. He drank a cup of coffee and a glass of water. Then he retired to his study on the second floor. It had a breathtaking view over the harbor, but he pulled the curtains shut. He liked the evenings best. He needed to keep the strong African sun away from his sensitive eyes. He sat down at the computer and went through his daily routine.

Somewhere deep inside that electronic world, an invisible clock was ticking. Falk had created it from Carter's instructions. It was Sunday, the twelfth of October, only eight days away from D-day.

He was done with his regular checks at a quarter past eleven.

He was about to turn off the computer when he froze. A small icon had just started flashing in the corner of the screen. The rhythm was two short flashes, then one long. He took out the manual that Falk had written for him and looked through it until he found the right page.

At first he thought there had to be a mistake. Then he realized it was all too true. Someone had just broken through the first layer of security into Falk's computer in Sweden. In that little town, Ystad, that Carter had only ever seen in postcards.

He stared at the screen, unable to believe his eyes. Falk had sworn that the system would be impossible to break into.

But still someone had done it.

Carter started sweating. He forced himself to remain calm. There were many layers to the security system in Falk's computer, and the innermost core of the program was buried under miles and miles of decoys and firewalls that no one could penetrate.

But someone was trying to get in.

Carter thought hard. He had immediately sent someone to Ystad after hearing of Falk's death. There had been several unfortunate incidents, but until now Carter had thought that everything was under control, especially since he had reacted so quickly and without hesitation.

He decided that everything was still under control, even though he couldn't deny that someone had broken through the first line of defense in Falk's computer and was possibly trying to go further. This needed to be taken care of as soon as possible.

Who could it be? Carter had trouble imagining that it was one of the policemen he had heard about through his informant, the ones who seemed to be sorting out the details surrounding Falk's death and the other events with what appeared to be complacency.

But who else could it be?

He found no answer and remained motionless in front of his computer as dusk fell over Luanda. When he finally got up from the desk he was still outwardly calm.

But a problem had arisen, and it was something that needed to be rectified.

He missed Falk more than ever.

He typed his message and sent it off into the electronic realm.

His answer came after about a minute.

Wallander was standing behind Martinsson. Robert Modin was sitting in front of the computer, where an ever-changing matrix of numbers was rushing by on the screen. Then the screen started to calm down. Only the occasional ones and zeroes flashed by. Then it became completely dark. Robert looked at Martinsson, who nodded. Robert continued to tap commands into the computer, and new hordes of numbers started flashing by. Then they stopped again. Both Martinsson and Wallander leaned over.

"I have no idea what this is," Robert said. "I've never seen anything like this."

"Could it be a computation of some kind?" Martinsson wondered.

Robert shook his head.

"I don't think so. It looks like a system of numbers awaiting a command."

It was Martinsson's turn to shake his head.

"Can you explain what you mean?" he asked.

"It can't be a calculation. There is no evidence of any equations here. The numbers only relate to themselves. I think it looks more like a code."

Wallander was unsatisfied. He wasn't sure what he had been expecting, but it was hardly a horde of meaningless numbers.

"Didn't people stop with codes after the Second World War?" he asked, but there was no answer from the other two.

They kept staring at the numbers.

"It's something to do with the number twenty," Robert said suddenly.

Martinsson leaned forward again, but Wallander's back was starting to hurt and he remained upright. Robert pointed and explained what he meant to Martinsson, who nodded and listened with interest. Wallander's thoughts started to drift.

"Could it be something to do with the year 2000?" Martinsson asked. "Isn't that when electronic chaos is supposed to break out and all computers are going to go haywire?"

"It's not 2000," Robert said stubbornly. "It's the number twenty. And no computers ever simply go haywire. It's people who do that."

"It will be the twentieth in eight days," Wallander said absently.

Modin and Martinsson kept bouncing ideas back and forth. They called up new numbers on the screen. Wallander was starting to get impatient, but he knew that what they were doing could be important.

The cell phone in his pocket rang. He walked over to the doorway and answered. It was Höglund.

"I may have found something," she said.

Wallander walked out into the little hallway.

"What is it?"

"You know how I told you I was going to root around in Lundberg's life?" she asked. "First I was going to talk to his sons. The oldest one's name is Carl-Einar Lundberg. Suddenly it hit me that I had seen that name before. I just couldn't remember where it was."

The name meant nothing to Wallander.

"I started combing through the computer registers."

"I thought only Martinsson could do that."

"Truth be told, I think soon you'll be the only one who *can't* do it."

"What did you find?"

"Something interesting. Carl-Einar Lundberg was tried for a crime a number of years ago. I think it was during that time that you were on sick leave."

"What did he do?"

"Well, apparently nothing, since he got off. But he was being tried for rape."

Wallander thought for a moment.

"It might be something," he said. "I guess it's worth looking into, though I have to admit I have trouble fitting it into either Falk's or Hökberg's death."

"All the same, I think I'll follow it through," Höglund said. "Like we agreed I would."

The conversation was over. Wallander went back to the others.

We're not getting anywhere, he thought in a sudden spasm of hopelessness. *We don't even know what we're looking for. We're totally lost.*

Chapter Twenty-two

Robert Modin stopped shortly after six o'clock. He was tired and complained of a headache.

But he wasn't giving up. He squinted up at Martinsson and Wallander through his glasses and said he was more than happy to keep going the following day.

"But I need some time to think," he said. "I need to come up with a plan of attack, and consult some of my friends."

Martinsson arranged for Modin to be driven back to Löderup.

"Do you think he meant what he said?" Wallander asked Martinsson when they had returned to the police station.

"That he needed time to think and plan his course of action?" Martinsson said. "That's what we do when we solve problems. Isn't that what we asked him to do?"

"He sounded like an old doctor who had a patient with unusual symptoms. He said he was going to consult with friends."

"That just means he's going to get in touch with other hackers. Maybe via the Internet. Comparing it to a doctor and an unusual case of illness is actually quite accurate."

Martinsson seemed to have gotten over the fact that they did not have official permission for working with Robert Modin. Wallander thought it was just as well not to go into that again.

Both Höglund and Hansson were in. Otherwise it was pleasantly empty at the station. Wallander thought in passing about the mountain of other work that was growing on his desk. Then he told the others to assemble for a quick meeting. Symbolically at least, they were at the end of a working week. What lay before them was as yet unclear.

"I talked to one of the canine units," Hansson said. "An officer called Norberg. He's actually in the process of getting a new dog, since Hercules is getting too old."

"Isn't that dog already dead?" Martinsson asked.

"Well, he's done for at any rate. He's blind, apparently."

Martinsson burst into tired laughter.

"That would be something to write about in the papers," he said. "The police and their blind search dogs."

Wallander was not amused. He would miss the old dog, perhaps even more than he would miss some of his colleagues when the time came.

"I've been thinking about this business of dog names," Hansson continued. "I guess I can understand calling a dog Hercules, but I still can't get my head around Steadfast."

"We don't have any police dogs by that name, do we?" Martinsson asked.

Wallander slammed his hands down on the table. It was the most authoritative gesture at his disposal.

"That's enough of that. Now, what did Norberg say?"

"That it was reasonable to assume that objects or bodies that were frozen or had been frozen could stop giving off a scent. Dogs can have trouble finding dead bodies in winter when it's very cold."

Wallander quickly proceeded to his next point.

"What about the van? Any news?"

"A Mercedes van was stolen in Ånge a couple of weeks ago."

Wallander had to think hard where that was.

"Where is Ånge?"

"Outside Luleå," Martinsson said.

"The hell it is," Hansson broke in. "It's closer to Sundsvall."

Höglund got up and went over to the map on the wall. Hansson was right.

"It could be the one," Hansson said. "Sweden isn't a big country."

"It doesn't sound right to me," Wallander said. "But there could be other stolen cars that haven't been reported yet. We'll have to keep an eye on incoming reports."

The discussion was turned over to Höglund.

"Lundberg has two sons who are as unlike each other as could be. Nils-Emil, the one who lives in Malmö, works as a janitor in a local school. I tried to get him over the phone. His wife said he was out training with his orienteering club. She was very talkative. Apparently Lundberg's death came as a hard blow to her husband, who is also a regular churchgoer. It's the younger brother who is of more interest to us. Carl-Einar was accused of rape in 1993. The girl's name was Englund. But he was never charged."

"I remember that case," Martinsson said. "It was a horrible incident."

Wallander's only memories from this time were of long walks on the beaches of Skagen in Denmark. Then a lawyer had been murdered and Wallander had returned to his duties, much to his own surprise.

"Were you in charge of that investigation?" Wallander asked.

Martinsson made a face.

"It was Svedberg."

The room fell silent as they thought about their dead colleague.

"I haven't made it through all the paperwork yet," Höglund continued after a while. "So I don't know why he wasn't found guilty."

"No one was ever found guilty of that crime," Martinsson said. "Whoever did it went scot-free. We could never find another suspect. I remember quite clearly that Svedberg was convinced it was Lundberg. I'd never thought about the fact that he was Johan Lundberg's son."

"Even if that's the case," Wallander said, "does that really account for the fact that his father was robbed and killed? Or that Sonja Hökberg was subsequently burned to death? Or that Tynnes Falk's fingers were cut off?"

"It was a brutal rape," Höglund said. "You have to at least imagine a perpetrator out there who was capable of horrendous violence. This girl Englund was in the hospital a long time with severe injuries both to her head and other parts of her body."

"Of course, we'll look at this more closely," Wallander said. "But I still don't think he'll turn out to have anything to do with this case. There's something else behind all of this, even if we don't yet know what that is."

Wallander went on to tell the group about the work that Robert Modin was undertaking with Falk's computer. Neither Hansson nor Höglund made any comments about an unauthorized expert who had served time for advanced computer crime being brought in.

"I don't really get this," Hansson said when Wallander finished. "What do you think is in that computer? A confession? An account of everything that's happened? A reason for all this?"

"I don't know if there's anything in there," Wallander said simply. "But we have to know what Falk was up to, just as we have to find out who he was. I have the impression that he was a strange man."

Hansson clearly doubted the value of spending so much time on Falk's computer, but he didn't say anything else. Wallander realized that the time had come to end the meeting. Everyone was tired and needed to rest.

"We have to continue in this same vein," he started, then interrupted himself and turned in Höglund's direction. "Whatever happened with Sonja Hökberg's bag?"

"I forgot about that," she said apologetically. "Her mother said she thought maybe an address book was missing."

"Maybe?"

"I think she was telling the truth. Sonja Hökberg was a very private person. Her mother simply thought she remembered Sonja having a little black address book where she wrote down people's phone numbers. In which case it was missing. But she couldn't be sure."

"If this is true, it's an important bit of information. Eva Persson should be able to confirm its existence."

Wallander thought for a while before continuing.

"I think we should reassign certain tasks," he said. "From now on I want Höglund to concentrate entirely on Sonja Hökberg and Eva Persson. There has to be a boyfriend out there somewhere, someone who could give her a ride out of town. Keep looking for any information that can tell us who she was and what she did. Martinsson will keep Robert Modin in a good mood. Someone else can check up on Lundberg's son—I can do that. And I'll keep checking into Falk's life. Hansson can be in charge of keeping things together. Keep Viktorsson informed of our activities, keep trying to locate potential witnesses, and keep trying to find possible explanations for how a body can disappear from a morgue. Last but not least, someone has to drive up to Växjö and speak with Eva Persson's father. Just so we can cross that off the list."

Wallander called the meeting to an end and they all stood up. Wallander got out as quickly as he could. It was already half past seven. Even though he had not had much to eat all day, he didn't feel hungry. He drove back to Mariagatan and looked around before unlocking the front door.

He spent the next hour cleaning up the apartment and gathering all his laundry. Now and again he stopped in front of the television set and looked at the news. One segment caught his eye. An American general was interviewed about what future wars would look like. He explained that they would be carried out on computers. The time of ground troops would soon be over, or at the very least their role would be much smaller in the future.

That made Wallander think of something, and since it was still early he looked around for the phone number and sat down at the phone.

Erik Hökberg picked up almost at once.

"How's the investigation going?" he asked. "We're not doing too well here. We really need to know what happened to Sonja."

"We're doing as much as we can."

"But are you getting anywhere? Who killed her?"

"We don't know that yet."

"I don't know how it can be so hard to find someone who murdered an innocent girl—in a substation, of all places."

Wallander didn't answer.

"I'm calling you because I need to ask you a question. Did Sonja know how to use a computer?"

"Of course she did. Don't all young people use computers nowadays?"

"Was she interested in computers?"

"She mainly surfed the web, I think. She was good at it, though I don't think she knew as much technical stuff as Emil."

Wallander couldn't think of anything else to ask. He felt somewhat helpless. Martinsson should have been the one asking these questions.

"You must have been thinking about what happened," he said. "You must be asking yourself why Sonja killed the taxi driver. And then why she in turn was killed."

Erik Hökberg's voice was close to breaking as he answered.

"I go into her room sometimes," he said. "I just sit in there and look around. I don't understand it."

"How would you describe Sonja?"

"She was strong-willed. Not always an easy person to deal with. She would have done well in life."

Wallander thought back to the room that had seemed frozen in time. The room of a little girl, not the person her stepfather seemed to be describing.

"Didn't she have a boyfriend?" Wallander asked.

"Not that I know of."

"Isn't that strange?"

"How so?"

"She was nineteen years old. And good-looking."

"She never brought anyone home."

"What about phone calls? Did anyone call her a lot?"

"She had her own line. She asked for it when she turned eighteen. Her phone often rang, but I don't know who was calling."

"Did she have an answering machine?"

"I've checked it. There were no calls."

"If anyone does call and leave a message, I'd like to get the tape."

Wallander suddenly thought of the movie poster he had seen in the closet in Sonja's room. It was the only object, apart from her clothes, that bore witness to the teenager who lived in the room, someone who was on her way to becoming an adult woman. He searched for the title in his mind. It was *The Devil's Advocate*.

"Inspector Höglund will soon be in touch with you," he said. "She will ask a number of questions, and if you are serious about wanting us to find Sonja's killer you'll have to answer in as much detail as much as possible."

"You don't think we've been helpful enough so far?" Erik Hökberg asked angrily. Wallander didn't blame him.

"No, on the contrary, I think you've being extremely helpful. I won't keep you any longer."

He hung up. The thought of the movie poster lingered in his mind. He looked at the time and saw it was nine-thirty. He dialed the number of the Stockholm restaurant where Linda worked. A distracted man with a heavy accent answered. He promised to get Linda. It took several minutes for her to come to the phone. When she heard who it was, she was furious.

"You know you can't call me here at this time! This is when we're the busiest. You'll get me in trouble."

"I know," Wallander said apologetically. "I just had a quick question."

"It had better be quick."

"It is. Have you seen a movie called *The Devil's Advocate* with Al Pacino?"

"Is that what this is all about? A movie?"

"That's it."

"I'm hanging up."

Now it was Wallander's turn to get angry.

"Can't you at least answer my question? Have you seen it?"

"Yes, I have," she hissed.

"What is it about?"

"Oh, my God! I don't believe this."

"It's about God?"

"In a way. It's about a lawyer who turns out to be the devil."

"Is that it?"

"Isn't that enough? Why do you need to know this, anyway? Are you having nightmares?"

"I'm in the middle of a murder investigation. Why would a nineteen-year-old girl have a poster of this movie on her wall?"

"Probably because she thinks Al Pacino is hot. Or else maybe she worships the devil. How the hell would I know?"

"Do you have to use that language?"

"Yes."

"Is there anything else to this movie?"

"Why don't you see it for yourself? I'm sure it's out on video."

Wallander felt like an idiot. He should have thought of this himself. He could have simply rented the movie without bothering Linda.

"I'm sorry I bothered you," he said.

Her anger had passed.

"It's okay. But I do have to go now."

"I know. Good-bye."

He put the receiver down and the phone rang immediately. He lifted it again with trepidation, fearing a journalist on the other end.

At first he didn't recognize the voice. Then he realized it was Siv Eriksson.

"I hope I'm not catching you in the middle of something," she said.

"Not at all."

"I've been thinking. I've been trying to find something that could help you."

Invite me over, Wallander thought. *If you really want to help me. I'm hungry and thirsty and I don't want to sit in this damned apartment any longer.*

"And did you think of anything in particular?"

"Not really. I guess his wife is probably the only one who really knew him. Or maybe his kids."

Wallander waited to see if she would say anything else.

"I have one memory of him that stands out as unusual. It isn't much. We only knew each other a few years."

"Tell me."

"It was two years ago, in October or the beginning of November. He came here one evening and was very upset. He couldn't hide it. We had a project due, I think it was something for the county. We had a deadline, but I saw that he was very upset and I asked him about it. He said he had just seen some teenagers accost an older man who had been a little drunk. When the man tried to brush them away, they hit him. He fell down and they kicked him as he was lying there on the sidewalk."

"Was that it?"

"Yes."

Wallander thought about it. Tynnes Falk had reacted strongly when a person was the victim of violence. It was interesting, but he couldn't immediately fit it into the case.

"Did he try to intervene in any way?"

"No. It just enraged him."

"What did he say?"

"That the world was chaos. That nothing was worth it anymore."

"What was it that wasn't worth it?"

"I don't know. I had a feeling he meant that mankind wasn't worth it any longer. That our animal nature was taking over, or something like that. When I tried to ask him about it he cut me off. We never talked about it again."

"How did you interpret his reaction?"

"I felt it was quite natural. Wouldn't you have felt that way?"

Maybe, Wallander thought. *But I wonder if I would have concluded that the world is in chaos.*

For some reason Wallander wanted to keep her on the line. But she was bound to see through him.

"I'm glad you called," he said. "Please call me again if you think of anything else. I'll probably call you myself tomorrow."

"I'm doing some programming for a restaurant chain. I'll be in the office all day."

"I'm curious. What will happen with your other projects now?"

"I don't know. I just hope I have enough of a reputation now to survive without Tynnes. If not, I'll have to think of something else."

"Like what?"

She laughed.

"Do you need this information for the case?"

"No, I was just asking."

"I might take off and see the world."

Everyone goes away, Wallander thought. *In the end it will just be me and all the misfits left.*

"I've had thoughts like that myself," he said. "But I'm locked in, like most people."

"I'm not locked in," she said cheerfully. "I'm my own woman."

After the conversation was over, Wallander thought about what she had said. *I'm my own woman.* She had a point. Just as Per Åkeson and Sten Widén had been right in their ways.

Suddenly he felt very pleased with himself for having sent in the ad to the dating service. Even though he wasn't expecting an answer, he had done something.

He put on his coat and went to the video store that was closest to his house, on Stora Östergatan. When he got there, it turned out the store closed at nine o'clock on Sundays. He continued up toward the main square, stopping from time to time to look in store windows.

Where the feeling came from he couldn't say, but suddenly he turned around. No one was there, apart from some teenagers and a security guard. He thought about what Höglund had said about being careful.

I'm imagining things, he thought. *No one is stupid enough to attack the same police officer twice in a row.*

Once he got to the main square, he turned down Hamngatan and then took Österleden home. The air was crisp. It felt good to be out.

He was back in his apartment at a quarter past ten. He found a solitary can of beer in the fridge and made some sandwiches. Then he sat down in front of the television and watched a discussion about the Swedish economy. The only thing he got out of the program was that the economy was both good and faltering. He nodded off and looked forward to finally getting an undisturbed night's sleep.

The case was going to have to get along without him for a few hours.

He turned out the light and went to bed at half-past eleven.

He had just fallen asleep when the phone rang.

He counted out nine rings before they finally stopped. Then he pulled the cord out of the jack and waited. Any of his colleagues would try his cell phone. He hoped that wouldn't happen.

The cell phone on his nightstand rang.

It was the patrol officer stationed outside Falk's apartment on Apelbergsgatan. His name was Elofsson.

"I don't know how important this is," he said. "But a car has been by here several times in the last hour."

"Did you see the driver?"

"That's why I'm calling, actually. You remember the orders you gave us."

Wallander waited impatiently.

"I think he looked Asian," Elofsson continued. "But I can't be totally sure."

Wallander didn't hesitate. The peaceful night he had been looking forward to was already ruined.

"I'll be there."

He hung up the phone and looked at the time.

It was one minute past midnight.

Chapter Twenty-three

Wallander turned off the Malmö highway.

Then he drove past Apelbergsgatan and parked his car on Jörgen Krabbes Way. It took him about five minutes to walk from there to the apartment building where Falk had lived. The wind was completely gone. There were no clouds in the sky and it was gradually getting chillier. October in Ystad was always a month that had trouble making up its mind.

The undercover car with Elofsson and his colleague inside was parked across the way and about half a block down from Falk's house. When Wallander reached the car, the back door was opened for him and he climbed in. There was a pleasant smell of coffee in the air. Wallander thought of all the nights he had spent in cars like this one, fighting the urge to sleep, fighting the cold.

They said hello and exchanged some casual remarks. Elofsson's colleague had only been in Ystad for about six months. His name was El Sayed and he had come originally from Tunisia. He was the first policeman with an immigrant background who had ever worked in Ystad. Wallander had been worried that El Sayed would be greeted with hostility and prejudice. He had no illusions about what his colleagues thought of getting a non-white recruit. His fears had been justified, as it turned out. El Sayed had to deal with his share of crude jokes and mean-spirited comments. How much of it he noticed and what he had been expecting, Wallander was still not sure. Sometimes he felt bad that he had never taken the time to invite El Sayed over for a meal. No one else had done so, either. But after a while the young man and his easygoing personality had grown on them, and he was slowly becoming part of the group.

"He came from a northerly direction," Elofsson said. "From Malmö in toward Ystad. At least three times."

"When was he here last?"

"Just before I called you. I tried your regular phone first. You must be a deep sleeper."

Wallander ignored his last comment.

"Tell me in detail what happened."

"You know how it is. It's only when they come by the second time that you really notice them."

"What kind of a car was it?"

"A navy blue Mazda sedan."

"Did he slow down when he passed by?"

"I don't know if he did the first time around, but definitely the second."

El Sayed broke in for the first time.

"He slowed down already that first time."

The comment clearly irritated Elofsson. Probably because he didn't want his colleague showing him up.

"But he never stopped?"

"No."

"Did he see you?"

"Not the first time. But probably on his second time around."

"What happened after that?"

"He came back a third time after about twenty minutes, but he didn't slow down."

"He was probably just checking that you were still here. Could you see if there was more than one person in the car?"

"We talked about that. We have no way of knowing for sure, but we think it was just one person."

"Did you check in with your colleagues at Runnerström Square?"

"They haven't seen it."

Wallander found that puzzling. If someone was keeping a check on Falk's apartment, he should also be interested in his office.

He thought about it. The only explanation he could find was that, whoever the person in the car was, he didn't know about the existence of the office. That is, if the officers on duty there hadn't been sleeping. Wallander didn't want to rule out that possibility at this point.

Elofsson turned around and gave Wallander a note with the license-plate number written on it.

"I take it you've already had this number checked out?"

"We tried, but the computer system was down."

Wallander held the note up so he could read it with the help of the streetlight. MLR 331. He memorized the number.

"When did they think they could access the registers again?"

"They couldn't say. Maybe by tomorrow morning."

Wallander shook his head.

"We need to know this as soon as possible. When do your shifts end?"

"At six o'clock."

"Before you head home I want you to write up a report on this and give it to Hansson or Martinsson. Then they'll take care of it."

"What do we do if he comes back?"

"He won't," Wallander said. "Not as long as he knows you're here."

"Should we intervene in any way in the unlikely event that he comes back?"

"No. He hasn't committed a crime. But call me. Use my cell-phone number."

He wished them luck, then walked back to Jörgen Krabbes Way. He drove down to Runnerström Square. Things there were not quite as bad as he imagined. Only one of the officers was asleep. They hadn't seen any navy blue Mazdas.

"Keep a close watch," Wallander said, giving them the license-plate number.

On his way back to his car he remembered he still had Setterkvist's keys in his pocket. Without really knowing why, he entered the building and walked all the way up to the top floor. Before unlocking the door he pressed his ear to it and listened. He walked in and turned on the light, looking around the room in the same way that he had the first time he was there. Was there anything he hadn't noticed that time? Something that both he and Nyberg had overlooked? He found nothing. He sat down at the computer and stared at the dark screen.

Robert Modin had talked about the number 20. Wallander had sensed intuitively that the boy was onto something. In the stream of numbers that were a nonsensical jumble to Martinsson and himself, Robert Modin had been able to see a pattern. The only thing Wallander could think of was that the 20th of October was approaching, and that the number 20 was the first part of the year 2000. But the question essentially remained unsolved. What did it mean? And did it mean anything for the investigation?

Suddenly the phone rang.

Wallander jumped. The sound rang out eerily in the room. He stared at the black phone and finally lifted the receiver on the seventh ring.

He heard static, as if it were a long distance call, and he strained to hear something on the other end. There was someone there.

Wallander said hello once, then a second time. The only thing he heard was the sound of breathing somewhere deep inside the buzz of static.

Then there was a clicking sound and the connection was lost. Wallander hung up. His heart was racing. He had heard that sound before, when he had listened to Falk's messages.

There was someone there, he thought. *Someone calling to talk to Falk. But Falk is gone. He's dead.*

Suddenly he thought of another possibility. Someone could be calling to talk to him. Had anyone seen him enter the building and walk up to Falk's apartment?

He remembered how he had stopped and turned around on the sidewalk earlier in the evening. As if he was expecting there to be someone behind him, observing him.

His anxiety returned. Up until now, he had been able to repress the knowledge that only a few days ago someone had tried to kill him. Höglund's words came back to him: he should take care.

He got up from the chair and walked over to the door. But he didn't hear anything.

He walked back to the desk. Without thinking about it, he lifted the keyboard.

There was a postcard lying underneath it.

He directed the lamp over it and put on his glasses. The card was old and the color had started to fade. It was a picture of a tropical bay. There were palm trees, a pier, small fishing boats in the water. Behind the shoreline, a row of tall buildings. He turned the card over and saw it was addressed to Tynnes Falk at his Apelbergsgatan address. So much for Siv Eriksson receiving all his mail. Had she lied to him, or did she not know about this other mail? There was no message on the card, just the letter "C." Wallander studied the postmark. The stamp was almost completely torn off, but he thought he could discern the letters *l* and *d.* That probably meant the other letters were vowels. But he couldn't tell what they were, nor could he read the date. There was nothing printed on the postcard to say where the picture had been taken. Wallander thought back to an unhappy and chaotic trip he had once taken to the West Indies. The palm trees were the same, but the city in this picture was foreign to him.

He studied the "C" again. That was the same as the C in Falk's diary. It must be a name. Falk had known who it was and had saved the postcard. In this bare room that contained nothing beyond the computer and a blueprint of a power substation, there had been this post-card. Wallander tucked the card into his breast pocket. Then he lifted the computer monitor to see if there was anything under that, but there was nothing. He lifted the phone. Nothing.

He looked around for another minute but finally turned out the light and left.

He was exhausted when he finally returned to Mariagatan. But before going to bed, he couldn't resist getting out the magnifying glass and studying the postcard again. But it didn't tell him anything more.

He went to bed shortly before two o'clock.

He fell asleep at once.

On Monday morning, Wallander made only a short stop at the station. He handed the apartment keys over to Martinsson and asked him about the car that had been seen the night before. Martinsson already had the report on his desk. Wallander didn't say anything about the postcard. Not that he wanted to keep it to himself, but because he was in a hurry. He didn't want to get bogged down in a long discussion. Before leaving the station he made two calls. One was to Siv Eriksson. He asked her about the number 20 and the letter C. She couldn't think of anything offhand but told him she would be in touch if anything came to her. He told her about the postcard he had found in Falk's office. Her exclamation of surprise was so strong that he didn't doubt it was genuine.

Wallander told her what the postcard depicted. But she couldn't shed light on where it came from.

"Maybe he had even more addresses," she said.

Wallander sensed a note of disappointment in her voice, as if Falk had betrayed her.

"We'll look into it," he said. "You could be right about him having more houses."

When the conversation was over, Wallander realized that the sound of her voice had cheered him up. He didn't let himself dwell on it. He picked up the phone and made the next call, which was to Marianne Falk. He told her he was coming over in half an hour.

For the next few hours, Wallander sat in Marianne Falk's living room and talked to her about the man she had been married to. He started at the beginning. When had they met? How had he been back then? Marianne Falk turned out to have an excellent memory. She rarely faltered or had to gather her thoughts. Wallander had brought his notebook, but he didn't make any notes. He wasn't planning to research what she told him; he was simply trying to get a better understanding of the man Falk had been.

According to Marianne, Falk had grown up on a farm outside Linköping. He was an only child. After graduating from high school he had done his military service and started studying in Uppsala. He hadn't been able to decide on anything and had taken courses in everything from law to literature. But after a year he had moved to Stockholm and started studying at the business school.

That was when they had met. It had been 1972. She had been training to be a nurse during those years and had gone to a big party held by a student organization.

"Tynnes didn't dance," she said. "But he was there. Somehow or other we were introduced. I remember thinking that he seemed boring. It certainly wasn't love at first sight, at least not from my side. He called a few days after that. I don't know how he got my number. He wanted to see me again, but not for the usual walk or movie. What he suggested surprised me."

"And what was that?"

"He wanted us to go out to Bromma and watch the airplanes taking off."

"Did he say why?"

"He liked airplanes. We went out there, and he could tell me everything about the planes that were parked there. I thought he was a little strange. He certainly wasn't how I had imagined the man in my life."

Tynnes had been very persistent, according to Marianne, although she had had her doubts.

"He wasn't pushy physically," she said. "I think it probably took him about three months even to think of kissing me. If he hadn't done so by that point, I would probably have tired of the whole thing. He probably sensed that and that's why he finally kissed me. He was very shy. Or at least he pretended to be."

"What do you mean by that?"

"Tynnes was very self-confident when it came down to it. He had a reserved manner, but I think he actually looked down on most of the rest of humanity, even if he often claimed the opposite."

A turning point in the relationship had come on a day in April or May about six months after they had met. They'd had no plans to meet that day, because Tynnes had said he had an important lecture at school to attend and she was running some errands for her mother.

On her way to the train station, she was forced to stop on the side of the road because a mass of demonstrators were walking by. It was a demonstration to raise awareness of Third World issues. The signs and banners had various messages about the World Bank and Portuguese colonial oppression. Marianne had come from a stable home with solid Social Democratic values. She had not been caught up by the swelling wave of left-wing radicals, nor had she ever detected such an interest in Tynnes, even though he always seemed to have the answer whenever they discussed political issues and he clearly liked showing off his political knowledge and sophisticated understanding of political theory. When she caught sight of him among the demonstrators that day, she couldn't believe her eyes. She had unconsciously taken a few steps back as he passed her on the street and he never saw her there.

Afterward she had asked him about it. When he realized that she had seen him in the demonstration, he became furious. It was the first time she witnessed his temper. But then he had calmed down. She never understood why it had affected him so strongly, but from that day she had known that there was a lot more to Tynnes than met the eye.

"I broke up with him that June," she said. "Not because I had met anyone else. I just didn't believe we were going anywhere. And his angry reaction about the demonstration had played a part in that."

"How did he take it?"

"I don't know."

"What do you mean?"

"We met at an outdoor café in Kungsträdgården. I told him straight out that I wanted to end the relationship and that I didn't think we had a future. He listened to what I had to say and then he just got up and left."

"And that was the end?"

"He didn't say a single word. I remember that his face was a complete blank. When I had finished talking, he left. Though he left some money on the table for our coffees."

"What happened after that?"

"I didn't see him again for several years."

"How long exactly?"

"Four years, I think."

"What did he do during that time?"

"I don't know for sure."

Wallander looked at her with curiosity.

"Do you mean to say that he was gone without a trace during those four years?"

"I know it seems hard to believe, but about a week after our date in Kungsträdgården I decided I needed to talk to him again. That's when I discovered that he had moved out of his student room without leaving a forwarding address. After a few weeks I managed to get in touch with his parents in Linköping, but they had no idea where he had gone, either. For four years he was gone, and I had no idea where he was. He had withdrawn from the business school. No one knew anything. And then he turned up again."

"When was that?"

"That I remember exactly. It was the 2nd of August, 1977. I had just accepted my first nursing position at Sabbatsberg Hospital. And there he was, waiting outside the hospital for me, carrying a big bouquet of flowers. He was smiling. I had gone through a failed relationship during those four years. When I saw him waiting there, it cheered me up. I think I was feeling pretty lost and lonely. My mother had just died."

"You started seeing each other again?"

"He thought we should get married. He asked me just a few days later."

"But he must have told you what he had been doing the past few years?"

"Actually, he didn't say a word about that. He said he wouldn't ask me about my life if I wouldn't ask him about his. He wanted us to pretend the past four years had never happened."

Wallander looked closely at her.

"Did he look different at all?"

"No. Not apart from having a tan."

"He was tanned? You mean from the sun?"

"Yes. But that was the only thing. It was only by accident that I ever found out where it was that he had been all that time."

At that moment Wallander's cell phone rang. He hesitated, but decided to answer. It was Hansson.

"Martinsson gave me the task of identifying the car that was seen last night," he said. "The computer registers keep crashing, but now I've finally been able to determine that it's a stolen car."

"The car, or just the license plate?"

"The plates. They were taken from a Volvo that was parked down by the Nobel Square in Malmö last week."

"Good," Wallander said. "Then Elofsson and El Sayed were right. That car was keeping an eye on things."

"I'm not really sure how to proceed with this now."

"Talk to the Malmö police about the Volvo. And send out a nationwide alert for the Mazda."

"What crime do we suspect the driver of?"

Wallander paused.

"We suspect he has something to do with Sonja Hökberg's murder. He may also have been the one who fired that shot at me."

"He was the one who shot at you?"

"Or been a witness," Wallander answered.

"Where are you right now?"

"I'm with Marianne Falk. I'll call you later."

She was serving him coffee from a beautiful blue-and-white coffee-pot. Wallander thought he remembered seeing similar china in his parents' home as a child.

"Why don't you tell me about that 'by accident' part," he said when she sat down again.

"It was about a month after Tynnes had turned up again in my life. He had bought a car, and he often came by to pick me up. One of the doctors I worked with at the hospital saw him come by one day. The following day he asked me if the man he had seen was Tynnes Falk. When I said yes, he told me he had met him the year before. But not in Sweden. In Africa."

"Where in Africa?"

"In Angola. The doctor had been there doing volunteer work, just after Angola had gained independence. One day he bumped into another Swede. They met in a restaurant late at night. Tynnes took out his Swedish passport to take out the money he kept in it, and when the doctor saw that, he said hello. They only spoke briefly, but the doctor remembered him. Not least because he thought Tynnes seemed so unfriendly to a fellow Swede, as if he didn't want to be recognized."

"You must have asked him what he was doing there?"

"You would think so, but I never did. I meant to, but I guess it came down to the promise we had made to each other not to ask. Instead I tried to find out what he had done through other channels."

"What other channels?"

"I called various relief organizations that had chapters in Africa. No one had any record of him. It was only when I called the Swedish Relief Agency that I got something. They said Tynnes had been in Angola for two months to help with the installation of various radio towers."

"But he was gone for four years," Wallander said. "Not just two months."

She didn't reply, perhaps lost in thought. Wallander waited.

"We married and had children," she said finally. "Apart from that meeting in Angola, I had no idea what he had done those four years.

And I never asked. It's only now that he's dead and we're divorced that I'm finally starting to find out."

She got up and left the room. When she returned she had a package in her hand. It was something wrapped in a torn plastic cloth. She lay it on the coffee table in front of Wallander.

"After he died, I went down into the basement. I knew he had a steel trunk down there. It was locked but I broke the lock. Apart from this there was nothing but dust."

She nodded for him to open the package. Wallander flicked the plastic cloth aside. Inside was a brown leather photo album. Someone had written ANGOLA 1973-1977 on the front cover in permanent ink.

Wallander hadn't even opened it when a thought came to him.

"My education isn't what it should be," he said. "What's the capital of Angola?"

"Luanda."

Wallander nodded. He still had the postcard in his breast pocket that had the letters "l" and "d" on it.

The postcard must have been sent from Luanda. What was it that had happened there?

And who was the man or woman whose name started with C?

He leaned forward and opened the album.

Chapter Twenty-four

The first picture was of a burned-out bus. It was lying by the side of the road, which was red, perhaps from sand or blood. The photograph had been taken from a distance. The bus looked like the body of a dead animal. A note under the picture said NORTHEAST OF HUAMBO, 1975. There was a small stain below that, similar to the one on the postcard. Wallander turned the page. A group of African women were gathered around a small water hole. The landscape looked parched. There were no shadows on the ground; the picture must have been taken at midday. None of the women was looking into the camera. The water level in the hole was low.

Wallander studied the picture carefully. Tynnes Falk, assuming he was the photographer, had chosen to capture these women on film. But it was the dried-up water hole that was the real focus of the photo. That was the story the photographer was telling, not the lives of the women. Wallander kept turning the pages. Marianne Falk sat quietly on the other side of the room. A clock ticked somewhere in the room.

Wallander kept leafing through the shots of villages, war sites, and radio towers until he came to a group photograph. In the picture were nine men, one boy, and a goat. The goat seemed to have entered the picture at random, from the right. One of the men had been trying to wave it away when the picture was taken. The boy had stared straight into the camera, laughing. Seven of the men were black, two were white. The black men looked cheerful; the white men had serious expressions on their faces. Wallander looked up from the page and asked Marianne Falk if she knew the names of any of the men. She shook her head. The place name scribbled under the picture was illegible, but it had a date: JANUARY 1976. Falk had been done with his radio towers for a long time at this point. Was he on a return trip to make sure the work had been done correctly? Was he returning at all, or had he simply stayed on in Angola after the job was done?

Wallander continued to page through the album until Marianne Falk leaned over and pointed out a picture to him. It was taken at something that looked like a party, with a small group of men in the foreground. There were only white people in the photo, their eyes red from the flash, like those of nocturnal animals. There were bottles and glasses on a table. Marianne was pointing to one man in particular with a glass in his hand. It was Falk. The young men around him were cheering and toasting each other. But Falk had his mouth shut and looked serious. He looked thin in the picture, dressed in a white shirt buttoned all the way to his throat. The other men were half-naked, flushed and sweaty. Wallander asked her again if she recognized any of them, but she shook her head.

Wallander stopped at another picture a few pages on. It was outside what looked like a whitewashed church. Tynnes Falk was standing against the wall, looking at the photographer. He was smiling for the first time in the album, and his shirt was not buttoned to the throat. Who was taking the picture? Was it "C"?

Next page. Falk was taking the pictures again. Wallander leaned in more closely to the next photo. For the first time he recognized a face from an earlier picture. It was a fairly close shot. The man was tall, thin, and tanned. His gaze was very determined, his hair shortly cropped. He looked like a Northern European, maybe German or even Russian. Wallander switched to examining the background. The picture was taken outside. There seemed to be a skyline of hills covered in thick green vegetation. But slightly closer than that, between the hills and the man, was something that looked like a large machine. Wallander thought the construction looked familiar, but it was only when he held the picture away from himself that he realized what it was. A power substation.

Here is a connection, he thought. *Though I have no idea what to make of it. Falk has taken a picture of a man outside a power substation, not unlike the one where Sonja Hökberg was found dead.* Wallander kept turning the pages in the hopes of finding more clues, but there was nothing of interest. There were several pages of animal pictures, clearly taken on tourist safaris in other parts of Africa.

But in the last picture, he was back in familiar territory. LUANDA, JUNE 1976. There was the thin man again with his cropped hair. He was sitting on a bench overlooking the ocean. For once Falk had managed to compose a pleasing arrangement. It was a good picture. Then the album ended. There were several empty pages remaining, but it didn't look as if anything had been taken out. The album just stopped there, with the picture of the man staring out over the sea. In the background Wallander saw the same city as in the postcard.

Wallander leaned back in his chair. Marianne Falk gave him a searching look.

"I don't know what these pictures tell us, but I'd like to borrow the album for a while," he said. "We may need to make some enlargements of individual shots."

She followed him out into the hall.

"Why do you think what he did back then was so important? It was such a long time ago."

"Something happened out there," Wallander said. "I don't know what. But I think it's something that followed him for the rest of his life."

He put on his coat and shook her hand.

"If you like, we can send a receipt for the loan of the album."

"That won't be necessary."

Wallander opened the door.

"There's one more thing," she said.

Wallander looked at her and waited. She looked suddenly unsure of herself.

"Maybe policemen only want facts," she said slowly. "The thing I've been thinking about is still very unclear even to me."

"Right now anything may be of help."

"I lived with Tynnes for a long time," she said. "And I thought I knew him. What he did during those years he was gone, I don't know. But I always knew there was something else in his life. Since he was so good-natured and treated me and the children so well, I never bothered pursuing it."

She stopped abruptly. Wallander waited.

"Sometimes I had the feeling I had married a fanatic, a person with two lives."

"A fanatic?"

"Sometimes he had such strange ideas about things."

"About what, for example?"

"About life. About people. About the world. About almost anything. He could suddenly come out with the most violent accusations, not directed at any individual, as if he were sending messages into space almost."

"He never explained himself?"

"It scared me. I didn't dare ask him about it. He would become so filled with hate. And besides, his rages would leave him as quickly as they had come. I always had the feeling they were something he wanted to hide, something that embarrassed him."

Wallander thought carefully.

"Do you maintain that he never got involved politically?"

"He despised politicians. I don't even think he used to vote."

"And, as far as you know, he had no ties to any political organizations?"

"No."

Wallander had nothing else to ask.

"If you think of anything else, let us know."

She promised to do so. The door closed behind him.

Wallander got in his car and placed the photo album on the passenger seat. He wondered about the man in the picture, the one in front of the power substation. The one Falk had met in a faraway land some twenty years ago.

Was he the one who had sent the postcard, the one who called himself "C"?

Wallander shook his head. He didn't understand it.

Suddenly he felt cold. It was a chilly day. He turned up the heat and drove back to the station. As he pulled into the parking lot, the phone rang. It was Martinsson.

"Trying to crack this code is like scaling a wall," he complained. "Modin is doing his best to get over it, but I couldn't tell you what he's actually up to."

"We just have to be patient."

"I take it we pay for his lunch?"

"Keep the receipt," Wallander said. "Give it to me later."

"I'm also wondering if now would be a good time to get in touch with the National Police computer experts. There's not really any reason to put it off, is there?"

Martinsson is right, Wallander thought. But he wanted to give Modin a little more time.

"We'll get in touch with them in due course," he said. "But let's just hold off for now."

Wallander walked into the police station. Irene told him that Gertrud had called. Wallander went into his office and called her back. Sometimes he drove out there on the weekend to visit, but it didn't happen very often. He felt guilty about it. Gertrud, after all, was the one who had taken pity on his father in those last few difficult years. Without her, he would never have made it as long as he had. But now that his father was gone, they didn't really have anything to talk about.

Gertrud's sister answered the phone. She was talkative and had strong opinions on most subjects. Wallander tried to get right to the point. She went to get Gertrud. It took a long time.

When Gertrud finally picked up, it turned out that nothing was wrong. There was no reason for Wallander to have been worried.

"I just wanted to see how you were doing," she said.

"I'm busy, but otherwise I'm doing fine."

"It's been a while since you were here."

"I know. I'll come by as soon as I have more time."

"One day it may be too late," she said. "At my age you never know how much more time you have."

Gertrud was just a little over sixty. A little too young for this brand of emotional blackmail. She was taking after his father in this respect.

"I'll be there," he said in a friendly tone. "Just as soon as I have more time."

Then he excused himself and said that people were waiting to talk to him. But when the conversation was over, he went out to the lunchroom to get some coffee. He bumped into Nyberg, who was drinking an unusual kind of herbal tea that was hard to find. For once he seemed well rested. He had even combed his hair, which normally stood on end.

"We have no fingerprints," Nyberg said. "The dogs have searched everywhere. But we did do a check on the ones we found in his apartment—that is, the ones we're assuming belong to Falk. They don't turn up anywhere in our registers."

"Then send them on to Interpol. By the way, do you know if that covers Angola?"

"How would I know that?"

"I was just wondering."

Nyberg left. Wallander stole a couple of rusks from Martinsson's private stash and returned to his room. It was already twelve o'clock. The morning had gone by quickly. The photo album lay in front of him, and he was momentarily unsure of how to proceed. He knew more about Falk now than he had a couple of hours ago, but nothing that could satisfactorily clarify a connection to Sonja Hökberg.

He pulled the phone toward him and called Höglund. No answer. Hansson wasn't in his office, either. Martinsson was of course still busy with Robert Modin.

Wallander tried to think of what Rydberg would have done. This time it was easier to imagine his voice. Rydberg would have taken time to think. That was the most important thing a policeman could do besides gathering facts. Wallander put his feet up on the desk and shut his eyes. He went through all the points of the case in his head once more, trying all the time to keep looking back toward the events that had taken place in Angola twenty years ago. He tried various scenarios and thought them through. Lundberg's death. Then Sonja Hökberg's. The large power outage.

When he opened his eyes it was with the feeling of being very close to the explanation. But he couldn't grasp it.

He was interrupted by the phone. Siv Eriksson was waiting for him in the reception area. He jumped up from his chair, ran his fingers through his hair, and went out to see her. She really was an extremely attractive woman. He asked her if she wanted to come back to his office, but she had no time. She handed him an envelope.

"Here is the list of clients you asked for."

"I hope it wasn't too much trouble."

"It took a little time, but it was no trouble."

She declined his offer of a cup of coffee.

"Tynnes left some loose threads behind," she said. "I have to attend to them."

"But you can't be sure he didn't have any other projects underway as well?"

"I don't think so. Just lately he was saying no to most new prospective clients. I know that because he asked me to deal with most of them."

"What did you make of that at the time?"

"I thought he needed time to rest."

"Had that ever happened before? That he turned down so many new jobs?"

"Now that you mention it, I think this was probably the only time."

"But he offered you no explanation?"

"No."

Wallander had no more questions. Siv Eriksson walked out the front doors to a taxi that was waiting for her. When the driver got out to open the door for her, Wallander noticed that he was wearing a black band of mourning around his arm.

He walked back to his office and opened the envelope she had given him. Inside was a long list of names of companies. Most were unknown to him—he recognized a couple of banks—but all, with one exception, were in Scania. The exception was a company in Denmark. It seemed to Wallander that the business involved the manufacture of loading cranes. Neither Sydkraft nor any utility companies were on the list, however.

After a few moments, Wallander called the Ystad branch of the North Bank. He had taken out several car loans with them on the few occasions when he had traded in his old cars for new models. He had gotten to know a man there named Winberg. He asked to speak with him, but when the telephone receptionist said his line was busy he decided to try again later. He left the station and went down to the bank in person. Winberg was busy with a client. He nodded at Wallander, who sat down and waited.

After five minutes Winberg was free.

"I've been expecting you," Winberg said. "Is it time for a new car?"

Wallander was always surprised by the fact that the bank employees were so young. The first time he had applied for a loan here Winberg had personally approved it even though he didn't look old enough to have a driver's license.

"I've come about something else, actually. Something work-related. The new car will have to wait."

Winberg's smile waned. He looked suddenly worried.

"Has anything happened here at the bank?"

"In that case I would have spoken to your boss. What I actually need is information about your automatic teller machines."

"I'm glad to be of assistance, though there's some information I can't disclose for security purposes."

Winberg was sounding as bureaucratic as Wallander sometimes did.

"The information I'm after is of a technical nature. The first thing is very simple. How often does a machine make a mistake on a withdrawal or with an account balance?"

"Very rarely, I think, though I have no exact figures to give you."

"Do I take it your phrase 'very rarely' means it almost never happens?"

Winberg nodded.

"And is there any chance that the date and time on a printed slip would be incorrect?"

"I've never heard of it. I imagine it must happen on occasion, but it certainly can't be very often. Security at financial institutions has to be very high."

"So one can usually rely on information from these machines?"

"Have you had an experience to the contrary?"

"No, but I need answers to these questions."

Winberg opened a drawer in his desk and looked for something. Then he pulled out a comic strip that showed a man being slowly being swallowed up by an ATM.

"It never gets quite this bad," he said smiling. "But it's a funny image. And when it comes down to it the bank computers are of course as vulnerable as all other computerized systems."

There it is again, Wallander said. *This talk of vulnerability.* He looked at the sketch and agreed it was good.

"North Bank has a client by the name of Tynnes Falk," Wallander said. "I need printouts of his activities for the past year. That includes his cash machine withdrawals."

"In that case you'll have to speak to someone higher up," Winberg said. "I'm not in charge of matters involving client privacy."

"Who should I speak to?"

"Martin Olsson is probably the best one. He's in an office on the second floor."

"Can you see if he's available?"

Winberg left his desk. Wallander feared a drawn-out bureaucratic process to get access to Olsson, but Winberg escorted him directly to the bank manager. Olsson was also surprisingly young. He promised to help Wallander. He said all he needed was an official police request. Once he found out that the request involved a deceased client, he said the widow could sign in his stead.

"He was divorced," Wallander said.

"A paper from the police is all we need then," Martin Olsson said. "I promise to see to it that this is taken care of quickly on our end."

Wallander thanked him and returned to Winberg. He had one more question.

"Can you check in your files to see if Falk kept a security box here?"

"I don't know if that's allowed," Winberg said doubtfully.

"Your boss has already cleared it," Wallander lied.

Winberg disappeared for a few minutes.

"There's no such box registered in his name," he said when he returned.

Wallander got up to leave, when it suddenly occurred to him he might as well take care of all his business at once.

"Let's do the paperwork for the new car while we're at it," he said. "You're right about it being time for me to get a new car."

"How much do you want?"

Wallander thought quickly. He had no other debt right now.

"One hundred thousand should do it. If I qualify for that much."

"No problem," Winberg said and reached for the right form.

They were done at half past one. Wallander left the bank with the feeling of being rich. When he walked past the bookstore by the main square, he remembered the book on refinishing furniture that he should have picked up a couple of days ago. He also remembered he had no cash on him. He turned around and walked to the cash machine next to the post office. There were four people ahead of him in line: a woman with a baby carriage, two teenage girls, and an older man. Wallander watched absently as the woman put in her card, then took out the cash and the printed slip. Then he started thinking about Tynnes Falk. The two girls took out a hundred crowns, then discussed the amount printed on the slip with great energy. The older man looked around before putting in his card and punching in his secret code. He took out five hundred crowns and put the printed slip in his pocket without looking at it.

Then it was Wallander's turn. He took out one thousand crowns and read through the account balance on the slip. Everything seemed to be in order. He crumpled up the piece of paper and tossed it into the garbage bin. Then he froze. He thought about the blackout that had cut power to most of Scania. Someone had known exactly which point to hit to affect as many areas as possible. However advanced technology became, there were always these occasional points of vulnerability. He thought about the blueprint they had found in Falk's office. It could not have been coincidence. Just as it had not been a coincidence that the electrical relay was found in the morgue.

Suddenly he was struck by what he had seen before but not fully absorbed: the realization that none of what had happened had been coincidence.

Perhaps it was a kind of sacrifice, he thought. There was an altar in Tynnes Falk's secret chamber, with Falk's face as a divine being. Perhaps Sonja Hökberg wasn't simply killed but also sacrificed. So that the point of vulnerability would become more visible. A black hood had been pulled down over Scania and everything had been brought to a halt.

The thought made him shiver. The feeling that he and his colleagues were fumbling around in the dark grew stronger.

He watched the stream of people who came up to the cash machine. *If you can control the power supply you can control this machine*, he thought. *And God only knows what else you control. Air traffic, trains, the water supply, and electricity. All of this can be brought to its knees if you know the right place to strike.*

He started walking again. Linda's book would have to wait. He returned to the station. Irene wanted to tell him something but he waved her away and continued to his office. He threw his coat down on a chair and pulled his pad of paper toward him. He wrote out the facts again, this time from the perspective that all that had happened was part of a well-planned act of sabotage. He thought back to the perplexing fact that Falk had been involved in the release of those minks.

Did that act foreshadow something even bigger? Was it a prelude to something much more sinister?

When he threw the pen down and leaned back in his chair he still was not convinced he had found the point that would truly break the case open, but it did offer new possibilities. Unfortunately Lundberg's murder fell outside these parameters, but was that perhaps an unforeseen development, something that had not been planned out in advance? It had to be the case that Sonja Hökberg was killed in order to keep her quiet. And why cut off Falk's fingers? To keep something from coming to light.

He kept working through his material. What happened if they assumed Lundberg was an accident, something that wasn't part of the larger pattern?

But after only half an hour he was less convinced of this idea. It was too early. The case still didn't hang together.

He cheered himself up with the thought that at least he had come a bit further along. He had realized there were probably more explanations and angles from which to view these events.

He had just gotten up to go to the bathroom when Höglund knocked on the door.

She got right to the point.

"You were right," she said. "Sonja did have a boyfriend."

"What's his name?"

"A more pertinent question would be to ask where he is."

"Why? Don't we know?"

"It looks like he's disappeared."

Wallander looked at her. That visit to the bathroom would have to wait.

It was a quarter to three in the afternoon.

Chapter Twenty-five

In hindsight Wallander would always feel he had made one of the biggest mistakes of his life that afternoon by sitting down and listening to what Höglund had to say. As soon as he heard that Sonja Hökberg had had a boyfriend, he should have realized that the truth was more complicated than that. What Höglund had discovered was a half-truth, and half-truths had a tendency to lead you into a mess of lies. The end result was that he didn't see then what he should have seen, and it was a costly mistake. In his darkest hours, Wallander would always feel it had cost a person his life. And it could have led to an even greater catastrophe.

That Monday, the thirteenth of October, Höglund had taken on the task of finding out once and for all if there had been a boyfriend in Sonja Hökberg's life. She had once more brought this topic up with Eva Persson, who had continued to deny the existence of a boyfriend in Sonja's life. The only name she gave was Kalle Ryss, who Sonja had been with at an earlier time. Höglund wasn't sure if Persson was telling the truth or not, but she had not been able to get any further and had finally given up.

Höglund then drove out to the hardware store where Kalle Ryss worked. They had gone out into the storeroom in order to speak undisturbed. In contrast to Eva Persson, Kalle Ryss answered simply and seemingly truthfully to all of Höglund's questions. She had the impression that he was still very fond of Sonja, although their relationship had been over for at least a year. He missed her, mourned her death, and was frightened by what had happened. But he couldn't shed much light on the direction her life had taken after their breakup. Even though Ystad was a small city, their paths had not crossed very often. And Kalle Ryss usually drove out to Malmö on the weekends. His new girlfriend lived there.

"But I think there was someone else," he said suddenly. "Someone that Sonja was with."

Kalle Ryss didn't know much about his successor except that his name was Jonas Landahl and that he lived all alone in a big house on Snappehanegatan. He didn't know the exact address, but it was by the corner of Friskyttegatan, on the left-hand side if you were coming from town. What Jonas Landahl did for a living he couldn't say.

Höglund immediately drove down there and saw a beautiful modern house on the left side of the street. She walked through the gate and rang the bell. The house seemed deserted, though she couldn't put her finger on why. No one came to the door. She rang the bell several more times, then walked to the back of the house. She banged on the back door and tried to look in through the windows. When she came back to the front she saw a man in a dressing gown and tall boots standing outside the front gate. It was a strange sight given the time of day and the cold. He explained that he lived in the house across the street and that he had seen her ringing the doorbell. He said his name was Yngve, but he didn't give his last name.

"No one's home," he said firmly. "Not even the boy."

Their conversation had been short but informative. Yngve was apparently a man who liked to keep his neighbors under surveillance. The Landahl family had been strange birds in these parts, he said, and had moved in about ten years ago. What Mr. Landahl did he didn't know. They hadn't even bothered to stop by and introduce themselves when they moved in. They had brought all their possessions and the boy into the house and then shut their doors. He hardly ever saw them. The boy couldn't have been more than twelve or thirteen when they arrived, but they often left him alone for long stretches of time. The parents took off on long trips to God knows where. From time to time they came back, only to disappear as suddenly as they had come. Neither one of them seemed to hold down a job, but there was always money. The last time he had seen them was sometime in September. Then the boy, now a grown man, was left alone again. But a couple of days ago a taxi had come for him and taken him away.

"So the house is empty?" Höglund asked.

"There's no one there."

"When was it that the taxi came?"

"Last Wednesday. In the afternoon."

Höglund imagined Yngve sitting in his kitchen with a big logbook of his neighbors' activities in front of him. *I guess it's not unlike watching trains come and go,* she thought.

"Do you remember what taxi company it was?" she asked.

"No."

You're lying, she thought. *You know exactly what company it was; you may even remember the make of the car and the license-plate number. But you're not going to tell me because you don't want me to know what I've already figured out. That you spy on your neighbors.*

She only had one more question.

"I'd be grateful if you would tell us when he turns up again."

"What's he done?"

"Absolutely nothing. We just need to ask him a few questions."

"What about?"

Clearly his curiosity knew no bounds. She shook her head and he didn't ask again, but she could see he was irritated. It was as if she had broken some unspoken rule of etiquette.

Höglund returned to the station and was lucky enough to locate the taxicab company and driver who had picked up Jonas Landahl on Snappehanegatan. The taxi driver stopped by the police station and she asked him a few questions. His name was Östensson and he was in his thirties.

She asked him about his passenger and he turned out to have a good memory.

"I picked him up shortly before two o'clock. I think his name was Jonas."

"Did he give a last name?"

"I think I thought it was a last name. Nowadays people have such strange names."

"And there was only one passenger?"

"Yes. A young man. He was friendly."

"Did he have a lot of luggage?"

"Just a little bag on wheels. That was all."

"Where did he want to go?"

"To the ferry terminal."

"Was he going to Poland?"

"Are there any other destinations?"

"What was your general impression of him?"

"I didn't really have one. But he was nice enough."

"Did he seem anxious?"

"No."

"Did he say anything?"

"He sat in the back seat and looked out the window, as far as I remember. But he gave me a tip. I remember that."

Östensson didn't have anything else to add. Höglund thanked him for his trouble. She decided to get a warrant to search the house on Snappehanegatan. She spoke to someone at the district attorney's office, who sent over the paperwork she needed.

She was just on her way over to the house when the day-care center called to say that her youngest child was sick and throwing up. She drove over and took her child home, then spent the next few hours there. But then the child seemed better and her godsend of a neighbor, who often jumped in and helped her in times of need, was available to look after the little one. By the time she returned to the station, Wallander had also come back.

"Do we have keys?" he asked.

"I thought we would bring a locksmith along."

"No need. Were the locks complicated in any way?"

"No, not really."

"Then I'll take care of them myself."

"Just remember that a man in a dressing gown and green boots will be watching us from his kitchen window."

"You'll have to go over and keep him busy, maybe sweet-talk him. Tell him his observations have helped us and that we would be grateful if he would take a special interest in the comings and goings on his street for the next few days. And of course keep everything he finds out to himself. If there's one curious neighbor, there could be more."

Höglund laughed.

"He's just the type to fall for it," she said.

They drove to Snappehanegatan in her car. As usual he thought she drove too fast and made unnecessarily jerky movements. He was going to tell her about the photo album but couldn't focus on anything but his hopes of not running into another car.

Wallander headed for the front door while Höglund went over to the neighbor's house. Just as she had described, he was also struck by a feeling of desolation as he regarded the house. He was about to get the doors open when she returned.

"The dressing-gown man is now part of our undercover team," she said.

"I take it you didn't say we wanted the boy in connection with Sonja Hökberg?"

"Who do you take me for?"

"A talented policewoman, of course."

Wallander opened the doors and they walked in, closing the doors behind them.

"Is anyone here?" Wallander shouted.

The words seemed to be swallowed up by the silence. There was no answer.

They proceeded slowly but deliberately through the house. It was a model of cleanliness and order. Everything stood in its place, nothing to point toward a sudden departure. There was something almost impersonal about the rooms, as if the furniture had been bought at the same time and brought in to give the rooms a lived-in look. There was a photograph of a young couple with a newborn baby on the mantelpiece. There were no other personal items. An answering machine with a blinking button stood on a table. Wallander pressed it and the messages came on. A computer company said his new modem was in. Then there was a wrong number. The person didn't leave a name.

Then there came the message Wallander had been hoping for.

It was Sonja Hökberg's voice.

Wallander recognized her voice immediately, although it took Höglund a few seconds to make the connection.

I'll call you again. It's important. I'll call you.

Then she hung up.

Wallander found the button that saved the message. They played it again.

"So now we know," he said. "Sonja was in contact with the boy who lived here. She didn't even say her name."

"Is this the call we've been looking for? When she escaped?"

"Probably."

Wallander went out into the kitchen, through the laundry room and opened the door to the garage. There was a car. A dark-blue Volkswagen Golf.

"Call Nyberg," Wallander said. "I want that car thoroughly searched."

"Do you think it's the one that delivered her to her death?"

"Could be. We can't rule that out, at any rate."

Höglund got out her phone and started the process of tracking down Nyberg. Wallander used the time to take a look around the second floor. There were four bedrooms, but only two of them looked like they had been used. One for the parents, one for the son. Wallander opened the closet in the parents' room and looked at the clothes that hung in neat rows. He heard Höglund come up the stairs.

"Nyberg is on his way."

Then she too looked at the clothes.

"They have good taste," she said. "And plenty of money by the looks of it."

Wallander found a dog collar and a little leather whip stuffed into the back of the closet.

"Perhaps their tastes run a little to the alternative side," he said thoughtfully.

"It's the in thing nowadays," Höglund said knowingly. "People think you screw better if you pull a plastic bag over your head and flirt with death."

Her choice of words startled and embarrassed Wallander, but he said nothing.

They continued into the boy's room. It was unexpectedly bare. There was nothing on the walls or the bed. There was a computer on a large desk.

"I'll ask Martinsson to take a look at this," Wallander said.

"Do you want me to start it up for you?"

"No, let's hold off."

They went back downstairs. Wallander searched through the slips of paper stuffed into a kitchen drawer until he found what he was looking for.

"I don't know if you noticed this or not," he said, "but there was no name on the front door. That's a little unusual. But here at least is some junk mail addressed to Harald Landahl, Jonas's father."

"Are we going to put out a search for him? I mean the boy."

"No, not just yet. We need a little more information first."

"Was he the one who killed her?"

"We don't know. But his departure can be interpreted as an attempt to flee."

They went through more drawers while they waited for Nyberg. Höglund found a number of photographs of what looked to be a newly built house in Corsica.

"Is that where they keep going?"

"It's not impossible."

"Where do they get their money?"

"The son is still the main focus of our investigation."

The doorbell rang. It was Nyberg and his team of technicians. Wallander led them out to the garage.

"Concentrate on fingerprints," he said. "They might correspond with some we've found in other places. On Sonja Hökberg's handbag, for example. Or in the office in Runnerström Square. Also, look for signs placing it at the power substation. Or that Sonja Hökberg has been in it."

"In that case we'll start with the tires," Nyberg said. "That will be the fastest. You remember we had one set of tire marks out there we couldn't account for."

Wallander waited, and it only took Nyberg ten minutes to give him the answer he had been hoping for.

"This is the car," Nyberg said after having compared the tread with pictures taken of the crime scene.

"Are you sure?"

"Of course not. There are thousands of tires out there that are almost identical. But if you look at this back left tire you'll see that it's low on air and is also worn on the inside since the tires haven't been balanced properly. That dramatically increases our chances of being right."

"So then you are sure."

"As sure as I can be without total certainty."

Wallander left the garage. Höglund was busy with the living room. He went to the kitchen. *Am I doing the right thing?* he thought. *Should I send out a description of him right now?* A sudden sense of anxiety drove him back upstairs to the boy's bedroom. He sat down at the desk and looked around. Then he got up and went over to the closet. There was nothing that caught his eye. He stood on tiptoe and felt around on the upper shelves. Nothing. He returned to the desk and looked at the computer. Impulsively he lifted the keyboard but there was nothing underneath. He paused before going to the top of the stairs and calling out to Höglund. They went back into the boy's bedroom together and Wallander pointed to the computer.

"Do you want me to start it up now?"

He nodded.

"So we're not waiting for Martinsson?"

There was no attempt to hide the irony in her voice. Perhaps she had been hurt by his earlier insistence that they wait for their colleague. But right now he didn't have time to think about that. How many times had he felt overlooked or humiliated during his years as a policeman? By other police officers, criminals, prosecutors, and journalists, and not least by those who were usually referred to as "members of the public."

Höglund sat down at the computer and started it. It made a little noise and the screen slowly came to life. She clicked open the hard drive and various icons emerged.

"What is it you want me to look for?"

"I don't know."

She chose an icon at random and double-clicked on it. In contrast to Falk's computer, this one didn't put up any resistance. It dutifully opened the file, the only problem being that the file was completely empty.

Wallander put on his glasses and leaned over her shoulder.

"Try the one called 'Correspondence,'" he said.

She clicked on the icon, but the same thing happened. There was nothing there.

"What does it mean?" he asked.

"That it's empty."

"Or it's been emptied. Keep going."

She tried file after file but kept getting the same result.

"It's strange," she said. "There really isn't anything here at all."

Wallander looked around to see if he could find any diskettes. But he couldn't find anything.

Höglund proceeded to the icon that held the information about computer activity.

"The last activity occurred on the ninth of October," she announced.

"That was last Thursday."

They looked questioningly at each other.

"The day after he went to Poland?"

"If the neighborhood spy is to be believed, which I actually think he is."

Wallander sat down.

"Explain it to me."

"Well, as far as I can see, that leaves us with two explanations. Either he came back, or else someone else has been here."

"And the person who was here could have emptied the computer of all content?"

"Quite easily, considering there were no security barriers."

Wallander tried to work with the little computer knowledge he had managed to absorb.

"Could this person also have removed the traces of such an existing barrier?"

"Yes, if they had already bypassed it themselves."

"And then emptied the computer at the same time?"

"There would always be prints left behind," she said thoughtfully.

"What do you mean?"

"It's something Martinsson explained to me."

"Tell me."

"You can try to understand it by comparing a computer to a house that has been emptied of its furniture. There are always a few traces left

behind. There might be scratches on the hardwood floors, or perhaps
there are patches of light and dark left from where the furniture once
was."

"Like a wall after the paintings have been taken down," Wallander
said. "There are lighter patches where they used to be."

"Martinsson used the example of a cellar. Somewhere deep inside
the computer there's a space where everything that is supposed to be
erased continues to live on. That means that until a hard drive has
been destroyed, it is theoretically possible to reconstruct everything
that was once in it."

Wallander shook his head.

"I understand what you're saying, though I don't understand how it
would be possible," he said. "But what interests me most right now is
the fact that someone used the computer on the ninth."

Höglund turned back to the monitor.

"Let me just check the games that are on here," she said and started
double-clicking on the icons she hadn't yet touched.

"That's funny," she mumbled. "I've never heard of this game. 'Jacob's Marsh'."

When she finished, she turned off the computer.

"There's nothing there. I just wonder why the icons were left on the
desktop."

They searched the room thoroughly, hoping to find some diskettes,
but had no luck. Wallander was intuitively convinced that getting to
the bottom of the use of the computer on the ninth was a key to
unlocking the entire case. Someone had deliberately cleaned out the
computer, and the only question was whether it was Jonas Landahl or
someone else.

They finally gave up looking and went downstairs. Wallander asked
Nyberg to go through the house with a fine-tooth comb after he was
done with the car. Looking for diskettes would be his highest priority.

Höglund was on the phone with Martinsson when Wallander came
back into the kitchen. She handed him the receiver.

"How is it going over there?"

"Robert Modin has a lot of energy, I'll give him that much," Martinsson said. "He took a lunch break and had a strange kind of quiche,
but he was ready to get back to work again before I was even ready for
coffee."

"Have there been any developments?"

"He keeps insisting that the number twenty is significant. It's returned in several different contexts. But he's not over the wall yet."

"What do you mean?"

"That's his own terminology. He hasn't cracked the code yet, though he's sure now it consists of two words. Or possibly a number and a word, though I'm not sure how he knows that."

Wallander told him briefly what they were doing. When the conversation was over he asked Höglund to go back to the neighbor and confirm the date of Jonas Landahl's departure. He also wanted her to ask if anyone else had been seen on the ninth.

She left, and Wallander sat down on the sofa to think. But he had not come up with anything when she returned twenty minutes later.

"It's pretty disturbing, really," she said. "He keeps a record of these events. Is that all one has to look forward to in retirement? In any case, he's absolutely sure the boy left on Wednesday."

"What about the ninth?"

"He didn't see anyone. But of course not even he spends every moment at the kitchen window."

"So that doesn't tell us anything," Wallander said. "It could as easily have been the boy as anyone else."

It was five o'clock. Höglund left to pick up her children. She offered to come back later that night, but Wallander told her to stay at home. He would call her if anything else developed.

He went to the boy's room for a third time, and knelt to peer under the bed. Höglund had already checked it but he wanted to see with his own eyes if there was anything there.

Then he lay down on the bed.

Suppose he's hidden something important in this room, Wallander thought. *Something he wants to be able to check on when he first wakes up in the morning and when he's going to bed at night.* Wallander let his gaze travel along the walls of the room. Nothing. He was about to sit up when he saw that one of the bookcases next to the closet leaned slightly in toward the wall. It was very apparent from the vantage point of the bed. He sat up, and the angle was no longer visible. He walked over to the bookcase and bent down. Someone had placed a small shim under each side, creating a sliver of space underneath. He slid his fingers in and immediately felt that there was something there. He coaxed out the object and knew what it was before he had a chance to look at it. A diskette. He had his cell phone out and was dialing a number even before he made it to the desk. Martinsson answered immediately. Wallander explained where he was and what he had found. Martinsson wrote down the address and said he was on his way. Robert Modin would have to be left unsupervised for a short while.

Martinsson was there within fifteen minutes. He started the computer and inserted the diskette. Wallander leaned forward to read the name of the diskette. JACOB'S MARSH. It reminded him of something Höglund had said about the games, and he felt a rush of disappointment. Martinsson double-clicked on it. There was only one file on the diskette, and it had last been opened on the twenty-ninth of September. Martinsson double-clicked on the file.

They were both startled by the text that came up on the screen.

Release the minks.

"What does that mean?" Martinsson asked.

"I don't know," Wallander said. "But we have another connection. This time between Jonas Landahl and Falk."

Martinsson stared at him uncomprehendingly.

"Don't you remember? Falk was involved in that animal-release heist a while back."

Now Martinsson remembered.

"I wonder if Jonas Landahl was involved in that job. He might have been one of the people who got away."

Martinsson was still confused.

"So this is all about minks?"

"No," Wallander said. "I don't think so. I think we need to find Jonas Landahl as soon as possible."

Chapter Twenty-six

It was early dawn on the fourteenth of October, and Carter had just been forced to make an important decision. He had opened his eyes in the dark and listened to the noise of the air conditioning unit. He heard that it was almost time to clean out the mechanism inside. There was a low hum that shouldn't have been there in the monotone gush of cold air from the machine. He had stood up, shaken out his slippers since there could be insects hiding inside, put on his robe, and gone down into the kitchen. Carter helped himself to a bottle of the previously boiled water that had spent the night inside the refrigerator. He slowly drank two large glasses, then went upstairs to his study and sat down in front of the computer. It was never turned off. It was connected to a large reserve battery in case of a blackout, and it was also hooked up to a surge protector that managed the constant ebbs and flows of power from the electrical outlet.

He had a message from Fu Cheng. He read it carefully.

Afterward he sat motionless in his chair for a while.

The news was not good, not good at all. Cheng had done what he had told him to do, but the police were apparently still trying to break into Falk's computer. Carter was convinced that they would never be able to break the codes, and even if they did they would never understand what they were looking at. But there was something in the message that worried him, and it was the fact that the police had brought in a young man to help them with their task.

Carter had a healthy respect for young men with glasses who spent a great deal of their time in front of computers. He and Falk had often spoken about these modern-day geniuses. They could break into secret networks, read through and even interpret the most complicated electronic programs.

Cheng had written that he believed Modin to be this kind of young man. Cheng pointed out that Swedish hackers had broken into the defense systems of other countries on more than one occasion.

He could be one of the dangerous ones, Carter thought. *A modern-day heretic. Someone who won't leave our systems and our secrets alone. In an earlier age, a person like Modin would have been burned at the stake.*

Carter didn't like it, as little as he had liked any of the developments after Falk's death. Falk had really left him in the lurch. Now Carter was forced to clean up around him, and he didn't have much time to weigh each decision carefully. Haste had led to mistakes, such as removing Falk's body. Maybe it hadn't even been necessary to kill that young woman? But she could have talked. And the police didn't seem to be losing interest.

Carter had seen this kind of behavior before—a person determined to follow a set of tracks leading to the wounded animal hiding in the bush.

After only a few days he realized it was the policeman called Wallander who was tracking them. Cheng's analysis had been very clear on the matter. That's why they had tried to take him out. But they had failed, and now the man was still tenaciously following their tracks.

Carter got up and walked over to the window. The city had not yet started to wake up. The African night was full of scents and sounds. Cheng was dependable. He was capable of a fanatic loyalty that Carter and Falk had once decided might be useful. The question now was only if that was enough.

He sat down at the computer and started typing. It took a little less than half an hour to list all the acts he felt constituted the alternatives. Then he cleared his mind of any emotion that would distract him from the best possible course of action.

He arrived at his decision in only a few minutes. After all, Carter had discovered Wallander's weakness, one that opened a possibility of getting to him.

Every person has his secret, Carter thought. *Even this Wallander. Secrets and weaknesses.*

He started typing again and heard banging and clattering starting to come from the kitchen before he was done. He read through his message three times before he was completely satisfied and sent it off.

Carter went down to the dining room and ate his breakfast. Every morning, he tried to tell if Celine was pregnant again. He had decided to fire her the next time it happened. He handed her the shopping list he had made the night before. He gave her the money, then unlocked the two front doors. Altogether there were sixteen different locks to unlock every morning.

Celine left the house. The city had begun to stir. But this house, built by a Portuguese doctor, had thick walls. When Carter returned to his study he had the feeling that he was surrounded by silence, the silence that always existed in the middle of the African din. There was a blinking light on his computer. He had mail.

It was now only a week before the electronic tidal wave would sweep the world.

Shortly after seven o'clock on Monday evening it was as if someone had let the air out of Martinsson and Wallander. That was after they had left the house in Snappehanegatan and returned to the police station.

They had tried to understand what must have happened. Had Jonas Landahl returned to erase all the files on his computer? In that case, why had he left the diskette behind? Was the content of the diskette unimportant? But why then had it been hidden with such care? There were many questions, but no good answers. Martinsson suggested carefully that the perplexing message—RELEASE THE MINKS—was a deliberate attempt to lead them astray. *But what direction was that?* Wallander wondered glumly. There seemed to be no direction that was any better than the rest.

They discussed whether or not they should put out an alert for Jonas Landahl. Wallander hesitated, since they had no real reason to bring him in—at least not until Nyberg had been able to examine the house. Martinsson did not agree with him, and it was at about this time that they were both overtaken by exhaustion. Wallander felt guilty because he couldn't steer the investigation in the right direction. He suspected that Martinsson silently agreed with him on this point.

Robert Modin had been sent home, though he had been eager to continue working all night. Martinsson started checking the police registers for the name "Jonas Landahl." He had focused on descriptions of animal-rights activists, but had found nothing. He had turned off his computer and joined Wallander, who was sitting in front of a plastic mug of cold coffee in the lunchroom.

They had decided to call it a day. Wallander remained in the lunchroom for a while, too tired to think, too tired to go home. The last thing he did was try to get in touch with Hansson. Someone finally told him that Hansson had gone to Växjö in the afternoon.

Wallander called Nyberg, but there was nothing new to report. The technicians were still working on the car.

On his way home, Wallander stopped at the grocery store. When he was in line to pay he realized he had left his wallet on his desk at work. The checkout clerk recognized him and let him buy his food on credit. The first thing Wallander did when he got home was write a note to himself in capital letters reminding him to pay his bill the following day. He put the note on his doormat so he would be unable to miss it as he was leaving. Then he cooked up a spaghetti dinner and ate it in front of the TV. For once the food was quite good. He flipped through the channels and finally decided on a movie. But it was already halfway through when he started, and he never got into it. Then he reminded himself that there was another movie he needed to see. The one with Al Pacino.

He went to bed at eleven o'clock and unplugged the phone. There was no wind, and the streetlamp outside the window was completely still. It didn't take long for him to fall asleep.

On Tuesday morning he woke up shortly before six o'clock, feeling well rested. He had dreamed of his father. And about Sten Widén. They had been in a strange landscape filled with rocks. In the dream Wallander had been afraid he was about to lose sight of them. *Even I can interpret this dream,* he thought. *I'm still as afraid of abandonment as a young child.*

The cell phone rang. It was Nyberg. As usual, he got straight to the point. He always assumed the person he was calling was fully awake, regardless of what time it was. But that never stopped him from complaining about other people calling him at all hours.

"I've just finished work on the garage at Snappehanegatan," he said. "I found something in the back seat of the car that I didn't see at first."

"What was it?"

"A piece of gum. It says 'Spearmint.'"

"Was it stuck to the back seat?"

"It was an unopened stick. If it had been a used piece of gum I would have found it much earlier."

Wallander was already out of bed and halfway across the cold floor to the bathroom.

"Good," he said. "I'll be in touch."

Half an hour later he had showered and dressed and was on his way to the station. His morning coffee would have to wait until he got to the office. He had planned to walk to work, but changed his mind at the last minute and took the car. He tried to quell his guilty conscience. The first person he looked for when he got in was Irene. But she wasn't in yet. *If Ebba was still working, she would already be here,* Wallander thought. *Even though she didn't officially start until seven. But she would have sensed intuitively that I needed to speak to her.* He realized he was being unfair to Irene. No one could compare to Ebba. He went to get a cup of coffee in the meantime. He spoke to some of the traffic police officers, who were complaining about speeding drivers and the rising incidence of driving under the influence. There was going to be a big crackdown today. Wallander listened absently, reflecting that policemen had a tendency to be whiny. He walked back to the reception area just as Irene was removing her coat and scarf.

"Do you remember me borrowing some gum from you the other day?"

"I don't think 'borrow' is the right word in that context. I gave it to you, or rather, to that girl."

"What kind was it?"

"A regular brand. 'Spearmint,' I think."

Wallander nodded.

"Was that it?" Irene asked, surprised.

Wallander returned to his office, walking so quickly that he almost spilled his coffee. He was in a hurry to confirm this trail of thought. He called Höglund at home and heard a child wail in the background when she picked up.

"I want you to do me a favor," he said. "I want you to ask Eva Persson what kind of gum she chews. I also want you to ask if she used to give any to Sonja."

"Why is this so important?"

"I'll explain it to you when you get down here."

She called him back after ten minutes. There was still a lot of noise in the background.

"I talked to her mother. She said Eva chewed different kinds of gum. I doubt she would lie about something like this."

"So she kept an eye on what kind of gum her daughter bought?"

"Mothers know a lot about their daughters," she said.

"Or think they do."

"In some cases."

"What about Sonja?"

"I think we can assume Eva sometimes shared her gum with Sonja."

Wallander smacked his lips.

"Why in God's name is this so important?"

"I'll let you know when you get down here."

"Everything is such a mess over here," she sighed. "For some reason Tuesday mornings are the worst."

Wallander hung up. *Every morning is the worst,* he thought. *Without fail. At least all those mornings that you wake up at five in the morning and can't fall back to sleep.*

He walked over to Martinsson's office. There was no one there. He was probably with Modin over at Runnerström Square. Hansson wasn't in either. Maybe he wasn't back yet from what was probably a completely unnecessary trip to Växjö.

Wallander sat down at his desk and tried to go through the latest findings on his own. They were now almost completely sure that the blue car over at Snappehanegatan was the same vehicle that had taken Sonja Hökberg to the power substation. Jonas Landahl had probably been the driver, letting her off to be killed, then preparing to take the ferry to Poland.

There were many gaps. Jonas Landahl may not have been the driver and he may not have been Sonja's killer, but he was definitely under suspicion. They needed to speak to him as soon as possible.

The computer was an even bigger mystery. If Jonas Landahl had not erased what was on it, then someone else had. And how could they account for the hidden diskette?

Wallander tried to come up with a plausible theory. After a few minutes he came up with a third alternative. Jonas Landahl did erase everything on his computer, but someone else also came in later to make sure he had done so.

Wallander turned to a fresh page on his pad of paper and wrote a list of names.

Lundberg, Sonja and Eva.
Tynnes Falk.
Jonas Landahl.

There was a connection among all of these people. But there was still no good motive for any of the crimes. *We're still looking for common ground,* Wallander thought. *We haven't found it yet.*

He was interrupted in his thoughts by Martinsson.

"Robert Modin has already started his day," he said. "He demanded to be picked up at six o'clock. He's a strange bird. He brought his own food with him today. Some funny-looking herbal teas and even funnier rusks. Made from organic ingredients in Bornholm. He also brought a Walkman with him, claiming he works best when he listens to music. I looked at his tapes. Here are the names."

Martinsson took a slip of paper out of his pocket.

"Handel's *Messiah,* Verdi's *Requiem.* What does that tell you?"

"That Modin has good taste in music."

Wallander told Martinsson about the phone calls with Nyberg and Höglund and the fact that they could now be fairly sure that Sonja had been driven in Landahl's car.

"It may not have been her last car ride, though," Martinsson said.

"I think for now we'll assume it was. We'll also assume that that's why Landahl decided to get away."

"So we put out an alert for him?"

"Yes. Can you arrange it with the DA's office?"

Martinsson made a face.

"Can't Hansson take care of it?"

"He's not in yet."

"Where the hell is he?"

"Someone claimed he went up to Växjö."

"Why?"

"That's where Eva Persson's alcoholic father is supposed to be."

"And is that really a priority? Speaking to her father?"

Wallander shrugged.

"I can't be the only authority on what to prioritize."

Martinsson got up.

"I'll talk to Viktorsson, and I'll also see what I can dig up on Landahl. As long as the computers are up."

Wallander detained him for a moment.

"What do we know about these groups?" he asked. "These—what do you call them—eco-terrorists?"

"Hansson compares them to motorcycle gangs, since they break into labs and sabotage animal experiments."

"Is that fair?"

"When was Hansson ever fair?"

"I thought most of these groups espoused nonviolence. Isn't it called civil disobedience? Has that gone out of style?"

"I think most of the time they're nonviolent," Martinsson said.

"And Falk was involved in this."

"Don't forget that he may not have been murdered at all."

"But Sonja Hökberg was, and so was Lundberg," Wallander said.

"Doesn't that just tell us that we don't have a clue about what's going on?"

"What about Robert Modin—do you think he's going to get anywhere?"

"It's hard to say. I hope so."

"And he claims the number twenty is important?"

"Yes. He's sure of that now. I only understand about half of what he says, but he's very convincing."

Wallander looked over at his calendar.

"It's the fourteenth of October today. That means we have a week left."

"If the number twenty refers to a date. We don't know that."

Wallander thought of something else.

"Have Sydkraft come up with anything else? They must have finished their internal investigation by now. How could the break-in occur? Why was the gate broken and not the inner door?"

"Hansson is in charge of that. He said that Sydkraft have taken the whole thing very seriously and he expects to see a number of heads roll."

"I wonder if *we* have taken it seriously enough," Wallander said thoughtfully. "How did Falk manage to get hold of the blueprint? And why?"

"Everything is so complicated," Martinsson complained. "Naturally we can't dismiss the idea of sabotage. The step from releasing minks to cutting power is perhaps not so great. Not if someone is a fanatic."

Wallander felt his anxiety tighten its grip.

"This thing with the number twenty worries me," he said. "What if it really does stand for the twentieth of October? What will happen then?"

"It worries me, too," Martinsson said. "But I don't have any answers for you."

Neither had anything more to say.

Martinsson left the room, and Wallander devoted the next couple of hours to catching up on paperwork and trying to make a dent in the piles that had built up on his desk. The whole time, he was searching for a clue that he might have overlooked. But he didn't think of anything new.

Later that afternoon they had a meeting. Martinsson had talked to Viktorsson, and Jonas Landahl was now officially wanted by the police. The alert had gone out internationally as well. The Polish authorities had responded very quickly and confirmed that Jonas Landahl had entered the country on the day that his neighbor saw him leave Snappehanegatan in a taxi. They had no confirmation as yet of any departure, but something told Wallander he wasn't in Poland anymore.

Nyberg had gone over the car again and sent a number of plastic bags with fiber and hair samples to the lab for further analysis. They would not be able to confirm the fact that Sonja had been in the car until the results came back. The question of the car sparked a heated discussion between Martinsson and Höglund. She maintained that if the tests came back positive Landahl must have been the person who drove Sonja to the power substation. But Martinsson argued that if Sonja Hökberg and Jonas Landahl had been dating, it would have been natural for her to have been in his car, so that wouldn't prove anything.

Wallander waited while they argued back and forth. Neither one of them was right. Both were tired. Finally the discussion died down on its own. Hansson talked about his trip to Växjö, which had been as meaningless as Wallander had suspected. He had also taken a wrong turn on the highway that had delayed him even further. When he finally located Eva Persson's father, the man turned out to be heavily intoxicated and had not been able to give Hansson any interesting information. He had burst into tears each time he said his daughter's name, and had talked despondently of her future. Hansson had tried to get away as quickly as he could.

There was no information as yet on the Mercedes van, but Wallander had received a fax from the American Express office in Hong Kong confirming that there was no one by the name of Fu Cheng at the address indicated on the card. Robert Modin was still wrestling with Falk's computer. After a long and, in Wallander's opinion, unnecessary discussion they decided to wait yet another day before bringing in the computer experts from the National Police.

At six o'clock they were exhausted. Wallander looked at the pale and tired faces around him. He knew that the only thing he could do now was let everyone go home. They decided to meet again at eight the following morning. Wallander kept working after the meeting was over, but at half past eight even he went home. He ate the leftovers of his spaghetti dinner and lay down on his bed to read a book. It was an account of Napoleon's various military campaigns, and it was incredibly boring. He soon fell asleep with the book draped over his face.

The phone rang. At first he didn't know where he was or what time it was. He answered. It was someone from the station.

"One of the ferries approaching Ystad has just contacted us," said the policeman on night duty.

"What's happened?"

"One of the axles for the propellers started malfunctioning, and when they located the problem they called us immediately."

"Yes?"

"There was a dead body down in the engine room."

Wallander caught his breath.

"Where's the ferry?"

"It's only half an hour from land."

"I'm coming right down."

"Should I notify anyone else?"

Wallander thought for a moment.

"Call Martinsson and Hansson. And Nyberg. We'll meet at the terminal."

"Anything else?"

"Call Chief Holgersson."

"She's at a police conference in Copenhagen."

"I don't care. Call her."

"What should I tell her?"

"That a suspected murderer is on his way back from Poland. But that unfortunately he's coming back dead."

They ended the conversation. Wallander knew he didn't need to spend any more time thinking about where Jonas Landahl was.

Twenty minutes later he met his colleagues by the ferry terminal and waited for the large ship to dock.

Chapter Twenty-seven

As Wallander was climbing down the steep stairs into the engine room, he had a strong feeling that he was descending into an inferno. Even though the ferry was securely docked and the noise from below had died down to an even hum, he felt as though there was still a hell down there waiting for him. Two pale engineers and an equally pale first mate had greeted them and escorted them to the engine room. They had managed to communicate that the body waiting for them in the oily water below had been mutilated beyond the point of recognition. Someone, perhaps Martinsson, said the pathologist was on her way. A fire truck with rescue personnel was waiting outside.

Despite his misgivings, Wallander wanted to be the first to go down. Martinsson was glad to be excused. Hansson had still not arrived. Wallander asked Martinsson to take charge of documenting the events surrounding the discovery of the body and asked him to send Hansson down as soon as he arrived.

Then Wallander set off downstairs, closely followed by Nyberg. The technician who had first discovered the body accompanied them. Once they had reached the bottom, he directed them to the stern. Wallander was astonished by the size of the room. Finally the technician stopped at a ladder and pointed down into the abyss. Wallander started climbing down. While they were still on the ladder, Nyberg stepped on his hand. Wallander cursed from the pain and almost lost his grip but managed to catch himself. Then they made it all the way down and there, under one of the two large, oily propeller axles, was the body.

The engineers had not been exaggerating. Wallander had the distinct impression that what he was looking at was no longer human. It was as if a newly-slaughtered animal carcass had been thrown in there. Nyberg groaned. Wallander thought he hissed something about his retirement. Wallander was surprised that he didn't feel the slightest bit queasy. He had been forced to endure so many terrible sights during his career. Car accidents. The remains of people who had died at home and not been discovered for months. But this was among the worst he had ever seen. There had been a picture of Jonas Landahl in his bedroom. A young man with a very normal appearance. Now Wallander tried to gauge if the body in front of him belonged to the person he had assumed it must be. But the face was almost completely gone. In its place was a bloody lump without any features.

The boy in the picture had been blond. The head in front of him, almost completely severed from the body, had a few tufts of hair remaining that were not matted with oil. They looked light. That was enough for Wallander, although it didn't necessarily prove anything. He stepped aside so Nyberg could take a closer look. Then Susann Bexell arrived, accompanied by two rescue workers.

"How in the hell did he end up down here?" Nyberg asked.

Even though the engine was idling at low speed, he had to shout to make himself heard. Wallander shook his head without answering. Then he felt an almost violent urge to get out of there, to leave this hell as soon as possible. If only to be able to think clearly. He left Nyberg, the pathologist, and the rescue workers and climbed the ladder. He made it all the way up to the deck, walked outside, and took some deep breaths. Martinsson turned up from somewhere and asked him how it was.

"Worse than you can imagine."

"Is it Landahl?"

They hadn't talked openly about this possibility until now. But clearly it had been in Martinsson's mind, too.

"It was too hard to tell," Wallander said. "But I'm sure it was him."

Then he tried to muster his organizational skills. Martinsson had found out that the ferry was not scheduled to leave again until the following morning. That would give them enough time to finish the forensic investigation and remove the body.

"I've already asked for a list of passengers," Martinsson said. "But there was no record of a Jonas Landahl, at least for this trip."

"But he was on board today," Wallander said firmly. "Whether or not he appears on the list. He may have used a different name. We'll need a printout of that list and all the names of the crew. Then we'll see if there isn't some name that looks familiar or like a version of Landahl."

"You're ruling out the possibility that it was an accident?"

"Yes," Wallander said. "It's about as much of an accident as what happened to Sonja Hökberg. And it's the same people."

Then he asked if Hansson had arrived. Martinsson said he was questioning the engineers.

They went back inside. The ferry seemed completely deserted. A small cleaning crew was working on the broad staircase that connected the different levels of the ship. Wallander directed Martinsson to the large cafeteria. There wasn't a single person to be seen, but there were noises coming from the kitchen. Through the windows they saw the lights of Ystad.

"See if you can get hold of some coffee," he said. "We need to talk."

Martinsson walked off in the direction of the kitchen. Wallander sat down at a table. What did it mean that Jonas Landahl was dead? He was slowly coming up with two different theories that he wanted to discuss with Martinsson.

Suddenly a man in a uniform appeared by his side.

"Why haven't you disembarked?"

Wallander looked at the man, who had a long beard and a ruddy complexion. There were several yellow stripes on his epaulettes. *This is a large ferry*, he thought. *Not everyone knows what happened down in the engine room.*

"I'm a police officer," Wallander said. "Who are you?"

"I'm third mate on this ship."

"That's good," Wallander said. "Go talk to your captain or first mate and they'll tell you why I'm here."

The man hesitated. But then he seemed to decide that Wallander was probably telling the truth and was not a lingering passenger that had to be dealt with. He disappeared. Martinsson came out of the kitchen with a tray.

"They were eating," he said when he sat down. "They hadn't heard anything about what happened, though they had of course noticed that the ferry cut back on power for part of the trip."

"The third mate came by," Wallander said. "He didn't know anything, either."

"Have we made a big mistake?" Martinsson asked.

"In what way?"

"Shouldn't we have detained everyone for a while? At least until we could have checked the names on the list and all the cars?"

Martinsson was right, but at the same time, that kind of an operation would have required more manpower than they could have mustered at such short notice. Wallander also doubted that they would have had any results.

"Maybe," he said. "But we should focus on the situation as is."

"I dreamed about going to sea when I was younger," Martinsson said.

"I did too," Wallander said. "Doesn't everyone?"

Then he dove right in.

"We have to come up with an interpretation," he said. "We had begun to suspect that Jonas Landahl was the one who drove Sonja Hökberg to the power substation and then killed her. We had assumed that that was why he later fled from Snappehanegatan. Now he himself is killed. The question is simply how this changes the picture."

"You still maintain it couldn't be an accident?"

"Is that what you think it was?"

Martinsson shifted slightly.

"As I see it, there are two conclusions that can be drawn," Wallander continued. "The first is that Landahl really did kill Sonja for some reason that we still don't know, although we suspect it has to do with keeping something quiet. Afterward Landahl takes off to Poland. Whether he is driven by panic or following some deliberate plan, we don't know. But then he is killed, perhaps as a kind of revenge. Perhaps because he has become a liability for someone else in turn."

Wallander paused, but Martinsson didn't say anything. Wallander continued.

"The other possibility is that an unknown person killed both Sonja Hökberg and now Landahl."

"How does that account for Landahl's quick getaway?"

"When he found out what happened to Sonja, he was scared. He fled, but someone caught up with him."

Martinsson nodded. It seemed to Wallander that they were thinking along the same tracks now.

"Sabotage and death," Martinsson said. "Hökberg's body is used to cause a huge blackout in Scania. Then Landahl's body is thrown down into the propeller axles of a huge ferry."

"Do you remember what we talked about a little while ago?" Wallander asked. "We put it this way: first the minks were released, then there was the blackout, and now a ferry incident. What's next?"

Martinsson shook his head despondently.

"It doesn't make sense," he said. "I can understand releasing the minks, that a group of animal-rights activists would plan and execute that task. I can perhaps even see some logic to the blackout—perhaps someone wants to demonstrate the enormous weaknesses built into our society. But what would be the point of causing chaos down in the engine room of a ferry?"

"It's like a game of dominoes. If one piece falls, the rest follow. And the first piece to fall was Falk."

"What about Lundberg's murder? How do you fit that in?"

"That's just the problem. I can't get it to fit, and therefore I've started thinking something else."

"That Lundberg's death is incidental to the rest of the events?"

Wallander nodded. Martinsson could think quickly when he tried.

"Do you mean that we should separate these two sequences of events? Even though Sonja figures so dominantly in both?"

"That's just it," Wallander said. "What if her role is far less important than we've thought?"

At that moment Hansson entered the cafeteria. He cast a longing glance at their coffee. Right behind him was a gray-haired, pleasant-looking man with many stripes on his epaulets who turned out to be the captain. Wallander got to his feet and introduced himself. When Captain Sund spoke, it was clear he was not from Scania.

"Terrible things," he said.

"No one has seen anything," Hansson said. "Even though you would think someone would have noticed the victim on his way down to the engine room."

"So there are no witnesses?"

"I spoke to the two engineers who were on duty on the trip over from Poland. Neither one of them saw anything."

"And the doors to the engine room aren't locked?" Wallander asked.

"Our security measures don't allow it. But they are clearly marked with signs that say 'No entry.' Everyone who works in the area knows to keep an eye out for stray passengers. Sometimes when people have had a bit too much to drink, they wander. But I never thought anything like this could happen."

"I take it the ferry is completely empty by now," Wallander said. "But there isn't by any chance a car that hasn't been claimed?"

Sund sent out a message on the radio in his hand. A crew member down in the car hold answered.

"All vehicles have been claimed," Sund reported. "The car hold is completely empty."

"What about the cabins? Is there any unclaimed luggage?"

Sund went off in search of an answer. Hansson sat down. Wallander noted that Hansson had been unusually careful in his questioning of the crew.

When the ferry left Swinoujscie the captain had estimated that the trip to Ystad would take about seven hours. Wallander asked if any of the engineers could point to a time when the body must have slipped into the axles. Could it have happened even before the ferry left Poland? Hansson had thought to ask this question and could report that yes, the body could indeed have been there at the very start of the trip.

There wasn't much to add. No one had seen anything unusual, let alone noticed Landahl. There had been a couple hundred passengers aboard, most of them Polish truckers. There had also been a delegation from the Swedish cement industry. They were returning from an investment conference in Poland.

"We need to know if Landahl was traveling with anyone," Wallander said when Hansson finished. "That's very important. What we need is a photograph of him. Then someone will have to take the boat back and forth tomorrow and see if anyone recognizes him."

"I hope that someone isn't me," Hansson said. "I get seasick."

"Then find someone else," Wallander said. "What I need you to do right now is to go up to Snappehanegatan and get his picture. Check with that boy who works in the hardware store to make sure it's a decent likeness."

"You mean that guy Ryss?"

"That's the one. He must have seen his successor at some point."

"The ferry leaves at six tomorrow morning."

"So you'll have to take care of all this by then," Wallander said patiently.

Hansson disappeared. Wallander and Martinsson remained in the cafeteria for a while longer. Susann Bexell came in after a while and sat down with them. She was very pale.

"I've never seen anything like this," she said. "First a young woman burned to death in a high-voltage area, and now this."

"Can you confirm if the victim is a young man?" Wallander said.

"Yes, it's a young man."

"Can you give us a cause of death? A time?"

"Of course not. You saw what kind of shape he was in. The boy was completely crushed. One of the rescue workers vomited. I have a great deal of understanding for that reaction."

"Is Nyberg still there?"

"I think so."

Bexell left. Captain Sund still had not returned. Martinsson's cell phone started to vibrate. It was Lisa Holgersson calling from Copenhagen. Martinsson stretched the phone out to Wallander, but he shook his head.

"You talk to her."

"What should I tell her?"

"Tell her the facts. What do you think?"

Wallander got up and started pacing up and down the empty cafeteria. Landahl's death had closed an avenue that had seemed promising. But what kept working its way to the front of his mind was the idea that his death might have been avoidable, if it was the case that Landahl had fled not because he was the killer but because he feared someone else. The real murderer.

Wallander chastised himself. He hadn't been thinking clearly. He had simply jumped to the easiest conclusion without keeping other theories in mind. And now Landahl was dead.

Martinsson finished his conversation and put his phone away. Wallander returned.

"I don't think she was completely sober, to tell you the truth," he said.

"She's at a police conference," Wallander replied. "But at least now she knows what our evening has been like."

Captain Sund returned.

"There is one bag that was left behind in one of the cabins," he said.

Wallander and Martinsson got up at the same time. They followed the captain through a myriad of corridors until they came to a cabin with a woman wearing the company uniform posted outside. She was Polish and spoke poor Swedish.

"According to our records this cabin was booked by a passenger named Jonasson."

Wallander and Martinsson exchanged glances.

"Is there anyone who can give us a description of him?"

It turned out that the captain spoke excellent Polish. He translated the question for the woman, who listened and then shook her head.

"He didn't share the cabin with anyone?"

"No."

Wallander went in. The cabin was narrow and windowless. Wallander shuddered at the thought of having to spend a stormy night in such quarters. On the bed that was attached to the wall there was a small suitcase with wheels. Martinsson handed him a pair of rubber gloves, which he put on. He opened the bag. It was empty. They searched the room for about ten minutes but without results.

"Nyberg will have to take a look in here," Wallander said when they had given up. "And the taxi driver who took Landahl to the ferry might be able to identify the bag."

Wallander went back out into the corridor. Martinsson made the arrangements to keep the cabin undisturbed and unoccupied until further notice. Wallander looked at the doors to the cabins on either side. There were used sheets and towels outside each one. The numbers on the doors were 309 and 311.

"Try to find out who the people were who were staying on either side," Wallander said. "They may have heard something or even seen someone come or go." Martinsson wrote it down in his notebook, then started speaking in English to the Polish woman. Wallander had often been envious of Martinsson's proficiency in that language. Wallander spoke it badly. Linda had often teased him about his poor pronunciation, especially when they traveled together. Captain Sund escorted Wallander back up the stairs.

It was almost midnight.

"Would it be in order for me to offer refreshments of a stronger nature after this ordeal?" Sund asked.

"Unfortunately not," Wallander said.

A call came through on Sund's radio. He excused himself. Wallander was actually glad to be left alone. His conscience kept gnawing at him. Could Landahl have had a chance if Wallander had made different assumptions from the beginning? He knew there was no answer to be found, just the reality of having to live with his self-accusations.

Martinsson turned up after twenty minutes.

"There was a Norwegian named Larsen in room 309. He's probably on the road to Norway as we speak, but I do have his phone number. In 311, however, there was a couple from Ystad, a Mr. and Mrs. Tomander."

"Talk to them first thing tomorrow," Wallander said. "That may give us something."

"I saw Nyberg on the stairs, by the way. He was covered in oil up to his waist. But he promised to take a look at the cabin once he had put on fresh clothes."

"I don't know that we can do much else tonight," Wallander said.

They walked together through the deserted ferry terminal, where a few young men were sleeping curled up on benches. The ticket counters were all closed. They stopped when they reached Wallander's car.

"We have to go through everything again tomorrow morning," Wallander said. "At eight o'clock."

Martinsson studied his face.

"You seem nervous."

"That's because I am. I'm always nervous when I don't understand what's going on."

"How is the internal investigation going?"

"I haven't heard anything new. No journalists have tried to call, either, but that may be because I keep my phone unplugged most of the time."

"It's too bad when these things happen." Martinsson said.

Wallander sensed a double meaning in his words. He was on his guard immediately, and angry.

"What exactly do you mean?"

"Isn't it what we're always afraid of? That we're going to lose control and start lashing out at people?"

"I slapped her. End of story. I was trying to protect her mother."

"I know," Martinsson said. "But still."

He doesn't believe me, Wallander thought after he sat down behind the wheel. *Maybe no one does.*

The insight came as a shock. He had never before felt truly betrayed or abandoned by his closest colleagues. He sat there without even turning on the engine. The feeling overwhelmed him, even overshadowing the image of the young man who had been crushed in the propeller axles.

For the second time that week he felt hurt and bitter. *I'm quitting,* he thought. *I'll turn in my pink slip first thing tomorrow and then they can shove this whole investigation up their ass.*

He was still upset when he got home. In his mind he continued a heated discussion with Martinsson.

It took a long time for him to fall asleep.

They met at eight o'clock the following morning. Viktorsson joined them, as did Nyberg, who still had oil under his fingernails. Wallander was in a better mood this morning than he had been the previous night. He was not going to quit, nor would he confront Martinsson. First he would wait for the results of the internal investigation. Then he would wait for the right moment to tell his colleagues what he thought of them and their lack of faith in him.

They talked at length about the events of last night. Martinsson had already spoken to Mr. and Mrs. Tomander, neither of whom had seen or heard anything from the cabin next door. The Norwegian, Larsen, had not yet reached his home, but his wife had assured Martinsson he would be back by mid-morning.

Wallander discussed his two theories regarding Landahl with the group, and no one had any objections to make. The discussion proceeded calmly and methodically, but Wallander sensed that under the surface everyone was impatient to return to their individual tasks.

When they finished, Wallander had decided to concentrate his energies on Tynnes Falk. He was more convinced than ever before that everything started with him. Lundberg's murder had to be pushed aside for now, and its exact connection with the other events still remained to be determined. The question Wallander kept returning to was very simple. What dark forces had been set in motion when Falk had died during his evening walk? Had he died from natural causes? Wallander spent the next few hours calling the coroner's office in Lund and talking again to the pathologist who had performed the autopsy on Falk. He also again called Enander, Falk's physician who had visited Wallander at the police station. As before, there was no consensus, but by lunchtime, when Wallander's stomach was screaming with hunger, he was convinced that Falk had in fact died a natural death. No crime had been committed per se, but this sudden death in front of a cash machine had set a certain course of events in motion.

Wallander pulled over a sheet of paper and wrote the following words:

Falk.

Minks.

Angola.

He looked at what he had written, then added a final item.

20.

The list formed an impenetrable matrix. What was it he was unable to perceive? In order to assuage his sense of irritation and impatience, he left the station and took a walk. He stopped in at a pizzeria and ate. Then he returned to his office and stayed there until five. He was on the verge of giving up. He couldn't see a motive or logic behind any of the events. He couldn't get through.

He was about to get a cup of coffee when the phone rang. It was Martinsson.

"I'm at Runnerström Square," he said. "It's finally happened."

"What?"

"Modin got through. He's in. And there are strange things happening on the screen down here."

Wallander threw down the receiver.

At last, he thought. *We have finally broken through.*

Chapter Twenty-eight

It was unfortunate that Wallander didn't think to look around as he got out of his car at Runnerström Square. If he had, he might have caught a glimpse of the shadow that quickly retreated into the darkness further up the street. He would then have known not only that someone was watching them, but that this someone was always in their presence and knew what they were doing—almost what they were thinking. The undercover cars that were posted on Apelbergsgatan and Runnerström Square had not stopped him.

But Wallander didn't look around. He locked his car and hurried over to Falk's building, eager to see for himself the strange things Martinsson claimed were happening on Falk's computer. When Wallander walked in, both Modin and Martinsson were staring at the screen. Wallander was surprised to see that Martinsson had brought in the kind of folding chair that people used on camping or hunting trips. There were also two additional computers in the room. Modin and Martinsson were mumbling and pointing. Wallander could almost feel the intense concentration emanating from them. He greeted the others without receiving much in the way of a reply.

The screen really did look different now. The chaotic swarms of numbers were gone, replaced by more orderly, fixed arrangements of numbers. Robert Modin had removed his headphones. His hands wandered back and forth between the three keyboards like a virtuoso playing three different instruments at once. Wallander waited. Martinsson had a pad of paper in his hands, and from time to time Modin asked him to write something down. It was clear that Modin was running the show. After about ten minutes it was as if they suddenly became aware of Wallander's presence. Modin stopped typing.

"What's happening?" Wallander asked. "And why are there now three computers?"

"If you can't get over the mountain, you have to go around it," Modin said. His face was shiny with sweat, but he looked happy.

"It's best if Robert explains," Martinsson said.

"I never did manage to find out what the password was," the boy said. "But I brought in my own computers and connected them to Falk's. Then I was able to get in through the back door, you could say."

Wallander felt the discussion was already getting too abstract. He knew computers had windows, but he had never heard anything about there being doors.

"How did that work?"

"It's hard to explain more precisely without getting into technical details. Moreover, it's kind of a trade secret that I'd rather not get into."

"Okay, so skip it. What have you found?"

Martinsson took over.

"Falk was connected to the Internet, of course, and in a file with the bizarre name 'Jacob's Marsh' we found a long row of phone numbers arranged in a particular order. Or at least that was what we thought. No more codes. There were two columns, one consisting of names and then a long number. Right now we're trying to figure out exactly what these are."

"There are actually both phone numbers and codes in there," Modin added. "And there are long number combinations that serve as code names for various institutions across the world. There are codes for the USA, Asia, Europe, even for Brazil and Nigeria."

"What kind of institutions are we talking about?"

"That's what we're trying to figure out," Martinsson said. "But we found at least one that Robert recognized right away. That was why we called you."

"What was it?"

"The Pentagon," Modin said.

Wallander couldn't decide if there was a note of triumph or fear in Modin's voice.

"What does that mean, then?"

"We don't know yet," Martinsson said. "But there is a lot of classified, perhaps even illegally obtained, information stored in this computer. It could mean that Falk had obtained access to all of these institutions."

"I have the feeling that someone like me has been working on this computer," Modin said suddenly.

"So Falk was breaking into other people's computer networks?"

"That seems to be the case."

Wallander understood less and less. But his sense of anxiety was returning.

"And what could all this classfied information be used for?" he asked. "Can you discern a purpose?"

"It's too early for that," Martinsson said. "First we have to identify more of these institutions. Then we might get a clearer picture. But it will take time. Everything is complicated, especially because Falk arranged it precisely so that no one from the outside would be able to look in and see what he was doing."

He got up from the folding chair.

"I have to go home for a while," he said. "It's Terese's birthday today. But I'll be back soon."

He handed Wallander the pad.

"Give her my congratulations," he said. "How old is she?"

"Sixteen."

In his mind Wallander remembered her as a little girl. Wallander had been to her fifth birthday party. He thought about the fact that she was two years older than Eva Persson.

Martinsson started walking away, then stopped.

"I forgot to tell you that I talked to Larsen," he said.

It took Wallander a few seconds to place his name.

"He had one of the cabins next to Landahl," Martinsson continued. "The walls were thin, so he heard him but never saw him. Larsen was tired and slept most of the way from Poland."

"What was it he heard?"

"Voices, but nothing indicating any trouble or tumult. He couldn't say exactly how many people he thought there were."

"People don't usually talk to themselves," Wallander said. "It seems reasonable to assume there was at least one other person there."

"I asked him to be in touch if he thought of anything else."

Martinsson left. Wallander sat down carefully on the portable chair. Modin kept working. Wallander realized the futility in asking more questions. This new age of electronic developments would eventually require a whole new type of police officer. As usual, criminals were way ahead of the game.

Modin hit the RETURN button and leaned back in his chair. The modem next to the monitor started blinking.

"What are you doing now?" Wallander asked.

"I'm sending an e-mail to see where it ends up. But I'm sending it from my own computer."

"But weren't you using the keyboard for Falk's computer?"

"I've connected them."

Modin jumped and leaned in toward the monitor. Then he started typing again. Wallander waited.

Suddenly everything on the screen went blank. Then the numbers came back. Modin furrowed his brow.

"What's happening?"

"I don't know exactly. But I was denied access. I have to cover my tracks. It'll take a couple of minutes."

The typing continued. Wallander was starting to get impatient.

"One more time," Modin mumbled.

Then something happened that made Modin jump again. He stared at the screen for a long time.

"The World Bank," he said finally.

"What do you mean?"

"One of the institutions Falk has access to is the World Bank. If I'm right, the code here is for a branch that deals with global finance inspections."

"The Pentagon and the World Bank," Wallander said. "That's not exactly the corner store."

"I think it's time I had a little conference with my friends," Modin said. "I've asked them to be on alert."

"Where are they?"

"One lives in Rättvik, the other one in California."

Wallander realized it was high time he contacted the National Police cybercrime division. He started imagining uncomfortable situations ahead. He didn't entertain any illusions regarding his actions: he would be strongly criticized for his decision to turn to Modin, even though Modin had turned out to be highly adept.

While Modin was communicating with his friends, Wallander paced around the room. He was thinking about the case, but his thoughts kept returning to the feeling that his colleagues mistrusted him. Perhaps this was a problem that extended beyond the incident with Eva Persson; perhaps they thought he was over the hill? Did they think it was time for Martinsson to take charge?

He was hurt and full of self-pity. But anger also pounded in his veins. He wasn't going to go without a fight. He had no exotic place waiting where he could start a new life. He had no stud ranch to sell. All he had to look forward to was a state pension, and a meager one at that.

The typing behind him had stopped. Modin got up from his chair and stretched.

"I'm hungry," he said.

"What did your friends say?"

"We're taking an hour to think. Then we're going to talk again."

Wallander was also hungry. He suggested they go get a pizza. Modin seemed almost insulted by the suggestion.

"I never eat pizza," he said. "It's not healthy."

"What do you eat?"

"Sprouts."

"Nothing else?"

"Egg and vinegar is good."

Wallander wondered if there was any restaurant, let alone in Ystad, that sported the kind of menu likely to appeal to Robert Modin. He doubted it.

Modin looked through the plastic bags filled with food that he had brought with him, but there seemed to be nothing that caught his fancy.

"A plain salad will do," he said.

They left the building. Wallander asked Modin if he wanted them to drive, but Modin preferred to walk.

They went to the only salad bar Wallander knew of in Ystad. Wallander ate heartily, but Modin scrutinized every lettuce leaf and vegetable before putting it in his mouth. Wallander had never seen a person who chewed so slowly. He tried conversing with Modin, but the latter only answered in monosyllables. After a while, Wallander realized he was still obsessed with the figures and patterns in Falk's computer.

They were back at Runnerström Square shortly before seven. Martinsson was still gone. Modin sat down at the computer to reconnect with his friends. Wallander imagined they looked exactly like the young man beside him.

"No one has managed to trace me," Modin said after he had performed some complicated operations on the computer.

"How can you see that?"

"I just see it."

Wallander shifted on the folding chair. *It really is like being on a hunting trip,* he thought. *We're hunting electronic elk. We know they're out there. But we don't know what direction they're going to come from.*

Wallander's cell phone rang. Modin flinched.

"I hate cell phones," he said with distaste.

Wallander walked out onto the staircase. It was Höglund. Wallander told her where he was and what they had managed to extract from Falk's computer.

"The World Bank and the Pentagon," she said, "They must be two of the world's most powerful institutions."

"We still don't know what all this means," Wallander said. "But why are you calling?"

"I decided I needed to talk to that guy Ryss again. After all, he was the person who led us to Landahl, and I'm becoming more and more convinced that Eva Persson actually knew very little about the friend she seems to have worshipped. In any case, we know she's lying."

"What did he say? His name is Kalle, isn't it?"

"Kalle Ryss. I wanted to ask him why he and Sonja broke up. I don't think he was expecting that question, and he clearly didn't want to answer it, but I wouldn't back down. And then he said something interesting. He said he broke up with her because she was never interested."

"Interested in what?"

"In sex, of course."

"He told you this?"

"Once he started, the whole story came pouring out of him. He fell in love with her from the moment he first saw her, but after they started dating it became clear that she had no interest in sex. Finally he grew tired of it. But it's the reason for her lack of interest that's important."

"What was it?"

"Sonja had told him that she was raped a few years ago. She was still traumatized by that experience."

"Sonja Hökberg was raped?"

"According to him she was. I started checking our files but didn't find any case involving Sonja."

"And it happened in Ystad?"

"Yes. So I started putting two and two together."

Wallander saw where she was heading.

"Lundberg's son. Carl-Einar?"

"Exactly. It's just a theory, but I think it has its merits."

"What do you think happened?"

"This is what I was thinking: Carl-Einar Lundberg has been implicated in a brutal rape case. He's acquitted, but there were several facts that pointed to his being the perpetrator. In which case, he could have committed an earlier rape. But Sonja never went to the police."

"Why not?"

"There are many reasons why a woman wouldn't go to the police in such a case. You should know that."

"So what's your conclusion?"

"It's just a theory."

"I still want to hear it."

"It's somewhat bizarre, I admit, but I think it's possible to see Lundberg's murder as a kind of revenge by proxy."

"Revenge?"

"At least that gives us a motive. And we also know something about Sonja."

"What is that?"

"That she was stubborn. And you said her stepfather described her as a strong person."

"I'm still not entirely convinced. How did the girls know that the father would be the one picking them up in the taxi? And how would she have known it was Carl-Einar's father?"

"Ystad is a small town. And we don't know how Sonja reacted to the rape. She could have been consumed by thoughts of revenge. Women are deeply affected by rape. Some withdraw and turn inward. But some do become possessed by violent thoughts of revenge."

Wallander realized that what Höglund had discovered could be important. It fit his idea that Lundberg's murder was incidental to the central chain of events surrounding Falk.

"I think you need to find out if Eva Persson knew any of this," he said.

"I agree. Then we need to check if Sonja ever came home with bruises. The rape that Carl-Einar Lundberg was accused of was violent."

"You're right."

"I'll get on it."

Höglund promised to call if she found anything else. Wallander put his phone in his pocket but stayed out on the dark landing. There was a thought that was bubbling up from his unconscious. Why was it that Sonja Hökberg had escaped from the police station? They had never dug very deeply into that matter. They had simply stopped at the most logical conclusion; that she wanted to skip out and avoid responsibility. After all, she had already confessed to the crime. But now Wallander saw another way to look at it. Sonja Hökberg may have left because she had something else to hide. What could that have been? Wallander instinctively sensed that he was getting closer to something important. But there was still something missing, a connection he was trying to make.

Then he thought of what it was. Sonja Hökberg could have left the station in the vain hope of getting away. So far so good. But somewhere out there waiting for her had been a person who was not as concerned about the fact that she had just confessed to killing Lundberg as about the fact that she might have told the police something else while she was there. Something that concerned a very different matter than personal revenge.

This works, Wallander thought. *This way Lundberg fits with everything else and there's a reasonable explanation for what follows. Something had to be kept quiet, something Sonja might have told us if she had lived. She is killed to keep her quiet. But her killer is done away with in turn. Just like Modin sweeps away any traces of himself in the computer. Someone has been trying to clean up.*

What was it that had transpired in Luanda? he thought again. *Who is "C"? And what does the number twenty refer to?*

Höglund's idea had cheered him up. He returned to Modin's side with renewed energy.

Fifteen minutes later, Martinsson came back. He described in detail the cake he had just eaten, while Wallander listened impatiently. Then Wallander asked Modin to fill Martinsson in on what they had discovered while he was gone.

"The World Bank?" Martinsson asked. "What does that have to do with Falk?"

"That's what we have to find out."

Martinsson removed his coat, sat back down on the folding chair, and rubbed his hands together. Wallander summarized his conversation with Höglund. Martinsson also sensed the importance of the discovery.

"That gives us a way in," he said when Wallander had finished.

"It gives us more than that," he said. "We're finally starting to make sense of this."

"I've never seen a case like this," Martinsson said thoughtfully. "We still have so much we can't account for. We don't know why the electrical relay was placed in the morgue. We don't know why Falk's body was removed. I just don't think cutting off his fingers was the driving motive."

"We'll do what we can to fill in these holes," Wallander said. "I'm going to head back to the office. But let me know if anything happens."

"We'll keep going until ten," Modin said suddenly. "But then I need to sleep."

Once Wallander was down on the street he was suddenly at a loss. Should he try to keep going for a few hours? Or should he head straight home?

He decided to do both. There was no reason he couldn't work at the kitchen table. All he needed was time to digest what Höglund had told him. He got into his car and drove home.

He sat down at the kitchen table and spread out his notes. Höglund's theory was on his mind and he wanted to go through the case methodically. At eleven he finally got up from the table and went to bed.

The holes are still there, he thought. *But it still seems that Höglund's insight has brought us forward.*

He went to bed shortly before midnight and fell asleep almost immediately.

Modin stopped at exactly ten o'clock. They packed up his computers, and Martinsson drove him out to Löderup personally. They agreed that he would pick him up at eight the following morning.

Modin did not go straight to bed after Martinsson left. He knew he shouldn't be doing what he was about to do. The memory of what happened after he broke into the Pentagon system was still strong. But the temptation was too great. And he had learned his lesson. Now he knew to erase all his tracks.

His parents had already gone to bed. The house was silent. Martinsson hadn't noticed when Modin started copying some of the material he had accessed in Falk's computer. Now he hooked up his two computers and started going through the files again, looking once more for clues and openings, new ways to climb the firewall.

A storm front came in over Luanda in the evening.

Carter had spent the evening reading a report that criticized the International Monetary Fund's operations in some East African countries. The criticisms were well-formulated and devastating. Carter couldn't have done a better job himself. But he remained convinced of the necessity of his actions. There was no other way to consider at this point. If the world's financial systems remained as they were, there could be no true reform.

He put the report down and walked over to the window and watched the lightning dance across the sky. His night guards huddled under the small rain shelter they had erected.

He was about to go to bed when something led him into the study. The air conditioning unit droned loudly.

He could tell immediately that someone was trying to break into the server. But something was different. He sat down at the computer. After a while he saw what it was.

Someone had become careless.

Carter dried his hands on a handkerchief.

Then he started chasing the person who was threatening to reveal his secret.

Chapter Twenty-nine

Wallander stayed at home until nearly ten o'clock on Thursday morning. He woke up early and felt fully rested. His joy at having been able to sleep undisturbed for a whole night was so great that it gave him a guilty conscience. He should have used the extra time to work. He often wondered where his overdeveloped work ethic had come from. His mother had been a housewife who had never complained about not being able to work outside the house. At least, she had never said anything about it.

His father had certainly never undertaken extra work if he could help it. Wallander had sometimes spied on him and discovered that his father did not spend a lot of time in front of the easel. Sometimes he had been reading a book or sleeping on the old mattress in the corner of the studio. Other times he had been seated at the rickety old table playing solitaire. Physically Wallander was starting to look more and more like his father, but on the inside he was driven by a constant state of unrest and dissatisfaction, demons he had never seen in either of his parents.

He had called the station at eight o'clock. The only person he could get hold of was Hansson. Everyone else was busy with their individual investigative tasks. He had decided they should postpone their meeting until the afternoon. Then he went down to the laundry room to sign up, only to discover that the morning hours were unclaimed. He had immediately booked the following hours and returned to the apartment to pick up his dirty clothes.

The letter had arrived while he was loading his clothes into the washer. It was lying on the floor in the hallway. There was no stamp, no return address on the envelope. His name and address were written by hand. He put it on the kitchen table, thinking that it must be some kind of invitation. It wasn't unheard of to get invitations delivered by hand. Then he hung his bedclothes out to air on the balcony. It was getting colder again, though there was no frost. He only opened the letter when it was time for his second cup of coffee. That was when he discovered that there was an unaddressed envelope inside. He opened it and read the letter. At first he couldn't make sense of it, but then he realized he had actually received an answer to his personal ad. He put down the letter, walked around the table, then read it again.

The woman who had written to him was named Elvira Lindfeldt. She had not included a photograph of herself, but Wallander decided she must be very beautiful. Her handwriting was elegant and firm, no fussy loops or curlicues. The dating service had forwarded his ad to her and she had found it interesting. She was thirty-nine years old and divorced. She lived in Malmö. She worked for a shipping company called Heinemann & Nagel. She ended her letter by giving her phone number and saying she hoped to hear from him soon. Wallander felt like a ravenous wolf who had finally managed to fell his prey. He wanted to call her right away. But then he controlled himself and decided he should throw the letter in the trash. The meeting was doomed to be a complete failure. She would be disappointed because she probably imagined him to be different.

He also had no time for this. He was in the middle of the most complicated murder investigation he had ever been in charge of. He walked around the table a few more times. Then he realized the futility of having written to the dating service. He picked up the letter, tore it into pieces, and threw it away. Then he sat down to think about the case. Before he drove into the station he put his laundry in the dryer. The first thing he did when he got to his office was write himself a note reminding him to get his laundry when he went home. In the corridor he met Nyberg, who was on his way somewhere with a plastic bag.

"We're going to be getting some results in today," he said. "Among other things, we've been cross-checking a number of fingerprints."

"Do you have a better idea of what happened in the engine room?"

"I don't envy the pathologist, I'll tell you that. The body was so crushed there wasn't a whole piece of bone in there. Well, you saw it. You know what it looked like."

"Sonja Hökberg was probably already unconscious or even dead by the time she was thrown against the high voltage wires," Wallander said. "Do you think that was the case with Jonas Landahl? If it really was Landahl."

"Oh, it was him," Nyberg said quickly.

"How do you know that?"

"He was identified by an unusual birthmark above his ankle."

"So there's no doubt about his identity?"

"Not as far as I can tell. The parents have apparently been contacted as well."

"Good. Then that's taken care of," Wallander said. "First Sonja Hök-berg. Then her boyfriend."

Nyberg raised his eyebrows.

"I thought he was suspected of having killed her? I know it's a grisly way to commit suicide, but wasn't that what it was?"

"There are other possibilities," Wallander said. "But the most important thing for now is having established his identity."

Wallander returned to his office. He had just taken off his coat and started to regret the fact that he'd thrown Elvira's letter away when the phone rang. It was Lisa Holgersson. She wanted to see him immediately. He walked to her office with a sense of dread. Normally he enjoyed speaking with her, but ever since she had openly displayed her mistrust of him a week ago he had been trying to avoid her. As he might have expected, the atmosphere when he came into the room was far from relaxed. Holgersson was sitting behind her desk, and her trademark smile was tense and forced. Wallander sat down. He felt his anger starting to bubble up inside him in anticipation of whatever was about to come his way.

"I'm going to get right to the point," she said. "The internal investigation into allegations made against you by Eva Persson and her mother is now underway."

"Who's in charge?"

"A man from Hässleholm."

"A man from Hässleholm? That sounds like the name of a bad TV series."

"He's a highly regarded police officer. I also need to inform you that you have been reported to the justice department ombudsman. And not just you. We have both been reported."

"Did you slap her, too?"

"I'm responsible for the conduct of my officers."

"Who filed the report?"

"Eva Persson's lawyer. His name is Klas Harryson."

"Thanks for letting me know," Wallander said and got up. He was furious now. The energy from the morning was quickly draining from his body, and he didn't want to lose it.

"I'm not finished yet."

"We're in the middle of a very complicated homicide investigation."

"I spoke to Hansson this morning. I know how it's going."

He said nothing about having talked to her, Wallander thought. The feeling that his colleagues were going behind his back returned.

He sat down heavily.

"This is a difficult situation," she said.

"Not really," Wallander said, interrupting her. "What happened between Eva Persson, her mother, and me happened in exactly the way that I told you. I haven't changed a single word of my story since the beginning. You should be able to tell that I don't flinch or get nervous when you press me on details. What makes me mad as all hell, however, is that you don't believe me."

"What do you expect me to do?"

"I want you to believe me when I talk to you."

"But the girl and her mother have a different story. And there are two of them."

"There could be a hundred of them and it wouldn't change a thing. You should believe me, not them. They have reason to lie."

"So do you."

"I do?"

"If you hit her without provocation."

Wallander got up a second time, even more forcefully.

"I won't even comment on the last thing you said. It's insulting."

She started to protest, but he interrupted her.

"Is there anything else?"

"I'm not done yet."

Wallander remained standing. The situation was almost unbearably tense. He was not going to back down, but he also wanted to get out of there as soon as possible.

"The situation we're in has become serious enough for me to be forced to take some action," she said. "While the internal investigation is underway I have to suspend you from your work."

Wallander heard her words and knew what they meant. Both Hansson and his now-dead colleague Svedberg had been suspended on earlier occasions. In Hansson's case, Wallander had been convinced that the allegations were false. In Svedberg's case he had not been so sure, and the allegations had later been corroborated. But in neither case had he supported Björk, who was chief back then, in going so far as to suspend his colleagues. It seemed to him to be calling them guilty before the investigation had yielded any results.

Suddenly his anger left him. He was completely calm.

"You do as you like," he said. "But if you suspend me now I will resign effective immediately."

"That sounds like a threat."

"I don't care what the hell it sounds like. It's just a fact. And don't think you can count on me coming back if the investigation proves that they were lying and I was telling the truth."

"I wish you would try to cooperate instead of threatening to resign."

"I have been a police officer for many years," Wallander said, "and I know enough to tell you that the steps you say you have to take are not necessary. There's someone higher up who's very nervous about that picture appearing in the paper and who wants to make an example of me. And you are choosing to go along with it."

"It's nothing like that," she said.

"You know as well as I do that it's exactly like that. When were you planning to suspend me, anyway? As soon as you dismissed me from this meeting?"

"The man from Hässleholm promised to work quickly. Since we are in the middle of a difficult homicide investigation right now, I was going to put it off."

"Why? Let Martinsson take charge. He'll do an excellent job."

"I thought we would finish out the week as usual."

"No," Wallander said. "Nothing is as usual right now. Either you suspend me as of this moment or else you don't do it at all."

"I don't understand why you have to resort to these threats. I thought we had a good working relationship."

"I thought so too. But clearly I was wrong."

They were silent.

"So how is it going to be?" Wallander asked. "Am I suspended or not?"

"You are not suspended," she said. "At least not right now."

Wallander left her office. As he walked through the halls he realized he was drenched with sweat. When he got to his office he locked the door behind him. Now the full force of his emotions came back. He wanted to sit down and write his resignation, clear out his office, and leave the station for good. Their afternoon meeting would have to take place without him. He was never coming back.

At the same time there was something inside him that resisted. If he left now, it would look like he was guilty. Then the final conclusion of the internal investigation wouldn't have much impact. He would always be tainted.

He slowly arrived at his decision. He would keep working for now, but he would inform his colleagues of the situation. The most important thing was that he had let Holgersson know where things stood. He did not intend to toe the line on this or ask for mercy.

He started to calm down. He opened his door wide and continued working. At noon, he went home and took his clothes out of the dryer. He carefully picked the pieces of Elvira's letter from the trash, although he couldn't exactly say why. At least she had nothing to do with the police.

He ate lunch at István's restaurant and chatted with one of his father's friends, who happened to be there. He returned to the police station shortly after one o'clock.

He walked in through the glass doors feeling somewhat on edge. Chief Holgersson could have changed her mind since their meeting and decided to suspend him after all. He didn't know how he would react to this. Secretly he found the idea of handing in his resignation appalling. He couldn't even begin to imagine what his life would look like after that. But when he reached his office there were only a few unimportant messages waiting for him. Holgersson had not tried to reach him. Wallander took a few deep breaths and then called Martinsson, who was at Runnerström Square.

"We're working slowly but surely," he said. "He's managed to break a couple more codes."

Wallander could hear the rustling of paper. Then Martinsson came back on the line.

"We now have a connection to a stockbroker in Seoul and to an English firm by the name of Lonrho. I contacted a person in Stockholm who was able to tell me that Lonrho was originally an African company that was involved in highly illegal operations in southern Rhodesia during the time of sanctions."

"But how are we supposed to interpret this?" Wallander broke in. "A stockbroker in Korea? And this other company, whatever its name is? How does it relate to Falk and our investigation?"

"We're trying to figure it out. Robert says there are about eighty companies entered into this program. But it will take us a while to find out what the connections between them are and what the program is."

"But if you were going to speculate? What would you say?"

Martinsson chuckled.

"I see money."

"And what else?"

"Isn't that enough? The World Bank, the Korean stockbroker, and this African company all share that as a common denominator. Money."

Wallander agreed.

"Who knows," he said. "Perhaps the key player in all of this isn't Falk but the cash machine where he died."

Martinsson laughed. Wallander suggested that they meet at around three.

After the conversation ended, Wallander started thinking about Elvira Lindfeldt. He tried to imagine what she could look like, but his mind always came up with a picture of Baiba. Or Mona. Or a very brief glimpse of a woman he had met briefly the year before at a roadside café outside Västervik.

He was interrupted in his thoughts by Hansson, who suddenly appeared in the doorway. Wallander felt guilty, as if his thoughts had been clearly visible.

"All the keys are accounted for," Hansson said.

Wallander looked at him without understanding what he was talking about. But he didn't say anything, since he had the feeling that he should know what Hansson meant.

"I have some documentation from Sydkraft," he went on. "The people who had keys to the substation can all account for them."

"Good," Wallander said. "It's always helpful to be able to strike something off our list."

"Unfortunately, I haven't been able to trace the Mercedes van."

Wallander leaned back in his chair.

"I think you can put that aside for now. We'll have to get the car eventually, but for now there are more important tasks."

Hansson nodded and wrote something in his notebook. Wallander told him about the three o'clock meeting. Hansson left.

Wallander put aside his thoughts of Elvira and her appearance. He got back to his paperwork and also thought about what Martinsson had said. The phone rang. It was Viktorsson, asking how the case was going.

"I thought Hansson kept you abreast of all developments."

"But you are in charge of this investigation."

Viktorsson's comment surprised Wallander. He had been sure that Holgersson had arrived at her decision to suspend him in consultation with Viktorsson. But he was fairly sure of the fact that Viktorsson was not being disingenuous when he said Wallander was in charge. Wallander automatically softened toward him.

"I can come and see you tomorrow morning."

"I'm free at half past eight."

Wallander made a note of it. Then he spent another half-hour preparing for the meeting. At twenty to three he went to get more coffee, but the machine was broken. Wallander thought once more about Erik Hökberg's observation about the vulnerability of society. That gave him a new idea. He went back to his office to give Hökberg a call. Hökberg picked up at once. Wallander gave him some details about the latest events and asked if he had ever heard the name Jonas Landahl. Hökberg answered with a definite no. That surprised Wallander.

"Are you completely sure?"

"The name is unusual enough that I would have remembered it. Was he the one who killed Sonja?"

"We don't know. But they knew each other, and we have some information indicating that they may even have been involved."

Wallander wondered if he should mention the idea of rape, but he decided it was the wrong moment. It wasn't something they should discuss over the phone. Instead, he moved on to the question he had been wanting to ask.

"When I was out to see you last, you told me about your computer transactions. I had the impression then that there were no real limitations to what you could do."

"That's right. If you connect to the large databases around the world, you're always at the center of things. It doesn't matter where you are physically."

"That means that you could do business with a stockbroker in Seoul if you felt like it."

"In theory, yes."

"And what would I need to know in order to do that?"

"First and foremost you would need his e-mail address. Then the security systems have to match up. He has to be able to see who I am, and vice versa. But otherwise there are no real problems. None of a technical nature, at any rate."

"What do you mean by that?"

"Each country naturally has its own set of laws and regulations governing trade. You would have to know what those are, unless you are operating illegally."

"Since there is so much money involved, the security measures must be pretty high. Do you think they are invincible?"

"I'm not the right man to ask those questions. But as a police officer you should know that anyone with a strong enough desire can do almost anything. What is it people say? If you really wanted to kill the president of the USA, you could do it. But now I'm getting curious about why you're asking me all these questions."

"You impressed me as having a great deal of technical expertise."

"Only on the surface. The electronic world is so complicated and is changing so fast that I doubt there's anyone out there who understands it completely. Or who has control over it."

Wallander promised to be in touch with him soon. Then he went to the conference room. Hansson and Nyberg were already there. They were talking about the coffee machine that was breaking down more and more often these days. Wallander nodded to them and sat down. Höglund and Martinsson arrived at the same time. Wallander had not yet decided if he was going to begin or end by talking about his meeting with Holgersson. He finally decided to wait. His hardworking colleagues were involved in a difficult investigation and he shouldn't burden them more than absolutely necessary.

They began by discussing the events surrounding Jonas Landahl's death. There were no eyewitness accounts. No one had seen him on the ferry, no one had seen him make his way to the engine room.

"I find it very strange," Wallander said. "No one saw him, either when he paid for his cabin or when he was moving about the ship. No one saw him enter the restricted area leading to the engine room. It makes no sense."

"He must have traveled with someone," Höglund said. "I spoke to one of the engineers before I got here, and he said it would have been impossible for Landahl to squeeze himself in between the axles on his own."

"So he must have been forced into that position," Wallander said. "Which means we now have two people who managed to find their way into the engine room without being seen. And one person who made his way back. But we can draw one conclusion from this, which is that Landahl must have accompanied this person willingly. If he had been coerced, someone would probably have noticed. It would also have been difficult for the killer to force Landahl down those steep ladders."

They kept discussing various aspects of the case until six o'clock, at which time Wallander decided they were no longer being productive. Everyone was tired. Wallander also decided not to mention his conversation with Holgersson at all. He simply didn't have the energy.

Martinsson returned to Runnerström Square, where Modin was working. Hansson brought up the point that Modin should probably be compensated in some way. Nyberg yawned. Wallander saw that he still had oil under his fingernails. Wallander stood around in the corridor with Hansson and Höglund and talked for a few more minutes. They assigned some of the tasks that remained. Then Wallander went to his office and closed his door.

He sat and stared at the phone for a long time without understanding his hesitation. Finally he picked it up and dialed Elvira Lindfeldt's number.

She picked up after the seventh ring.

"Lindfeldt."

Wallander quickly put the phone down. Then he waited a few minutes before dialing her number again. This time she answered immediately. He liked the sound of her voice.

Wallander told her who he was, and they chatted in a casual way for a few minutes. It was apparently quite windy in Malmö, more so than in Ystad. Elvira also complained that many of her colleagues at work were coming down with colds. Wallander agreed. Fall was always such a difficult time that way. He was recovering from a sore throat himself.

"It would be nice to get together sometime," she said.

"I'm not a big believer in dating services," he said, regretting it as soon as the words left his mouth.

"It's really no better or worse than any other way to meet people," she said. "We're both adults, after all."

Then she said another thing that surprised him. She asked him what he was doing that evening. She suggested that they meet in Malmö.

I can't, Wallander thought. *This is way too fast. And I have work to do.*

Then he said yes.

They decided to meet at eight-thirty at the Savoy Bar.

"We'll skip the carnations," she said. "I think we'll be able to pick each other out."

The conversation came to an end.

Wallander wondered what he was getting himself into. But he was also excited.

Then he realized it was already half past six. He had to get ready.

Chapter Thirty

Wallander parked outside the Savoy at exactly twenty-seven minutes past eight. He had driven way too fast on his way from Ystad because he thought he would be late. He had taken a long time deciding what to wear. He'd finally picked a fresh but unironed shirt from the pile of clean clothes, and then he couldn't decide on a tie. Finally he decided against one altogether. But his shoes were scuffed and needed polishing. The end result was that he left the apartment later than he intended.

Hansson had also called him in the middle of his preparations and asked him if he knew where Nyberg was. Wallander had not managed to find out why it was so important to him. He had kept his answers so short that Hansson had asked him if he was in a hurry. Wallander had been secretive enough that Hansson had not asked any further questions. When he was about to leave, the phone rang again. This time it was Linda. There was a lull at the restaurant and her boss was on vacation, so she thought she would check in with him. Wallander almost told her where he was going. Linda was the one who had spurred him to get into this in the first place. She immediately sensed he was in a hurry. Wallander knew he could never put anything past her. But he still tried to tell her as convincingly as possible that he was about to attend to a work-related matter. They agreed she would call him the following evening.

Once Wallander was on the road, he realized he had almost no gas. He thought he could almost make it to Malmö, but didn't want to take any chances. He pulled into a gas station outside Skurup and doubted that he would be able to make it in time. He didn't even know why it was so important to him. But he still remembered the time when he had been ten minutes late for a date with Mona and she had simply left.

But he did make it in time. He stayed in the car for a moment and looked at his face in the mirror. He was thinner now than he'd been a few years ago, and his features were more sharply defined. She wouldn't know that he had his father's face. He closed his eyes and took a few deep breaths. He forced all his expectations away. Even if he wasn't likely to be disappointed, she probably would. They would meet in the bar, have a drink, and then it would be over. He would be back in his bed by midnight. When he woke up the next day he would already have forgotten her and also be confirmed in his suspicions that this dating-service business was nothing for him.

He stayed in the car until almost twenty to nine, then got out and walked across the street to the Savoy.

They saw each other at the same time. She was sitting at a table in the far corner. Apart from some men at the bar there weren't many guests, and she was the only unaccompanied woman. Wallander caught her gaze and she smiled. When she stood up to greet him he saw that she was very tall. She was wearing a dark-blue suit. Her skirt came to just above her knees and he saw that she had beautiful legs.

"Am I right?" he asked as he stretched out his hand.

"If you are Kurt Wallander, I am Elvira."

He sat down across the table from her.

"I don't smoke," she said. "But I do drink."

"So do I," Wallander said. "But not tonight. I'm driving, so I'll have to stick to mineral water."

He was dying for a glass of wine. Or better yet, several. But since that time many years ago when he had been stopped by his colleagues Peters and Norén after having had one too many, he had been very careful. They had not said anything, but Wallander knew he had been so drunk that it could have meant immediate dismissal. It was one of the worst memories of his career. He didn't want to risk anything like it again.

The waiter came to the table and took their order. Elvira ordered another glass of white wine.

Wallander felt self-conscious. Ever since he was a teenager he had been under the impression that he looked best in profile. Therefore he now turned his chair so that he sat sideways to the table.

"Don't you have enough room for your feet?" she asked. "I can pull the table over, if you like?"

"Not at all," Wallander said. "I'm fine."

What the hell do I say now? he wondered. *Do I tell her I fell in love with her from the moment I stepped in the door? Or rather, when I first read her letter?*

"Have you ever done this before?" she asked.

"Never."

"I have," she said cheerfully. "But it's never led to anything."

Wallander noticed that she was very direct in her approach, in direct contrast to himself. He was still mostly concerned over whether or not to appear in profile.

"Why hasn't it worked out before?"

"Wrong person, wrong sense of humor, wrong attitude, wrong expectations. Some have been pompous or had too many drinks. A lot can go wrong."

"Perhaps I've already done something wrong, too?"

"You look nice enough," she said.

"I think that's a word that is only rarely applied to me," he said. "But I guess I'm no ogre."

At that moment he suddenly thought of the picture of Eva Persson that had been circulated in the press. Had she seen it? Did she know he was accused of assaulting a juvenile?

But the picture never came up in the conversation that ensued over the following hours. Wallander started to believe she hadn't seen it. Perhaps she never read the evening papers. Wallander sat with his mineral water in front of him and longed for something stronger. She kept drinking wine. She asked him what it was like to be a policeman, and Wallander tried to answer her questions as truthfully as he could. But he noticed that he kept bringing up the more difficult aspects of his work, as if he was trying to elicit sympathy from her.

Her questions were well thought-out, sometimes even unexpected. He had to keep his wits about him in order to give her meaningful answers.

She told him about her own work. The shipping company she worked for did a lot of moving of household goods for Swedish missionaries who were either setting off abroad or coming home. He began to realize that she held a position of some responsibility, since her boss was often away on business. She clearly enjoyed her work.

The time flew by. Shortly after eleven, Wallander was in the middle of telling her about his failed marriage with Mona. She listened attentively, seriously but also supportively.

"And afterward?" she asked when his story trailed off. "You've been divorced for some time now. There must have been someone else."

"I've been alone for long periods of time," he said. "But for a while I was seeing a woman from Lettland, from Riga. Her name was Baiba.

I had high hopes for the relationship and for a while I thought she shared those hopes. But it didn't work out."

"Why not?"

"She wanted to stay in Riga, and I wanted to stay here. I had made all kinds of plans. We were going to live in the country, start over."

"Perhaps your dreams were too big," she said. "You got burned."

Wallander had the feeling that he had talked too much, that he had said too much about himself and perhaps even Mona and Baiba. But the woman across from him was easy to confide in.

Then she told him about herself. Her story was much the same as his, except that in her case it was two failed marriages rather than one. She had one child from the first marriage and one from the second. Without saying anything explicit, she gave Wallander the impression that her first husband had been physically abusive. Her second husband had been Argentinean, and she told Wallander with equal measures of insight and self-irony how his passionate nature, which at first had been a breath of fresh air, had finally become stifling.

"He disappeared two years ago," she said. "The last I heard of him he was in Barcelona and had run out of money. I helped him get a ticket back to Argentina. Now I haven't heard from him for a year. His daughter is distraught, of course."

"How old are your kids?"

"Alexandra is nineteen, Tobias twenty-one."

They paid their bill at half-past eleven. Wallander wanted to treat her, but she insisted on splitting it.

"It's Friday tomorrow," Wallander said once they were out on the street.

"I've never been to Ystad. Isn't that funny?"

Wallander wanted to ask if he could call her. He didn't really know what he was feeling, but she seemed not to have found too many faults in him yet. For now that was enough to be encouraged.

"I have a car," she said. "I could even take the train. Do you have any time?"

"I'm in the middle of a difficult homicide case right now," he said. "But I guess even policemen need occasional time off."

She lived out in a Malmö suburb, toward Jägersro. Wallander offered to give her a ride, but she said she wanted to walk for a while and then take a taxi.

"I take as many long walks as I can," she said. "I hate to jog."

"Me too," Wallander said.

But he said nothing about his diabetes, the reason he was now an avid walker.

They shook hands and said goodnight.

"It was nice to meet you," she said.

"Yes," Wallander said. "Likewise."

He watched her until she had rounded the corner of the hotel. Then he walked over to his car and drove back toward Ystad. He put on a cassette tape of the tenor Jussi Björling. Music filled the car as he drove. As he passed the turn off to Stjärnsund, where Sten Widén's ranch was, he thought that his normal sting of jealousy was not as strong now.

It was half past one by the time he parked the car. He walked up to his apartment and sat down on the sofa. It had been a long time since he had felt as happy as he did this evening. The last time must have been when he started to sense that Baiba reciprocated his feelings.

He went to bed without even thinking about the case.

For the first time in a long while, work had taken a back seat.

Wallander arrived at the station on Friday morning with explosive energy. The first thing he did was cancel the surveillance on Falk's apartment on Apelbergsgatan. He did, however, want the surveillance at Runnerström Square to continue. Then he walked over to Martinsson's office. It was empty. Hansson was also not in yet. But he bumped into Höglund in the hall. She looked unusually tired and grumpy. He thought he should say some encouraging words to her but couldn't think of anything that would sound genuine.

"Sonja Hökberg's phone book still hasn't turned up," she said. "The one she carried in her purse."

"Have we established that she had one?"

"Eva Persson has corroborated Sonja's mother's claim. It was a small, dark-blue book with a rubber band around the middle."

"Then we're assuming that whoever killed her and tossed her handbag had first pocketed this book?"

"That seems plausible."

"The question is what phone numbers were in there. And what names."

Höglund shrugged. Wallander looked more closely at her.

"How are things with you, anyway?"

"Things are as they are," she said. "But they sure as hell could be better."

She went into her office and closed the door. Wallander hesitated but decided to knock on her door. When he heard her voice, he went in.

"We have some other things to talk about," he said.

"I know. I'm sorry."

"Don't be."

He sat down. As usual, her office was perfectly neat.

"We have to sort out this business with the rape," he said. "I haven't spoken to Sonja's mother yet. I have a meeting with Viktorsson at half past eight, but then I'm going to head over to their house. I take it she's back from staying with her sister?"

"They're planning the funeral. I think it's very hard on them."

Wallander got up.

"What's going to happen to Eva Persson?" he asked.

"I don't know."

"Even if she manages to lay the blame on Sonja, her life has been destroyed."

Höglund made a face.

"I don't know if I would go that far. Eva Persson seems like one of these people who can let everything wash over her and not let it affect her. How you get like that, I don't know."

Wallander thought about what she had said. Perhaps he would understand it better later.

"Have you seen Martinsson?" he asked as he was leaving.

"I saw him come in."

"He wasn't in his office."

"I saw him go into Lisa's office."

"I didn't think she ever came in this early."

"They were having a meeting."

Something in her voice made him stop. She saw his hesitation and seemed to make a decision. Then she gestured for him to come back inside and close the door.

"A meeting about what?"

"Sometimes you really surprise me," she said. "You see and hear everything. You're a great police officer and you know how to keep your investigative team motivated. But at the same time it's as if you see nothing that's going on around you."

Wallander felt something cramp up in his gut. He didn't say anything, he just waited for her to go on.

"You always speak well of Martinsson, and he always follows where you lead. You work well together."

"I'm constantly worried that he's going to get fed up and leave."

"He won't, believe me."

"That's what he always tells me. And it would be a shame. He is a good police officer."

She looked squarely at him.

"I shouldn't be telling you this, but I will anyway. You trust him way too much."

"What do you mean?"

"I mean that he's going behind your back. What do you think is going on in Lisa's office right now? They may very well be talking about it being high time for some changes around here. Changes, I might add, that would be to your detriment rather than Martinsson's."

Wallander heard what she said but couldn't believe it.

"How do you mean 'going behind my back'?"

She threw her letter opener across her desk in an angry gesture.

"It took me a while to see it. Martinsson is smart. He's manipulative, and good at it. He goes and complains to Lisa about the way you're handling this investigation."

"He tells her I'm incompetent?"

"I don't think he would ever express himself so directly. He simply implies certain deficiencies. Weak leadership, strange priorities. He went straight to Lisa when you brought in Robert Modin, for example."

Wallander was amazed.

"I can't believe what you're telling me."

"You should. But I hope you understand that I'm telling you this in confidence."

Wallander nodded. His stomach was hurting now.

"I just thought you should know. That's all."

Wallander looked at her.

"Do you agree with him?"

"If I did, I would tell you to your face. Not go behind your back."

"What about Hansson? Nyberg?"

"This is Martinsson's game. No one else's. He's going after the throne."

"But what about his constant complaints about work? He doesn't even know if he wants to stay in the force."

"Aren't you the one who's always telling us to look past the surface to the very bottom? You always take Martinsson at face value. But I can tell you I've seen what's underneath, and I don't like what I see."

Wallander felt almost paralyzed. The energy and joy he had felt when he woke up was gone. Somewhere inside him, anger was starting to bubble up.

"I'm going to get him for this," he said. "I'm going to grab him right now and see what he has to say for himself."

"That is not a good idea."

"How am I supposed to keep working with someone like him?"

"I can't tell you that. But you have to wait for a better opportunity to confront him. If you say anything now, you'll just give him more reasons to complain about you being unbalanced. He also thinks that the slap you gave Eva Persson was no coincidence."

"Maybe you know that Lisa is thinking of suspending me."

"It wasn't Lisa's idea," Höglund said grimly. "It was Martinsson."

"How do you know all this?"

"He has a weakness," she said. "He trusts me. He thinks I agree with him, even though I've told him I think he should stop going behind your back."

Wallander got up from the chair.

"Don't do anything rash," she repeated. "Try to think of this information as having a leg up on him. Use it when the time comes."

She was right.

Wallander went back to his office. His anger was tinted with sadness. He could have believed it about almost anyone, just not Martinsson. Not Martinsson.

He was interrupted in his thoughts by the phone. It was Viktorsson, calling to see where he was since he hadn't shown up for the meeting. Wallander walked over to the district attorney's office, nervous about running into Martinsson. But then he realized Martinsson had probably already left to be at Robert Modin's side in Falk's office.

The conversation with Viktorsson didn't take long. Wallander forced himself to put all other thoughts aside and focused on the main events of the case. He told Viktorsson where they thought they were and what direction they were planning to take. Viktorsson asked a few questions but had no objection to what he had heard.

"What do you think you will find in Falk's computer?"

"I don't know. But I think it may help us clarify the issue of motive."

"Did Falk commit any kind of a crime?"

"Not as far as we know."

Viktorsson scratched his head.

"Do you know enough about these things? Shouldn't experts from the National Police be stepping in here?"

"We have a local expert working on it for us. But we have decided to contact Stockholm."

"I would urge you to do so as soon as possible. They can be touchy about these kinds of things. Who is this local expert?"

"His name is Robert Modin."

"And he's very good?"

"Better than most."

Wallander realized he should tell Viktorsson the truth about Modin's criminal past, but before he had gathered himself enough to do so, the moment was past. Wallander had in effect chosen to safeguard the investigation rather than himself. He had taken the first step on a path that could lead straight into personal disaster. Even if he escaped suspension for the business with Eva Persson, this could be the clincher. And Martinsson would have more than enough grounds to crush him.

"I take it you have been informed about the internal investigation that is now underway?" Viktorsson said abruptly. "The girl's lawyer has filed a complaint with the Justice Department ombudsman as well as charging you with assault."

"That picture tells a lie," Wallander said. "Whatever anyone says, I was simply protecting the mother."

Viktorsson didn't say anything.

Is there anyone who believes me? Wallander thought. *Anyone?*

Wallander left the station at nine o'clock. He drove directly to the Hökbergs' house. He had not called them in advance to notify them of his visit. The most important thing was to get away from the station for a while. He still felt it was too early to run into Martinsson. It would happen sooner or later, but right now he still didn't trust his ability to control himself.

When he stepped out of his car the cell phone rang. It was Siv Eriksson.

"I'm sorry to have to bother you," she said.

"No problem."

"I'm calling because I need to talk to you."

He suddenly could tell that she was upset. He pressed the phone closer to his ear and tried to turn out of the wind.

"Has anything happened?"

"I don't want to talk about it over the phone. Please come as soon as possible."

It must be urgent. He promised to drive over right away. The conversation with Sonja's mother would have to wait. He drove back toward Ystad and parked in Lurendrejargränd. A wind from the east was bringing colder air into the region. Wallander pressed the bell to her apartment. She buzzed him in and came out to meet him on the landing. He saw that she was frightened. When they walked into the living room together, she stopped to light a cigarette. Her hands were shaking.

"What happened?" he asked.

It took a while for her to get the cigarette lit. She inhaled deeply, then put it out.

"I often go to see my mother," she began. "She lives in Simrishamn, and I went to visit her yesterday. It got late and I decided to spend the night. When I got back this morning I saw what had happened."

She interrupted herself and walked out into her study. Wallander followed her. She pointed to her computer.

"I had just sat down to work, but when I turned on the computer, nothing happened. At first I thought the computer had been unplugged, but then I realized what it was."

She pointed to the screen.

"I don't follow you," Wallander said.

"Someone has deleted all my files," she said. "My hard drive is completely empty. But it gets worse."

She walked over to a cabinet and opened the doors.

"All of my backup disks are gone. Nothing is here. Nothing. I even have a reserve hard drive. That's gone, too."

Wallander looked around.

"So someone broke into your apartment last night."

"But there are no signs of burglary. And how did they know I wasn't going to be here last night?"

Wallander thought for a moment.

"Did you happen to leave a window open? Were there any marks on the front door?"

"No, I checked."

"Does anyone else have the keys to your apartment?"

Her answer came slowly.

"Yes and no," she said. "I gave Tynnes a set of spare keys."

"Why did you do that?"

"So that he would have access to my apartment when I was away. In case anything happened. But he never used them as far as I know."

Wallander nodded. He understood why she was so upset. Someone had used her spare keys to enter her apartment when she was away, and the only person who had had access to those keys was dead.

"Do you know where he kept them?"

"He said he was going to keep them in his apartment on Apelbergsgatan."

Wallander nodded. He thought about the man who had tried to shoot him.

Perhaps he had finally been given the answer to what the man had been looking for.

The spare keys to Siv Eriksson's apartment.

Chapter Thirty-one

For the first time since the beginning of the investigation, Wallander felt that he had a clear picture of what had happened. After checking the front door and the windows of the apartment, he was convinced that Siv Eriksson was right. The person who had cleaned out her computer had used keys to enter her home. There was another conclusion he could also draw. Someone had been watching her and waiting for the right moment to strike.

They returned to the living room. She was still upset, and lit another cigarette that she also immediately put out. Wallander decided to wait a while before calling in Nyberg. There was something else he wanted to clarify first. He sat down across from her.

"Do you have any idea who might have done this?"

"No. It's totally incomprehensible to me."

"Your computer equipment must be quite valuable, but the burglar didn't come for money. He wanted what was inside."

"Everything is gone," she repeated. "Everything. All my work. Even the hard drive I kept in reserve."

"I imagine you must have used some kind of password to protect your work."

"Of course I did."

"But the burglar must have known what it was?"

"Or been able to get around it somehow."

"Which means this was no ordinary burglar. It was someone who was very skilled with computers."

She followed his train of thought now and understood where he was trying to go.

"I haven't even been able to think that far," she said. "I've been too distraught."

"That's understandable. What was your password?"

"'Cookie.' That was my nickname when I was a child."

"Did anyone else know about it?"

"No."

"What about Falk?"

"No."

"Are you sure?"

"Yes."

"Did you have it written down anywhere?"

"No."

"Are you sure?"

She paused before she replied.

"Yes."

Wallander sensed that they were homing in on a crucial point. He proceeded carefully.

"Did anyone else know about this nickname?"

"My mother, but she's basically senile."

"No one else?"

"I have a girlfriend who lives in Austria. She knows it."

"Do you exchange letters with her?"

"Yes. But the past few years it's been mainly e-mail."

"Do you sign those with your nickname?"

"Yes."

Wallander sat back and took a minute to think.

"I don't know exactly how this works," he said, "but I take it those letters are stored in your computer somewhere."

"Yes, that's right."

"So if someone accessed them they would have been able to see your nickname, and perhaps guessed it might have been used as a password."

"That's impossible. To gain access to my letters they would need the password up front. It can't happen the other way around."

"But someone did manage to break into your computer and delete your files," Wallander said.

She shook her head obstinately.

"Why would anyone do that?" she said.

"You're the only person who can answer that question. It's an important question, as I hope you realize. What did you have in your computer that someone could have wanted?"

"I never worked with classified information."

"This is very important. You have to think carefully."

"You don't have to remind me."

Wallander waited. She looked as though she was thinking hard.

"There was nothing," she said finally.

"Perhaps there was something there that you didn't realize was valuable?"

"And what would that have been?"

"Again, only you can tell me that."

Her voice was very firm when she answered him.

"I pride myself on keeping all areas of my life, particularly my work, in meticulous order," she said. "I am constantly cleaning and sorting files. And I never worked on particularly advanced projects, I've already told you that."

Wallander also thought hard before proceeding.

"Did Falk ever come over and use your computer?" he asked.

"Why would he do that?"

"I have to ask. Could he have come here without your knowledge? He had keys to your apartment."

"I would have noticed it on the computer. It's hard to explain without getting too technical."

"I see. But Falk was very good at these things. Isn't it possible that he could have erased all traces of his activities? It's always a question of who is better at staying a step ahead—the intruder or the investigator."

"I still don't see what the point would be of him using my computer."

"Maybe he wanted to hide something. The cuckoo hides his eggs in other birds' nests."

"But why?"

"We don't know why. It may also simply be that someone *thought* he hid something here. And now that Falk is dead, they need to make sure there isn't something here that you would eventually discover."

"Who would these people be?"

"That's what I want to know."

This is what must have happened, Wallander thought. *There is no other reasonable explanation. There's a lot of frenetic cleaning going on around this town. Something needs to be kept secret at any cost.*

He repeated the words in his head. *Something needs to be kept secret at any cost.* That was the case in a nutshell. If only they could find the secret, the case would solve itself.

Wallander sensed that he was running out of time.

"Did Falk ever mention the number twenty?" he asked.

"Why is that important?"

"Just answer the question, please."

"Not as far as I remember."

Wallander got out his cell phone and called Nyberg. There was no answer. He called Irene and asked her to find him.

Siv Eriksson escorted him to the door.

"I'll be sending over a forensic team," he said. "I'd be grateful if you could avoid touching anything in your study. They might find some fingerprints."

"I don't know what I'm going to do," she said desperately. "Everything is gone. My whole career has vanished overnight."

Wallander didn't know how to comfort her. He recalled Erik Hökberg's words about society's vulnerability.

"Was Falk a religious man?" he asked.

Her surprise was genuine.

"He never said anything that would suggest such a thing."

Wallander had no more questions. He promised to be in touch. When he came out on the street he was at a loss. The person he most needed to talk to was Martinsson, but the question was if he should take Höglund's advice. He wanted to confront him with what she had told him. Then he was overcome by fatigue. The betrayal was so hurtful and unexpected. He still had trouble accepting it, but deep down he knew it must be true.

Since it was still early, he decided to wait. Hopefully his anger would subside over the course of the day. First he would pay a visit to the Hökbergs. Just then he remembered something that he had forgotten to do. He drove to the video store that had been closed when he visited it last, went in, and rented the movie with Al Pacino that he wanted to see. He then continued on to the Hökberg house and stopped outside. Just as he was about to ring the bell, the door opened.

"I saw you pull up," Erik Hökberg said. "You were also here about an hour ago, but you didn't come in that time."

"Something else came up that I had to attend to."

They went inside. The house was quiet.

"I actually came to speak to your wife."

"She's resting in the bedroom upstairs. Or crying. Or both."

Erik Hökberg's face was ashen. His eyes were bloodshot.

"My son is back in school," he said. "I think it's the best thing for him."

"We still don't know who killed Sonja," Wallander said. "But we're optimistic that we're closing in on whoever is responsible."

"I always considered myself against the death penalty," Hökberg said. "But I don't know about that anymore. Just promise not to let me get close to whoever did this. I don't know what I would do to him."

Wallander promised, and Hökberg went upstairs to get his wife.

Wallander walked around the living room while he waited. The silence was oppressive. It took about a quarter of an hour, then he heard footsteps on the stairs. Hökberg came down alone.

"She's very tired," he said. "But she'll be down shortly."

"I'm sorry that this conversation can't wait."

"Both she and I understand."

They waited for her in silence. Then she turned up, barefoot and wearing black. Beside her husband she looked very small. Wallander shook her hand and expressed his condolences. She wobbled slightly then sat down. She reminded Wallander of Anette Fredman. Here was yet another mother who had lost a child. When he looked at her, he wondered how many times he had found himself in this situation. He was going to have to ask questions that were the equivalent of pouring salt in already painful wounds.

This situation was perhaps even worse than many of the others. Sonja Hökberg had not only been killed. Now he was about to confront them with the idea that she may also have been raped on an earlier occasion.

He groped around for a way to begin.

"In order to find Sonja's killer, we have delved into the past. There is a particular incident that has come to our attention and that we need some more information about. You are probably the only people who can tell us about it."

Both Hökberg and his wife regarded him intently.

"Let's look back about three years," Wallander said. "Sometime in 1994 or 1995. Can you remember anything unusual that happened to Sonja during that time?"

Ruth, Sonja's mother, spoke very quietly. Wallander had to lean forward to catch her words.

"What kind of thing are you looking for?"

"Did she ever come home looking as if she had been involved in an accident? Did she have unexplained bruises?"

"She broke her ankle once."

"Sprained," Erik Hökberg said. "She didn't break her ankle. She sprained her ankle."

"I'm thinking more of bruises on her face and body. Did that ever happen?"

Ruth Hökberg jumped in abruptly.

"My daughter was never naked in the house."

"She may have been unusually upset or depressed during this time," Wallander continued.

"She was a moody girl."

"So neither one of you can think of anything unusual along these lines?"

"I don't even understand why you're asking these questions."

"He has to," Erik Hökberg said. "It's his job."

Wallander was grateful for this.

"I can't ever recall her coming home with bruises."

Wallander decided he couldn't keep going around in circles.

"We have some information to indicate that Sonja was raped at some point during this time. But she never reported it."

Ruth flinched as if she had been burned.

"It's not true."

"Did she ever speak of it?"

"That she had been raped? Never."

She started laughing helplessly.

"Who said this? It's a lie. It's nothing other than a lie."

Wallander had the feeling that she was withholding something. Perhaps she had suspected something of the kind. Her objections were forced.

"The information we have is quite compelling."

"Says who? Who is spreading these lies about Sonja?"

"Unfortunately I cannot reveal our sources."

"Why not?"

Erik Hökberg had jumped back into the conversation.

"It's standard practice during investigations of this nature."

"Why?"

"For now it has to do with making sure the informant remains protected."

"What about my daughter?" Ruth screamed. "Who is protecting her? No one! She's dead!"

The situation was getting out of hand. Wallander regretted not letting Höglund handle this questioning. Erik calmed his wife, who had started to sob. It was a horrible scene.

After a while he continued asking questions.

"She never talked about having been raped?"

"Never."

"And neither one of you noticed anything unusual in her behavior?"

"She was a hard person to gauge."

"In what way?"

"She kept to herself. She was often in a bad mood, which I guess is normal for teenagers."

"Was she angry with you?"

"It was mostly directed toward her younger brother."

Wallander thought back to the only conversation he had ever had with Sonja. She had complained then about the fact that her younger brother always got into her things.

"Let's go back to the years 1994 and 1995," Wallander said. "She had returned from England. Did you notice anything at that time? Any sudden change?"

Erik jumped out of his chair so violently that it fell backward.

"She came home one night with bleeding from her mouth and her nose. It was in February of 1995. We asked her what had happened but she wouldn't say. Her clothes were dirty and she was in shock. We never found out what happened. She said she had fallen down. Of course it was a lie. Now I realize that, now that you come here and tell us she was raped. Why do we have to keep lying about this?"

Ruth started crying again. She tried to say something, but Wallander couldn't tell what it was. Erik gestured for him to follow him into the study.

"You won't get anything else out of her for now."

"I only have a few more questions."

"Do you know who raped her?"

"No."

"But you suspect someone?"

"Yes. But I can't give you any names."

"Was he the same person who killed her?"

"I doubt it. But it may still help clarify the events that led to her death."

Hökberg was silent.

"It was toward the end of February," he said after a pause. "It snowed all day. By evening everything was white. And she came home bleeding. The following day you could still see her blood on the snow."

Suddenly it was as if he was overcome by the same helplessness as his wife crying in the room next door.

"You have to get him. A person who can do something like this deserves whatever's coming to him."

"We will do what we can," Wallander answered. "We will get the person who is responsible, but we need your help."

"You have to understand my wife," Hökberg said. "She's lost her daughter. How is she supposed to react to the news that Sonja was also raped?"

Wallander understood.

"So it was the end of February, 1995. Do you remember anything else? Did she have a boyfriend at the time?"

"We never knew who she associated with."

"Did any cars ever stop outside the house? Did you ever see her with a man?"

Anger flashed in Hökberg's eyes.

"A man? I thought you were talking about boyfriends?"

"That's what I meant."

"It was a grown man who did this to her?"

"I've already said I can't give you any information."

Hökberg lifted his hands defensively.

"I've told you everything I know. I should get back to my wife."

"Before I leave I'd like to take a look around Sonja's room again."

"You'll find it the way it was last time. We haven't changed anything."

Hökberg went into the living room and Wallander went upstairs. When he walked into Sonja's room he was struck by the same feeling he'd had the first time. It was not the room of a grown woman. He opened the door to the closet to look at the movie poster. It was still there. *The Devil's Advocate. Who is the Devil?* he thought. *Tynnes Falk worshipped his own image. And Sonja Hökberg has a picture of the devil in her closet.* But he had never heard rumors of Satan-worshippers in Ystad.

He closed the closet door and was about to leave when a boy turned up in the doorway.

"What are you doing here?" he asked.

Wallander told him who he was. The boy regarded him suspiciously.

"If you're police you should be able to get the guy who killed my sister."

"We're trying," Wallander answered.

The boy didn't move. Wallander couldn't decide if he seemed scared or simply curious.

"You're Emil, aren't you?"

The boy didn't answer.

"You must have liked your sister."

"Sometimes."

"Only sometimes?"

"Isn't that enough? Do you have to like people all the time?"

"No, you don't."

Wallander smiled. The boy didn't smile back.

"I think I know one time when you liked her," Wallander said.

"When?"

"A couple of years ago. She came home and was hurt."

The boy shifted.

"How do you know that?"

"I'm a policeman," Wallander said. "I have to know. Did she ever tell you what happened?"

"No. But someone hit her."

"How do you know that if she didn't tell you?"

"I won't tell you."

Wallander thought hard about how to proceed. If he pushed too much, the boy might stop talking completely.

"You asked me just now if I was going to find the guy who killed your sister. But if I'm going to be able to do that, I need your help. The best thing you can do right now is tell me how you know that someone hit her."

"She made a drawing."

"She drew?"

"She was good at it, but she never showed it to anyone. She drew pictures and then tore them up. But I went into her room sometimes when she wasn't here."

"And you found something?"

"She drew a picture of what happened."

"Did she say that?"

"Why else would she draw a picture of a guy hitting her in the nose?"

"Do you still have that picture?"

The boy didn't answer. He left the room. After a few minutes he came back with a pencil drawing in his hand.

"I want it back."

"I promise."

Wallander took the picture over to the window. It was a disturbing picture. He saw that Sonja Hökberg was good at drawing. He recognized her face. But it was the man who dominated the picture. His face loomed over her and his fist hit her nose. Wallander studied his face. If it was as accurate as her self-portrait they should be able to identify the man from this drawing. Something on the man's wrist also caught his attention. At first he thought it was a bracelet. Then he realized it was a tattoo.

Wallander was suddenly in a hurry.

"You did the right thing when you kept this drawing," he told the boy. "I promise you'll get it back."

The boy followed him down the stairs. Wallander carefully folded the drawing and put it in his inner pocket. There were still sobs coming from the living room.

"Is she always going to be like that?" the boy asked.

Wallander suddenly felt a lump in his throat.

"It will take time," he said. "But it will get better. Sometime."

Wallander didn't go in to the adults. He stroked the boy's head and carefully closed the front door behind him.

Wallander tried to reach Höglund on his cell phone, but she didn't answer. He called Irene, who told him that Höglund had been forced to go home. One of her kids was sick. Wallander didn't have to think twice. He drove to the house on Rotfruktsgatan where she lived. It had started to rain. He folded his arms over his chest to make sure no rain would penetrate his coat and reach the drawing inside his pocket. Höglund opened the front door with a child on her arm.

"I wouldn't have bothered you if it wasn't important," he said.

"It doesn't matter," she said. "She just has a low-grade fever. My neighbor can't take her until later in the day."

Wallander went in. It had been a while since he was last there. When he stepped into the living room, he saw that the Japanese masks had disappeared from the wall. She followed his gaze.

"He took his travel mementos with him," she said.

"Does he still live in town?"

"He moved to Malmö."

"Are you going to stay here?"

"I don't know. I don't know if I can afford it."

The girl in her arms was almost asleep. Höglund softly put her down on the couch.

"In a moment I'm going to show you a drawing," Wallander said. "But first I need to ask you something about Carl-Einar Lundberg. I know you haven't met him, but you've seen pictures of him and read through the case files on him. Can you recall if there was any mention of a tattoo?"

She didn't need time to think.

"He had a snake design on his right wrist."

Wallander smacked his hand down on the coffee table. The child jerked and started to cry, but soon stopped and returned to sleep. At last they had arrived at a conclusion that held water. He took the drawing out and showed it to her.

"That's Carl-Einar. Without a doubt. How did you get hold of it?"

Wallander told her about his encounter with Emil, and about learning of Sonja's hidden talent for drawing.

"I doubt we'll ever be able to prosecute him for this," Wallander said. "But that's not the most important thing right now. What we've done is prove your theory. You were right. It's no longer simply a working hypothesis."

"I still find it hard to believe that she would kill his father."

"Keep in mind that there may be other factors we still don't know about. But now we can lean on Lundberg and see what we get. We're going to assume she killed his father out of revenge. And Eva Persson may be telling the truth when she said that Sonja was the one who did both the stabbing and the hitting. Eva Persson is a riddle unto herself that we'll have to attend to later."

They both thought for a moment about the new developments. Finally Wallander broke the silence.

"Someone became worried that Sonja was going to tell us something. So we have three questions we need answers to: What was it she knew? What did it have to do with Falk? Who was the person who became worried?"

The girl on the sofa started to whimper. Wallander took that as his cue.

"Have you seen Martinsson since this morning?" she asked.

"No, but I'm going over there now. Don't worry, I'm planning to take your advice. I won't say anything."

Wallander left the house and hurried to his car.

He drove down to Runnerström Square in the pouring rain.

He stayed in his car for a long time, trying to summon all his energy.

Then he walked into the building to face Martinsson.

Chapter Thirty-two

Martinsson greeted Wallander at the door with his widest smile. "I've been trying to call you," he said. "Things are happening."

Wallander had opened the door to Falk's office with a great deal of pent-up aggression in his body. He was itching to punch Martinsson in the face. How could he have done this to him? But Martinsson smiled and immediately led the conversation to the latest news about Falk's computer. Wallander realized he was somewhat relieved. It gave him breathing space. There would be time enough for him to have it out with Martinsson later. And Martinsson's smile gave him pause. What if Höglund had misunderstood Martinsson's intentions? Martinsson may have had other reasons to consult with Holgersson. Höglund may also have taken some of his comments the wrong way.

But in his heart he knew she was right. Höglund had not exaggerated the situation. She had said what she did because she was also upset by it.

Wallander walked around the table to say hello to Modin.

"Tell me what's happened," he said.

"Robert is breaking through one layer of defense after another," Martinsson said with satisfaction. "We're getting deeper and deeper into the strange and fascinating world inside Falk's computer."

Martinsson offered Wallander the folding chair, but he declined. Martinsson checked his notes while Modin took a sip of what looked like carrot juice.

"We've identified another four institutions in Falk's network. The first is the National Bank of Indonesia. Don't ask me how Robert managed to confirm that. He's a wizard when it comes to getting around security."

Martinsson kept flipping the pages.

"Then there's a bank in Liechtenstein called Lyder Bank. It gets somewhat harder after this. If we're right, then the next two companies are a French telecommunications firm and a commercial satellite company in Atlanta."

Wallander furrowed his brow.

"What do you make of it?"

"The thought from before that it's all about money still stands, as far as I'm concerned. But we're not sure how the telecom company or the Atlanta satellites are involved."

"Nothing is here by coincidence," Modin said abruptly.

Wallander turned toward him.

"Try to explain it to me in a way that I'll understand."

"Everyone arranges their bookshelf in their own way. Or their folders, or whatever. After a while you learn to see people's patterns, even in their computers. The person who worked on this one was very deliberate. Everything is tidy. There's nothing superfluous. But it also isn't arranged in any mundane way following the alphabet or numerical sequences."

Wallander interrupted him.

"Say that again."

"Well, usually people arrange things alphabetically or according to some numerical sequence. A comes before B comes before C. One comes before two and five before seven. But here there isn't any of that."

"What's the pattern, then?"

"Something else entirely."

Wallander tried to sense where Modin was going.

"You see another kind of pattern?"

Modin nodded and pointed to the screen. Wallander and Martinsson leaned forward.

"Two components turn up repeatedly," Modin continued. "The first one I discovered was the number twenty. I tried to see what would happen if I added a few zeroes or changed the order around. If I do that, something interesting happens."

He pointed to the digits on the screen: a two and a zero.

"See what happens when I do this."

Modin typed something and the numbers were highlighted. Then they disappeared.

"They're like frightened animals that run and hide," Modin said. "It's as if I were shining a bright light on them. Then they rush back into the darkness. But after a while they come out again, and always in the same place."

"So how do you interpret this?"

"That they're important somehow. There's also another component that behaves in this way."

Modin pointed to the screen again, this time to the initials "JM."

"They do the same thing," he said. "If you try to home in on them, they disappear."

Wallander nodded.

"They turn up all the time," Martinsson said. "Every time we identify a new institution on the list, they're there. But Robert has also found something else."

Wallander stopped them so he could polish his glasses.

"If you leave them alone," Modin said, "you start to see after a while that they move around."

He pointed to the screen again.

"The first company we identified was the first on the list," he said. "And here the nocturnals are at the top of the column."

" 'Nocturnals'?"

"That's what we call them," Martinsson said. "We thought it was a fitting name."

"Keep going."

"The second item we managed to identify lay a bit farther down on the list in the second column. Here the nocturnals have moved to the right and lower down. If you continue through the list, you'll see that they move according to a strict pattern. They move down toward the lower right-hand corner."

Wallander stretched out his back.

"This still doesn't tell us what they're doing."

"We're not quite done," Martinsson said. "Now is when it gets really interesting."

"I've found a time element," Modin said. "The nocturnals change their coordinates with time. That means there's an invisible time-keeper in here somewhere. I amused myself by constructing a calculation. If you assume that the upper left corner is zero, and that there are seventy-four identities in the network, and that the number twenty refers to the twentieth of October, then you see the following."

Modin typed away until a new text emerged on the screen. Wallander read the name of the satellite company in Atlanta. Modin pointed to the last two components.

"This is number four from the end," he said. "And today is the seventeenth of October."

Wallander nodded slowly.

"You mean the pattern will reach some sort of high point on Monday? That the twentieth represents some kind of end point for these nocturnals?"

"It seems possible."

"But what about the other component? This 'JM'? What does it mean if we take the twenty to refer to the date?"

No one had an answer to that question. Wallander continued.

"What happens on Monday the twentieth of October?"

"I don't know. But I can tell you that some kind of countdown is underway."

"Maybe we should just pull the plug."

"It wouldn't help, since this is just a monitor," Martinsson pointed out. "We can't see the network clearly and we don't know if one or more servers are involved."

"Let's assume the countdown is for a bomb of some kind," Wallander said. "Where is it actually being controlled, if not from here?"

"We don't know."

Wallander suddenly had the feeling they were on the wrong track. Was he misguided in his assumption that the answer to the whole case lay in Falk's computer? Wallander hesitated. The doubt that had come over him was very strong.

"We have to rethink this," he said. "From the beginning."

Martinsson looked shocked.

"Do you want us to stop?"

"I mean we have to rethink this. There have been some developments you aren't aware of."

They walked out onto the landing. Wallander told him about Carl-Einar Lundberg. He felt uncomfortable in Martinsson's presence now, but he tried to hide his feelings.

"We should move Sonja Hökberg's role out of the center," he concluded. "I'm convinced now that someone was simply afraid of what she could tell us."

"And how do you explain Landahl's death?"

"They had been in a relationship. Perhaps she had told him what she knew, and in some way this had to do with Falk."

He also told him what had happened in Siv Eriksson's apartment.

"But that seems to contradict our ideas," Martinsson said.

"But we still can't explain why the electrical relay turned up in the morgue, or the fact that Falk's body was removed. There's an air of desperation in all of this, combined with an extreme ruthlessness. Why do people behave in this way?"

Martinsson thought it over.

"Maybe they're fanatics," he said. "The only thing that matters to them is what they believe in."

Wallander gestured toward Falk's office.

"Robert Modin has done a great job, but the time has come for us to bring in experts from the National Police cybercrimes division. We can't take any risks regarding a countdown to Monday."

"So Robert is done here?"

"Yes. I want you to contact Stockholm immediately. Try to get someone down here today."

"But it's Friday."

"I don't care. Monday is just around the corner."

They went back in. Wallander congratulated Modin on his excellent work and told him he was no longer needed. Modin was clearly disappointed but didn't say anything. He simply turned back to the computer to finish up.

Both Wallander and Martinsson turned their backs to him and started discussing the matter of his compensation in low tones. Wallander said he would take this on.

Neither one of them noticed the fact that Modin had quickly copied the remaining material onto his computer.

They said good-bye outside in the rain. Martinsson was going to drive Modin back to his home.

Wallander shook his hand and thanked him.

Then he drove down to the police station. He thought about the fact that Elvira Lindfeldt was coming up from Malmö to see him that evening. He was both excited and nervous. But before then, he had to meet with the others about rethinking the case. Sonja's rape had dramatically altered the significance of certain events.

When Wallander stepped in through the front doors, he saw that someone was waiting in the reception area. The man came over and introduced himself as Rolf Stenius. The name was familiar to Wallander, but he couldn't place it until the man explained that he was Falk's accountant.

"I should have called you before coming down here," Stenius said. "But I happened to be in town for another meeting and thought perhaps I could drop in."

"Unfortunately it's not a good time," Wallander said. "I can only spare a couple of minutes."

They went to his office. Rolf Stenius was a gaunt man about his own age with thinning hair. Wallander remembered seeing in a memo that

Hansson had been in contact with him. Stenius took out a plastic folder from his briefcase.

"I had already been informed of Falk's death when the police contacted me."

"Who told you about it?"

"Falk's ex-wife."

Wallander nodded for him to continue.

"I've made a spreadsheet for you covering the past two years, as well as including other things that may be of interest to you."

Wallander accepted the plastic folder without looking at it.

"Was Falk a rich man?" he asked.

"That depends on what you mean by rich. He had about ten million kronor."

"Then he was rich in my book. Did he have any outstanding debt?"

"Nothing of any consequence. His operating costs were also quite low," Stenius said.

"His income came from his various consulting projects. Is that correct?"

"I've provided you with all this information in the folder."

"Was there any one project that was significantly more lucrative than the others?" Wallander asked.

"Some of his projects in the U.S. paid very well, but nothing unusual."

"What kind of projects were those?"

"Among other things, he worked for a national advertising chain. Apparently he helped improve their graphic design program."

"And what else?"

"He worked for a whiskey importer by the name of DuPont. He made some kind of advanced warehouse storage program."

Wallander tried to gather his thoughts.

"Did his accumulation of wealth increase less rapidly in the past year?"

"I don't think one could say that. He always made wise investments and never put his eggs in one basket. He had money in Swedish, Scandinavian, and American funds. He always kept a good amount of cash on hand, and then he invested in several reputable companies. Ericsson, for example."

"Who handled his stock-market account?"

"He did that himself, mostly."

"Did he have any interests in Angola?"

"Where did you say?"

"Angola," Wallander repeated.

"Not that I know of."

"Could he have had such interests without you knowing about it?"

"Of course. But I doubt it. Falk was a very honest man. He felt strongly about paying his share of taxes. When I suggested he think about moving his assets abroad in order to achieve a more favorable tax rate, he became very upset."

"What did he do?"

"He threatened to get a new accountant."

Wallander felt tired.

"Thank you," he said. "I'll look through these papers as soon as I have the chance."

"It's a sad affair," Stenius said and closed his briefcase. "Falk was a good man. Overly reserved, perhaps, but amiable."

Wallander escorted him back to the reception area.

"An incorporated company always has a board of directors," he said. "Who was on it?"

"Falk, of course. My boss, and my secretary."

"And you held regular meetings?"

"I took care of most of the business over the phone."

"So the board doesn't have to meet in person?"

"It's often enough to circulate documents and have people sign them on their own time."

Stenius left the station, unfolding his umbrella as he walked outside. Wallander returned to his office and wondered if anyone had had a chance to speak to Falk's children. *We don't even have time for the most important tasks,* he thought. *Even though we're working ourselves to the bone. The Swedish justice system is degenerating into a crumbling warehouse of unsolved cases.*

At three-thirty, the investigative team gathered for a meeting. Höglund relayed Nyberg's apologies—he was suffering from vertigo. They speculated gloomily about which of them would be the first to suffer a heart attack. Then they launched directly into the discussion about Sonja Hökberg's rape and its possible consequences for the case. Wallander demanded that Carl-Einar Lundberg be brought in for questioning as soon as possible and looked over to Viktorsson, who nodded his assent. Wallander also asked Höglund to find out if Lundberg senior had been involved in any way.

"You think he had been after her, too?" Hansson exclaimed. "What kind of a family was that?"

"We have to know the facts," Wallander said. "We can't afford any gaps."

"I have trouble accepting the theory of a revenge by proxy," Martinsson said. "I'm sorry, but that just seems too farfetched to me."

"We're not discussing how we feel about these things," Wallander said. "We're talking about facts."

His voice was sharper than he intended. He saw that the others around the table had noticed it. He hurried on in a friendlier tone.

"What about the National Police and their cybercrime experts? What did they say?"

"Well, they whined when I insisted that someone come down immediately. But someone will be here by nine o'clock tomorrow morning."

"Does this someone have a name?"

"His name is actually Hans Alfredsson."

Everyone burst out laughing. Hans, or rather Hasse, Alfredsson was a legendary Swedish comedian. Martinsson volunteered to meet his plane at Sturup.

"Do you think you'll be able to show him what's been done so far?" Wallander asked.

"Yes. I made plenty of notes while Modin was working."

They finished the meeting by talking about Jonas Landahl. Hansson had been allotted the unpleasant task of getting in touch with his parents. They had been in Corsica and were now on their way home. Nyberg had sent Höglund a memo in which he stated that Sonja Hökberg had indeed been in Landahl's car, and that the car had been at the substation that night. They now also knew that Landahl had no previous criminal record, but that didn't mean that he hadn't been involved in releasing the minks at the farm in Sölvesborg, where Falk was apprehended.

It was almost six o'clock. Wallander felt they were not going to get any further and ended the meeting. They would meet again on Saturday. Wallander was now in a hurry. He needed to clean the apartment and get himself ready before Elvira arrived. But he walked by his office and called Nyberg. It took so long for him to answer that Wallander was starting to get worried. Finally he answered, furious as usual, and Wallander was able to relax. Nyberg said he was feeling better and would be back at work the following day.

Wallander had just managed to tidy up in his apartment and change his clothes when the phone rang. Elvira was on her way to Ystad and was calling from her car. She had just passed the exit to Sturup. Wallander had booked a table at a fancy Ystad restaurant. He gave her the directions to the main square, where they arranged to meet. He put the receiver down so clumsily that it fell to the floor. He picked it up again, cursing, while he suddenly remembered that he and Linda had agreed to talk on the phone this evening. After an internal debate he decided to leave the number of the restaurant on his answering machine for anyone who wanted to reach him. There was a chance that a journalist would call, but he decided it was only a small one. Right now public interest in the scandal seemed to be low.

Then he left the apartment. He left the car at home and walked. It had stopped raining and the wind had also died down. Deep inside Wallander felt a twinge of disappointment over the fact that she had decided to take the car and not the train. He wondered if she had been afraid of missing the last train and being stuck in an awkward situation with him. But there was no point in speculating. He concentrated on the fact that for once he was going to have the pleasure of dining with a beautiful woman.

He stopped outside the bookstore on the main square and waited. After about five minutes he saw her come walking along Hamngatan. He felt suddenly shy, and was baffled by her directness. While they were walking up Norregatan to the restaurant, he felt her take his arm. It was just as they were passing the building where Svedberg had lived. Wallander stopped and told her about what had happened there that time. She listened attentively.

"How do you think about it now?" she asked when he had finished.

"I don't know. Like a bad dream. Something I'm not convinced actually happened."

The restaurant was small and had only been open about a year. Wallander had never been there, but Linda had recommended it. Wallander had been expecting it to be full, but only a few tables were taken.

"Ystad is hardly a bustling metropolis," he said as an excuse. "But the food is supposed to be good."

A waitress that Wallander recognized from the Continental Hotel showed them to their table.

"You took the car," Wallander said as he studied the wine list.

"Yes, I'm planning to drive back after we're done."

"Then I'll be having the wine today."

"What do the police say about blood alcohol levels?"

"That it's best not to have any alcohol at all if you're planning to drive. But I think one glass is fine with a meal. If you like we can go up to the station after dinner and give you a sobriety test."

The food was excellent. Wallander finished his first glass of wine and pretended to hesitate before ordering another. The conversation so far had been mainly about his work. For once he was enjoying it. He told her how he had been a rookie cop in Malmö and almost been stabbed to death. She asked him about the cases he was currently involved in and he became more and more convinced she knew nothing about the picture in the paper. He told her about the strange death at the power substation, the man who had been found outside the ATM, and the boy who had been thrown between the propeller axles on the ferry from Poland.

They had just ordered coffee when the door to the restaurant opened.

Robert Modin walked in.

Wallander spotted him immediately. When Modin saw that Wallander was not alone he seemed to hesitate, but Wallander gestured for him to come over. He introduced Modin to Elvira. Wallander saw that he looked worried. He wondered what had happened.

"I think I've found something," Modin said.

"If you would like to speak privately, I can leave," Elvira said.

"There's no need."

"I asked my dad to drive me out from Löderup," Modin said. "I found out where you were from your answering machine."

"You said you thought you had something?"

"It's hard to explain without the computer in front of me, but I think I've managed to crack the last codes."

Modin looked sure of himself.

"Call Martinsson tomorrow," Wallander said. "I'll inform him in advance of this development."

"I'm pretty sure I'm right."

"There was no need for you to come out here in person," Wallander said. "You could have called me."

"I get a little carried away sometimes."

Modin nodded nervously in Elvira's direction. Wallander thought he should ask him more closely about the new breakthrough, but decided it could wait until the next day. He wanted to be left alone right now. Modin understood. He walked out again. The conversation had taken two minutes.

"He's a very talented young man," Wallander said as he left. "He's a computer whiz and he's helping us with part of our investigation."

Elvira smiled.

"He seemed like a nervous type. But I'm sure he's very good at what he does."

They left the restaurant around midnight and walked slowly back toward the main square. Her car was parked on Hamngatan.

"I've had a wonderful time," she said when they said good-bye.

"You're not tired of me yet?"

"No. What about you?"

Wallander wanted her to stay longer, but realized he had to let her go. They said they would talk again over the weekend.

He gave her a hug. She left. Wallander walked home. Suddenly he stopped in the middle of the street. *Is it possible?* he thought. *Have I really met someone?*

He continued on to Mariagatan and fell asleep shortly after one o'clock.

Elvira Lindfeldt drove to Malmö through the darkness. Shortly before Rydsgård she pulled into a parking lot by the side of the highway. She got out her cell phone.

The number she dialed was registered to a person in Luanda.

She tried three times before she was put through. It was not a good connection. When Carter answered, she got right to the point.

"Fu Cheng was right. The person who is killing our system is named Robert Modin. He lives in a village outside Ystad called Löderup."

She repeated her statement twice, and then she was sure that he had understood what she had said.

The connection was broken.

Elvira swung back onto the highway and continued on to Malmö.

Chapter Thirty-three

Wallander called Linda on Saturday morning.

He had woken up at dawn but had managed to fall back to sleep and not get up until shortly after eight. When he had finished breakfast he called her apartment in Stockholm. He woke her up. She immediately asked him why he hadn't been at home the evening before. She had tried to call the number he had left on the answering machine twice but it had been busy both times. Wallander decided to tell her the truth. She listened without interrupting him.

"I never would have thought it," she said when he was done. "I would never have thought you had enough brains in your head to follow my advice for once."

"I had my doubts."

"But not anymore?"

She asked about Elvira Lindfeldt and they talked for a long time. She was very happy for him, though he kept trying to play it down. It was too early, in his opinion. For now it was enough not to have spent another Friday night alone.

"That's not true," she objected. "I know you. You're hoping this is going to turn out to be the real thing. So do I."

Then she changed the subject.

"I want you to know that I saw that picture in the paper. It was a bit of a shock. Someone at the restaurant showed it to me and asked if that was my dad."

"What did you say?"

"I thought about saying no, but I didn't."

"That was nice of you."

"I just decided it couldn't be true."

"It's not."

He told her what had actually happened, and about the internal investigation that was underway. He told her he was confident the truth would come out.

"It's important for me to hear this right now," she said.

"Why?"

"I can't tell you why. Not yet."

Wallander's curiosity was piqued. During the past few months, he had begun to suspect that Linda's plans for the future had taken a new turn. But in what direction he had no idea, and she had always changed the subject.

They ended their conversation by talking about when she was coming to Ystad next. She thought she could make it in the middle of November, but not before.

Wallander put the phone down and wondered if she would ever get a real job and try to settle down in Ystad.

She's got something on her mind, he thought. *But for some reason she won't tell me what it is.*

It was senseless to try to figure it out. He looked at the time. It was twenty minutes past eight. Martinsson would soon be picking up the cybercrime expert named Alfredsson from Stockholm. Wallander thought about how Modin had turned up so unexpectedly at the restaurant the night before. He had seemed very sure of his discovery. Wallander should let Martinsson know. Something inside Wallander, however, resisted having more contact with Martinsson than absolutely necessary. He still had lingering doubts about what Höglund had told him. He knew these doubts were caused mainly because he wanted it to be untrue. To lose Martinsson as a trusted friend would create an impossible work environment. The betrayal would be too hard to bear. He felt he had trained Martinsson the way Rydberg had trained him, but Wallander had never been tempted—had never *wanted*—to overthrow Rydberg's authority.

The force is a wasp's nest, he thought angrily. *Nothing but envy, gossip, and intrigue. I've always liked to imagine that I remained above it all, but now it seems I've been pulled into the very center. I'm a ruler whose successor is getting impatient.*

Despite his resistance, he made himself call Martinsson's cell phone. After all, Modin had forced his father to drive him in all the way from Löderup the night before. They had to take him seriously. He may have already been in touch with Martinsson, but if not, Wallander's call could be important. Martinsson picked up immediately. He had just parked the car and was on his way to the terminal. Modin had not contacted him. Wallander briefly explained the situation.

"It seems a little strange," Martinsson said. "How could he have thought of this when he didn't have access to the computer anymore?"

"You'll have to ask him about that."

"He's wily," Martinsson said. "I wouldn't put it past him to have copied some of that material over onto his own computer."

Martinsson promised to call Modin, and they agreed they would be in touch again in the afternoon.

As Wallander was putting his phone back, he thought that Martinsson sounded completely normal. *Either he's much better at this game of deception than I could have imagined,* he thought, *or else what Höglund told me isn't right.*

Wallander got to the station at a quarter to nine. When he reached his office there was a message on his desk. "Something has come up," he read in Hansson's jerky handwriting. Wallander sighed over his colleague's inability to communicate more effectively. "Something" was his trademark. The question was always what this "something" referred to. He left and walked to the lunchroom.

The coffee machine had been fixed. Nyberg sat at a table eating his breakfast. Wallander sat down across from him.

"If you ask me about my vertigo, I'm leaving," Nyberg said.

"I guess I'll pass, then."

"I feel fine," Nyberg said. "I just wish retirement would hurry up and get here. Even though the money will be bad."

Wallander knew it wasn't true. Clearly Nyberg was tired and worn out, but he probably feared his retirement more than anything else.

"Is there any word on Landahl from the coroner's office?"

"He died about three hours before the ferry arrived in Ystad. I guess that means whoever killed him was still aboard, unless he jumped ship, of course."

"That was a mistake on my part," Wallander admitted. "We should have checked the passengers before allowing them to get off."

"What we should have done was choose a different career," said Nyberg.

He didn't say anything else, and Wallander decided it was best to leave him alone. This was an easy choice, since he never had to direct him in any way. Nyberg was thorough and well-organized and could always judge which aspects of a case were most urgent and which could wait. Wallander got up to leave.

"I've been thinking," Nyberg said suddenly.

Wallander looked attentively at him, since he knew that Nyberg sometimes had an uncanny ability to come up with crucial observations. In more than one instance, what he had said had helped to completely turn a case around.

"What have you been thinking?"

"About that relay that we found in the morgue. About the handbag that was thrown down by the fence. And the body put back by the cash machine, without two of its fingers. We've been trying to find a meaning in all of this, to get it to fit into a pattern. Isn't that right?"

Wallander nodded.

"We've been trying. But it's not going very well. At least not so far."

Nyberg scraped up the rest of his muesli from his bowl before continuing.

"I talked to Höglund yesterday. She filled me in on what you talked about at the meeting. Apparently you stressed the double meanings in the events of this case. You said there was something both deliberate and accidental about the events. Is that right?"

"Something like that."

"Well, what happens if we take this more seriously, that there is both deliberate planning and coincidence at work here?"

Wallander shook his head. He had nothing to say and waited for Nyberg to go on.

"So I had an idea. What if we're over-interpreting what's happened? First, we find out the murder of the taxi driver is much less significant than we thought. What if that's true about other things as well? What if much of what has happened is for our benefit—to lead us astray, as it were?"

Wallander sensed that Nyberg was onto something important.

"What are you thinking of, specifically?"

"First of all, this relay."

"Are you trying to say that Falk had nothing to do with Sonja's murder?"

"Not really. But I think someone wants us to think that Falk had much more to do with it than was actually the case."

Wallander was starting to get very interested.

"Or this business about his body turning up again. What if we assume it doesn't mean anything? Where does that get us?"

Wallander thought about it.

"It leaves us in a swamp. We don't know where to put our feet to get to solid ground."

"Good image," Nyberg said approvingly. "I didn't think anyone would ever be able to top Rydberg as far as fitting analogies went, but I wonder if you aren't even sharper than he was. We're wading through a swamp, exactly where someone wants us to be."

"And we need to find our way back to solid ground?"

"Take the business with the fence, for example. We've been driving ourselves crazy trying to figure out why the outer gate was forced and the inner door was unlocked."

Wallander understood what Nyberg was driving at. It irritated him that he hadn't picked up on this himself.

"So the person who unlocked the door later banged up the gate simply in order to confuse us. Is that what you mean?"

"Seems like the easiest explanation to me."

Wallander nodded in agreement.

"Good job," he said. "I'm embarrassed I haven't seen this myself until now."

"You can hardly be expected to think of everything yourself."

"Any other details we should ignore?"

"No. We just need to proceed carefully and evaluate the events as they come up. Decide if they're important or not."

Nyberg rose to his feet, signaling the end of the conversation. He walked over to the sink to wash his plate. The last thing Wallander heard before leaving the lunchroom was Nyberg complaining about the old bristles on the brush.

Wallander continued to Hansson's office. His door was open, and Wallander saw that he was busy filling in his tip sheets. Wallander knocked in order to give Hansson a moment to put them away before he walked in.

"I saw your note," he said.

"The Mercedes van has turned up," he said.

Wallander leaned against the doorjamb while Hansson searched through his growing piles of paper.

"I did like you said and went through the programs again yesterday. A small-car rental company in Malmö finally reported a stolen vehicle. A dark-blue Mercedes van which should have been returned on Wednesday."

"What was the name it was rented under?"

"You'll like this," Hansson replied. "It was a man named Fu Cheng."

"Who paid with American Express."

"Exactly."

Wallander nodded grimly.

"He must have given them a local address."

"Hotel Saint Jörgen. But the rental company already checked with them and they have no record of a guest with that name."

Wallander frowned.

"That's strange. You would think this Fu Cheng wouldn't run the risk of being exposed like that."

"There's a possible explanation," Hansson said. "There was a man of Asian appearance who was staying at the Hotel Saint Jörgen, only his name was Andersen and he came from Denmark. But the rental company checked his description with the hotel personnel and are convinced it was the same man."

"How did he pay for his room?"

"Cash."

Wallander thought for a moment.

"He would have had to give them his home address."

Hansson searched for another piece of paper in his pile. A tip sheet fell to the ground without his noticing and Wallander kindly ignored it.

"Here we go. Andersen gave them a street address in Vedbæk."

"Has anyone checked it out?"

"The rental company has been extremely persistent. I guess the van was valuable. It turns out the street he wrote down doesn't exist."

"And that's where the tracks stop," Wallander said.

"The car hasn't been found, either. Do we keep looking for it?"

Wallander didn't take long to make up his mind.

"Hold off on that for now. You have more important things to do. We'll get back to it."

Hansson gestured toward the heaps of paper.

"I don't know how we're supposed to be able to get all this other work done at the same time."

Wallander didn't have the energy to be pulled into yet another discussion of chronic police understaffing.

"We'll talk later," he said and left. He cast a quick eye on the latest papers to have landed on his own desk, then grabbed his coat and got ready to go down to Runnerström Square to check out Alfredsson. He was curious how the encounter between him and Robert Modin would go.

But after he got behind the wheel, he did not immediately start up the engine. His thoughts went to his dinner with Elvira the night before. It was a long time since he had felt so good. He still had trouble believing that it was true. But Elvira Lindfeldt was real. She was no mirage.

He couldn't resist the impulse to call her up. He took out his cell phone and quickly dialed the number he had already memorized. She picked up after the third ring. Although she said she was happy to hear from him, Wallander got the distinct impression that he had interrupted her. He couldn't put his finger on it, but he knew there was something there. A wave of unexpected jealousy came over him, but he kept it out of his voice.

"I wanted to thank you again for coming out here last night."

"Oh, there's no need to do that. But it's sweet of you."

"Was the drive home all right?"

"I almost ran over a rabbit. But apart from that it was fine."

"I'm here in my office and I was trying to imagine what you do on Saturday mornings. But I must be disturbing you."

"Not at all. I was in the middle of cleaning my apartment."

"This is probably not a good time, so I won't keep you. But I wonder if you have any time to get together later this weekend?"

"Tomorrow would be best for me. Could you call back later this afternoon?"

Wallander promised to do so.

Afterward, he sat and stared at the phone. He knew he had disturbed her. He could hear it in her voice. *I'm imagining things,* he thought. *I once made that mistake with Baiba. I even went to Riga without telling her in advance just to see if my suspicions were correct. But there wasn't another man in her life. I was wrong.*

He decided to take her at her word. She was in the middle of cleaning up, nothing more. When he called back later in the afternoon she would be back to normal.

Wallander drove down to Runnerström Square. He stayed in the car after turning off the engine, lost in thought until suddenly someone knocked on the windowpane. He jumped. It was Martinsson, who was smiling and holding up a bag of Danishes in his hand. Wallander felt almost happy to see him. Normally he would have talked to him about the events of the day. But he didn't say anything. He just got out of the car.

"Were you napping?"

"I was thinking," Wallander said curtly. "Is Alfredsson here?"

Martinsson laughed.

"The funny thing is, he actually looks like his namesake. But that's just the surface. I don't think he's much of a comedian at heart."

"Is Modin here as well?"

"I've arranged to pick him up at one o'clock."

They walked across the street and up the stairs, where they paused.

"Alfredsson is a thorough sort," Martinsson said. "I'm sure he's very good. He's still working his way through what we've done so far. His wife keeps calling every so often and chastizing him for not being at home."

"I'm just going to say hello," Wallander said. "Then I'll leave you two alone until Modin gets here."

"What was it he claimed to have done, by the way?"

"I don't know exactly, but I think he said he had broken the rest of the codes."

They walked in. Martinsson was right. Alfredsson bore an unnatural resemblance to the comedian. Wallander couldn't help smiling a little. It lifted his mood, if only for the moment.

"We're grateful you could come down here on such short notice," Wallander said.

"I wasn't aware of having a choice," Alfredsson replied sourly.

"I've bought some Danishes," Martinsson said. "That may help some."

Wallander decided to leave immediately. It was only once Modin was in place that it would be worth his while.

"Call me when Modin gets here," he said to Martinsson. "I'll be back then."

Alfredsson made an exclamation. He was sitting in front of the computer.

"There's a letter to Falk," he said.

Wallander and Martinsson walked over to take a look. A small cursor indicated that there was mail. Alfredsson retrieved it.

"It's for you," he said in a surprised tone of voice and looked at Wallander.

Wallander put on his glasses and read the brief message.

It was from Robert Modin.

They have traced me. I need help. Robert.

"Damn," Martinsson said. "I thought he said he always covered his tracks!"

Not another one, Wallander thought helplessly. *I can't cope with another one.*

He was already on his way down the stairs with Martinsson at his heels.

Martinsson's car was closer. Wallander put the police light on the roof.

Together they sped out of Ystad. It was ten o'clock in the morning. The rain was pouring down.

Chapter Thirty-four

After the hair-raising drive to Löderup, Wallander finally met Robert's mother. She was overweight and seemed very nervous. She had plugs of cotton wool in her nostrils and was lying on the sofa with a damp towel on her forehead.

Robert Modin's father had opened the door when they had pulled into the driveway. Wallander searched in vain for his first name. He looked over at Martinsson.

"His name is Axel Modin."

They got out of the car, and the first thing Axel Modin said was that Robert had taken the car. He repeated this sentence again and again.

"The boy took the car. He doesn't even have a license."

"Does he know how to drive?" Martinsson asked.

"Hardly. I've tried to teach him. I have no idea how I got such an impractical son."

But he knows his way around a computer, Wallander thought. *However you explain that.*

They ran across the yard to get out of the heavy rain. Once they were in the hall, Axel Modin said in a low voice that his wife was in the living room.

"She has a nosebleed," he said. "She always gets one when she is upset."

Wallander and Martinsson walked in to meet her. She started to cry when she heard that they were from the police.

"We'd better sit down in the kitchen," Axel Modin said. "That way we won't disturb her. She has a tendency to get anxious."

Wallander sensed a note of sadness in his voice as he spoke of his wife. They walked out into the kitchen and Axel closed the door part of the way. During the entire conversation, Wallander had the feeling that he was listening for any sound from his wife.

He asked them if they wanted coffee and they both declined. They shared a feeling of urgency. During the ride out to Löderup Wallander had grown increasingly afraid. He wasn't sure what was going on but he knew Robert could be in severe danger. They already had two dead youngsters in the case and Wallander couldn't stand it happening a third time.

While they had been speeding down the highway toward Löderup, Wallander had been too nervous about Martinsson crashing the car to say anything, but once they reached the smaller roads where he was forced to slow down, he started asking some questions.

"How could he have known we were in Falk's office? And how could he have used Falk's account?"

"He probably tried to call you first," Martinsson said. "Is your phone turned on?"

Wallander took it out. It was turned off. He swore.

"He must have guessed that we were likely to be there," Martinsson continued. "And of course he had simply memorized the information about Falk's e-mail. There's nothing wrong with his mind."

They didn't get any further before it was time to turn into Modin's yard. Now they were sitting in the kitchen.

"What happened?" Wallander asked. "We got what amounts to an SOS from Robert."

Axel Modin stared at him in disbelief.

"An SOS?"

"He sent us an e-mail. But the most important thing now is that you tell us what happened on your end."

"I don't know anything," Axel Modin said. "I didn't even know you were on your way. But I have noticed that he's been up late the past couple of nights. I don't know what he's been up to, but I know it has to do with those damned computers of his. This morning when I woke up around six he was still up. He must not have slept at all. I knocked on his door and asked if he wanted a cup of coffee. He said yes. He came down after about half an hour, but didn't say anything. He seemed completely absorbed in his thoughts."

"Was that typical of him?"

"Yes, it didn't surprise me at all. I could see in his face that he hadn't slept."

"Did he tell you anything about what he was doing?"

"No, he never did. It wouldn't have done any good. I'm an old man and I don't understand the first thing about computers."

"What happened after that?"

"He drank the coffee, had a glass of water, and went back upstairs."

"I didn't think he drank coffee," Martinsson said. "I thought he was very particular about his dietary habits."

"Coffee is the big exception. But you're right. He's vegan, he says."

Wallander wasn't sure what the criteria for a vegan were. Linda had tried to explain it all to him once and had mentioned things such as environmental consciousness, buckwheat, and sprouts. But it was beside the point in this discussion. He pressed on.

"So Robert returned to his bedroom. What time was it then?"

"A quarter to seven."

"Did you receive any calls this morning?"

"He has a cell phone. I can't hear it."

"Then what happened?"

"At eight I went upstairs with breakfast for my wife. When I walked past his door I didn't hear anything. I actually stopped and tried to hear if he might have gone to bed."

"Do you think he had?"

"It was quiet and I think he was lying in bed. But I don't think he was sleeping. I got the impression that he was thinking."

Wallander wrinkled his nose.

"How could you know that?"

"I can't, of course. But I don't think it's so hard to tell if a person behind that closed door is thinking with great concentration. Don't you think you can sense it?"

Martinsson nodded in an understanding manner that irritated Wallander. *The hell you'd be able to tell if I was thinking hard if the door was closed,* he thought to himself.

"Let's move on. You gave your wife breakfast in bed."

"Not in bed, actually. She has a little table in the bedroom. She's often unsettled in the morning and needs a little time to herself."

"And then?"

"I went back down to the kitchen to wash the dishes and feed the cats. And the chickens out back. We have a couple of ducks as well. Then I went down to the mailbox and got the morning paper. Then I had some more coffee and read the paper."

"And the whole time you didn't hear any noise from upstairs?"

"No. It was after this that it happened."

Martinsson and Wallander grew more attentive. Axel Modin got up and walked over to the living-room door. He pulled it a little closer, then came back to the table and sat down.

"I suddenly heard Robert's door open with a bang. He came rushing down the stairs with incredible speed. I only had time to stand up before he reached the kitchen. He looked completely in shock, as if I were a ghost. Before I had time to say anything he ran out into the hall and locked the front door. Then he came back and asked me if I had seen anyone. He screamed it at me, that is."

"That was what he said? 'Have you seen anyone?'?"

"He was beside himself. I asked him what the matter was, of course. But he didn't listen to me. He was looking out the window, here in the kitchen and in the living room. My wife started yelling from upstairs. She was frightened by the noise. It was pretty hectic in here for a few minutes, I can tell you."

"What happened?"

"When he came back into the kitchen, he had my shotgun with him and ordered me to get the ammunition for it. That scared me, and I asked him again what had happened but he didn't say anything. He just wanted that buckshot. But I didn't give him any."

"Then what happened?"

"He threw the shotgun on the sofa in there and grabbed the car keys. I tried to stop him, but he shoved me aside and ran out."

"What time was it?"

"I don't know. My wife was screaming at the top of the stairs and I had to take care of her. But it was probably a quarter to nine."

Wallander looked at the time. It was now about an hour later. Robert Modin had sent out his e-mail asking for help and then he had left.

Wallander stood up.

"Did you see what he direction he was taking?"

"He went north."

"One other thing. Did you see anyone when you went out to get the paper? Or when you fed the chickens?"

"Who would I have seen? And in this weather?"

"There may have been a car parked somewhere. Or someone who drove past."

"There was no one here."

Wallander nodded to Martinsson.

"We have to look at his room," Wallander said.

Axel Modin had buried his face in his hands.

"Can someone explain to me what's going on?"

"Not right now," Wallander said. "But we're going to try to find your son."

"He was frightened," Axel Modin said softly. "I had never seen him so frightened. He was as frightened as his mother sometimes gets."

Martinsson and Wallander walked upstairs. Martinsson pointed to a shotgun that was leaning against the railing. The flickering screens of two monitors greeted them in Robert's room. There were clothes all over the floor, and the wastepaper basket next to the desk was over-flowing.

"What happened shortly before nine this morning?" Wallander asked. "Something scared him, he sent us the e-mail and then ran. He was desperate, literally afraid for his life. He wanted to use the shotgun for protection. He looked out the window and then took the car."

Martinsson pointed to the cell phone that was lying right between the two computers.

"He may have received a call," he said. "Or else he could have made a call and heard something that frightened him. It's too bad he didn't take the phone with him when he left."

Wallander pointed to the computers.

"If he sent us a message, he may also very well have received one. He told us that someone had traced him and that he needed our help."

"But he didn't wait for us."

"Either something else happened after he wrote to us, or else he didn't want to wait any longer."

Martinsson sat down at the desk.

"We'll leave this one for now," he said pointing to the smaller of the two computers.

Wallander didn't ask how Martinsson could determine which of the two was more important. Right now he was dependent on his knowl-edge. It was an unusual situation for Wallander. For once one of his colleagues knew more than he did.

While Martinsson started typing on the keyboard, Wallander looked around the room. The rain was whipping against the window. On one wall there was a large poster with a carrot on it. It was the only thing that stood out in a room devoted to the electronic sphere. There were computer books, diskettes, and cables. Some of the computer cords were wrapped around each other like a nest of vipers. There were a modem, a printer, a TV, and two VCRs. Wallander walked over to Martinsson and bent his knees. What could Robert have seen through his window as he was sitting at the desk? There was a road far away in the distance. *He could have seen a car,* Wallander thought. He looked around the room again, lifting things carefully, until he found a pair of binoculars under a pile of papers. He directed them at the window and looked. A raven flew past and Wallander flinched involuntarily. Oth-erwise there was nothing. A fence that was falling down, some trees, and a small road that snaked through the fields.

"How's it going?" he asked.

Martinsson mumbled something incoherent. Wallander put on his glasses and looked at the pieces of paper that lay closest to the computers. Robert Modin's handwriting was hard to read. There were some half-finished equations and phrases, without beginning or end. The word "delay" occurred several times. Sometimes it was underlined, other times it appeared with a question mark beside it. Wallander kept looking. On another page Robert had written "completion date of programming?" and then two additonal words: "insider necessary?" *A lot of question marks*, Wallander thought. *He's been searching for answers, just as we have.*

"Here," Martinsson said suddenly. "He got some e-mail. Then he sent his message to us."

Wallander leaned in and read the message.

YOU HAVE BEEN TRACED.

Nothing else. Only those four words.

"Is there anything else?" Wallander asked.

"There have been no messages since then."

"Who sent the letter?"

Martinsson pointed at the screen.

"The person's identity is hidden behind all these scrambled codes. This is someone who didn't want to say who he was."

"But where did it come from?"

"The name of the server is 'Vesuvius,'" Martinsson said. "We can certainly have it traced, but it may take a while."

"You don't think it's here in Sweden?"

"I doubt it."

"Vesuvius is a volcano in Italy," Wallander mused. "Can that be where it came from? What happens if we return the message?"

"I'm not sure. We can try."

Martinsson prepared a return message.

"What do you want the text to say?"

Wallander thought about it.

"'Please repeat your message,'" he said. "Try that."

Martinsson nodded approvingly and wrote the message in English.

"Should I sign it 'Robert Modin'?"

"Yes."

Martinsson hit SEND, and the text vanished into cyberspace. Then a message came up on the screen saying that the address was unknown.

"You'll have to tell me what you want me to do next," Martinsson said. "What should I look for, do you think? Where 'Vesuvius' is, or something else?"

"Send a message to someone over the Internet asking about this server," Wallander said. "Ask if anyone knows where to find it."

But then he changed his mind.

"Put the question this way. Is the server 'Vesuvius' located in Angola?"

Martinsson was taken aback.

"Are you still thinking about that postcard from Luanda?"

"No, I think the postcard is incidental. But I think Falk met someone in Luanda a number of years ago and that it was a turning point in his life. I don't know what happened there, but I'm sure it's important. Crucial, in fact."

Martinsson looked hard at him.

"Sometimes I think you put too much stock in your intuition, if you'll pardon me for saying so."

Wallander had to control himself in order not to fly off the handle. His rage at Martinsson boiled up inside him. But he took a deep breath. They had to focus on Robert Modin. But Wallander did file away what Martinsson had said, word for word. He could have a long memory, as Martinsson was going to learn firsthand.

But for now, he had an idea he wanted to try out.

"While Robert was working for us, he often consulted with a couple of friends on line," Wallander said. "One in California and one in Rättvik. Did you ever make a note of their e-mail addresses?"

"I wrote everything down," Martinsson said in a hurt voice. Wallander assumed he was upset because he hadn't thought of it himself.

Wallander cheered up.

"They won't hold anything against us for asking about Vesuvius," Wallander continued. "Make it clear that we're asking on Robert's behalf. While you do that, I'm going to start looking for him."

"What does this message mean, anyway?" Martinsson said. "He didn't manage to clean up after himself. Is that it?"

"You're the one who knows about these things," Wallander said. "Not me. But I have a feeling that has only been growing stronger. You'll have to correct me if I'm wrong, and this feeling has nothing to do with my intuition, only with facts. But I feel as if the people we're dealing with are supremely well informed of our activities."

"We know someone has been observing our activities at Apelbergsgatan and Runnerström Square. You almost ran into him, in fact, when he took a shot at you."

"That's not it. I'm not talking about this person, who may or may not be called Fu Cheng. What I'm getting at is that it almost seems as if we have a leak inside the station."

Martinsson burst out laughing. Wallander couldn't tell if it was derisive or not.

"You're not serious! You don't think one of us is mixed up in this, do you?"

"No, I don't. But I'm wondering if there might be another kind of leak."

Wallander pointed at the computer.

"What I'm wondering is if someone has been doing the same thing we were doing with Falk's computer. Breaking in to get secret information."

"The national registers are extremely secure."

"But what about our personal computers? Are they so watertight that someone with the right amount of expertise and drive couldn't break into them? You and Höglund write all your reports on them. I don't know about Hansson. I do it some of the time. Nyberg tussles with his machine. The coroner's report comes both in a hard copy and electronically. What would happen if someone had a way in and was watching everything that came in to our computers? Without us being aware of it?"

"It isn't plausible," Martinsson said. "Our security is very good."

"It's just a thought," Wallander said. "One of many." He felt around in his pocket for his cell phone, then remembered he had left it in Martinsson's car.

He left Martinsson and walked down the stairs. Through the half-open door to the living room he could see Axel Modin put an arm around his giant wife, who still had cotton balls in her nostrils. It was an image that filled him with pity and, mysteriously, with joy. Which feeling dominated he wasn't sure. He knocked carefully on the door.

Axel Modin came out into the kitchen.

"I need to use your phone," Wallander said.

"Do you know what happened? Why is Robert so afraid?"

"We're still trying to determine that. But don't worry."

Wallander said a silent prayer that his words would turn out to be true. He sat down by the phone in the hall. Before lifting the receiver, he reflected on what needed to be done. The first thing he had to address was whether or not there was real cause for worry. But the e-mail message addressed to Robert was real. There was someone out there who had sent it. And the case so far was characterized by secrecy and silence, and by people who did not hesitate to kill.

Wallander decided the threat to Robert was real. He couldn't take the chance of being wrong. He lifted the receiver and called the station. He was lucky enough to reach Höglund right away. He told her what was going on and asked her to send patrol cars to search the area around Löderup. Since Robert was an inexperienced driver, he had probably not managed to get very far. There was also the chance that he had already caused or been in an accident. Wallander called out to Axel Modin to give him the license plate number as well as a description of the car. Höglund wrote it down and promised to take care of it. Wallander put the phone down and walked back up the stairs. Martinsson still hadn't heard anything from Modin's hacker friends.

"I need to use your car," Wallander said.

"The keys are in the ignition," Martinsson said without taking his eyes off the screen.

Wallander decided to take a look at the little road that ran through the fields and that Robert could see through his window. There was probably nothing there, but Wallander wanted to be sure. He drove out onto the road and started looking for the turnoff. He drove much too fast down the muddy road between the fields, but since it was Martinsson's car it was a way to take another small revenge. He stopped when he got to the point he had found through the binoculars. He got out of the car and looked around. The rain was almost completely gone now. If Martinsson looked up, he would be able to see his car and its driver. Wallander looked down at the road and saw that another car had been there. He thought he could tell that it had stopped nearby, but the tracks were not easy to see. The rain had almost washed them away. *But someone probably stopped here,* he thought.

Wallander felt uneasy. If someone had been keeping an eye on the house from here, he would easily have seen Robert dash out and leave in the car.

He felt the sweat start to break out over his body. It's my responsibility, he thought. *I should never have gotten him mixed up in this. It was too dangerous and irresponsible.*

He had to force himself to stay calm. Robert had panicked and wanted a gun. Then he had decided to leave in the car. The question he had to answer was where the boy had gone.

Wallander looked around one more time, then drove back to the house, remembering to bring his cell phone with him this time. Axel Modin met him at the door and raised his eyebrows.

"I haven't found Robert," Wallander said. "But we are looking for him, and there's no need to be concerned."

Axel Modin did not believe him. Wallander could see it in his face, but Modin didn't say anything. He looked away, as if he found Wallander's concern insulting. There was no sound from the living room.

"Do you have any idea where he may have gone?" Wallander asked.

Axel Modin shook his head.

"I don't know."

"But he had friends. When I came here that first night he had been at a party."

"I've called all his friends. No one has seen him. They promised to let me know if they did."

"You have to think hard," Wallander said. "He's your son. He's scared and he fled in your car. What could he be thinking of as a safe hiding place?"

"He likes to walk on the beach," Modin said doubtfully. "Down by Sandhammaren or on the fields around Backåkra. I don't know of any other place."

Wallander was also doubtful. A beach was too open, just like a field. Of course, there was the fog. A better hiding place than the Scanian fog was hard to imagine.

"Keep thinking," Wallander said. "You may be able to think of something else, some hiding place from his childhood."

He went to the phone and called Höglund. The patrol cars had already been dispatched. The police in Simrishamn had been alerted and were helping them. Wallander told her about Sandhammaren and Backåkra.

"I'm going up to Backåkra," he said. "Get another car to Sandhammaren."

Höglund told him she'd handle it and said she was going out to Löderup.

Wallander hung up as Martinsson came dashing down the stairs.

"Rättvik got back to me," he said. "You were right. The server 'Vesuvius' is registered in Luanda."

Wallander nodded. He was not surprised.

But it increased his fear.

Chapter Thirty-five

Wallander stood there in the hallway staring at Martinsson as the seconds ticked by. The only thing he was sure of was that they had to find Robert before it was too late. Images of Sonja Hökberg's scorched body and Jonas Landahl's butchered remains swept through his mind. Wallander wanted to dash out into the fog and start to look. But the situation was still unclear. Robert was out there somewhere, terrified. He had fled just as Jonas Landahl had fled. But someone had caught up with Landahl.

And now Robert Modin was in the same situation.

Martinsson had established that some Brazilian entrepreneurs were responsible for the installation and upkeep of the server called Vesuvius. But they had not yet identified the person who had written to Robert, even if Wallander suspected it to be "C." Who this person was, or if there was even a group of individuals hiding behind the letter, remained unknown.

Martinsson returned to the computers upstairs. Wallander had encouraged him to keep talking to Robert's hacker friends in Rättvik and California. They might even know about a possible hiding place.

Wallander walked to the window and looked out. A strange silence seemed to accompany the fog. Wallander had never experienced it anywhere except here in Scania in October and November, before winter struck. The landscape seemed to be holding its breath when the fog came in.

Wallander heard a car pull up. He went to the front door and opened it. It was Höglund. She introduced herself to Axel Modin while Wallander walked to the stairs and asked Martinsson to come down. Then they all sat down around the kitchen table. Axel Modin hovered in the background, attending to his wife and her debilitating anxiety.

For Wallander, nothing else mattered right now except the task of finding Robert. Everything else was unimportant. It was not enough that they put patrol cars on the job; they needed to send out a regional alert. All nearby police districts should be involved in the search. Wallander gave this task to Martinsson.

"We don't know where he is," Wallander said. "But he fled in a state of panic. We can't know for sure the extent of the threat against him, and we don't know if his movements were actually being monitored by someone, but for now that is what we're going to assume to be the case."

"They're very good, whoever they are," Martinsson said from the doorway with the telephone receiver pressed against his ear. "I know he was conscientious about erasing his tracks."

"That must not have been enough," Wallander said. "Especially if he copied material and kept working on it through the night after he got home. After he had said good-bye to us."

"I haven't found anything to indicate that," Martinsson said. "But you may be right."

Once Martinsson had seen to the regional alert, they decided to establish their temporary headquarters at the house. It was possible that Robert would contact someone here. Höglund would go down to Sandhammaren with a few cars while Wallander went to Backåkra.

On the way out to the cars, Wallander noticed that Höglund was carrying her gun. Once she had left, Wallander went back up to the house. Axel Modin was sitting in the kitchen.

"I'd like the shotgun," Wallander said. "And some rounds of buckshot."

Wallander could see the anxiety flare up in Modin's face.

"It's a precautionary measure," Wallander said in an attempt to allay his fears.

Modin got up and left the kitchen. When he came back he had the shotgun and a box of ammunition with him.

Wallander was back in Martinsson's car, headed to Backåkra. Cars were crawling along the highway. Headlights emerged from the fog and were swallowed up again. The whole time, he was racking his brains to figure out where Robert Modin must have gone. Had he left without a thought in his head, or did he have a plan? Wallander realized he wasn't going to get anywhere. He didn't know Robert well enough.

He almost missed the turnoff for Backåkra. He turned sharply and sped up, even though he was now on a smaller road. But he didn't expect to meet any other cars here. The grounds as well as the house were owned by the Swedish Academy, the elite group of writers and intellectuals responsible for awarding the Nobel Prize in Literature, and it was probably deserted this time of year. He got out of the car when he reached the parking lot and took the shotgun with him. He heard a foghorn in the distance, and he could smell the sea. Visibility was only about one meter. He walked around the parking lot but didn't see any other cars. He walked up to the house and its outer buildings, but it was thoroughly locked. *What am I doing here?* he wondered. *If there's no car, then there's no Robert either.* But something drove him onward toward the fields. He went to the right, where he knew he would find the small meditation garden. A bird squawked nearby. The fog made it impossible to judge distances accurately. He reached the ring of stones that bordered the meditation garden. Now he could hear the sea clearly. No one was there, and no one seemed to have been there, either. He got out his phone and called Höglund. She was in Sandhammaren. There were still no traces of Modin's car.

"The fog is very localized," she told him. "Air traffic is normal at Sturup. A bit north of Brösarp everything is clear."

"I don't think he's gone that far," Wallander said. "I think he's still in the area. In fact, I'm sure of it."

He ended the conversation and started back. Suddenly something caught his attention. He listened. A car was approaching the parking lot. He concentrated intensely. Robert Modin had fled in a Volkswagen Golf sedan. But the engine sound from this car sounded different. Instinctively he loaded the shotgun. Then he pressed on. The engine noise stopped. Wallander waited. A car door was opened, but not closed. Wallander was sure it was not Modin who had just arrived. Perhaps it was a caretaker coming to see to the place. Or to find out who it was who had just arrived, to make sure it wasn't a burglar. Wallander thought about getting closer but something warned him not to. What it was he couldn't say. He left the little path he was on and made a wide circle back, heading toward the other end of the parking lot. From time to time he stopped. *I would have heard someone unlock the door and enter the house,* he thought.

But it's too quiet out there. Much too quiet.

He looked at the house again. He was directly behind it. He took a few steps back and the house disappeared from view into the gray fog. Then he walked around toward the parking lot. He arrived at the fence, and climbed over with some difficulty. Then he slowly examined the parking lot. Visibility was even worse now. He thought that it was probably a bad idea to get too close to Martinsson's car. It was better to go around it. He stayed close to the fence so he wouldn't lose his sense of direction.

He stopped short when he reached the entrance to the parking lot. There was the car. Or rather, the van. At first he wasn't sure what it was, but then it dawned on him that he was looking at a dark-blue Mercedes van.

He took a few quick steps back into the fog and listened. His heart was beating faster. He undid the safety catch on the shotgun. The door to the driver's side had been open. He was standing completely still now. There was no doubt in his mind that this was the van they had been looking for. It was the same one that had brought Falk's body back to the cash machine. And now it was out in the fog looking for Modin.

But Modin isn't here, Wallander thought.

Then it suddenly occurred to him that they could just as well be looking for him. If they had seen Modin leave the house, they could also have been observing him. He tried to think back to his drive here. No car had overtaken him, but hadn't there been a pair of headlights in his rearview mirror?

His cell phone rang in his pocket. Wallander jumped and answered as quickly as he could with a low voice. But it wasn't Martinsson or Höglund. It was Elvira Lindfeldt.

"I hope I'm not disturbing you," she said. "But I wonder if we could set a date for tomorrow. That is, if you still want to."

"I'm a bit busy right now," Wallander said.

She asked him to speak up, saying it was hard to hear him.

"Can I call you back?" he asked. "I'm busy right now."

"Can you repeat that?" she asked. "I really can't hear you very well."

He raised his voice slightly.

"I can't talk now. I'll call you back."

"I'm at home," she replied.

Wallander turned off his phone. *This is insane*, he thought. *She doesn't understand. She thinks I'm avoiding her. Why did she have to pick this time to call, for heaven's sake?*

Then he had a thought that made his head spin. He didn't know where it came from and he brushed it aside before it had a chance to catch. But it had been there, like a dark undercurrent in his mind. *Why did she call just now? Was it a coincidence?*

It was an unreasonable thought and it was a symptom of his fatigue and his growing sense of being the object of his colleagues' conspiracies to get rid of him. He stared at the phone before putting it away. He would call her as soon as this was over. He was about to put the phone in his pocket when it slipped. He bent down to try to catch it before it fell on the wet ground.

It saved his life. At the same moment that he bent down he heard a loud noise like a gunshot above and behind him. He left the phone where it was and raised his shotgun. Something was moving in the fog. Wallander threw himself to the side and then stumbled away as fast as he could. His heart was beating wildly. He didn't know who had fired the gun and he didn't know why. *He must have heard my voice,* Wallander thought. *He heard me and was creeping up toward me. If I hadn't dropped the phone I wouldn't be here now.* The thought terrified him. The shotgun shook in his arms. He didn't know where his phone was, nor the car. He lost all sense of direction as he ran. He just wanted to get away. He crouched down with the shotgun in his arms and waited. The man was out there somewhere. Wallander tried to see through the thick white mass and strained his ears. But there was no sound. Wallander realized he shouldn't stay. He made a quick decision and fired into the air. The bang was deafening and he ran a few meters to one side, then listened again. He was close to the fence now and knew which way to go to get away from the parking lot.

Then there was a new sound. The sound of sirens rapidly approaching. *Someone heard that first shot,* he thought. There are plenty of police out on the roads right now. He hurried down to the entrance. Now he had a leg up on his opponent, and that feeling was transforming his fear to rage. He had just been shot at for the second time in the space of a few days. But he also tried to think clearly. The Mercedes van was still there, and there was only one way out of the parking lot. If the man chose to take the car, it would be easy to get him. If he fled on foot it would be much harder.

Wallander reached the entrance and ran down along the road. The sirens were close now, signaling one, maybe even two or three, patrol cars. Hansson was in the first car. Wallander had never been so happy to see him.

"What's happening here?" Hansson shouted. "We got a report of a gunshot in the area. And Höglund said you had gone down here."

Wallander tried to explain what had happened as quickly as he could.

"No one goes down there without the proper protection," he finished. "We also need dogs. But first we have to be prepared for the possibility that he tries to shoot his way out."

They quickly erected a barrier and started putting on their vests and helmets. Höglund arrived, closely followed by Martinsson.

"The fog is about to lift," Martinsson said. "I've talked to the National Weather Service. It's very localized."

They waited. It was now one o'clock on Saturday, the eighteenth of October. Wallander had borrowed Hansson's phone and gone off to one side. He dialed Elvira's number but changed his mind and hung up before she answered.

The fog didn't lift until half past one. But then it disappeared quickly. It was gone in a matter of minutes and the sun came out. They saw the parked van and Martinsson's car. No one was around. Wallander walked over and found his phone.

"He must have taken off on foot," he said. "He abandoned the van."

Hansson called Nyberg, who promised to come as quickly as possible. They searched the car but found nothing that told them anything about its driver.

"Did you catch sight of him at all?"

Höglund was the one who asked the question. It irritated Wallander and made him defensive.

"No," he said. "I didn't see him. You wouldn't have been able to, either."

She was taken aback.

"It was just a question," she said sourly.

We're all tired, Wallander thought. *She and I both. Not to mention Nyberg. Martinsson might be the exception, since he had the energy to sneak around the police station and talk behind people's backs.*

Two canine units had been dispatched and were now searching the area. They immediately picked up a scent that led down toward the water. Nyberg arrived with his forensic technicians.

"I want fingerprints," Wallander said. "That's the main thing. I want to know if anything matches what we found at Apelbergsgatan or Runnerström Square. Or the power substation and Sonja Hökberg's purse. And don't forget Siv Eriksson's apartment."

Nyberg took a quick look into the van.

"I'm so grateful every time I'm called out to look at something that doesn't involve mutilated bodies," he said. "Or so much blood that I have to put on waders."

Robert Modin was still missing without a trace. The canine units came back at three. They had lost the track some distance up the coast.

"Everyone looking for Robert Modin should also be keeping an eye out for a man with an Asian appearance," Wallander said. "But it's important that he not be directly approached. This man is armed and dangerous. He's been unlucky twice, but don't count on a third time. We should also remain alert to incoming reports of stolen cars."

Wallander gathered the members of his closest team. The sun was shining and there was no wind. He led them to the meditation garden.

"Were there any police during the bronze age?" Hansson asked.

"Probably," Wallander said. "But I doubt there was a justice department breathing down their necks."

"They played horns," Martinsson said. "I was at a concert recently at the Ale stone formation. They had tried to re-create prehistoric music. It sounded like foghorns."

"Let's try to focus on the situation at hand," Wallander said. "Further discussion of the bronze age will have to wait. Robert Modin receives a threat on his computer and he flees. He has now been gone for about five or six hours. Somewhere out here is a person who is looking for him, but we can also assume this person is after me. This will naturally come to extend to all of you."

He looked around at them.

"We need to ask ourselves why," he continued, "and I can only find one reasonable explanation. He, or someone, is worried that we know something. And even worse, this person—or persons—is worried that we're in a position to prevent something from occurring. I'm completely convinced that everything that has happened has been a result of Falk's death, and has to do with whatever is in his computer."

He paused and looked at Martinsson.

"How's Alfredsson doing?"

"I last spoke to him over two hours ago. At that point he could only tell us what Modin told us—that there is some kind of ticking time bomb built into the program. Something is going to happen. He was going to apply various probability calculations and reduction programs to see if he could isolate some kind of pattern. He is also in contact with Interpol cybercrime experts to see if any other countries have experience with this kind of thing. I have the impression that he's thorough and knows what he's doing."

"Then we'll leave it in his hands," Wallander said.

"But what if something is really going to happen on the twentieth? That's on Monday. It's less than thirty-four hours away," Höglund said.

"Quite honestly, I don't know what to tell you," Wallander said. "But we know it must be something important, since these people are prepared to commit murder."

"Could it be anything other than an act of terrorism?" Hansson asked. "Shouldn't we have contacted the National Guards a long time ago?"

Hansson's suggestion was met with hearty laughter. Neither Wallander nor any of his colleagues had the slightest confidence in the

Swedish National Guards. But Hansson had a point, and Wallander should already have thought of it, since he was leading the investigation. His head was the one on the block, and it would roll if a situation developed in which the National Guards could have played a role in preventing what happened.

"Call them," Wallander told Hansson. "If they actually stay open for business during the weekend."

"What about the blackout?" Martinsson said. "It seems that whoever is behind this has developed a sophisticated knowledge of power stations. Could there be a plot to knock out the power grid?"

"We can't rule anything out," Wallander answered. "But that makes me think of the blueprint we found in Falk's office. Do we know how it got there?"

"According to Sydkraft, the original was in Falk's office and a copy had been left in its place in their files," Höglund said. "They gave me a list of people who would have had access to these files. I gave it to Martinsson."

Martinsson made an embarrassed gesture.

"I haven't had time," he said. "I'll feed it through our registers as soon as I get a chance."

"That is now a priority," Wallander said. "It may give us something."

A soft wind had started blowing cold air over the fields. They talked a moment longer about the most important tasks at hand, and then Wallander delegated them. Martinsson was the first to leave. He was going to bring Modin's computers to the station, as well as cross-check the names that Sydkraft had sent them. Wallander put Hansson in charge of the search for Modin. Wallander felt a need to talk through the situation with someone, in this case Höglund. Ordinarily he would have chosen Martinsson, but now that was unthinkable.

Wallander and Höglund started walking back toward the parking lot together.

"Have you talked with him?" she asked.

"Not yet. It's more important to focus on finding Modin and the reasons for all of this."

"You've just been shot at for the second time this week. I can't understand how you can take it so well."

Wallander stopped and looked at her.

"Who says I'm taking it well?"

"You give that impression."

"Well, it's not true."

They kept walking.

"Tell me how you see the case now," he asked her. "Take your time.

How would you explain it to someone? What can we expect in the near future?"

She swept her coat tightly around her.

"I can't tell you any more than you already know."

"But you'll tell me in your own way. And if I hear your voice, at least I won't be hearing my own thoughts for a while."

"Sonja Hökberg was definitely raped," she began. "I see no other reason for her crime. I think if we were to keep digging into her life we would find a young woman consumed by hatred. Sonja Hökberg is not the stone that is thrown into the water, she's one of the outer rings. I think perhaps timing is the most important factor in her case."

"Tell me what you mean."

"What would have happened if Falk hadn't died so close to the time she was arrested? Let's say a few weeks had gone by, and say it wasn't so close to the twentieth of October."

Wallander nodded. So far her thinking was right on track.

"The fact that it's close to some important event in time leads to hasty and unplanned actions on the part of our perpetrator? Is that what you mean?"

"There are no margins. Sonja Hökberg is being held by the police. Someone is afraid of what she can tell us. Specifically, something she may have heard from her friends, first and foremost Jonas Landahl, who is later also killed. All of these events are an attempt to keep something inside a computer a secret. The nocturnals, as Modin apparently calls them, want to keep doing their work in the dark. If one disregards some loose details, I think this about sums it up. It then also makes sense that Modin was threatened. And that you were attacked."

"Why me? Why not any other police officer?"

"You were in the apartment when they came the first time. You have consistently been on the frontlines of this investigation."

They kept walking in silence. The wind was gusty now. Höglund hunched her shoulders against it.

"There's one more thing," she said, "that we know, but that they don't know."

"What's that?"

"That Sonja Hökberg never told us anything. In that sense, she actually died for nothing."

Wallander nodded. She was right.

"I keep wondering what could be in that computer," he said after a while. "The only thing that Martinsson and I have come up with is that it has something to do with money."

"Perhaps there's a big heist in the works? Isn't that the way it's done nowadays? A bank computer goes haywire and starts transferring money into the wrong account."

"Maybe. We just don't know."

They had reached the parking lot. Höglund opened her mouth to say something when they both saw Hansson running toward them.

"We've found him!" Hansson shouted.

"Modin or the man who shot at me?"

"Modin. He's in Ystad. One of the patrol cars spotted him when they drove back to change shifts."

"Where was he?"

"He had parked at the corner of Surbrunnsvägen and Aulingatan. By the People's Park."

"Where is he now?"

"At the station."

Wallander saw the relief in Hansson's face.

"He's okay," Hansson said. "We got to him first."

"Yes, it seems like it."

It was a quarter to four.

Chapter Thirty-six

The phone call that Carter had been waiting for came at five o'clock. It was a bad connection, and it was difficult to interpret Cheng's broken English. Carter thought that it was like being transported back to the 1980s, when communications between Africa and the rest of the world was still very poor. He remembered a time when it was still a challenge to do something as simple as send or receive a fax.

But in spite of the time difference and the static, Carter had still managed to understand Cheng's message. When the phone call ended, Carter had walked out into the garden to think. He had trouble controlling his irritation. Cheng had not lived up to his expectations, and nothing was more infuriating to him than when people were not able to handle the tasks that he asked them to carry out. The latest news report was unsettling, and he knew he had to make an important decision.

The heat, after he'd left the cool and air-conditioned house, was oppressive. Lizards ran to and fro around his feet. The sweat was already trickling down inside his shirt, but it was not from the heat. It was from the anxiety he felt. Carter had to think clearly and calmly. Cheng had failed him, but his female watchdog was doing a better job. Nonetheless, she had her limits. He knew he had no real choice now. But it was not too late. There was a plane leaving for Lisbon at eleven o'clock in the evening. That was in six hours. *I can't take any more chances*, he thought. *Therefore, I have to go.*

The decision was made. He went back inside and sent the necessary e-mails.

Then he called the airport to book his flight.

He ate the dinner that Celine had prepared. Then he showered and packed his bag. He shivered at the thought of having to travel to the cold.

At ten minutes past eleven, the TAP Portuguese Airlines plane headed for Lisbon took off from Luanda airport. It was only ten minutes late.

They arrived at the station shortly after four o'clock. For some reason Modin had been set up in Svedberg's old office that was now mainly used by police officers on temporary assignments. Modin was drinking a cup of coffee when Wallander came in. He smiled uncertainly when he saw Wallander, but Wallander could still see the fear underneath.

"Let's go into my office," he said.

Modin took his cup of coffee and followed him. When he sat down in the chair across from Wallander's desk, the armrest fell off. He jumped.

"That happens all the time," Wallander said. "Leave it."

He sat down in his chair and cleared all his paperwork from the middle of his desk.

"I'm going to present you with a hypothesis I'm working on. I think that when we weren't looking, you copied a bunch of material from Falk's computer and transferred it to your own. What do you think of that?"

"I want to speak to a lawyer," Modin said firmly.

"We don't need lawyers," Wallander said. "You haven't actually broken any laws. At least not as far as I know. But I need to know exactly what you did."

Modin didn't believe him.

"You're here now so that we can protect you," Wallander continued. "Not for any other reason. You are not being held here on charges. We don't suspect you of anything."

Modin still seemed to weighing Wallander's words. He waited.

"Can I have that in writing?" he asked finally.

Wallander reached out for a pad of paper and wrote a guarantee for him. He signed it and wrote the date.

"I don't have a stamp," he said. "But this ought to work."

"It's not good enough," Modin said.

"It will have to do," Wallander said. "This is between you and me. I would accept it if I were you. If you don't, there's always the chance I'm going to change my mind."

Modin realized he meant business.

"Tell me what happened," Wallander said. "You received a threatening e-mail in your computer. I've read it myself. Then you looked up and saw that there was a car parked on that little road that goes between the fields behind your house. Is that right?"

Modin looked disbelievingly at him.

"How can you know all that?"

"I just know," Wallander said. "You were scared and you left. The question I have is why you were so scared."

"They had traced me."

"So you weren't careful enough at erasing your steps? Did you make the same mistake as last time?"

"They're very good."

"But so are you."

Modin shrugged.

"The problem is that you started taking chances, isn't that so? You copied material from Falk's computer onto your own, and something happened. The temptation was too great. You kept working on the material through the night, and somehow they caught on to you while you weren't looking."

"I don't know why you keep asking if you already know everything."

Wallander decided to make his point.

"You have to understand that this is serious."

"Of course I do. Why would I have tried to get away otherwise? I don't even have my driver's license."

"Then we see eye to eye on this. You realize you're involved in a dangerous business. From now on you need to do as I say. By the way, has anyone brought you any food?" he asked. "I know you have un-usual food preferences."

"A tofu pie would be nice," Modin answered. "And some carrot juice."

Wallander called Irene.

"Could you get us a tofu pie and a carrot juice, please."

"Can you repeat that?"

Ebba would not have asked any questions, Wallander thought.

"Tofu pie."

"What on God's earth is that?"

"Food. It's vegetarian. Please try to get it as quickly as you can."

He hung up before Irene had a chance to ask anything else.

"Let's start by talking about what you saw from your window," Wallander said. "At some point you discovered a car out there."

"There are never any cars on that road."

"You took out your binoculars and took a closer look."

"You already know everything I did."

"No," Wallander said. "I know part of it. What did you see?"

"A dark-blue car."

"Was it a Mercedes?"

"I don't know anything about cars."

"Was it big? Did it look like a van?"

"Yes."

"And there was someone standing next to the car?"

"That was what scared me. When I looked through the binoculars I saw a man who was looking at me with some binoculars of his own."

"Could you see his face?"

"I was scared."

"I know. What about his face?"

"He had dark hair."

"What was he wearing?"

"A dark raincoat. I think."

"Did you see anything else? Had you ever seen him before?"

"No. And I didn't notice anything else."

"You left. Could you tell if he followed you?"

"I don't think he did. There's a little road you can take just a little bit past our house. I don't think he saw it."

"Then what did you do?"

"I had sent you the e-mail, but I didn't feel I could go to Runnerström Square. I didn't know what to do. At first I was planning to go to Copenhagen. But I didn't feel up to driving down to Malmö. I'm not a very good driver. Something could have happened."

"So you simply drove into Ystad. What did you do then?"

"Nothing."

"You stayed in the car until some policemen found you?"

"Yes."

Wallander tried to think about where they should go from here. He wanted Martinsson to be present, as well as Alfredsson. He got up and left the room. Irene was at her desk. She shook her head when she saw him.

"How is the food coming?" he asked sternly.

"Sometimes I think all of you are nuts."

"That's probably true, but I have a boy back there who doesn't eat hamburgers. I guess there are people like that. And he needs food."

"I called Ebba," Irene said. "She said she would take care of it."

That put him in a better mood. If she had talked to Ebba, everything would be taken care of.

"I'd like to speak to Martinsson and Alfredsson as soon as possible," he said. "Please get hold of them as soon as you can."

At that moment Lisa Holgersson hurried in through the front doors.

"More shooting?" she asked. "That's what I heard. What happened?"

Talking to Holgersson right now was the last thing he wanted, but Wallander knew he had no choice. He briefly filled her in on the latest events.

"Have you sent out an alert to the neighboring districts?"

"It's been taken care of."

"When can we have a meeting about this?"

"As soon as everyone comes back in."

"It feels to me like this investigation is getting out of hand."

"We're not quite at that point," Wallander said, and he didn't bother to hide his irritation. "But feel free to relieve me of my responsibilities if you like. Hansson is the one who's been in charge of the search operation."

She had a few more questions, but Wallander had already turned his back and started walking away.

Martinsson and Alfredsson came in at five o'clock. Wallander and Modin met with them in one of the smaller conference rooms. Hansson had called to say there was still no trace of the man in the fog. No one knew exactly where Höglund was. Wallander barricaded the door to make sure no one could interrupt them. Modin's computers were up and running.

"We're going to go through everything from the beginning," Wallander said when everyone had sat down.

"I'm not sure we can do that yet," Alfredsson said. "There are too many things we can't see clearly yet."

Wallander turned to Modin.

"You said you had thought of something new," he said.

"It's hard to explain," Modin said. "And I'm very hungry."

Wallander felt irritated with him for the first time. Modin might be a computer whiz, but he was far from satisfactory in other respects.

"The food is on its way," Wallander said. "If you need something right now we have good old Swedish rusks, and some leftover pizza. Take your pick."

Modin got up and sat down in front of his computers. The others gathered behind him.

"It took me a while to figure all this out," he began. "At first I was convinced that the number twenty that kept turning up had something to do with the year 2000. We already know that Y2K will cause a number of problems in many computer systems. But I never found the missing zeroes, and I also noticed that the countdown, whatever it's for, looked like it was set to go off much sooner than the end of the year. So I concluded that it had to do with the twentieth of October instead."

Alfredsson shook his head and looked like he wanted to protest, but Wallander held him back.

"Go on."

"I started looking for the other pieces of the puzzle. We know something here proceeds from the left to the right. There is an end point, and that's how we deduce that something is going to happen. But we don't know what. I decided to surf the Web for information about the financial institutions we had already identified. The National Bank of Indonesia, the World Bank, the stockbroker in Seoul. I tried to see if they had anything in common—the point you're always searching for."

"What point would that be?"

"The point of weakness. The one spot where someone could enter the system without anyone noticing."

"But there's a lot of awareness about hackers these days," Martinsson said. "And the business world is getting faster at responding to computer viruses when they emerge."

"The United States already has the capacity to conduct computer wars," Alfredsson said. "Earlier, the talk was about computer-programmed missiles, or 'smart' bombs. But soon that will be as antiquated as a cavalry. Now the goal is to dismantle the enemy's networks and kill their missiles. Or better yet, to direct the enemy's missiles against themselves."

"Is this really true?" Wallander asked skeptically.

"It is definitely in the works," Alfredsson said. "But we should also be honest about the fact that there are many things we just don't know. Weapons systems are complicated."

"Let's return to Falk's computer," Wallander said. "Did you find those weak points?"

"I'm not sure," Modin said hesitantly. "But I think there's a way to see a connection between all of these institutions. They all have one thing in common."

"And what is that?"

"They're the cornerstones of the global financial network. If you compromised them enough, you'd be able to set in motion an economic crisis that could wipe out all of the world's financial systems. The stockmarkets would crash. There'd be widespread panic. Everyone would rush to take out their money. Currency exchanges would go wild until no one could be sure what the rates should be."

"And who would be interested in causing anything of this nature?"

Martinsson and Alfredsson spoke at the same time.

"Many people," Alfredsson said. "It sounds like the highest form of terrorism imaginable. And there are many people out there eager to cause chaos and destruction."

"Taking out the global financial network would be the ultimate act of sabotage." Martinsson added.

"Does everyone in this room think that that's what we're looking at here? And that something like this is based in a computer in Ystad?" Wallander asked.

"It's definitely something like this," Martinsson said. "I've never come across anything like it before."

"Is it harder to break into than the Pentagon?" Alfredsson asked.

Modin narrowed his eyes.

"It's certainly not any less complicated."

"I'm not sure how best to proceed in this kind of a situation," Wallander said.

"I'll talk to my people in Stockholm," Alfredsson said. "I'll send in a report that will later get sent on all over the world. We have to alert the institutions involved so that they can take precautions."

"If it isn't already too late," Modin mumbled.

Everyone heard him, but no one made any comment. Alfredsson left the room in a hurry.

"I still have trouble believing it," Wallander said.

"Well, whatever it is in Falk's computer, there are people ready to kill in order to keep the system and countdown going," Martinsson said.

Wallander pointed at Modin so that Martinsson would understand that he should choose his words with greater care.

"The question is what we can do," Wallander said. "Is there anything we can do?"

"There's often a button to push," Modin said abruptly. "If you infect a computer system with a virus, you often hide it in an innocent and common command. But in order to set it off, several things have to come together at once. The commands often need to be carried out at a precise time, for example."

"The best thing we can do now is carry on with what we've been doing," Martinsson said. "We need to let the institutions know that they're in danger of an attack so that they can inspect their security procedures. Alfredsson will handle the rest."

Martinsson scribbled a few words on a piece of paper. He looked up at Wallander, who bent over to read them:

THE THREAT AGAINST MODIN IS SERIOUS.

Wallander nodded. Whoever had been spying on Modin from the road between the fields had known how important he was. Right now he was in the same situation that Sonja Hökberg had been in.

Wallander's phone rang. Hansson was calling to let him know that the search for the attacker had not yet yielded any results. But they would continue unabated.

"How is Nyberg doing?"

"He's already comparing fingerprints."

Hansson was still out near Backåkra, where he would stay for now. He didn't know where Höglund was.

They ended the conversation. Wallander tried to phone Höglund, but her phone was out of range.

There was a knock on the door, and Irene came in with a box.

"Here's the food," she said. "Who's supposed to take care of the bill? I had to pay the delivery man out of my own pocket."

"I'll take care of it," Wallander said and stretched out his hand for the receipt.

Modin ate. Wallander and Martinsson watched him in silence. Then Wallander's phone rang again. It was Elvira Lindfeldt. He went out into the hall and closed the door behind him.

"I heard on the radio that shots were fired in an incident close to Ystad," she said. "And there were policemen involved. I hope that wasn't you."

"Not directly," Wallander said vaguely. "But we have a lot going on right now."

"It made me worried, that's all. I had to ask. Now of course I'm getting curious but I won't ask any more questions."

"There isn't much I can tell you," Wallander said.

"I understand that you don't have a lot of free time at the moment."

"It's too early to say. But I'll be in touch."

When the conversation was over Wallander thought about the fact that it had been a long time since anyone had cared about him. Let alone worried about him.

He went back into the room. It was twenty minutes to six. Modin was still eating. Wallander and Martinsson left to get some coffee.

"I forgot to tell you that I cross-checked the list of names I got from Sydkraft. But I didn't find anything."

"We didn't expect to," Wallander said.

The coffee machine was on the blink again. Martinsson pulled out the plug and then put it in again. Now it was working.

"Is there a computer program inside the coffee machine?" Wallander asked.

"Hardly," Martinsson said. "Though I guess you can imagine more sophisticated machines that would be controlled with tiny computer chips."

"What if someone went in and changed the program? Could they change it so tea came out instead of coffee? And milk when someone wanted espresso?"

"Of course."

"But how would it get triggered? How could you get it to start?"

"Well, you could imagine that a certain date has been entered in. A date and a time, perhaps an interval of an hour. Then the eleventh time that someone presses the button for coffee, the virus is triggered."

"Why the eleventh?"

"That was just an example. It could have been any number that you'd chosen."

"Is there anything you can do once that change occurs?"

"You could pull out the plug and restart it," Martinsson said. "You can hang a sign saying the machine is broken. But the program that runs the machine would have to be replaced."

"Is this what Modin is talking about?"

"Yes, but on a larger scale."

"But we have no idea where Falk's coffee machine is."

"It could be anywhere in the world."

"And that would mean that whoever sets off the chain reaction wouldn't even have to be aware of it."

"It would even be an advantage if the responsible party was nowhere near where the virus first arises."

"So we're looking for the symbolic equivalent of a coffee machine," Wallander said. He walked over to the window and looked out. It was already dark. Martinsson walked over to where he was.

"I want you to do something," Wallander said. "I'd like you to write a memo about what we just talked about. The threat of a global financial collapse. Get Alfredsson to help you. Then send it on to Stockholm and all of the internationl police agencies you can think of."

"If we're wrong, we'll be the laughing stock of the world."

"We have to take that chance. Give me the papers and I'll sign them."

Martinsson left. Wallander stayed in the lunchroom, deep in thought. He didn't notice when Höglund slipped in. He jumped when she turned up at his side.

"You know the poster of that movie," she said. "The one that you saw in Sonja Hökberg's closet?"

"*The Devil's Advocate*. I have the movie at home, I just haven't had
time to see it."

"I don't think the movie is so important, actually," she said. "But I've
been thinking about Al Pacino. He resembles someone."

Wallander looked at her.

"Who does he resemble?"

"The man in her sketch. Carl-Einar Lundberg. He actually looks a
little like Al Pacino."

Wallander realized that she was right. He had seen a picture of
Lundberg in a file she had put on his desk. He just hadn't thought
about the resemblance until now. Another detail fell into place.

They sat down at a table. Höglund was tired.

"I went over to talk to Eva Persson," she said. "I thought I would be
able to get something more out of her. Silly me."

"How was she?"

"She's still completely nonchalant. That's the worst thing. I wish she
looked like she slept badly and cried at night. But she doesn't. She just
sits there chewing her gum and seems mildly irritated at having to
answer my questions."

"She's hiding her feelings," Wallander said. "We just can't see it."

"I hope you're right."

Wallander filled her in on Modin's hypothesis of an impending
financial collapse.

"We've never even been close to something like this," she said when
he finished. "If it's true."

"We'll find out on Monday, I guess. Unless we think of some way to
intervene."

"Do you think we will?"

"Maybe. Martinsson is contacting police all over the world, and
Alfredsson is getting in touch with all of the institutions on Falk's list."

"There isn't much time. If it really is set for Monday. And it's the
weekend."

"There's never enough time," Wallander answered.

By nine o'clock, Robert Modin was completely exhausted. They had
decided that he was not going to be spending the next few nights at
home. But when Martinsson suggested he sleep at the station, he
flat-out refused. Wallander thought about calling Sten Widén to see if
he could accomodate an extra person, but he decided against it. For
security reasons Modin could not spend the night with anyone on the

investigative team, since they could also be considered a target. They had to be careful.

Finally, Wallander thought of a person to ask. Elvira Lindfeldt. She was a complete outsider, and it would also give him a chance to see her, if only for a short while.

Wallander didn't say her name, but he said he would take Robert to a safe place for the night.

He called her shortly before nine-thirty.

"I have a question that may seem a little strange," he said.

"I'm used to strange questions."

"Could you take an extra person for the night?"

"Who would that be?"

"Do you remember the young man who came to the restaurant that night?"

"His name was Kolin?"

"Modin."

"He has nowhere to sleep?"

"I'm only going to say that he needs a place to stay for a few nights."

"Of course he can stay here. How is he going to get here?"

"I'll give him a ride. We'll be there shortly."

"Do you want anything to eat when you arrive?"

"Some coffee would be nice. That's all."

They left the station shortly before ten. When they passed Skurup Wallander was sure no one was following them.

Elvira Lindfeldt slowly put down the receiver. She was happy, in fact more than happy. She was overjoyed. This was an amazing stroke of luck. She thought about Carter, who was about to take off from the Luanda airport.

He would be happy, too.

After all, this was exactly what he had wanted.

Chapter Thirty-seven

The night of Sunday the nineteenth of October would go down as one of the worst in Wallander's life. Afterward he would think back to a near accident that night as a sign. As they passed the exit for Svedala, a car had suddenly decided to overtake him just as a huge truck was bearing down on them in the oncoming lane. Wallander turned his steering wheel as sharply as he could without driving off the road, but it was close. Robert Modin was sleeping in the front seat next to him and didn't notice anything. But Wallander's heart was pounding inside his chest.

As he kept driving, his mind returned uneasily to what Höglund had told him about Martinsson and his games. He had an unpleasant feeling of being on trial and not being sure of his own innocence. The anxiety and worry was nagging at him from all sides.

When he exited the highway to Jägersro, Robert Modin woke up.

"We'll be there soon," Wallander said.

"I was dreaming," Modin said. "Someone tried to attack me."

Wallander found the house easily. It lay in the corner of a housing development that looked like it had been built between the wars. He parked and turned off the engine.

"Who lives here?" Modin asked.

"A friend of mine," Wallander said. "Her name is Elvira. You'll be safe here. I'll send someone to pick you up in the morning."

"I don't even have a toothbrush with me," Modin said.

"We'll take care of it somehow."

It was almost eleven o'clock. Wallander had imagined that he would have a cup of coffee, look at her lovely legs, and stay until about midnight.

But it didn't turn out that way. They had only just gone inside when his phone rang. It was Hansson. Wallander could tell that something was up by the tension in his voice. They had finally found traces of the man they thought had shot at Wallander. Once again it was a person out walking a dog who had helped them, this time by notifying them of a man who seemed to be hiding in the bushes and generally behaving strangely. Since he had been seeing police cars driving to and fro all day, the dog owner thought it best to call in with his information. The dog owner had told Hansson that the man appeared to have been dressed in a black raincoat.

Wallander quickly thanked Elvira for her hospitality, introduced Modin to her again, and then left. He thought about the curious fact that dog owners had been such a big help during the investigation. Perhaps these civilians were a resource that the police should make more use of in the future? He drove much too fast and soon arrived at the spot north of Sandhammaren that Hansson had described to him. On the way he had stopped at the station and picked up his gun.

It had started raining again. Martinsson arrived a few minutes before Wallander. Police officers in full protective gear were in place, as well as several canine units. The man they were closing in on was located in a small pocket of forest that was bordered on one side by the highway to Skillinge and some open fields on the other. Although Hansson had been very effective in mobilizing police into the area, Wallander immediately realized that the man would have a good chance of being able to get away. They tried to come up with a reasonable plan of attack. While they were discussing their options, something came in on Hansson's radio. A police patrol toward the north thought they had spotted the suspect. The radio contact broke off. In the distance came the sound of a shot closely followed by another. Then the radio came on again: "The fucker's shooting at us." Then silence.

Wallander immediately feared the worst. Martinsson seemed to have disappeared. It took him and Hansson six minutes to reach the spot where the radio transmission had come from. When they saw the patrol car with its lights on they readied their weapons and got out of their own vehicle. The silence was deafening. Wallander shouted out to the others, and to his and Hansson's great relief there was an answer. They ran over to the patrol car in a crouched position where they found two policemen who were scared out of their wits. One of them was El Sayed, the other Elofsson. The man who had shot at them appeared to be in a clump of trees on the other side of the road. They had been standing next to the car when they heard the sound of breaking twigs. Elofsson had directed his flashlight toward the trees while El Sayed had established radio contact with Hansson. Then the shots had come.

"What's beyond those trees?" Wallander hissed.

"There's a path down to the sea," Elofsson said.

"Are there any houses down there?"

No one knew.

"We'll try to surround him," Wallander said. "Now at least we have a better idea of where he is."

Hansson managed to locate Martinsson and tell him where they were. Meanwhile Wallander dispatched Elofsson and El Sayed deeper into the shadows. The whole time he expected the suspect to turn up alongside the car with his gun cocked.

"What about a helicopter?" Martinsson asked.

"Good idea. Make sure it has strong spotlights. But don't let it turn up until all of us are in place."

Martinsson turned to his radio and Wallander carefully looked out at the terrain. Since it was dark, he couldn't really see anything, and since the wind had picked up it was hard for him to hear anything, either. It was impossible for him to determine if the sounds he heard were real or imagined.

Martinsson crept over to him.

"They're on their way. Hansson has dispatched a helicopter."

Wallander never had time to answer. At that moment another shot was fired. They steeled themselves.

The shot had come somewhere from the left. Wallander had no idea who the intended target was. He called out to Elofsson, and El Sayed called back. Then he also heard Elfosson's voice. Wallander knew he had to do something. He called out into the darkness.

"Police! Lay down your weapon!"

Then he repeated the phrase in English.

There was no answer, only the wind.

"I don't like this," Martinsson whispered. "Why is he still there shooting at us? Why doesn't he leave? He must know there are reinforcements on the way."

Wallander didn't reply. He had started thinking the same thing.

Then they heard police sirens in the distance.

"Why didn't you tell them to be quiet?"

Wallander didn't try to hide his irritation.

"Hansson should have known better."

At the same moment El Sayed cried out. Wallander thought he glimpsed a shadow running across the road and out into the field that lay to the left of the car. Then it was gone.

"He's getting away," Wallander hissed.

"Where?"

Wallander pointed in the direction where the shadow had been, but there was no point. Martinsson couldn't see anything. Wallander realized he had to act fast. If the suspect made it across the field he would reach a larger stretch of forest and then it would be harder to get him. He told Martinsson to move, then he jumped into the car, started it, and pulled it around violently. He hit something but didn't stop to look what it was. But now the headlights were shining straight out into the field.

The man was out there. When the light hit him he stopped and turned around. The raincoat flapped in the wind. Wallander saw the man raise one arm. He threw himself to the side. The bullet went straight through the windshield. Wallander rolled out of the car while he yelled to the others to get down. Another shot rang out. It took out a headlight. Wallander wondered if the man was just a lucky shot or if he had meant to hit it. It was much harder to see now.

The police sirens were getting closer. Suddenly Wallander was afraid that the approaching cars were going to be a target. He yelled out to Martinsson to radio the cars and tell them not to approach until they received an all-clear.

"I've dropped the radio," Martinsson said. "I can't find it in this shit."

The man in the field was quickly disappearing. Wallander saw him trip and almost fall. Wallander knew he had to make a quick decision. He got to his feet.

"What the hell are you doing?"

"We have to take him," Wallander said.

"We have to surround him first."

"Before we do that, he'll get away."

Wallander looked at Martinsson, who shook his head. Then he started running. The mud immediately started caking up under his shoes. The man was beyond the reach of the light now. Wallander stopped and made sure his gun was cocked. Behind him he heard Martinsson shouting to El Sayed and Elofsson. Wallander stayed slightly outside the light from the remaining headlight and sped up. Then one of his shoes sank down in the mud and came off. Wallander angrily ripped off the other. His feet immediately became cold and wet, but it was easier to walk over the mud. He suddenly caught sight of the man, who was also having trouble crossing the plowed mud.

The distance between them was still so great that Wallander did not dare try to immobilize him by shooting at his legs. In the distance he heard a helicopter, but it did not come closer. It seemed to be awaiting further orders. They were out in the middle of the field now and the light from the car was very weak. Wallander knew he had to do something, he just didn't know what. He was a mediocre shot. The man in front of him had missed his mark twice in a row, but Wallander still sensed he was better with his weapon than Wallander was with his. He had hit the headlight from very far away. Wallander frantically tried to think of something that would work. He didn't understand why neither Hansson nor Martinsson ordered the helicopter to advance.

Suddenly the man tripped and fell. Wallander stopped. Then he saw that the man was looking for something. It took Wallander a split second to understand that he had dropped his gun and was looking for it. They were about thirty meters apart. *I don't have enough time*, he thought, but then he was running and jumping across the stiff furrows. A few times he almost lost his balance. Then the man saw him. Even though it was dark, Wallander could tell he looked Asian.

Wallander's left foot slipped out from under him as if he were on an ice floe. He didn't manage to recover and ended up falling headfirst into the mud. At that moment his opponent found his gun. Wallander had one knee up and saw that the gun was aimed straight at him. Wallander pulled his own trigger. The gun didn't work. He tried again with the same result. In a last desperate attempt to survive, Wallander threw himself to the side and tried to sink down into the mud. That was when the shot was fired. Wallander flinched, but he had not been hit. He lay motionless and waited for his opponent to fire again. But nothing happened. Wallander had no sense of how long he lay there. He felt as if he were watching himself from a distance, observing the situation. So this was how it would end: a meaningless death in a muddy field. This is where he had brought his dreams and intentions. Now nothing would come of them. He would disappear into the final darkness with his face pressed down into the cold wet clay, and he wasn't even wearing any shoes.

It was only when he heard the sound of a rapidly approaching helicopter that he dared to think he might survive. He carefully looked up.

The man lay on his back with his arms spread. Wallander got up and slowly walked closer. He could see the floodlights on the helicopter starting to search the far end of the field. Some dogs were barking and somewhere far away he heard Martinsson's voice.

The man was dead. The shot Wallander had heard had not been meant for him after all. The man lying in the mud had shot himself in the temple. Wallander was overcome by a sudden onset of nausea and dizziness and had to sit down. His clothes were cold and wet and now he finally started shaking.

Wallander looked at the body in front of him. He didn't know who this man was or why he had come to Ystad, but his death was a relief. This was the man who had entered Falk's apartment when Wallander was there waiting for Marianne Falk. He had tried to shoot Wallander on two separate occasions. Most likely he had also dragged Sonja Hökberg to the power substation, and thrown Jonas Landahl into the propeller axle on the Polish ferry. There were many question marks, but as Wallander sat there on the muddy field he felt that at least something had come to an end.

Now Wallander no longer had to fear for his colleagues' or Robert Modin's safety.

There was no way for him to know that he was wrong about this assumption. It was something he would only come to understand in time.

Martinsson was the first person to reach Wallander. The latter stood up. Elofsson was also nearby. Wallander asked him to find his shoes and bring them over.

"Did you shoot him?" Martinsson asked in disbelief.

Wallander shook his head.

"No, he shot himself. If he hadn't, I wouldn't be standing here right now."

Lisa Holgersson suddenly appeared, as if out of thin air. Wallander let Martinsson do the explaining. Elofsson turned up with Wallander's shoes, which were covered in thick clay. Wallander wanted to get away as soon as possible. Not only to be able to change his clothes, but to get away from the memory of what it was like to lie there in the mud expecting the end. The depressingly pathetic end.

Somewhere deep inside there was probably a flicker of happiness, but for the moment a feeling of emptiness dominated.

The helicopter was gone now. Hansson had dismissed it, and the large operation was now being dismantled. The only people left were the team who were going to do the investigation surrounding the suspect's death.

Hansson made his way through the mud. He was wearing bright orange boots.

"You should go home," he said, looking at Wallander.

Wallander nodded and started walking the same way he had come.

All around him he saw the flickering of flashlights. Several times he almost tripped.

Shortly before he got to the road, Holgersson caught up with him.

"I think I have a fairly complete picture of what happened," she said. "But tomorrow we'll have to have a thorough debriefing. It's lucky things turned out as well as they did."

"Soon we should be able to determine if this is the individual who was responsible for Sonja Hökberg's and Jonas Landahl's deaths."

"But why did all of this happen?"

"We don't know why, but Falk is in the center of it all. Or rather, whatever is in his computer."

"This hypothesis still seems unfounded to me," Holgersson said.

"There's no alternative, as far as I see."

Wallander had no more energy for this discussion.

"I have to get into some dry clothes," he said. "If you'll excuse me, I'm heading home now."

"One more thing," she said. "I have to say this to you. It was completely irresponsible of you to have gone after this man alone. You should have taken Martinsson along as backup."

"Everything happened so fast."

"But you should not have ordered him to stay behind."

Wallander had been brushing clay from his clothes. Now he looked up.

"Ordered him?"

"Yes, ordered him to stand back while you went in. You know as well as I do that one of the most basic rules of police work is never to act alone."

Wallander had forgotten all about the mud now.

"Who says I ordered him to stay behind?"

"It has emerged from various reports."

Wallander knew there was only one possible explanation for this version of the events. Martinsson must have said this to her. Elofsson and El Sayed had been too far back to be able to hear anything.

"Perhaps we should talk about this tomorrow," he said.

"I had to bring this up with you right away," she said. "It's my duty as your commanding officer. You're in a delicate enough situation as it is."

She left him and continued on toward the road.

Wallander realized he was trembling with fury. Martinsson had lied. He claimed Wallander had ordered him not to follow him out onto the field, where Wallander had subsequently become trapped and had thought he was going to die.

He looked up and saw that Martinsson and Hansson were on their
way toward him. The light from their flashlights bobbed up and down.
From the other direction he heard Holgersson start up her car and
drive away.

Martinsson and Hansson stopped when they reached him.

"Could you hold Martinsson's flashlight for a moment?" Wallander
asked, looking at Hansson.

"Why?"

"Just do it, please."

Martinsson handed Hansson his flashlight. Wallander took a step
forward and hit Martinsson in the face. However, since it was hard to
judge the distance between them in the poor light from the flashlights,
the blow didn't land squarely on his jaw as intended. It was more of a
gentle nudge.

"What the hell are you doing?"

"What the hell are *you* doing?" Wallander yelled back.

Then he threw himself on Martinsson and they fell back into the
mud. Hansson tried to get between them but slipped. One of the
flashlights went out, the other landed some distance away.

"You told Holgersson I ordered you to stay behind! You've been
spreading lies about me this whole time!"

Wallander pushed Martinsson away and stood up. Hansson was also
standing. A dog was barking in the background.

"You've been going behind my back," Wallander continued, and
heard that his voice had become completely steady.

"I don't know what you're talking about."

"You go behind my back and say that I'm a bad at my job. You sneak
away into Holgersson's office when you think no one sees you."

Hansson entered the conversation for the first time.

"What is going on between you two?"

"We're discussing the issue of good teamwork," Wallander answered. "If it's best to say what you think to someone's face, or whether
you should go behind someone's back and complain about them to
their superior officer."

"I still don't get it," Hansson said.

Wallander sighed. He saw no point in dragging this out.

"That was all I wanted to say," he said and threw a flashlight at
Martinsson's feet.

Then he walked over to a patrol car and asked the officer behind
the wheel to take him home.

He took a bath and then went and sat in the kitchen. It was close to
three o'clock. He tried to think, but his head still felt empty. He went

to bed but couldn't sleep. His thoughts returned to the field, and to the terror he had experienced as he lay with his face pressed into the wet clay. The intense sense of humiliation at dying without his shoes on. And then his confrontation with Martinsson.

I've reached my limit, he thought. *Not only in relation to Martinsson but perhaps in relation to everything I do.*

He wondered what the consequences of his fight with Martinsson would be. He had struck him in the face. It would come down to word against word, just like the case with Eva Persson and her mother. Holgersson had already proved that she put greater stock in Martinsson's accounts than his own. And now Wallander had shown himself guilty of excessive force for the second time in only two weeks.

As he lay in the dark, he wondered if he regretted his behavior. He couldn't honestly say that he did. It was motivated by a sense of personal dignity. The assault had been a necessary reaction to Martinsson's betrayal. All of the rage that he had been feeling since Höglund had told him about Martinsson had finally bubbled up to the surface.

It was shortly after four when he finally fell asleep.

It was Sunday, the nineteenth of October.

Carter landed in Lisbon on the TAP Portuguese Airlines flight 553 at exactly six thirty in the morning. The connecting flight to Copenhagen was leaving at eight fifteen. As usual, his entry into Europe disturbed him. He felt protected in Africa. Here he was in foreign territory.

At home he had looked carefully at his selection of passports and finally settled on the identity of Lukas Habermann, a German citizen born in Kassel in 1939. After going through customs in Portugal, he went into the nearest bathroom and cut the passport into small pieces that he then flushed down the toilet. He would continue his journey as the Englishman Richard Stanton, born in Oxford in 1940. He put on another coat and slicked his hair down with water. After checking his luggage to Copenhagen, he went through the passport control again, this time studiously avoiding the line to the customs officer from the time before. He did not run into any problems. He walked through the terminal until he reached an area that was under construction. Since it was Sunday, there were no workers around. He took out his cell phone only after making sure that he was alone.

She answered immediately. He didn't like talking on the phone, so he only asked short questions and received equally brief and concise answers.

She was not able to tell him anything about Cheng's whereabouts. He was supposed to have contacted her in the early evening, but he had never called.

Carter listened to her big news with some skepticism. He could not fully believe that it was true. He was not used to being lucky.

But he was finally convinced. Robert Modin had indeed been brought straight into their trap.

After the conversation was over, Carter thought about Cheng. Something must have happened to him. But on the other hand, they now had access to Modin, and he was their biggest threat.

Carter put away his phone and went to the executive lounge, where he had an apple and a cup of tea.

The plane to Copenhagen took off five minutes later than scheduled.

Carter sat in seat 3D, on the aisle. The window seat made him feel too trapped.

He told the flight attendant that he would not be requiring breakfast.

Then he closed his eyes and fell asleep.

Chapter Thirty-eight

Wallander and Martinsson met in the corridor outside the lunchroom at the police station at exactly eight o'clock on Sunday morning. It was as if they had decided on the time and place in advance. Since they approached the lunchroom from opposite ends of the corridor, Wallander felt as if they were participating in a duel. But instead of drawing pistols, they nodded curtly at each other and went in to get coffee. The coffee machine had broken down again. They read the handwritten sign that had been affixed to the front. Martinsson had a black eye and his lower lip was swollen.

"I'm going to get you for what you did," Martinsson said. "But first we have to finish this case."

"It was wrong of me to hit you," Wallander said. "But that's the only thing I'll take back."

They said nothing more about what had happened. Hansson came in and stared nervously at them.

Wallander suggested that they may as well have their meeting in the lunchroom rather than move to a conference room. Hansson put on a pot of water and offered to make them coffee from his private stash. Just as they were pouring it out, Höglund arrived. Wallander assumed it must be Hansson who had notified her of the latest events, but it turned out to be Martinsson. Wallander gathered that he had said nothing about the fight, but he noticed that Martinsson looked at her with a new coldness. He must have spent the brief night figuring out just who could have snitched on him to Wallander.

Once Alfredsson had joined them, they were ready to begin the meeting. Wallander asked Hansson to inform Viktorsson of the night's events. In the present situation it was even more important that the district attorney's office was kept up to date. There would probably be a press conference later in the day, but Chief Holgersson would have to take care of it. Wallander asked Höglund to assist her if she had time. She looked surprised.

"But I wasn't even there."

"You don't need to say anything. I just want you there so you can hear what Holgersson says. Especially if she happens to say something stupid."

There was a stunned silence in the room after his last comment. No one had heard him openly criticize Holgersson before. It was not premeditated on his part; it had just slipped out. He felt another wave of exhaustion, of being burned out, maybe even old. Of course, his age gave him an excuse for speaking plainly.

He moved on to the most pressing matter.

"We have to concentrate our efforts on Falk's computer. Whatever is programmed into it is going to take effect on the twentieth of October. We therefore have less than sixteen hours to figure out what that is."

"Where is Modin?" Hansson asked.

Wallander drained the last of his coffee and got up.

"I'm going to pick him up. Let's get going, everybody."

As they filed out of the lunchroom Höglund grabbed his arm, but he tried to shake her off.

"Not now. I have to get Modin."

"Where is he?"

"With a friend of mine."

"Can nobody else get him?"

"Sure they could. But I need the time to collect my thoughts. We need to figure out how to use the short amount of time we have most effectively. What does it mean that Cheng is dead?"

"That's exactly what I wanted to talk to you about."

Wallander stopped.

"All right," he said. "You have exactly five minutes."

"It seems as if we haven't posed the most important question."

"And what might that be?"

"Why he shot himself and not you."

Wallander was getting irritated. He was irritated at everything and everyone and made no attempt to hide it.

"And what's your opinion?"

"I wasn't there. I don't know how things looked out there or exactly what happened. But I know that it takes a lot, even for a person like that, to actually pull the trigger on himself."

"And how do you know this?"

"You have to admit I have some experience after all these years."

Wallander knew he was lecturing her as he answered. He couldn't help it.

"The question is what your experience is really worth in this case. This person killed at least two people before he died, and he wouldn't have hesitated one moment to kill me. We don't know what was driving him, but he must have been a completely ruthless person. What happened was that he heard the helicopter approaching and he knew he wasn't going to get away in time. We know the people involved in this case are fanatical in some way. In this instance that fanaticism was turned on himself."

Höglund wanted to say something, but Wallander was already on his way out the front doors.

"I have to get Modin," he said. "We can talk more later. If our world still exists, that is."

Wallander left the station. It was a quarter to nine and he was in a hurry. He drove at a very high speed and inadvertently ran over a hare. He tried to swerve but one of his back wheels hit the animal. He could see its legs jerking when he looked back in the rearview mirror. But he didn't stop.

He reached the house in Jägersro at twenty minutes to ten. Elvira opened the door very quickly after he rang the bell. She was already fully dressed, but Wallander sensed that she was very tired. In some way she seemed different than when he had seen her last. But her smile was the same. She asked if he wanted a cup of coffee. Wallander looked past her and saw Robert Modin drinking a cup of tea in the kitchen. Wallander wanted nothing more than to drink a cup of coffee with her but declined her offer. They had so little time. She insisted, took his arm, and almost pushed him into the kitchen. Wallander also saw her cast a quick glance at her watch. That made him suspicious. *She wants me to stay*, he thought. *But not too long. She's expecting someone else later.* He declined the coffee again and told Modin to get ready.

"People who are always in a hurry make me nervous," she complained after Modin had left the kitchen.

"Then you've found my first flaw," Wallander said. "I'm sorry about this, but it can't be helped. We need Modin in Ystad right away."

"What is it that is so urgent?"

"I haven't got time to explain," Wallander said. "Let me just say that we're a bit worried about the twentieth of October. And that's tomorrow."

Even though Wallander was tired, he noticed the slight cloud of worry that appeared in her face. Then she smiled again. Wallander wondered if she was afraid, but then he dismissed the whole thing as imagination.

Modin came down the stairs. He carried a small computer under each arm.

"And when will I be seeing you again?" she asked.

"I'll call you," Wallander said. "I don't know yet."

Wallander drove Modin back to Ystad. He stuck to a slightly slower speed.

"I woke up early," Modin said. "I had some new ideas that I'd like to try out."

Wallander wondered if he should tell him what had happened during the night, but he decided to wait. Right now it was important for Modin to stay focused. They kept driving in silence. Wallander realized that it was pointless for him to ask Modin about his ideas, since he wouldn't understand the explanations.

They drove past the place where Wallander had run over the hare. A flock of crows took off as they approached. The hare was already dismembered to the point of unrecognizability. Wallander told Modin that he was one who had run it over.

"You always see hundreds of run-over hares along this road," Wallander remarked. "But it's only once you kill one yourself that you really see it."

Modin suddenly looked at him.

"Could you say that last part again? About the hare?"

Wallander repeated what he had said.

"Exactly," Modin said thoughtfully. "That's it. Of course."

Wallander looked inquiringly at him.

"I'm thinking about what we're looking for in Falk's computer," Modin explained. "The way to think about it may be to look for something we've seen a hundred times without really noticing."

Then Modin sunk back into thought. Wallander was still not sure he had understood this insight.

At eleven o'clock he stopped the car by Runnerström Square. Wallander knew that from here on out he was dependent on what Alfredsson and Modin were able to accomplish, with Martinsson's assistance. The best he could do would be to try to maintain the larger perspective and not think he would be able to dive into the electronic world with the others. He hoped Martinsson and Alfredsson had the good sense not to tell Modin about what had happened last night. He should really have taken Martinsson aside and told him that Modin knew nothing about the events, but he couldn't stand talking to him any more than absolutely necessary.

"It's eleven o'clock," he said when they had gathered around the desk. "That means we have thirteen hours left until it is officially the twentieth of October. Time is of the essence, in other words."

"Nyberg called," Martinsson said, interrupting him.

"What did he have to say for himself?"

"Not much. The weapon was a Makarov, nine millimeter. He thought it would turn out to be the same weapon used in the apartment on Apelbergsgatan."

"Did the man have any identification?"

"He had three different passports. Korean, Thai and, strangely enough, one from Romania."

"None from Angola?"

"Nope."

"I'm going to talk to Nyberg."

Wallander returned to his general remarks. Modin sat impatiently in front of the computer.

"We only have thirteen hours left until the twentieth of October," he continued. "And right now we have three main points of interest. Everything else can wait."

Wallander looked around. Martinsson's face was devoid of expression. The swelling at his lower lip was starting to turn blue.

"The first question is if the twentieth of October is the real date," Wallander said. "If it is, what will happen? The third question that follows from this is, if something is about to happen, how can we prevent it? Nothing else matters except these three things."

Wallander finished.

"There haven't been any responses from abroad," Alfredsson said.

Wallander suddenly remembered the paper he should have signed and authorized before it was sent out to police organizations across the world.

Martinsson must have read his mind.

"I signed it. Just to save time."

Wallander nodded.

"And no one has written back or sent further inquiries?"

"Nothing yet. But it hasn't been long, and it's still Sunday."

"That means that we're on our own for now."

Then Wallander looked at Modin.

"Robert told me on the way over that he had some new ideas. Hopefully they will lead us to new information."

"I'm convinced it's the twentieth of October," Modin said.

"Then your job is to convince the rest of us."

"I need an hour," Modin said.

"We have thirteen," Wallander said. "And let us all assume for now that we really don't have more than that."

Wallander walked away. The best thing he could do now was leave them alone. He drove to the station.

What is it I've overlooked? he thought. *Is there a clue in all of this that could bring everything together in a single stroke?* The thoughts in his head tumbled around without connecting. Then he thought back to when he had seen Elvira in Malmö. She had seemed different. He couldn't say exactly what it was, but he knew it was something, and it worried him. The last thing he wanted was for her to start finding fault with him at this stage. Perhaps taking Robert to her had been a mistake. Perhaps he had involved her too quickly and too abruptly to the re-alities of his life.

He tried to shake off these thoughts. When he got to the station, he tried to find Hansson. He was sitting in his office researching compa-nies from a list that Martinsson had compiled. Wallander asked him how it was going and Hansson shook his head despondently.

"Nothing hangs together," he said. "The only thing that seems to be a common denominator is that most of them are financial institutions. But there's also a telecommunications firm and a satellite company."

Wallander frowned.

"What was the last one?"

"A satellite company in Atlanta, Telsat Communications. As far as I can tell, they rent broadcasting space on a number of communications satellites."

"Which would fit with the field of telecommunications."

"I suppose you can even get it to fit with the financial companies, from the standpoint that they're also involved in the large-scale elec-tronic transfer of sums."

Wallander thought of something.

"Can you see if any of the company's satellites cover Angola?"

Hansson typed something into the computer. Wallander noticed that he had to wait longer than he usually did with Martinsson.

"Their satellite coverage covers the globe," he said finally. "Even to the poles."

Wallander nodded.

"It may mean something," he said. "Call Martinsson and tell him."

Hansson took the opportunity to ask something else.

"What was it that happened out there on the field anyway?"

"Martinsson is full of shit," Wallander said. "But we won't go into that right now."

Chief Holgersson organized a hasty press conference for two o'clock in the afternoon. She had tried to reach Wallander beforehand, but he'd made himself unavailable and instructed Höglund to say he was out of the office. Now he stood in front of his window for a long time and stared at the water tower. The clouds had disappeared. It was a cold and clear October day.

At three o'clock he couldn't stand it any longer and drove down to Runnerström Square, and walked in on an intense debate about how best to interpret a new combination of numbers. When Modin tried to involve Wallander, the latter simply shook his head.

At five he went out and had a hamburger. When he came back to the station he called Elvira, but there was no answer, not even an answering machine. He was immediately suspicious again, but too tired and distracted to hang on to these thoughts.

At half past six Ebba turned up unexpectedly. She had some food with her for Modin. Wallander asked Hansson to drive her down to Runnerström Square. Afterward he realized he hadn't thanked her enough.

At seven he called the team at Runnerström Square and Martinsson answered. Their conversation was brief. The team were not yet able to answer a single one of Wallander's questions. He put down the phone and went to find Hansson, who was sitting in front of the computer with bloodshot eyes. Wallander asked if there had been any messages from the international community, and Hansson had only one word in reply: "Nothing."

At that moment Wallander was overcome by rage. He grabbed one of the chairs in Hansson's office and threw it against the wall. Then he left the room.

At eight o'clock he was back in Hansson's office.

"Let's go down to Runnerström Square," he said. "We can't go on like this. We have to get an idea of where we stand."

They stopped by Höglund's office on the way out. She was half-asleep at her desk. They drove in silence. When they reached the apartment they saw Modin seated against the wall, Martinsson on his folding chair, and Alfredsson lying on the floor. Wallander asked himself if he had ever led a more exhausted and dispirited team. He knew that the physical exhaustion was due more to their lack of progress rather than to the events of the night before. If only they had come a few steps closer to the truth, if only they could break down the wall, they could each summon sufficient energy to see it through. But for now the dominant mood was one of hopelessness.

Wallander sat down on the chair in front of the computer. The others gathered around him, except Martinsson, who positioned himself in the background.

"Let's sum up where we are," he said. "What is the situation right now?"

"There are several indications that the date in question is the twentieth of October," Alfredsson said. "But we have no indications of a precise time for the event, so we cannot know if it will begin on the stroke of midnight or later. Quite possibly the intended event is a form of computer virus that targets all of these financial institutions we've identified. Since they are mostly large and powerful financial institutions, we imagine the event has something to do with money, but if we're talking about a form of electronic bank robbery or not we don't know."

"What would be the worst thing that could happen?" Wallander asked.

"Total collapse of the world financial markets."

"But is that even possible?"

"We've been through this point before. If there were a significant enough disruption of the markets or a severe fluctuation in the dollar, for example, it could incite a panic in the public that could be hard to control."

"That's what's going to happen," Modin said.

Everyone stared at him. He was sitting on the floor next to Wallander with his legs crossed.

"Why do you say that? Do you know it for a fact?"

"No, not for a fact. But I think this is going to be so big we can't even imagine it. We're not going to be able to deduce what's going to happen before it's too late."

"How does the whole thing start? Isn't there a starting point, some kind of button that needs to be pressed?"

"I imagine it will be started by some action that's so ordinary we would have trouble accepting it."

"The hypothetical coffee machine," Martinsson said.

Wallander was quiet. He looked around.

"The only thing we can do right now is keep going," he said. "We don't have a choice."

"I left some diskettes in Malmö," Modin said. "I need them in order to keep working."

"I'll send out a car to get them for you."

"I'll go too," Modin said. "I need to get out. And I know of a store in Malmö that stays open late and has the kind of food I like."

Wallander nodded and got up. Hansson called for a patrol car that would take Modin to Malmö. Wallander called Elvira. The line was busy. He tried again. Now she answered. He told her what had happened, that Modin needed to come by and pick up the diskettes he had left behind. She said it was no problem. Her voice sounded normal now.

"Can I expect to see you as well?" she asked.

"Unfortunately, I don't have the time right now."

"I won't ask you why."

"Thank you. It would take too long to explain."

Alfredsson and Martinsson were leaning over Falk's computer again. Wallander, Hansson, and Höglund returned to the station. When Wallander reached his office, the phone rang. It was the reception desk, telling him he had a visitor.

"Who is it and what is it about?" Wallander asked. "I don't have any time right now."

"It's someone who says she's your neighbor. A Mrs. Hartman."

Wallander immediately worried that something had happened. A few years ago there had been a bad water leak in his apartment. Mrs. Hartman was a widow who lived in the apartment beneath his. That time she had called him at the station.

"I'll be right there," Wallander said and hung up.

When he reached the waiting area, Mrs. Hartman was able to assuage his fears. There was no water leak, just a letter for him that had been delivered to her.

"It must be the mailman," she complained. "It probably came on Friday, but I've been away this whole time and only returned earlier today. I just thought it might be important, that's all."

"You shouldn't have taken the trouble of coming down here," Wallander said. "I rarely get mail that is so important it can't wait."

She handed him the letter. There was no return address on the envelope. After Mrs. Hartman had left, Wallander went back to his room and opened the letter. To his surprise he saw it was a notice from the dating service thanking him for his subscription and assuring him that they would forward any replies as they arrived.

Wallander crumpled the piece of paper and threw it in the trash. For the next couple of seconds his mind was a total blank. Then he frowned, took out the letter from the trash, smoothed it, and read it again. Then he looked for the envelope, still without knowing exactly why. He stared at the postmark for a long time. The letter had been posted on Thursday.

His mind was still empty.

Thursday. But at that point he had already received a reply from Elvira Lindfeldt. Her letter had arrived in an envelope that had been brought directly to his door. A letter without a postmark of any kind.

His thoughts were swirling around in his head.

Then he turned and looked at his computer. He wondered if he was going crazy. Then he forced himself to think logically and clearly. As he kept staring at his computer, a picture started to emerge. A plausible sequence of events. It was horrifying.

He ran out into the corridor and into Hansson's office.

"Call the patrol car!" he shouted as soon as he came in.

Hansson jerked back and stared at him.

"Which patrol car?"

"The one that took Modin to Malmö."

"Why?"

"Just do it. Quickly!"

Hansson grabbed the phone. He got through to them in less than two minutes.

"They're on their way back," he said putting the phone down.

Wallander breathed a sigh of relief.

"But they left Modin at the house."

Wallander felt as if he had been punched in the stomach.

"Why did they do that?"

"Apparently he came out and told them that he was going to keep working from the house."

Wallander didn't move. His heart was beating very hard. He still had trouble believing that it was true. But he himself had suggested the risk of someone breaking into their computers on an earlier occasion. These break-ins weren't necessarily limited to material surrounding the investigation. Someone could just as easily access more personal information—such as a letter that someone sent to a dating service.

"Take your gun with you," he said. "We're leaving."

"Where to?"

"Malmö."

Wallander tried to explain the situation along the way, but Hansson seemed to have trouble understanding the full story. Wallander kept asking him to try Elvira's number, but there was no answer. Wallander put the police siren on the roof and increased his speed. He prayed silently to all the gods he could think of to spare Modin's life. But he already feared the worst.

They stopped in front of the house shortly after ten o'clock. The house was dark. They stepped out of the car. Wallander asked Hansson to wait in the shadows down by the gate. Then he cocked his gun and walked up the path. When he reached the front door, he stopped and listened. Then he rang the bell. There was no answer. He rang again. Then he felt the doorknob. It was unlocked. He gestured for Hansson to come up.

"We should send for reinforcements," Hansson hissed.

"There's no time."

Wallander slowly opened the door. He listened. He didn't know what was waiting for them in the dark. He remembered that the light switch was on the wall to the left of the door, and after fumbling around for a while he found it. As soon as the light came on he took a step to the side and crouched down.

The hall was empty.

Some light fell into the living room. He could see that Elvira was sitting on the sofa. She was looking at him. Wallander took a deep breath. She didn't move. Wallander knew that she was dead. He called out to Hansson. They carefully went into the living room.

She had been shot in the neck. The pale yellow sofa was drenched in blood.

Then they searched the house, but they didn't find anything.

Robert Modin was gone. Wallander knew that could only mean one thing.

Someone had been waiting for him in the house.

The man in the field had not been working alone.

Chapter Thirty-nine

He didn't know what it was that kept him going that night. He imagined it was equal parts self-reproach and rage. But the overriding emotion was his fear for what might have happened to Modin. His first terrified thought when he realized that Elvira was dead was that Modin had also been killed. But once they had searched the house and established that it was empty, Wallander realized that Modin might still be alive. Everything up to this point in the case seemed to have been about concealment and secrets, and that must be the reason for Modin's abduction as well. Wallander didn't have to remind himself of Sonja Hökberg's and Jonas Landahl's fates. But this was not precisely the same situation. That time the police had not known what was going to happen. Now that they knew more, they had a better starting point, even though they didn't yet know what had happened to Modin.

Wallander also had to acknowledge that part of what was fueling him that night was his sense of betrayal, and his bitter disappointment that life had once more cheated him out of the promise of companionship. He could not claim to miss Elvira herself. Her death had mainly frightened him. She had accessed his letter to the dating service and approached him with the intention of tricking and manipulating him. And he had been thoroughly taken in. It had been a masterful performance. The humiliation was intense. The rage that coursed through him came from many different sources at once.

But Hansson would later tell him how collected and calm he had seemed. His evaluation of the situation and his suggested course of action had been quick and impressive.

Wallander had realized he needed to return to Ystad as soon as possible. That was where the heart of the case still was. Hansson would stay in the house, alert the Malmö police, and fill them in as necessary.

But Hansson was also to do something else. Wallander had been very firm on this matter. Even though it was the middle of the night, he wanted Hansson to try to find out more about Elvira Lindfeldt's background. Was there anything that linked her to Angola? Who did she know in Malmö?

"Who was she, anyway?" Hansson asked. "Why was Modin here? How did you know her?"

Wallander didn't answer, and Hansson never repeated the question. Afterward he would sometimes ask people about it when Wallander was not present. He discussed the fact that Wallander must have known her since he placed Modin in her care. But no one knew anything about this mysterious woman. Despite the intensive investigations that they conducted, there was always the sense that her relationship to Wallander was not a matter to be delved into. No one ever found out exactly what had happened.

Wallander left Hansson and returned to Ystad. He concentrated on a single question in his mind: What had happened to Modin?

As Wallander drove through the night he had a feeling that the impending catastrophe was very close. What it was exactly that needed to be stopped, and how he was going to prevent it, he was not sure. The most important thing was saving Modin's life. Wallander drove at a ridiculous speed. He had asked Hansson to call ahead and let the others know he was on his way. Hansson had asked if he should call and wake up Chief Holgersson, and Wallander had lost his temper and screamed at him. He did *not* want him to call her. It was the first time he showed some of the intense strain that he was under.

At half past one, Wallander slowed down and turned into the station parking lot. He shivered from the cold as he ran toward the front doors.

The others were waiting for him in the conference room. Martinsson, Höglund, and Alfredsson were already there, with Nyberg on his way. Höglund handed him a cup of coffee that he almost immediately managed to spill down the front of his trousers.

Then he got down to business. Robert Modin had disappeared without a trace, and the woman he had been staying with had been found murdered.

"The first conclusion we can draw," Wallander said, "is that the man in the field was not working alone. It was a fatal mistake to assume that this was the case. I should have realized it earlier."

Höglund was the one who asked the inevitable question.

"Who was she?"

"Her name was Elvira Lindfeldt," Wallander said. "She was an acquaintance of mine."

"But how did she know Modin was coming by tonight?"

"We'll have to tackle that question later."

Did they believe him? Wallander thought he had lied convincingly but he couldn't tell. He knew he should have told them about sending in the ad to the dating service, and that someone must have broken into his computer and read the letter. But he didn't say any of these things. He tried to tell himself, in his own defense, that the most important thing was finding Modin.

At this point the door opened and Nyberg came in. His pajama top peeked out from under his sport coat.

"What the hell happened?" he asked. "Hansson called from Malmö and seemed out of his mind. It was impossible to understand a word he was saying."

"Sit down," Wallander said. "It's going to be a long night."

Then he nodded to Höglund, who summarized the current situation for Nyberg.

"Don't the Malmö police have their own forensic team?" Nyberg asked.

"I want you to go out there," Wallander said. "Not only in case anything else turns up but also just so I can hear what you think."

Nyberg nodded without saying anything. Then he took out a comb and started pulling it through his unruly thinning hair.

Wallander continued.

"There is one more conclusion we can draw here, and it is simply this: something else is going to happen. And this something is somehow based here in Ystad."

He looked over at Martinsson.

"I take it someone is still stationed outside Runnerström Square?"

"No, the surveillance has been canceled."

"Who the hell made that call?"

"Viktorsson thought it was a waste of our resources."

"Well, I want a car reposted there immediately. I canceled the surveillance of Apelbergsgatan, which maybe was a mistake. I think I want a car there, too, from now on."

Martinsson left the room, and Wallander knew he would see to it that the patrol cars were dispatched immediately.

They waited in silence for his return. Höglund offered Nyberg, who was still combing his hair, her make-up mirror so he could see what he was doing but he simply growled at her. Martinsson came back.

"Done."

"What we're looking for is the catalyst," Wallander said. "It could be something as simple as Falk's death. At least that's how I see it. As long as he was alive, everything was in control. But then he died, and everything threatened to unravel."

Höglund raised her hand.

"Do we know for sure that Falk died from natural causes?"

"I think it must have been natural causes. My conclusion is based on the fact that Falk's death was unexpected. Falk was in excellent health. But he died, and that's what started the chain reaction. If Falk had continued to live, Sonja Hökberg would have been tried and convicted of Lundberg's death. Neither she nor Jonas Landahl would have been killed. Landahl would have kept running errands for Falk. And we would have had no idea of whatever it is that Falk and his companions were planning."

"So it's only thanks to his death that we know something is going to happen, something that might affect the whole world?"

"That's how I see it, yes. If someone else has a better hypothesis, I'd like to hear it."

No one had anything to say.

Alfredsson took out his briefcase and poured out a number of loose papers, some torn, some folded in half.

"These are Modin's notes," he said. "They were lying in a corner and I gathered them up. Do you think it's worth our time to go through them?"

"That will be up to you and Martinsson," Wallander said. "You are the only two who will understand what he's talking about."

The phone rang and Höglund answered. She handed the receiver to Wallander, saying it was Hansson.

"A neighbor claims she heard a car drive away with squealing tires at about nine-thirty," he said. "But that's all we have been able to establish. No one seems to have seen or heard anything else. Not even the shots."

"There was more than one?"

"The doctor says she was shot twice in the neck. There are two entry wounds."

Wallander felt sick to his stomach. He forced himself to swallow hard.

"Are you still there?"

"I'm here. No one heard the shots?"

"At least not the immediate neighbors, and they're the only ones we've had time to wake up so far."

"Who is leading the work down there?"

"A guy named Forsman. I've never met him before."

Wallander couldn't recall hearing the name, either.

"What does he say?"

"He says he has trouble getting a coherent picture from what I tell him. There's no motive, for a start."

"You'll have to placate him the best you can. We don't have time to fill him in right now."

"There was one more thing," Hansson said. "Didn't Modin say he was on his way down here to pick up some diskettes?"

"That was what he said."

"I think I know what room he was staying in, but there are no diskettes in there."

"He must have taken them with him. Have you found anything else that belongs to him?"

"Nothing."

"Any signs that anyone else was in the house?"

"A neighbor claims a taxi came by earlier in the day. A man stepped out of it."

"That could be important. Try to find that taxi. Make sure Forsman makes that a priority."

"You know I have no control over what police from another district choose to do or not."

"Then you'll have to do this yourself. Did the neighbor give a description of the man?"

"All he said was that the man looked lightly dressed for this time of year."

"He said that?"

"Yes, I think so."

It's the man from Luanda, Wallander thought. *The one whose name starts with "C."*

"This business with the taxi is very important," Wallander repeated. "It probably came from one of the ferry terminals, or Sturup International Airport."

"I'll see what I can do."

Wallander told the others about their conversation.

"I think the reinforcements have arrived," Wallander said. "Maybe even from as far away as Angola."

"I haven't been able to get a single answer to any of my inquiries," Martinsson said. "I've been researching known sabotage and terrorist groups that focus on financial targets. But no one seems to have any data on them."

"You think people like that would be based here in Ystad?"

Nyberg put his comb down and stared disapprovingly at Wallander, who thought that Nyberg suddenly seemed very old. Did the others see Wallander himself in this way?

"A man of Asian heritage turns up dead in a field outside Sandhammaren," Wallander answered. "He was posing as a man from Hong Kong and we know this identity was forged. This is not the kind of thing that should happen around here. But it does. There are no truly remote parts of the world anymore. If I understand anything about the new technology it is that it enables you to be at the center of things from any geographic location."

The phone rang again. Wallander answered again. It was Hansson.

"Forsman is actually pretty good," he said. "Things are moving right along. He's found the taxi."

"Where did it come from?"

"Sturup. You were right."

"Has anyone spoken to the driver?"

"He's right here. His shifts seem to be very long. Forsman says hello, by the way. Apparently you met at a conference last spring."

"Then give him my regards as well," Wallander said. "Let me talk to this driver."

"His name is Stig Lunne. Here he is."

Wallander gestured to the others to hand him a piece of paper and a pen.

The taxi driver spoke with such a thick Scanian dialect that it was almost impossible, even with Wallander's extensive experience, to understand him. But at least his answers were impressively short and concise. Wallander told him who he was and what he wanted to know. He had picked his passenger up at two minutes past twelve from Sturup and the trip had not been booked in advance.

"Can you describe your passenger?"

"Tall."

"Anything else?"

"Thin."

"Is that all? Is there anything else you might have noticed?"

"Tan."

"So this man was tall, thin, and suntanned?"

"Yes."

"Did he speak Swedish?"

"No."

"What language did he speak?"

"I don't know. He showed me a piece of paper with the address."

Wallander sighed. After continued questioning, he found out that the man had been wearing a light summer suit. He asked Lunne a few other routine questions, then finished. He thanked him and asked him to be in touch if he thought of anything else.

It was three o'clock. Wallander gave the others the description that Lunne had given him. Martinsson and Alfredsson had already left to go read through Modin's notes. Now they returned.

"It's hard to get anything out of Modin's notes," Alfredsson said. "Not least because he writes things like 'What we need to find is a coffee machine that's right in front of our eyes.'"

"He's talking about the process that triggers the intended event," Wallander said. "We discussed that it was probably something very common, something most of us do every day without thinking twice about it. When the right button is pushed at the right time and place, then something is set in motion."

"What button?" Höglund asked.

"That's what we were trying to figure out."

They kept talking. Shortly before four-thirty, Hansson called again. Wallander listened and made some notes. From time to time he asked a short question. The conversation took a little longer than fifteen minutes.

"Hansson has managed to dig up a friend of Elvira Lindfeldt," Wallander said. "She had some interesting information for us. Apparently Lindfeldt worked in Pakistan for a couple of years during the '70s."

"I thought we were still focused on Angola," Martinsson said.

"The important thing is what she was doing in Pakistan," Wallander said and looked closer at the back of the envelope that he had used to make notes. "According to this friend, she was working for the World Bank. That gives us a connection. But there's more. The friend also said that she expressed strange opinions from time to time. She was convinced that the current financial order had to be completely restructured, and that this could only be accomplished if everything was essentially torn down first."

"That seems to settle it," Martinsson said. "There must be a number of people involved in this, even if we still don't know where or who they are."

"So we're looking for a button." Nyberg said. "Is that it? Or a lever? Or a light switch? But one that could be anywhere."

"Yes."

"So in other words, we know nothing."

The room was tense. Wallander looked at his colleagues with something nearing desperation. *We're not going to make it,* he thought. *We're not going to find Modin in time.*

The phone rang again. Wallander had lost count of the times Hansson had called them.

"Lindfeldt's car," he said. "We should have thought of it earlier."

"Yes," Wallander said, "you're right."

"It was normally parked on the street outside her house, but it's gone now. We've alerted the district. It's a dark-blue VW Golf with the license plate FHC 803."

All the cars in this case seem to be dark blue, Wallander thought.

It was ten minutes to five. The feeling in the room was tired and heavy. Wallander thought they all looked defeated. No one seemed to know what to do. Martinsson got up.

"I have to have something to eat," he said. "I'm going down to the fast-food kiosk on Österleden. They're open late. Does anyone want anything?"

Wallander shook his head. Martinsson made a note of what the others wanted, then he left. A few seconds later he was back.

"I don't have any money," he said. "Can anyone lend me some?"

Wallander had twenty crowns. Strangely enough, no one else had any cash.

"I'll have to stop at the cash machine," Martinsson said and left again.

Wallander stared blankly at the wall. His head was starting to hurt.

But somewhere behind the growing headache he had a thought. He didn't know where it had come from, but suddenly he jumped. The others stared at him.

"What did Martinsson say?"

"He was going to get some food."

"Not that. Afterward."

"He said he had to stop by a cash machine."

Wallander nodded slowly.

"How about that?" he asked. "Something right in front of our eyes. Is it our coffee machine?"

"I don't think I follow," Höglund said.

"It's something we do without thinking twice."

"Buying some food?"

"Sticking a card into an automatic teller machine. Getting cash and a printed receipt."

Wallander turned to Alfredsson.

"Was there anything in Modin's notes about a cash machine?"

Alfredsson bit his lip. He looked up at Wallander.

"You know, I actually think there was."

Wallander stretched.

"What did he write?"

"I can't remember exactly. It didn't strike either me or Martinsson as important."

Wallander slammed his fist onto the table.

"Where are his notes?"

"Martinsson took them."

Wallander was already on his feet and on his way out the door.

Alfredsson followed him to Martinsson's office.

Modin's crumpled notes lay on the desk beside Martinsson's phone. Alfredsson started leafing through them while Wallander waited impatiently.

"Here it is," Alfredsson said and handed him a piece of paper.

Wallander put on his glasses and looked it over. The paper was covered with drawings of roosters and cats. At the bottom, among some complicated and to him completely meaningless calculations there was a sentence that Modin had underlined so many times that he had ripped the paper. *Suitable trigger. Could it be an ATM?*

"Is that the kind of thing you were looking for?" Alfredsson asked.

But he didn't get an answer. Wallander was already on his way back to the conference room.

Suddenly he was convinced. What better place? People were always using cash machines day in and day out at all times of day. Somewhere, at some point in time on this day, someone would make a transaction at an unknown location and thereby trigger an event that Wallander did not yet understand but had come to fear. He could not even be sure that this hadn't in fact already taken place.

"How many ATMs are there in Ystad?" he asked the others after explaining his new idea.

No one knew.

"We can find out from the phone book," Höglund said.

"If not, you'll have to dig up a bank employee and find out."

Nyberg raised his hand.

"How can we be so sure that what you say is right?"

"You can't," Wallander said. "But it beats sitting here twiddling our thumbs."

Nyberg didn't back down.

"What can we do about it, anyway?"

"Even if I'm right," Wallander said, "we don't know which bank machine is the trigger. There may even be more than one involved. We don't even know when or how something is going to happen. But what we can make sure of is that nothing happens."

"So you're thinking we could have all cash machine transactions suspended?"

"For now, yes."

"Do you realize what that means?"

"That people will have even more reason to dislike the police. That we'll be hearing about this for a long time. Yes, of course I do."

"You can't even do this without permission from the D.A.'s office. And after consultation with the bank directors."

Wallander got up and sat down in the chair directly across from Nyberg.

"Right now I don't give a shit about any of that. Not even if it becomes the last thing I ever do as a police officer in Ystad. Or as a police officer, period."

Höglund had been looking through the phone book while they talked.

"There are four cash machines in Ystad," she said. "Three downtown and one up in the department-store area. Where we found Falk."

Wallander thought about it.

"Martinsson probably went to one of the machines downtown. They're closer to Österleden. Call him. You and Alfredsson will have to guard the other two. I'm going up to the one by the department stores."

He turned to Nyberg.

"I'm going to ask you to call Chief Holgersson. Wake her up. Tell her exactly what's going on. Then she'll have to take it from there."

Nyberg shook his head.

"She'll put a stop to the whole thing."

"Call her," Wallander said. "But if you like you could wait until six."

Nyberg looked at him and smiled.

Wallander had one more thing to say.

"We can't forget about Robert and this tall, thin, suntanned man. We don't know what language he speaks. It might be Swedish, it could very well be something else. But we have to assume that he or someone else associated with him is keeping an eye on the cash machine in question. If you have the slightest suspicion or hesitation about someone, you have to call the others immediately."

"I've staked out many things in my day," Alfredsson said. "I don't think I've ever staked out a cash machine."

"Sometime has to be the first. Do you have a gun?"

Alfredsson shook his head.

"Get him one," Wallander said to Höglund. "And now let's get going."

It was nine minutes past five when Wallander left the station. He drove up to the department-store area with mixed feelings. Most likely he was completely wrong about this, but they had gotten as far as they could back there in the conference room. Wallander parked outside the Tax Authority building. The area was dark and deserted. Dawn was still some time away. He zipped his jacket and looked around. Then he walked over to the cash machine. There was no reason to remain concealed. The radio he had brought along made a noise. Höglund was broadcasting that they were all in place. Alfredsson had immediately run into problems. Some drunk young people had insisted they be allowed to make a withdrawal. He had called in for a patrol car to help him out.

"Let the car circulate between us," Wallander said. "It will only get worse in an hour or so when people start waking up."

"Martinsson took out some cash," she said. "But nothing happened."

"We don't know that," Wallander said. "Whatever happens, we're not going to see it."

The radio fell silent. Wallander looked at a knocked-over shopping cart in the parking lot. Apart from a small pickup truck, the lot was empty. It was twenty-seven minutes past five. Up on the highway, a large truck rattled past on its way to Malmö. Wallander started thinking about Elvira but decided he didn't have the energy. He would have to come back to it, figuring out how he could have let himself be taken in like that. How he could have been such a fool. Wallander turned his back to the wind and stamped his feet. He heard a car approaching. It was a sedan painted with the logo of a local electrical firm. The man who jumped out was tall and thin. Wallander flinched and grabbed his gun, but then he relaxed. He recognized the man as an electrician who had once done some work for his father out in Löderup. The man nodded.

"Is it broken?" he asked.

"We're not letting anyone make any withdrawals right now."

"I'll have to go across town, then."

"Unfortunately that won't be possible, either."

"What's wrong?"

"It's only a temporary malfunction."

"And they called in the police for that?"

Wallander didn't answer. The man got back into his car and drove away. Wallander knew he would be able to keep warding people off with the explanation of a temporary malfunction, but he was already dreading the moment when it got out into the public. How had he thought it would work? Lisa Holgersson would put a stop to it the moment she found out. Their reasons were still mere speculation. He would not be able to do anything, and Martinsson would have more grist for his mill.

Then he caught sight of a man walking across the parking lot. It was a young man. He had emerged from behind the pickup truck, and he came walking toward Wallander. It took a few seconds for him to realize who it was. Robert Modin. Wallander was frozen to the spot. He held his breath. He did not understand. Suddenly Modin stopped and turned his back to Wallander, who sensed instinctively what was about to happen. He threw himself to the side. The man behind him had come from the direction of the department stores. He was tall, thin, and suntanned and he was carrying a gun. He was ten meters away and there was nowhere for Wallander to run. Wallander closed his eyes. The feeling from the field returned. The bitter end. Here but no longer. He waited for the shot that didn't come. Slowly he opened his eyes. The man had the gun pointed directly at him, but he was looking down at his watch. *The time*, Wallander thought. *It's time. I was right. I still don't know what is going to happen but I was right.*

The man gestured for Wallander to come closer and to put his arms in the air. He pulled out Wallander's gun and threw it into a garbage can next to the cash machine. Then he held out a plastic card in his left hand and said some numbers in broken Swedish.

"One, five, five, one."

He dropped the card on the pavement and pointed at it with his gun. Wallander picked it up. The man took a few steps to the side and looked down at his watch. Then he pointed to the bank machine. His movements were more violent now. For the first time the man looked nervous. Wallander walked up to the machine. When he turned slightly he could see Modin still standing in the spot where he had stopped. Right now Wallander didn't care what would happen when he put the card in and entered the numbers. Modin was alive. That was all that was important. But how could he continue to protect him? Wallander was searching for a way out. If he tried to attack the man behind him he would immediately be shot. Modin would probably not have time to run away. Wallander fed the card into the machine. At the same time a shot rang out. A bullet hit the ground nearby and whined away. The man spun around. Wallander turned and saw Martinsson about thirty meters away on the other side of the street. As the man aimed at Martinsson, Wallander leaped at the garbage can and pulled his gun out of the trash. The man shot at Martinsson but missed. As he turned back around, Wallander shot him in the chest and he collapsed.

"What's happening?" Martinsson yelled.

"It's safe to come over," Wallander yelled back.

The man on the pavement was dead.

"What made you come here?" Wallander asked Martinsson.

"If your hypothesis was right, it had to be here," Martinsson answered. "It makes sense that Falk would have chosen the bank machine closest to his house and that he always went past on his evening walks. I asked Nyberg to keep an eye on the cash machine downtown where I was."

Martinsson pointed at the dead man.

"Who is he?"

"I don't know. But I think his name starts with the letter 'C.'"

"Is everything over now?"

"Maybe. I think so. But I don't even know what it is that's over."

Wallander should have thanked Martinsson, but he didn't say anything. Instead he walked over to Modin, who was still standing in the same spot. There would be time enough for him and Martinsson to talk later.

Robert Modin's eyes were filled with tears.

"He told me to walk over to you. He said otherwise he would kill my mother and father."

"We'll talk about all that later," Wallander said. "How are you feeling?"

"He told me to say I had to stay and finish my work in Malmö. Then he shot her. And we left. I was in the trunk and could hardly breathe. But we were right."

"Yes," Wallander said. "We were right."

"Did you find my notes?"

"Yes."

"I didn't start taking it seriously until much later. A cash machine. A place where people come to take out their money."

"You should have said something," Wallander said. "But maybe I should have thought of it myself. We knew it had something to do with money, after all. It should have been an obvious choice to hide something like that."

"An ATM as the launching pad for their virus-bomb," Modin said. "It has a certain finesse, don't you think?"

Wallander looked at the boy by his side. How much longer could he handle the strain? Suddenly he was hit by the feeling of having stood like this before with a young boy at his side. Then he realized he was thinking of Stefan Fredman. The young boy who was now dead and buried.

"What was it that happened?" Wallander asked. "Do you think you can tell me?"

Modin nodded.

"He was already there when she let me in. And he threatened me. They locked me in the bathroom. Then I heard him start screaming at her. I could understand him since he was speaking English. At least the parts I could hear."

"What did he say?"

"That she hadn't done her job. That she had shown weakness."

"Did you hear anything else?"

"Only the shots. When he came to unlock the bathroom door I thought he was going to kill me as well. He had the gun in his hand. But he said I was his hostage and that I had to do as he said. Otherwise he would kill my parents."

Modin's voice started to wobble.

"We'll talk about the rest later," Wallander said. "That's enough. That's plenty, in fact."

"He said they were going to knock out the global financial system. It was going to start here, at this cash machine."

"I know," Wallander said. "But we'll talk about that later. You need to sleep. You have to go home to your parents now. Then we'll talk."

They heard sirens approaching. Now Wallander could see a dark blue Volkswagen Golf parked behind the pickup. It had been impossible to see from where he was standing.

Wallander felt how exhausted he was. And how relieved.

Martinsson came walking over.

"We need to talk," he said.

"I know," Wallander said. "But not now."

It was nine minutes to six on the Monday, the twentieth of October. Wallander wondered absently what the rest of the winter was going to be like.

Chapter Forty

On Tuesday, the eleventh of November, all charges against Wallander in the Eva Persson assault case were dismissed. Höglund was the one who told him the news. She had also played a central role in the direction the investigation had taken, but he only found that out later.

A few days before, Höglund had paid a visit to Eva Persson and her mother. No one knew exactly what was said during that visit; there had been no transcription of the conversation and no third party present, although these had been court-ordered. Höglund did tell Wallander that she applied "a mild form of emotional blackmail." What that entailed she never told him, but in time Wallander was able to put together a clearer picture. He assumed that she had told Eva Persson to turn her thoughts to the future. Even if she was now cleared in the murder of Lundberg, bringing false charges against a policeman could have unpleasant consequences. The following day Eva Persson and her mother withdrew the charges against Wallander. They acknowledged that Wallander's version of the events had been correct, and that Eva Persson had tried to hit her mother. Wallander could still have been held accountable for his actions in the situation, but the whole matter was hastily dropped, much to everyone's relief.

Höglund had also seen to it that a number of journalists were informed of the dropped charges, but the news never made it into the paper.

This particular Tuesday was an unusually cold fall day in Scania, with gusty northerly winds that occasionally neared storm strength. Wallander had woken up early after an unsettled night. He could not recall his dreams in any detail, but they had involved being hunted and almost choked to death by shadowy figures and objects bearing down on him.

When he arrived at the station around eight o'clock, he decided he would only stay for a short while. The day before he had decided he would finally get to the bottom of a question that had been troubling him for a long time. After casting his eye over a few forms and making sure that the photo album Marianne Falk had lent to the police had been returned to her, he left the station and drove to the Hökbergs' house. He had spoken to Erik Hökberg the day before and arranged a meeting. Sonja's brother Emil was at school, and Erik's wife was on one of her frequent trips to see her sister in Höör. Erik Hökberg looked pale, and as if he had lost weight. According to a rumor that had reached Wallander, Sonja Hökberg's funeral had been an intensely emotional affair. Wallander stepped into the house and assured Erik that his business would not take long.

"You said you wanted to see Sonja's room," Erik said. "But you never said why it was so important."

"I'll explain it to you when we get up there. Why don't you come with me?"

"Nothing has been changed in there. We don't have the energy. Not yet."

They walked upstairs and into the pink room where Wallander had once immediately sensed that something was off.

"I don't think this room has always looked the way it does now," he said. "At some point Sonja redecorated her room, didn't she?"

Erik Hökberg looked baffled.

"How do you know that?"

"I don't know. I'm asking you."

Erik swallowed. Wallander waited patiently.

"It was after that time," Erik said. "The rape, I mean. Suddenly she took everything down from the walls and got out all of her old things from when she was a little girl. Things that had been stored in boxes in the attic for years. We never understood why she did it, and she never said anything about it."

Something was taken from her, Wallander thought. And she tried to run away from it in two ways: by running back to a childhood where everything was still all right, and by planning a revenge by proxy.

"That was all I wanted to know," Wallander said.

"Why is it so important to you now? Nothing matters anymore. It won't bring Sonja back. Ruth and Emil and I are living half a life, if that."

"Sometimes one feels a need to get to the bottom of things," Wallander said apologetically. "Unanswered questions can hang on and on. But you're right, of course. It doesn't change anything."

They left the room and went back downstairs. Erik Hökberg asked if he wanted a cup of coffee, but Wallander declined. He wanted to leave this depressing place as soon as possible.

He drove downtown, parked on Hamngatan, and walked up to the bookstore that had just opened for the day. He was finally picking up the book on refinishing furniture that he had ordered for Linda. He was shocked at the price. He had them gift-wrap it and took it back to the car. Linda was coming to see him the following day and he would give her the book then.

He was back in his office by nine. At nine-thirty he gathered up his folders and went to one of the conference rooms. Today they were having a final meeting to discuss the Tynnes Falk case before handing the documents over to the prosecutor. Since the murder of Elvira Lindfeldt had involved the Malmö police, Inspector Forsman was also present at the meeting.

At the meeting Wallander had not yet heard about the dropped charges against him, but this was not anything that weighed heavily on his mind. The most important thing was still the fact that Robert Modin had survived. This helped him even when he was overwhelmed by thoughts that he might have been able to prevent Jonas Landahl's death if he had been able to think just a little further ahead. Part of him knew that this self-accusation was unreasonable, but these thoughts came and went, regardless.

For once, Wallander was the last to enter the conference room. He said hello to Forsman and did in fact remember his face from the police conference they had both attended. Only two people were absent: Hans Alfredsson had returned to Stockholm and Nyberg was sick with the flu. Wallander sat down, and they started reviewing the case material. They had so much to cover that the meeting ran on until one o'clock, but at that point they could finally close the books on it.

Wallander's memories of the case had started losing clarity in the three weeks that had gone by since the shooting incident by the cash machine. But the facts that they had uncovered since then strongly supported their initial conlusions.

The dead man's name was Carter, and he came from Luanda. They had pieced together an identity and history for him now, and Wallander thought he had finally been able to answer the question he had asked himself so many times during the investigation: *What had hap-*

pened in Angola? Now he knew at least the bare bones of the answer. Falk and Carter had met in Luanda during the 1970s, probably by accident. Exactly what that first meeting had been like or what had been said was impossible to reconstruct, but the two men had clearly had a great deal in common. They had shared many traits in which pride, a taste for revenge, and a confused sense of being among the chosen few had predominated. Together they had started laying the plans for an attack on the global financial system. They were going to fire their electronic missile when the time was right. Carter's extensive familiarity with the structures of financial organizations, coupled with Falk's innovative technological knowledge of the electronic world that connected those institutions, had been a powerful and potentially le-thal combination.

Together they had built up a secretive and strongly controlled or-ganization that came to include such disparate individuals as Fu Cheng, Elvira Landfeldt, and Jonas Landahl. They had been pulled in, indoctrinated, and forever ensnared. The picture that had emerged was of a highly hierarchical organization in which Carter and Falk made all the decisions. Even if the evidence was as yet insubstantial, there were indications that Carter had personally executed more than one unsatisfactory member of the group.

To Wallander, Carter seemed like the archetypal crazed and ruthless sectarian leader, driven by cold calculation. His impression of Falk remained more complicated, since he had never been convinced that Falk shared the same capacity for ruthlessness. But Falk did appear to have had a carefully guarded but deep-seated need for affirmation. During the 1960s he had swung from the extreme right to the radical left. Finally he had broken with conventional politics entirely and em-barked on his demonic plottings against the human race.

The police in Hong Kong had been able to establish the true iden-tity of Fu Cheng. His real name had been Hua Gang. Interpol had identified his fingerprints at the scene of several crimes, including bank robberies in Frankfurt and Marseilles. Though he couldn't prove it, Wallander suspected that this money had been used to finance parts of Falk's and Carter's operations. Hua Gang had been involved in organized crime for a long time and had figured as a suspect in several murder cases, both in Europe and Asia, without ever being convicted. There was no doubt that he had been the killer of both Sonja Hökberg and Jonas Landahl. Fingerprints and reports from several witnesses confirmed this. But Hua Gang had been working under the direction of Carter, and perhaps of Falk. There was still work to be done in mapping the entire workings and reach of the organization, but the information they already had suggested that there was no longer a reason to fear the group. With Carter and Falk dead, the organization had essentially ceased to exist.

Wallander was never able to determine exactly why Carter had shot Elvira Lindfeldt. Modin had reported as much as he could about the angry accusations Carter had flung at her before she died. Wallander assumed she had simply known too much and become a liability. Carter must have been in a state of near desperation when he reached Sweden.

Still, he had come uncomfortably close to succeeding. If either Wallander or Modin had put the bank card into the machine at exactly five thirty-one that Monday, the twentieth of October, they would have unleashed an electronic avalanche. The experts who had been tracing the infiltrations that Falk had made into the bank networks had been amazed. Falk and Carter had managed to render the major financial institutions of the world shockingly vulnerable to attack. Right now, security experts around the world were working around the clock to rectify these deficiencies, while yet other groups were trying to construct an accurate picture of what would have happened had the plan actually been set in motion.

Luckily, of course, neither Modin nor Wallander had entered Carter's password into the machine. And nothing had happened, other than that a selection of cash machines in Scania had gone haywire that day. Many of them had been shut down, but as yet no problem had been located. Eventually they had resumed working normally just as mysteriously.

They never did manage to find a satisfying answer to why Sonja Hökberg was thrown against the high voltage wires at the power substation, nor why Falk had been in possession of the blueprint. They had, however, managed to find out how the perpetrators had gained access to the station. That had been thanks to Hansson's doggedness. It turned out that one of the technicians, Moberg, had come home from a vacation to find that his house had been broken into. The keys to the station had still been there, but Hansson maintained that whoever committed the burglary must have made an imprint and then had copies made by bribing the American manufacturer. Simple fact-checking had revealed an entry visa in Jonas Landahl's passport proving that he had been in the United States in the month following the break-in at Moberg's house. The money may have come from Hua Gang's bank robberies in Frankfurt and Marseilles.

Some loose ends were painstakingly tied up; others remained un-solved. They found out that Tynnes Falk had kept a post-office box in Malmö—but they could never figure out why he had told Siv Eriksson that he had his mail sent to her address. His journal was never recov-ered, nor were the fingers that had been severed from his hand. The coroner's office did, however, finally determine that he had died from natural causes. Enander had been right about one thing: it was not a heart attack. Falk's death was the result of a burst blood vessel in his brain.

Other information slowly trickled in. One day Wallander found a long report on his desk from Nyberg in which he described how they had determined that the empty suitcase found in Jonas Landahl's cabin on the ferry had belonged to him. Nyberg had not determined exactly what had happened to the contents but assumed that Hua Gang had thrown them overboard in an effort to delay the identifica-tion of the body. They only ever recovered his passport. Wallander put the report aside with a sigh.

The most important task had been the mapping of Carter's and Falk's strange world. Wallander knew now that their ambitions had known no bounds. After their intended crippling of the world finan-cial markets, they'd had plans to strangle important utilities worldwide. They had been motivated in no small part by their own vanity and an intoxication with their sense of power. Wallander thought that it was this weakness that had tempted Carter to have the electrical relay brought to the morgue and to have Falk's fingers cut off. There had been religious overtones in their macabre world, and Carter and Falk had figured as not only as overseers but as deities.

Although Carter and Falk had lived in the idiosyncratic realm of their own deranged fantasies, Wallander had started to sense that at least their plan had cast attention on an important insight: the incred-ible vulnerability of modern society.

Sometimes he thought about it for a long time late at night. During the past thirty years, a society had been emerging that he did not fully recognize. In his work he was constantly confronted with the results of brutal forces that ruthlessly flung people to the outer margins. The walls surrounding these outcasts were dauntingly high: drugs, unem-ployment, social indifference.

These changes were accompanied by a parallel development in which members of society were being connected ever more tightly by new technological innovations. But this highly efficient electronic net-work came at the cost of increased vulnerability to sabotage and terror.

At the heart of his thinking on these changes was his heightened sense of his own vulnerability. He knew he was in danger of being mowed down by Martinsson. He also felt intimidated by the constantly changing conditions of the workplace and the new demands that were being made. In the future, society would need a new kind of policeman. Not that his kind of experience and knowledge were no longer valuable, but now there were whole domains of knowledge he knew nothing about. He was forced to accept the fact that he had simply become old. An old dog who could no longer be taught new tricks.

During those long nights in his apartment, he often thought he no longer had the energy for policework. But he knew he had no choice but to continue, at least for another ten years. There were no real alternatives open to him anymore. He was an investigative police officer, a homicide detective. Traveling around to schools to lecture about the dangers of drugs or drunken driving was not a viable option for him. That would never be his world.

The meeting ended at one o'clock and the material was handed over to the district attorney's office. No one would be charged, since all of the suspects were already dead. But the D.A. already had a report on his desk that could very well lead to an indictment of Carl-Einar Lundberg.

It was after the meeting was over that Höglund came by his office to tell him that Eva Persson and her mother had recanted their story regarding the slap. Naturally Wallander was relieved, but he was not particularly surprised. Although he had his share of doubts about the ability of justice to prevail in the Swedish judicial system, he had always expected that the truth in this particular case would eventually come out.

They sat and talked for a while about the possibility that he could now counter the accusations. Hölgund urged him to make an example of his mistreatment for the sake of the whole force, but Wallander was reluctant. He thought the best thing would be for the whole affair to be buried in silence.

Once Höglund had left, Wallander sat in his chair staring into space for a long time. His head was empty. Finally he got up to get a cup of coffee.

In the doorway to the lunchroom he bumped into Martinsson. During the past few weeks Wallander had felt a strange and, for him, an unfamiliar ambivalence. Normally he did not shy away from conflicts, but what had happened between him and Martinsson was more difficult and went deeper. There were elements of lost friendship, betrayal, camaraderie. But now he knew the moment had come. He couldn't put it off any longer.

"We should talk," he said. "Do you have a minute?"

"I've been waiting for you."

They went back to the conference room, where they had spent the whole morning. Wallander got straight to the point.

"I know you've been going behind my back. I know you've been spreading lies about me. You questioned my ability to lead this investigation. Why you've done all this in secret instead of coming to me directly, only you can say. The only way I can explain your behavior is that you're laying the groundwork for your future career, and that you're willing to do anything to get where you want to go."

Martinsson was calm when he spoke. Wallander noticed that his words seemed well rehearsed.

"I can only tell you how it is. You've lost your grip. I think the only thing I'm guilty of is that I didn't say this earlier."

"Why didn't you tell me directly?"

"I tried to, but you don't listen."

"I do listen."

"You think you do, but that's not the same thing as really listening."

"Why did you tell Lisa that I had ordered you not to follow me into the field that time?"

"She must have misunderstood what I said."

Wallander looked at Martinsson. The urge to hit him in the face was still there, but he knew he wouldn't do anything like that. He didn't have the energy for it. He wasn't going to be able to shake Martinsson. He seemed to believe his own lies. At the very least, he would not be able to get him to change his official line.

"Was there anything else you wanted to talk about?"

"No," Wallander said. "I don't have anything else to say."

Martinsson got up and left.

Wallander felt as if the walls had come tumbling down around him. Martinsson had made his choice and their friendship was gone, broken off. Wallander wondered with growing despondence if it had ever really been there in the first place. Or had Martinsson always been waiting for his opportunity to strike?

Waves of grief washed over him. And then there came a wave of rage.

He was not going to give up. For the next few years at least, he would remain in charge of the most complicated investigations in Ystad.

But the feeling of having lost something was stronger than this rage. He asked himself again how he would have the energy to carry on.

Wallander left the station directly after his conversation with Martinsson. He left his cell phone in his office and didn't tell Irene anything about where he was going or when he would be back. He got in his car and took the highway to Malmö. When he approached the exit for Stjärnsund, he decided to take it. He didn't know why. Perhaps the thought of two broken friendships was too much to bear.

Wallander's thoughts often returned to Elvira. She had entered his life under false pretenses, and in the final analysis he suspected she would even have been prepared to kill him. But he could not stop himself from thinking about her the way he had actually experienced her. A woman who sat across from him at the dinner table and listened to what he had to say. A woman with beautiful legs who had dispelled his loneliness for a short time.

When he turned into Sten Widén's ranch, he saw that it looked deserted. Widén had posted a FOR SALE sign some time ago, but now there was an additional sign announcing that the ranch was sold. The house was empty. Wallander walked over to the stables. The horses were all gone. A lone cat sat in a pile of hay and looked at him suspiciously.

Wallander found it upsetting. Sten Widén had already left, and he hadn't even bothered to say good-bye.

Wallander left the stables and drove away as fast as he could.

The following day he did not go into the office at all. He drove around on the small roads outside Ystad all afternoon. A couple of times he stepped out of his car and stared out over the barren fields. When it started getting dark, he headed back. He stopped at the grocer's on the way and paid his bill. That evening, he listened to the entire score of Verdi's *La Traviata* twice in a row. He also spoke to Gertrud over the phone, and they arranged that he would stop by in the morning.

The phone rang shortly before midnight. Wallander fumed. *Oh, God, not again,* he thought. *Don't let anything have happened. Not now, not yet. None of us can handle it.*

It was Baiba calling from Riga. It had been about a year since they had spoken last.

"I just wanted to know how you were doing," she said.

"Fine. How about you?"

"Fine."

The silence bounced from Ystad to Riga and back again.

"Do you ever think about me?" he asked.

"Of course. Why would I have called otherwise?"

"I was just wondering."

"And you?"

"I always think about you."

Wallander knew she would see through him. He was lying, or at least exaggerating. He didn't know exactly why. Baiba was something that was over, that was fading. But he still could not completely let go of the thought of her, or of the memories of their time together.

They exchanged some casual remarks on other topics, and then the conversation ended. Wallander put the phone down slowly.

Did he miss her? He didn't know. It was as if firewalls were not a phenomenon relegated to the world of computers. He had a firewall inside himself, and he didn't always know how to get past it.

The next day, Wednesday, the twelfth of November, the gusty winds had died down. Wallander woke up early even though he had the day off. He couldn't remember the last time he had had a day off in the middle of the week. He had decided to use some of his comp time, since Linda was coming to visit. He was going to meet her plane at one o'clock at Sturup Airport. He would use the morning to trade in his car and visit Gertrud.

At eight o'clock he got out of bed. He drank his coffee and read the paper. He cleaned the apartment, changed the sheets in Linda's old room, and put the vacuum cleaner away. The sun was shining, and that cheered him up. He drove out to the car dealership, which was located on Industrigatan. He chose another Peugeot, this time a 306 from 1996. It had few miles on it, and the car dealer, Tyrén, gave him a good price on his old car. Wallander was done at ten-thirty. It always gave him a good feeling to get a new car, as if he had scrubbed himself clean.

He continued on to the house in Svarte where Gertrud lived with her sister. He had a cup of coffee and listened somewhat absentmindedly to their chatter.

He left their house at a quarter to twelve. When he got to Sturup there was still a half-hour left.

As usual he felt nervous about seeing Linda again. He wondered if it was always the case that parents eventually became afraid of their own children. He sat down in the airport café and had another cup of coffee. Suddenly he noticed Höglund's ex-husband sitting a few tables away. Wallander assumed he was leaving on another business trip. A woman that Wallander didn't recognize was with him. Wallander felt hurt on Höglund's behalf. He moved to another table and sat with his back to the man so he wouldn't be recognized. He wondered why he was reacting so strongly but found no answer.

The plane landed on time. Linda was one of the last people to get off the plane. When they saw each other, Wallander's nervousness disappeared. She was just as open and cheerful as before. Her easygoing nature was the direct opposite of his own. She was also not as outrageously dressed as she had been on some previous occasions. They picked up her suitcase at the baggage claim, and then Wallander showed her to the new car. He wasn't sure that she would have noticed the difference if he hadn't said anything.

They drove toward Ystad.

"How are things?" he asked. "What are you doing these days? You've been a bit secretive this past while."

"It's such a nice day," she said. "Can't we drive down to the beach?"

"I asked you a question."

"You'll get an answer."

"When?"

"Not just yet."

Wallander took the next exit and drove down to Mossby Beach. The parking lot was deserted, the fast-food kiosk closed for the year. She opened her suitcase and took out a thick sweater, and they walked down toward the water.

"I remember coming here when I was little," she said. "It's one of my earliest memories."

"Often it was just you and me. When Mona needed time to herself."

There was a ship far out at sea on the horizon. The sea was very calm.

"What about that picture in the paper?" she asked suddenly.

Wallander felt his stomach tighten up.

"It's over now," he said. "The girl and her mother recanted. It's over."

"I saw another picture," she said. "In a magazine. Something happened outside a church in Malmö. I think it said you threatened a photographer."

Wallander thought back to Stefan Fredman's funeral and the film he had pulled out of the camera. The photographer must have had an extra roll. He told her about the incident.

"You did the right thing," she said. "I hope I would have done the same thing."

"Luckily you're not going to find yourself in these situations," Wallander said. "You're not a police officer."

"Not yet."

Wallander stopped short and looked at her.

"What did you say?"

She kept walking and didn't answer immediately. Some seagulls flew over their heads, screeching.

"You think I've been secretive," she said. "And you want to know what I've been up to. I didn't want to tell you about it until I had made up my mind."

"Do you mean what you just said?"

"I want to be a police officer. I've already applied to the police academy, and I think I'm going to get in."

Wallander still couldn't believe it.

"Is this true?"

"Yes."

"But you've never talked about it before."

"I've been thinking about it for a long time."

"Why didn't you say anything?"

"I didn't want to."

"But I thought you were going to go into the antique business and refinish old furniture."

"I thought so, too—for a while. But now I know what I really want to do. And that's why I came down here—to tell you. Ask you what you think. Get your blessing."

They started walking again.

"This comes right out of the blue," Wallander said.

"You've talked about what it was like when you told Grandfather that you were going to be a policeman. If I remember correctly, his answer came pretty quickly."

"He said no before I had finished talking."

"And what do you say?"

"Give me a minute and I'll let you know."

She went and sat down on an old tree trunk that was half-buried in the sand. Wallander walked down to the water. He had never imagined that Linda would want to follow in his footsteps. It was still hard for him to sort out what he had heard.

He looked out over the ocean. The sunlight reflected on the water.

Linda shouted out to him that his minute was up. He walked back.

"I think it's a good thing," he said. "I think you'll be the kind of police officer we're going to need in the future."

"Do you mean it?"

"Every word."

"I was nervous about telling you. I was worried about how you'd react."

"You didn't have to worry."

She got up from the log.

"We have a lot to talk about," she said. "And I'm also hungry."

They returned to the car and continued to Ystad. Wallander tried to digest the news as he drove. He didn't doubt that Linda would make a good policewoman. But did she realize what was in store for her? The fatigue, and the burnout?

But he also felt something else. Her decision somehow justified the one he had made so long ago in life.

This feeling was buried underneath the others. But it was there, and it was strong.

They sat up talking for a long time that evening. Wallander told her about the extremely challenging case that had started and ended by the same nondescript cash machine.

"Everyone talks about power," she said when Wallander had finished. "But no one really questions institutions like the World Bank, or the enormous power they wield. How much human suffering have they caused?"

"You mean to say you're sympathetic to Carter and Falk and their cause?"

"No," she said. "At least not to the way they chose to fight back."

Wallander became more and more convinced that her decision was the result of a long process. This was not an impulse decision that she would come to regret.

"I'm sure I'm going to need to ask you for advice," she said just before going to bed.

"Don't be so sure I have any good advice to give."

Wallander stayed up for a while after she had gone to bed. It was half past two in the morning. He had a glass of wine in his hand and had put on one of Puccini's operas. The volume was low.

Wallander shut his eyes. In his mind he saw a burning wall in front of him. He readied himself.

Then he ran straight through the wall. He only singed his hair and skin.

He opened his eyes again and smiled.

Something was behind him.

Something else was only just beginning.

The following day, on Thursday, the thirteenth of November, the stock markets in Asia unexpectedly started to fall sharply.

Many explanations were offered, most of them contradictory.

But no one ever managed to answer the most important question: What was it that had set the process in motion?